Down These
Green Streets

First published in 2011 by
Liberties Press
Guinness Enterprise Centre | Taylor's Lane | Dublin 8
Tel: +353 (1) 415 1224
www.libertiespress.com | info@libertiespress.com

Trade enquiries to Gill & Macmillan Distribution
Hume Avenue | Park West | Dublin 12
Tel: +353 (1) 500 9534 | Fax: +353 (1) 500 9595
sales@gillmacmillan.ie

Distributed in the United States by
Dufour Editions | PO Box 7 | Chester Springs | Pennsylvania | 19425

Paperback ISBN: 978-1-907593-19-2
Harback ISBN: 978-1-907593-32-1
A CIP record for this title is available from the British Library.

Cover design by Ros Murphy
Internal design by Liberties Press
Printed by ScandBook AB

The publishers grateful acknowledge financial assistance from the Arts Council.

Down These
Green Streets

Irish Crime Writing in the 21st Century

Edited by Declan Burke

LIB
ERT
IES

Contents

Part II: Thieves Like Us

Part III: Kiss Tomorrow Goodbye

Editor's Note

Veronica Guerin's murder. The end of the thirty-year 'Troubles' in Northern Ireland. The economic boom of the Celtic Tiger, with its attendant greed and corruption. A country awash in cash and drugs. The rise and rise of criminal gangs, and soaring gangland murders. The declining reputations of the Church and the political, legal and financial institutions.

There have been many reasons mooted for the current explosion in Irish crime fiction. A more practical reason, and one offered in these pages by John Connolly, is the work of authors such as Maeve Binchy, Roddy Doyle and Marian Keyes, writers who stepped out of the long shadow cast by the Irish literary tradition of Joyce, Beckett, Wilde et al, to prove that an appetite existed for stories that were more relevant to the day-to-day concerns of a whole new generation of readers.

It's true, of course, that Irish novelists have always engaged with the crime genre, from Gerald Griffin to Liam O'Flaherty, Flann O'Brien to Brian Moore, and on to John Banville (there are even some, including Supreme Court Justice Adrian Hardiman, who argue that a murder mystery lies at the heart of James Joyce's *Ulysses*). There have also been pioneers, in the years prior to the current upsurge in crime writing, who wrote dedicated crime and mystery fiction, among them Patrick McGinley, T. S. O'Rourke, Jim Lusby, Seamus Smyth, John Brady, Philip Davison, Rory McCormac, Hugo Hamilton and – last but by no means least – Vincent Banville.

The generation of crime writers contributing to *Down These Green Streets* have for the most part been published since the mid-1990s. Eoin McNamee's

Resurrection Man appeared in 1994; Colin Bateman published *Divorcing Jack* in 1995; Ken Bruen's *Rilke on Black* appeared in 1996; Paul Charles's *I Love the Sound of Breaking Glass* was published in 1997; Julie Parsons's *Mary Mary* appeared in 1998; and John Connolly's *Every Dead Thing* was published in 1999. All of these writers have continued to both set the standard and expand the parameters of what is now the established sub-genre of Irish crime writing, and in their wake came Tana French, Declan Hughes, Alex Barclay, Adrian McKinty, Alan Glynn, Ingrid Black, Gene Kerrigan, Arlene Hunt, Benjamin Black, and many more. The roll-call expands by the year: notable additions in the last couple of years alone include Stuart Neville, Niamh O'Connor, Conor Fitzgerald, Kevin McCarthy, Rob Kitchin, William Ryan, Ava McCarthy, Gerard O'Donovan and Gerry O'Carroll.

It may be stretching the point to suggest that they are prophets without honour in their own country, but for the most part Irish crime writers are more celebrated outside of Ireland than they are at home. That's a little bit odd, given that the Irish public appears to have a healthy appetite for crime writing, albeit of the US, UK and Scandinavian variety; it's also not a little unfortunate, given that Irish crime writers are more than capable of holding their own on the international stage, not least when it comes to awards season. Further, as Fintan O'Toole notes in the afterword, reprinted from his original article in the *Irish Times*, which was published in November 2009, 'Irish-set crime writing has not merely begun to blossom but has become arguably the nearest thing we have to a realist literature adequate to capturing the nature of contemporary society.'

It is hoped that the publication of *Down These Green Streets: Irish Crime Writing in the 21st Century* will go some way to alerting the Irish public to the quality of the indigenous crime writers. Not all of the writers in this collection set their novels in Ireland; not all of them are concerned with engaging with contemporary criminality and its consequences; few are concerned with directly addressing issues of national identity. Indeed, there is very little that is homogenous about the current crop of Irish crime writers, and the sheer diversity of the kinds of stories told, the styles and approaches employed, is arguably the most potent charm of a group that can only be loosely described as a body of Irish crime writers. This collection incorporates offerings – essays, interviews, short stories – from writers who variously write hard-boiled crime, comic capers, police procedurals, historical mysteries and urban noir, and who bring a distinctly Irish flavour to private eye tales, high-concept thrillers, psychological studies, serial killers, playful meta-fiction and genre-blending. Taken as a whole, it can at times be a bewildering brew; but it is rarely less than satisfying, and is as often as not exhilarating.

Success, they say, has many fathers, but in this case it has at least one mother: *Green Streets* would never have got off the ground were it not for the support and encouragement of Sarah Bannan at the Irish Arts Council, to whom I'm deeply grateful. Heartfelt thanks are also due to the peerless Jonathan Williams, who provided the necessary grace under pressure. I'd also like to thank all of the writers who committed so comprehensively to the collection, without whom this would have been a very slim volume indeed; and Seán O'Keeffe at Liberties Press, who had the vision to bring the project to fruition, and in such elegant fashion.

Last, but by no means least, I'd like to express my gratitude to my family, Aileen and Lily, for somehow managing to put up with me and my frequent absences, or more accurately my infrequent appearances, throughout the process.

This book is dedicated to Michael Gallagher, former owner of the crime and mystery fiction bookstore Murder Ink on Dawson Street in Dublin, who was for many years a patron and supporter of Irish crime writers, long before such was fashionable or profitable.

Declan Burke, January 2011

*

Declan Burke was born in Sligo, Ireland, in 1969. He is the author of four novels: *Eightball Boogie* (2003), *The Big O* (2007), *Crime Always Pays* (2009) and *Absolute Zero Cool* (2011). He hosts an online resource dedicated to Irish crime fiction called Crime Always Pays.

Foreword

by Michael Connelly

At first I thought I didn't belong here. My name got me the invite but the truth was that I didn't belong. I am a full and direct descendant of Ireland all right. My grandparents were Scahan, McEvoy, McGrath and Connelly, but still, what did I know of the true Irish experience? I'd been to Dublin and Belfast, quaffed a Guinness at the place on the river where it's made and drank another pint at Davy Byrnes in an effort to conjure the ghost and inspiration of Joyce. But it hardly qualified me to introduce this book.

But then I started reading the stories and the essays and I came to realise there is a universal language in the crime story. What Tana French does in Dublin I try to do in Los Angeles. What John Connolly (spelling not withstanding) hopes to say with Charlie Parker is what I want to say with Harry Bosch. Same goes with Black, Bateman, Burke, and any of the other writers whose work is contained herein. We're all in this together and there is only the language of storytelling.

Great storytelling knows no boundaries such as oceans or borders. It is universal and it is in embedded in the twisting helix of our DNA. It is arguable that the Irish DNA is indeed different, that it has extra chromosomes for metaphor, legend and wit. For such a relatively small place, it's impact on and contribution to the world of literature has been disproportionately huge.

So, too, now in the shorter field of crime fiction. What you have in this book is the acknowledgement of some of the finest writers in the world in the understanding of the crime story's important place in literature. These writers know the secret. That the examination of a crime is an examination of society. The form is simply the doorway we go through as we enter lives and worlds as fully realised as any in fiction, as we examine issues and societies and moral dilemmas that are important to all of us. I am drawn to these stories as an outsider with this inside information. As someone who knows the power and importance of what these pages hold.

*

Michael Connelly is the best-selling and award-winning author of the Harry Bosch and Mickey Haller series of novels. He served as President of the Mystery Writers of America 2003-04. His latest novel is *The Fifth Witness*.

Introduction

by Professor Ian Campbell Ross

Crime fiction has a long history. Whether that history goes back nearly two centuries or three thousand years depends, though, on how we choose to consider what exactly constitutes that body of writing. To take the longer perspective is to be aware that the literary treatment of themes of crime, investigation, judgment and punishment has a very extended history indeed. The second, more narrowly focused approach takes us back to the emergence of a distinctive form of prose fiction that began in the 1840s, so literary historians usually agree, with Edgar Allan Poe's three 'tales of ratiocination': 'The Murders in the Rue Morgue', 'The Mystery of Marie Rogêt', and 'The Purloined Letter'. Any account of Irish crime writing, past and present, should consider both approaches. Beginning with the broader definition, we find crime – or detective – writing to have exceptionally ancient origins. Pre-eminent in the pre-history of detective fiction is Sophocles' *Oedipus Rex*, written in Athens around 500 BC. Oedipus is solver of the riddle of the Sphinx – 'what walks on four legs in the morning, two legs at noon, and three legs in the evening?' – literature's first great puzzle and a forerunner of those puzzles which literary detectives seek to solve. More importantly, and having been warned that he will shed the blood of his father and sleep with his mother, Oedipus commits the very transgressions the Oracle at Delphi has predicted. Investigating the identity of the man he has slain at the crossroads, Oedipus discovers himself to be guilty of the crimes of murder and incest, leading him to try to assuage his guilt by blinding himself. The detective who investigates a crime only to discover that the culprit is, literally or metaphorically, himself is one of the most frequently used tropes in the history of crime writing.

Oedipus kills his father. In the Judaeo-Christian version of history, Adam's son Cain kills his brother (Genesis, 4.8). Murder, then, is both the archetypal crime and the first committed in the fallen world. Cain, though, cannot escape detection, for 'the LORD said unto Cain, where is Abel thy brother?', before cursing Cain and making him a 'fugitive and vagabond'. An omniscient God perhaps has unfair advantages as a detective – especially given the limited number of suspects in the case of Abel's murder. The Bible also provides influential examples of human detection of guilt in the interest of the restoration of justice. With his god-like wisdom, Solomon discovers the real mother of the child, contested by two women who have just given birth, by offering to resolve the dispute by having the infant cut in two, leading the birth mother to intervene to save her child's life (1 Kings 3:16-28). Already, here, we are on the way to the Great Detective – Poe's Dupin, Conan Doyle's Sherlock Holmes or Agatha Christie's Hercule Poirot – blessed with more than ordinary powers of insight and judgement. A more ordinary but very determined biblical detective is Ioachim, in the story of Susanna and the Elders (Daniel 13:1-64), who traps the old men who attempted to rape his wife by means of a contradiction between their stories – a trope that is a staple in any number of modern police procedural novels. This renders Ioachim the forerunner of the ordinary detective, whom criminals often overlook to their later regret: Baroness Orczy's 'The Old Man in the Corner', G. K. Chesterton's Father Brown, or Agatha Christie's Miss Marple. Leaping forward two thousand years from Old Testament times to the Renaissance, we find Elizabethan and Jacobean drama anticipating many characteristic features of modern crime fiction, from the use of clues, through re-enactment of the crime, to plot structure. Of all such plays, the most famous is *Hamlet* and it is unsurprising that Shakespeare's play has influenced crime writing directly. *Hamlet* is a play about murder and Hamlet himself a forerunner of many other investigators who will attempt to confirm his suspicions of the murderer's guilt by watching his reactions when faced by a re-enactment of his crime: in this case, when Claudius is part of the audience for the play within the play. As Hamlet declares, in an aside: 'The play's the thing/Wherein I'll catch the conscience of the king' (*Hamlet*: 2.2. 605-6). The title of the work the players act is 'The Mousetrap', from which Agatha Christie would take the title of her own best-known work for the stage: a play that began in London's West End in 1952 and is still running.

Changing times result in changing methods of uncovering the truth. In the eighteenth century, Enlightenment, faith in the power of reason, led Voltaire, in chapter 3 of his satirical fiction *Zadig* – 'The dog and the horse' – to anticipate the acute powers of reason of Dupin, Holmes and a host of later literary detectives, describing accurately two animals he has never seen and of whose very existence he was unaware. This is the passage Umberto Eco so brilliantly evokes at the opening of *The Name of the Rose,* when his detective figure, the Franciscan William of Baskerville, performs a similar feat of deduction.

If the eighteenth century was an 'Age of Reason', however, then that same century also saw the rise of a quite different form of writing: Gothic fiction. Characteristically offering tales of horror involving extreme, and often extremely perverse, passions – set in such sinister, unfamiliar locations as medieval castles and ruined abbeys – Gothic fiction describes a world where the forces of night seem more powerful than those of the day, as the obscurantist forces of a dark past return to challenge Enlightenment's optimistic rationalism. Influenced by Edmund Burke's *Enquiry into the Origin of our Ideas of the Sublime and the Beautiful* (1757), Gothic fiction counts the Irish historian Thomas Leland's *Longsword* (1762) as well as Horace Walpole's *The Castle of Otranto* (1764) among early exemplars.

The eighteenth century was an age preoccupied by crime in many forms – a period when the number of capital offences rose in England from fifty in 1700 to two hundred in 1800 – and which produced many works of true and fictional crime writing, from the real-life *Newgate Calendar* to Daniel Defoe's psychological thriller, *Roxana* (1724). It was only at the very end of the century, however, that the eighteenth century's innovative and predominantly realistic fiction merged with the Gothic romance of Horace Walpole or Ann Radcliffe. And it was at the height of the Terror that followed the French Revolution of 1789 that the English radical William Godwin created, in *Caleb Williams* (1794), a novel in which the protagonist sets out to investigate a murder committed by his master, convinced that reason and justice will triumph, only to find himself accused of the crime, becoming an outcast like Cain, the pursued not the pursuer, and who ends, in the tale's gripping climax, convinced like Oedipus of his own guilt.

The entwined influence of Enlightenment rationalism and the Gothic is perhaps nowhere more obvious in crime fiction than in those short stories that are most often thought of as the founding texts of crime writing as more narrowly conceived – Edgar Allan Poe's tales of ratiocination, featuring the Chevalier C. Auguste Dupin: 'The Murders in the Rue Morgue' (1841), 'The Mystery of Marie Rogêt' (1842), and 'The Purloined Letter' (1845). A master of inductive reasoning, Dupin is also a down-at-heel aristocrat in bourgeois Paris, who lives in a decaying mansion, emerging onto the streets only by night. A contradictory personality, Poe's 'double Dupin' is both mathematician and poet. Poe's stories are distinctively different from one another, but this doubleness is a feature common to all three and one that would prove highly influential in the later history of crime writing.

Doubling is not confined to detective (or crime) fiction but it is certainly characteristic of a great deal of it. Historically, the line between those who committed crimes and those charged with investigating it was a thin one. In eighteenth-century England, two notorious thieves and thief-takers, Jack Shepherd and Jonathan Wild, who finished their lives on the gallows, were both remembered by William Harrison Ainsworth in his novel *Jack Sheppard* (1839). In early nineteenth-century France, Eugène Vidocq, formerly a thief, became the first head of the Paris police force, the Sûreté and author of a renowned volume of autobiography, *Mémoires* (1829-30). It was also the formation of the forerunners of modern police forces, in the early decades of the nineteenth century, which gave further impetus to the development of crime fiction. In England, the Metropolitan police force was formed in 1829 while, in New York, police reform was a major issue of concern in the 1830s and 1840s. Still more significant was the foundation, in 1842, of the first detective police in England, though this was initially a tiny and generally despised force.

The rising fame of these new enforcers of law and order owed a good deal to Charles Dickens, who wrote about them in his journal *Household Words* in 1850. Dickens, for whom crime was a major social concern, also wrote at least two novels that can usefully be thought of as detective fiction: *Bleak House* (1852-3), which features one of the first fictional policemen, Inspector Bucket, and *The Mystery of Edwin Drood* (1870), unfinished at his death. By then, Dickens's friend and brother-in-law, Wilkie Collins, had written what the poet T. S. Eliot considered 'the best of modern English detective novels', *The Moonstone* (1868-9), which mixes amateur detectives with the police detective, Sergeant Cuff, and which was based on a notorious recent murder, theRode Case.

Modern readers know *Bleak House* and *The Moonstone* as novels in book form but both started life as magazine serialisations in popular periodicals founded by Dickens: *Household Words* and *All the Year Round*. In the later nineteenth century, detective fiction figured importantly in the magazines that appeared with increasing frequency. One the best known of these cheap periodicals – typically priced at 2d or even 1d – was *The Strand*, which ran Arthur Conan Doyle's Sherlock Holmes stories. Holmes first appeared in a short novel, *A Study in Scarlet*, published in *Beeton's Christmas Annual* for 1887. It was in the magazines that crime writing really thrived, however. Even *The Hound of the Baskervilles* was initially published as a serialisation in *The Strand*. Although the most enduringly popular writer of the new detective fiction, Conan Doyle had many rivals among writers of late nineteenth and early twentieth-century detective novels and stories, including Grant Allen, Fergus Hume, Arthur Morrison, and G. K. Chesterton, whose Father Brown retains his popularity. Notable female authors, who often used crime writing to explore women's social and political issues in popular fiction, included Mary Elizabeth Braddon, Ellen Wood (or Mrs Henry Wood as she was better known), and Baroness Orczy.

*

Ireland and Irish writers rarely feature prominently in accounts of early crime fiction. If this is so, however, the reasons may lie in the ways in which the critical codification of the genre took place in Britain and Ireland. In the 1920s and '30s, influential writers such as Dorothy L. Sayers (of Irish stock herself) subordinated many elements of crime writing's pre-history, not least its links with the Gothic, in order to privilege the rational and scientific detection that the 'Golden Age' writers valued above all else. In the same period, in newly independent Ireland, much eighteenth- and nineteenth-century Anglo-Irish writing across all genres was neglected, as nationalist critics sought to define a more narrowly 'authentic', nationalist tradition of Irish writing in English and Irish. Looked at from the pluralist perspective of the twenty-first century, however, the importance of Irish authors in early crime writing was far from negligible.

This is not to say that there were no indigenous reasons why Irish crime writing was not immediately perceived as a distinct and distinctive body of work. In the nineteenth century Irish writers might either address themselves predominantly to an English audience, as did Gerald Griffin in *The Collegians* (1829), or draw on elements of Irish life and legend that had no place in an 'English' tradition. So, Samuel Lover's 'The Priest's Story' (1831), for instance, tells of a Roman Catholic priest who learns the identity of his brother's murderer under the seal of the confessional. Here, the criminal is eventually brought to justice by human agency but elsewhere crimes might be detected by magic, as in 'The Holy Well and the Murderer', retold by Lady William Wilde in *Ancient Legends, Mystic Charms, and the Superstitions of Ireland* (1887).

The continuing importance of indigenous explanations of 'crime' in nineteenth-century Ireland is illuminatingly discussed in Angela Bourke's fine study, *The Burning of Bridget Cleary* (1999). In the same decade that saw Sherlock Holmes solving two dozen mysteries, each in the space of a few pages, a far more perplexing case occupied the attention of newspaper readers in

Ireland and England. In 1895, the burned body of Bridget Cleary, the young wife of Michael Cleary, was found in a shallow grave outside Clonmel. She had been sick. The local priest was called and folk-remedies attempted, one of which resulted in her death. By the time the case was investigated, Michael Cleary seemed convinced that his wife had been taken by the fairies and that the body he acknowledged burning had been that of a changeling. Following a trial that brought withering though deeply-rooted Irish folk beliefs in conflict with English law, Michael Cleary was convicted of manslaughter, a verdict that satisfied neither his detractors nor his supporters.

Irish suspicion of nineteenth-century English law enforcement, even among the respectable middle classes, did not end with such extreme cases. In his short story, 'The Keening Woman', the barrister and schoolteacher Patrick Pearse, later executed after the 1916 Easter Rising, related a tale of crime and its consequences that might easily have been told very differently. Here, though, sympathy lies with the naïve country boy, framed by a shadowy government agent and a perjured 'peeler', who dies in prison the victim of an oppressive colonial power that pays no heed to the petitions of his mother, the keening woman of the title.

Old belief systems and modern nationalist politics both worked against an easy acceptance – at least among part of the population – of crime fiction as it was developing in the neighbouring island. Yet Pearse's 'The Keening Woman' points to a different problem for the Irish writer. Pearse originally wrote the story in Irish, as 'An Bhean Chaointe', as part of his project to revitalise the language. In the event, his stories quickly became as well, or better known in an English translation by the poet Joseph Campbell. Attempts at crime fiction in Irish have generally foundered, despite the efforts of short story writers such as Micheál Ó Gríobhtha, author of *Lorgaireacht* (1927), or those publishing in periodicals, like Father Seoirse Mac Clúin, Art Ó Riain, and Father Gearóid Ó Nualláin, uncle of Brian O'Nolan (Flann O'Brien) and of Ciarán Ua Nualláin, whose *Oidhche i nGleann na nGealt* (1939) was the first full-length crime fiction in the language. Noteworthy too are Seoirse Mac Liam's *An Doras do Plabadh* (1940), Pól Ó Muirí's *Dlithe an Nádúir* (2001), featuring Bangarda

Paloma Pettigrew, and Seán Ó Dúrois' *Crann Snola* (2001) and *Rí na gCearrbhach* (2003), both set in the North of Ireland in the 1860s, along with Eilís Ní Dhuibhne's *Dúnmharú sa Daingean* (2000) and *Dún an Airgid* (2008), whose central characters are the amateur detective Saoirse Ní Ghallchóir and Garda Máirtín Ó Flaithearta. Most prolific was the English-born Cathal Ó Sándair, whose Réics Carló series, written between the 1950s and 70s, was published by the state-sponsored Irish-language publisher An Gúm.

The realities of the market-place offer a simpler but equally pressing reason for the perceived failure of crime fiction to take root in nineteenth-century Ireland: the lack of a sufficiently large readership to sustain a local popular culture comparable to that of late nineteenth-century England. The much larger and more literate population of Britain, coupled with the rise of railway travel, and commuting by Underground in London, helped foster a literary culture in which cheap magazines formed an important part of what English men and women read. In Ireland, the market for such popular literature was much smaller, where it existed at all. The result was to persuade even such convinced patriots as M. McDonnell Bodkin, a lawyer and nationalist politician, to publish in England. Equally importantly, and despite the fact that he was author of a fictional life of Lord Edward Fitzgerald and of other Irish historical novels, Bodkin set his detective fiction predominantly in England, a practice followed by many of his contemporaries.

Yet while such circumstances need to be taken into account, it remains equally true that the role of Irish authors in the history of crime writing, more broadly considered, is a significant one. If Gothic fiction is acknowledged as an important precursor of modern crime writing, then nineteenth-century authors such as Charles Robert Maturin and Sheridan Le Fanu were exceptional Irish exponents of the genre. Maturin's most famous novel, *Melmoth the Wanderer* (1820), is constructed in a manner that prefigures later detective fiction, as the hero John Melmoth obsessively investigates the mysterious figure of his ancestor, the Wanderer himself. The supernatural elements employed by Maturin touch but do not define the varied fiction of Sheridan Le Fanu, which includes *Uncle Silas*, *The Wyvern Mystery* (1867), and *In a Glass Darkly* (1872), a collection including the lesbian vampire story 'Carmilla'.

Uncle Silas first appeared, entitled 'Maud Ruthyn and Uncle Silas', as a serialisation in the *Dublin University Review* in 1864, being published in novel form in London later that same year. Introducing Le Fanu's novel in 1947, Elizabeth Bowen remarked that '*Uncle Silas* has always struck me as being an Irish story transposed to an English setting'. Bowen's intuition has subsequently been confirmed. Le Fanu's novel originated in a short story 'A Passage in the Secret History of an Irish Countess', set in Ireland and published as early as 1838, giving the tale good claim to the first 'locked-room' mystery, written three years before Poe's more celebrated 'The Murders in the Rue Morgue'. When republished, as 'The Murdered Cousin' in *Ghost Stories and Tales of Mystery* (1851), the story retained its Irish setting and it was at his publisher's insistence that Le Fanu relocated his tale to Derbyshire, when incorporating it into *Uncle Silas*.

By the end of the nineteenth century, detective stories were among the most widely read genre of popular fiction, along with science fiction, ghost stories, and romance. Unsurprisingly, even authors not usually associated with the form were alert to its popularity. So, Oscar Wilde published *Lord Arthur Savile's Crime and Other Stories* in 1891: the volume including tales that had already appeared in magazines and which offered in the title story a comically oblique version of crime writing, as 'The Canterville Ghost' does of the ghost story. That Wilde should have written 'Lord Arthur Savile's Crime' seems appropriate, too, since Conan Doyle's characterisation of Sherlock Holmes – part energetic man of science, part violin-playing, cocaine-taking aesthete – owed something not only to the example of Dr Joseph Bell, who lectured Doyle when the latter was a medical student at the University of Edinburgh, but also to Oscar Wilde, whom Doyle met at a dinner in 1889, during which the two writers were invited to contribute to *Lippincott's Magazine*, Wilde subsequently writing *The Picture of Dorian Gray* and Doyle *The Sign of the Four*.

Prominent among the contemporaries of Wilde and Doyle, and among the best-known writers of crime and mystery fiction in the nineteenth century, was L. T. Meade – the most frequently used pen-name of Elizabeth Thomasina

Meade Smith – born in Bandon, County Cork. Astoundingly prolific – author of some three hundred volumes published between 1875 and 1915 – Meade was celebrated as a writer of children's literature. She was also author, along with Robert Eustace, of crime and mystery stories which appeared in *Harmsworth Magazine* and *The Strand,* among others. It was to the former that Meade and Eustace contributed a series of tales detailing the 'detections' and 'adventures' of Miss Cusack, one of a number of female, or 'lady', detectives to appear in fiction after the 1860s. In 1910, under her own name, she published another collection: *Micah Faraday, Adventurer.* Meade's crime novels, variously set in Ireland, England, and continental Europe, include *The Voice of the Charmer* (1895), *The Home of Silence* (1907), and *The Fountain of Beauty* (1909). Collections of crime fiction included the two series of *Stories from the Diary of a Doctor* (1894; 1896), co-authored with Edgar Beaumont, and *The Sorceress of the Strand* (1903), with Robert Eustace. *Silenced* (1904), *The Oracle of Maddox Street* (1904), *Twenty-four Hours: A Novel of To-day* (1911) and *Ruffles* (1911) followed. A number of Meade's works were illustrated by Sidney Paget, famous for his definitive illustrations of Sherlock Holmes in *The Strand.* Given that Meade was perhaps best known for her writing for girls – she was editor of the progressive girls' magazine, *Atalanta,* for some years – it is worth noticing that she not only included female detectives and criminals, including the evil Madame Koluchy in *The Brotherhood of the Seven Kings* (1899), in her fiction, but attempted to suggest a particular role for women in criminal inves-tigation and crime writing. This aim, shared by many of her female contem-poraries, notably anticipated the different waves of feminist crime writing of the past half century.

Among L. T. Meade's Irish contemporaries, the Clonmel-born Richard Dowling (1846-1898) is little known today yet he was an author popular as a writer of romance, mystery, and of crime fiction with English or Irish settings, including *A Baffling Quest* (1891), featuring the London private investigator, George Tufnell, and *Old Corcoran's Money* (1897), set in what is most likely a fictionalised Waterford. Less known still is Kathleen O'Meara (1839-1888), whose eccentric oeuvre includes, alongside religious fiction such as *The Bells of the Sanctuary* (1871), a thriller entitled *Narka, the Nihilist* (1887), involving intrigue and murder, which concludes with its noble heroine's triumph at La Scala opera house, singing the title-role of Bellini's *Norma*.

Better remembered is M. McDonnell Bodkin, another prominent writer of crime fiction. Born in Tuam, he was educated by the Jesuits and at the Catholic University in Dublin, becoming a lawyer (later a judge) and Nationalist MP for North Roscommon. From the late 1880s until the 1920s, Bodkin managed to combine his legal and political work with the writing of historical novels and Irish-based short stories, as well as frequently extravagant detective fiction, featuring 'impossible' crimes. Beginning with *Paul Beck: The Rule of Thumb Detective* (1898), Bodkin introduced a female counterpart in *Dora Myrl, Lady Detective* (1900), before pitting the one against the other in *The Capture of Paul Beck* (1909), in which the pair are married. Not content with anticipating similar couples in crime fiction – Christie's Tommy and Tuppence, or Nick and Nora in Dashiell Hammett's *The Thin Man* (and subsequent movies), to say nothing of such modern-day counterparts as Arlene Hunt's John Quigley and Sarah Kenny of QuicK Investigation in *False Intentions* (2005) and *Undertow* (2008) – Bodkin moved on to the next generation with a sequel, *Young Beck: A Chip off the Old Block* (1911), featuring the son of Paul and Dora.

Since Bodkin was a staunch nationalist and author of several Irish historical novels, it is the more striking that Dora Myrl is the daughter of a Cambridge don who, at eighteen, misses her chance to study medicine when her father dies, leaving her to a life initially composed of such humdrum jobs as telegraph and telephone girl, before setting up as a 'Lady Detective'. Though Bodkin disclaimed feminist views on his heroine's behalf, recent critics have found Dora Myrl to be the very personification of the New Woman: independent, athletic and (in her case) handy with a 'six-shooter'. Yet Dora Myrl also follows in the path of female detectives like C. L. Pirkis's Loveday Brooke, who solve their cases by a combination of intuition and attention to the kind of domestic detail their duller and more impatient male counterparts often overlook. While she outwits Paul Beck in crime and courtship – Ellery Queen ungallantly suggested that she would do anything to get her man, 'be he criminal or husband' – marriage persuades Dora to abandon detection in favour of domesticity. It was a problem common enough for women in crime fiction in the first half of the twentieth century. A more elaborate variation on the inequalities of sexual and romantic liaisons in the first half of the twentieth century is to be found in the relationship between Dorothy L. Sayers's Lord Peter Wimsey and Harriet Vane. A detective novelist herself, Harriet Vane enters an Oxford college, in *Gaudy Night*, under the pretext of researching the work of Sheridan Le Fanu. Lord Peter and Harriet will eventually outdo Paul and Dora by having three children – though none of these will become the 'chip off the old block' by turning their hand to detection, like Young Beck.

McDonnell Bodkin set his detective fiction in England, as did his more influential contemporary, Freeman Wills Crofts – though Ireland is the location for *Sir John Magill's Last Journey* (1930) and *Fatal Venture* (1939). Born in Dublin and brought up in the North of Ireland, Crofts long worked as an engineer on the Belfast and Northern Counties railways, writing a number of railway crime fictions. He came to prominence in 1920, the same year as Agatha Christie, eventually becoming, like her and Sayers, a member of the influential Golden Age 'Detection Club'. His debut novel, *The Cask* (1920), is also one of his best books, an ingenious narrative set in Paris and London. Perhaps Crofts's greatest contribution to crime writing was to make a police detective, Inspector (later Superintendent) French of Scotland Yard, the hero of his fiction. Early crime fiction had featured policemen but rarely as the heroes of the narrative. It is the amateur detective, Dupin, who outwits the Prefect of Police in 'The Purloined Letter', while Dickens's Inspector Bucket comes belatedly on the solution to the mystery he investigates, and social pressures force Wilkie Collins's Sergeant Cuff off the case of the missing moonstone altogether. Sherlock Holmes invariably defeated his habitual antagonist, Inspector Lestrade, and did much to establish the vogue for the consulting or private detective.

Freeman Wills Crofts's creation of a sympathetic police detective in fiction was a notable achievement, then, and the more so since Inspector French is a model of the determined but undemonstrative investigator. Other police detectives followed in crime series. In England, Ngaio Marsh began to write about the aristocratic Superintendent Roderick Alleyn in 1934, and John Creasey created Inspector West in 1940. French, Alleyn and West are all fore-runners not only of more recent notable police detectives, such as Colin Dexter's Inspector Morse or Ian Rankin's D.I. John Rebus, but also of their Irish counterparts, including Eugene McEldowney's Superintendent Cecil McGarry, Brian McGilloway's Inspector Ben Devlin, and Detective Superintendent Jo Birmingham in Niamh O'Connor's debut, *If I Never See You Again* (2010).

Among the next generation of Irish writers, arguably the most important was Nicholas Blake, pen-name of the poet (and eventual Poet Laureate), Cecil Day-Lewis, most of whose twenty crime novels – from *A Question of Proof* (1935) to *The Morning after Death* (1966) – featured a detective, Nigel Strangeways, supposedly based on W. H. Auden. Among the most notable is *The Beast Must Die* (1938), which, three decades later, Claude Chabrol turned into one of his best films, *Que la Bête Meure* (1969). Blake also wrote four stand-alone novels, of which the last and most personal is *The Private Wound* (1968), which offers a carefully framed story that explores a theme of belong-ing and alienation, characteristic of much Irish fiction of the nineteenth and twentieth centuries. (Day-Lewis lived his earliest years in Queen's County – now County Laois – the son of a Church of Ireland clergyman.)

Had Day-Lewis written the book under his own name, instead of that of Nicholas Blake, *The Private Wound* would certainly have received more serious critical attention. But prejudice against crime fiction is deep-rooted. It was in response to a crime novel by Eilís Dillon – a younger contemporary of Day-Lewis, from a very different background – that an *Irish Times* reviewer wrote in 1954: 'I cannot help feeling that, if Miss Dillon is so good a writer, perhaps she should be encouraged to launch in the wider seas of the real novelist'. The occasion of the *Irish Times* reviewer's faint praise was the first of three crime fictions by Dillon. Author of many novels for adult and young readers, Dillon wrote fiction with Irish settings: *Death at Crane's Court* (1953) and *Sent to His*

Account (1954), located in counties Galway and Wicklow, and *Death in the Quadrangle* (1956), whose action takes place in a Dublin university where motives for murder abound. Other admired Irish writers include Sheila Pim, whose Irish village mysteries share a common thread indicated by the title of the first of the four novels she wrote between 1945 and 1952: *Common or Garden Crime* economically indicating their shared gardening theme. Nigel Fitzgerald, whose *Suffer a Witch* (1958) was chosen as a classic of crime fiction of the third quarter of the twentieth century, was author of over a dozen novels. Fitzgerald set his fiction mainly in Ireland and created, as series characters, Inspector Duffy and the actor-manager Alan Russell. More recently, Gemma O'Connor's best works, including *Sins of Omission* (1995), *Falls the Shadow* (1996) and *Following the Wake* (2002), evoke the 1940s and 1950s.

Like that of Eilís Dillon, Pim's achievement as a writer of crime fiction is happily not entirely forgotten. The detective fiction, featuring Chief Inspector Ellis McKay of Scotland Yard, by the prolific L. A. G. Strong has been so completely ignored as not even to receive mention in the author's Oxford Dictionary of National Biography entry. A poet and biographer of, among others, Thomas Moore and John McCormack, Strong was born in England of an Irish father and half-Irish mother. He spent part of his childhood in Ireland, however, with the result that the country featured largely in his life and fiction, with novels set both in Dublin and the west. Like others before him, though, Strong looked to a bigger market in setting his detective fiction – from *Slocombe Dies* (1942) to *Treason in the Egg* (1958), published shortly before his premature death – in England. The Irish-born Ruth Dudley Edwards, an immensely versatile writer, also uses English settings, though her Robert Amiss series, running from *Corridors of Death* (1981) to *Murdering Americans* (2007), does not overlook Ireland, offering characteristic political satire in *The Anglo-Irish Murders* (2000). Another Irish-born author, Jane Casey, has recently set two psychological thrillers in England, including *The Burning* (2010), featuring the London Metropolitan Police detective Maeve Kerrigan.

Among earlier Irish authors whose work included some element of crime, mystery or espionage writing, Edward Plunkett, Lord Dunsany, deserves mention. A vastly prolific writer in many genres, Dunsany was author of an early crime mystery drama, *The Murderers* (1919), and among his short stories, featuring Mr Linley, the much anthologised 'Two Bottles of Relish' (1932) has been included in many collections, such as *The Fifty Greatest Mysteries of All Time*. As was the case with many authors, crime writing formed only a small part of Dunsany's extensive output. This included thrillers and spy stories, genres with which crime fiction shares occasionally ill-defined boundaries. So 'How Ryan got out of Russia' (1934) has been anthologised, by Michael Cox, in *The Oxford Book of Spy Stories* – but Dunsany's antecedents and successors in such forms of writing include Erskine Childers, author of the classic *The Riddle of the Sands* (1913), Liam O'Flaherty with *The Informer* (1925) and Frank O'Connor with 'Guests of the Nation' (1931). In the second half of the twentieth century, Brian Moore who, sometimes under the pen-names of Bernard Mara or Michael Bryan, began his career with luridly-entitled works such as *Wreath for a Redhead* (1951) and *A Bullet for My Lady* (1955), also wrote, among quite different kinds of fiction, highly praised works that bear strong resemblance to Graham Greene's 'entertainments', including *The Colour of Blood* (1987) and *Lies of Silence* (1990).

In *Lies of Silence*, Moore engaged with the Troubles that had dominated Irish life since the late 1960s. Few of his contemporaries dared address such matters in the form of crime fiction or, perhaps, thought it appropriate to do so. Yet the Troubles did produce works that might be characterised as crime fiction, including Eoin McNamee's chilling *Resurrection Man* (1994), based on the notorious Shankhill Butcher murders, and *The Ultras* (2004); McNamee also returned to an earlier moment in Northern Ireland's past with *Orchid Blue* (2010), a remorseless anatomy of the circumstances surrounding another real murder investigation, this time in Newry in 1961. An unblinking approach to the aftermath of the Troubles characterises Stuart Neville's compelling debut novel, *The Twelve* (2009), whose central character, Gerry Fegan, is haunted by the victims of his own murderous past, while his fellow paramilitaries divide between political respectability and republican dissidence. A very different response to the Troubles is to be found in *Mohammed Maguire* (2001), a funny, satirical and decidedly irreverent work by the prolific Colin Bateman. Author between 1995 and 2005 of seven Dan Starkey novels, featuring an investigative journalist, Bateman has also created Detective Jimmy Murphy and, most recently, the eponymous (and anonymous) hero of *Mystery Man* (2008), a Belfast crime fiction bookshop owner who has already featured in two subsequent novels. Some of Bateman's work has been written for children, the principal audience for Derek Landy's series, featuring the skeletal detective Skulduggery Pleasant, which reached its fifth title with *Mortal Coil* (2010). Also successful in blending crime writing with humour for a wide audience has been Pauline McLynn, author of three Leo Street novels. Humour of a very much darker kind characterises Hugo Hamilton's *Headbanger* (1996) and *Sad Bastard* (1998), featuring the Garda Pat Coyne, the eponymous headbanging sad bastard, as well as Declan Burke's *The Big O* (2007) and its sequel *Crime Always Pays* (2009).

As Hamilton's work suggests, not all police detectives created by Irish writers are as basically decent and principled as the quiet, conservative Protestant Inspector French or Brian McGilloway's mass- and confession-going family man Inspector Benedict Devlin. Among contemporary variations on the police detective are Ken Bruen's tormented, alcoholic, drug-addicted former Garda, Jack Taylor, introduced in *The Guards* (2001) and most recently featured in *The Devil* (2010), and the endlessly malevolent London policeman, Inspector Brant, central character of seven novels, from *A White Arrest* (1998) to *Ammunition* (2008).

Like many of his contemporaries, Bruen has been much influenced by American crime writing, and Declan Burke's first novel, *Eightball Boogie* (2003), is a daring homage to Chandler that can stand the comparison. Such writing lies at the opposite end of the crime writing spectrum from the 'cosy' – the kind of book in which, at their most complacent, authors play with their readers as the great detective plays with the suspects until he gathers them together to expose the guilty and restore order to a society only temporarily disrupted by crime. The great change in crime fiction between the puzzle and hard-boiled mystery was largely the creation of the American pulp fiction writers of the 1920s and '30s, of whom Dashiell Hammett and Raymond Chandler are the most widely admired.

Instead of flamboyant detectives such as Sherlock Holmes or S. S. Van Dine's Philo Vance, readers discovered investigators enmired in altogether dirtier worlds. As Chandler famously wrote in 'The Simple Art of Murder' (1950), 'Hammett took murder out of the Venetian vase and dropped it into the alley'. In the Continental Op, Hammett created a (literally) anonymous character who works – for the Continental Detective Agency – as anyone might work at any job, only the Op's job is to solve crime. Sam Spade, the 'blond Satan' who is Hammett's most famous creation, appears only slightly more engaged in the rights and wrongs of crime, declaring of his intention to solve the murder of his partner Archer (with whose wife he has been conducting an affair): 'it happens we were in the detective business. Well, when one of your organisation gets killed, it's bad business to let the killer get away with it' (*The Maltese Falcon*). Despite the vividly metaphorical wisecracking, Raymond Chandler's Philip Marlowe is an altogether more chivalric figure, introduced on the opening page of Chandler's first novel, *The Big Sleep* (1939), as a kind of knight-errant. The seedy Los Angeles of the 1940s in which he operates, though, is for the most part very much at odds with the alluring images of the Golden State or Hollywood's silver screen. Likewise, the third of the great California detectives, Ross Macdonald's Lew Archer (named for Spade's murdered partner), works his way through a series of cases haunted by tragically dysfunctional families anxious to conceal murderous secrets.

These three great writers have continued to exercise an influence on their successors both in the United States and beyond. Among contemporary Irish writers openly influenced by Macdonald is one of the most admired and successful, Declan Hughes. In a series of novels, from *The Wrong Kind of Blood* (2006) to *City of Dead Girls* (2010), the south Dublin-born Ed Loy returns to his native city from the States, following a failed marriage and decline into near alcoholism, to find a country very different from the one he had left. The Dublin he observes is a capital initially marked both by the Celtic Tiger's material affluence and the disintegration of the stable, conservative, Catholic world he had left. It is an Ireland of violent, often drug-related crime, facing up to a past tainted by religious hypocrisy and the long-concealed physical, sexual and emotional abuse of children. Like many contemporary detectives, Loy must battle personal demons as he struggles to expose – and understand – the new Ireland: a materialistic society facing catastrophic economic decline. Other Irish crime writers have anticipated, as much as chronicled, the collapse of the Celtic Tiger, as Alan Glynn shows in his second novel, *Winterland* (2009), set against the background of property speculation in an economically imploding Dublin, or Gene Kerrigan's unsettling account of gang warfare in the Irish capital in his aptly titled *Dark Times in the City* (2010).

Such fictions probe the metropolitan heart of modern Ireland, as, variously, do works by Paul Carson, beginning with *Scalpel* (1997), K. T. McCaffrey, in eight novels written between 1999 and 2010, and Cormac Millar, whose civil servant hero, Séamus Joyce, finds himself suddenly in charge of drug-related crime, in *An Irish Solution* (2004). Prominent among writers who have worked variations on this theme is Benjamin Black – alter ego of the Booker Prize-winning novelist John Banville – who, like a Victorian novelist, has chosen to recess his crime fiction in time, writing of the 1950s from the vantage point of the twenty-first century, laying bare the underbelly of the conservative Ireland of half a century previously. Unflinching rational enquiry conducted in worlds still clinging on to older images of themselves characterised Banville's early novels *Dr Copernicus* (1976) and *Kepler* (1981), while crime and its aesthetic responses to it formed the matter of *The Book of Evidence* (1989). In works from *Christine Falls* (2006) to *Elegy for April* (2010), the pathologist Quirke anatomises the Ireland of the 1950s, as he does its victims, Black casting a retrospective eye on a country described in its day by precursors like Edna O'Brien or John McGahern.

Crime writing with more distant historical settings ranges from the work of such established writers as Peter Tremayne (Peter Berresford Ellis), author of over twenty Sister Fidelma mysteries set in seventh-century Ireland, to that of newcomers like Kevin McCarthy, the action of whose *Peeler* (2010) takes place in 1920 during the War of Independence. Irish writers, however, have more usually preferred to attempt the constant regeneration genre fiction demands by the use of geographical shift. In the United States, Californian crime fiction has a special place, thanks to the way in which it fed, from the 1920s onwards, on potent American literary myths, including Eldorado and the frontier. When that frontier, pushing westwards, met the Pacific, it had nowhere left to go, leaving crime writers like Hammett and Chandler among the earliest to question the contemporary understanding of the American Dream, as articulated in 1931 by James Truslow Adams. Contemporary writers as different as Walter Moseley, Sue Grafton, Michael Connelly, Robert Crais, Faye Kellerman and James Ellroy have variously turned back to the world first described by the early writers of pulp fiction, but American crime writing is now remarkable for geographical diversity. New York was always important, with older writers like Chester Himes or Ed McBain making use of the city's ethnic diversity. The writing of recent decades has left few parts of the States untouched by crime writing. Chicago has Sarah Paretsky and Robert Campbell; Boston, Robert B. Parker and Dennis Lehane; New Orleans, James Lee Burke; the Twin Cities John Sanford; Washington, George Pelecanos; while Detroit and south Florida alike have their criminal laureate in Elmore Leonard.

Strikingly, given the relative sizes of the two countries, Irish writing too is increasingly marked by decentralisation (less evident elsewhere in contemporary Ireland). Dublin remains the preferred setting for crime writing – including the Ken Bruen-edited short-story collection, *Dublin Noir* (2006) – but recent fiction has learned lessons from quite different kinds of popular writers – Maeve Binchy or Roddy Doyle, for instance – as to ways of using and often exposing the social and geographical differences of Ireland's capital. Declan Hughes initially focused on the south Dublin coastal strip before moving his hero into the heart of the city, while Tana French, in her powerful, unsettling debut novel, *In the Woods* (2007), featuring two Gardaí, Rob Ryan and Cassie Maddox, made original use of the south Dublin suburbs. Outside of the capital, the North of Ireland figures strongly in the work of McEldowney, Bateman, McNamee and Neville; Galway in Ken Bruen's Jack Taylor series; Sligo in Declan Burke's dark *Eightball Boogie*, with the fiercely memorable PI, Harry Rigby.

Most recently, Brian McGilloway has taken the border between the Republic and the North of Ireland as the location for his fiction. Crime writing has often been understood in terms of borders – between good and evil, right and wrong, justice and injustice. It is precisely this borderland that much good crime writing, past and present, occupies, with detectives and investigators frequently straying from one side of the border to the other. McGilloway moves this notion of liminality – of an indeterminate state of being – away from the metaphorical to the literal, locating the Garda detective hero of four novels, *Borderlands* (2007) to *The Rising* (2010), in Lifford in County Donegal, on the left bank of the River Foyle, facing Strabane in County Tyrone, in Northern Ireland. Here, this troubled political border also marks a line between past and present – the novels subtly evoking rather than engaging directly with the area's recent history – and between Roman Catholics and Protestants, variously united and divided by a shared past. Inspector Benedict Devlin, meanwhile, finds a sympathetic counterpart in Inspector Hendry of the Police Service of Northern Ireland, the PSNI, suggestive of very different relationships that existed until recently between the Garda Síochána and the Royal Ulster Constabulary.

The quiet confidence of McGilloway's handling of this central conceit in his fiction also points to another of the ways in which recent Irish crime fiction has developed new directions for itself. The fact that the market in Great Britain was for long so important for writers of different kinds undoubtedly influenced the settings and characterisations of Irish crime writing. In the global market of the twenty-first century, the United Kingdom, while remaining important – Ken Bruen and Paul Charles, creator of D.I. Christy Kennedy, are among Irish writers to set fiction in London – no longer looms quite so large for Irish authors. The legacy of American crime writing being so strong, it is not surprising that elements of American plotting and prose style are variously evident in the work of writers like Bruen, Burke and Hughes. Some Irish writers have gone further, locating their fiction in the United States. (Only occasionally is the reverse true, though American authors such as Bartholomew

Gill (1943-2002), whose Peter McGarr series includes *The Death of a Joyce Scholar* (1989) and, more recently, Erin Hart, have written fiction set in Ireland.) One such writer is Adrian McKinty, in three novels featuring the Irish fugitive Michael Forsythe, beginning with the stunning *Dead I Well May Be* (2003), besides equally accomplished stand-alone novels, including *Fifty Grand* (2009). Another is Alex Barclay, whose New York detective Joe Lucchesi is first encountered, in *Darkhouse* (2005), in Ireland but who returns to home ground in *The Caller* (2006), while Barclay's *Blood Runs Cold* (2008) and *Time of Death* (2010) feature the female FBI agent, Ren Bryce. Ingrid Black (pen name of Eilís O'Hanlon and Ian McConnell) has imported a female former FBI agent turned crime novelist, Saxon, into Ireland, alongside her partner, the Dublin policewoman Detective Superintendent Grace Fitzgerald, in a series beginning with *The Dead* (2003). More recently, *American Skin* (2006) was marketed as Ken Bruen's long-awaited 'American' novel, Benjamin Black's short fiction, *The Lemur* (2008), is set in New York, where Stuart Neville's Gerry Fegan is also to be found in *Collusion* (2010), while Ireland and the United States meet in Bruen's *Once Were Cops* (2008).

Most determined in his relocation of Irish crime writing is certainly John Connolly. Born, educated and living in Ireland, Connolly may have seemed to make a strange decision to set his Charlie Parker novels in Maine, a state well known to readers of Stephen King's fiction. The series now includes nine novels and a novella, from *Every Dead Thing* (1998) to *The Whisperers* (2010), this last evoking the experience of veterans returning from the second Iraq war. Each work features the PI Charlie Parker, an ex-NYC cop haunted by the knowledge that he could not prevent the deaths of his own wife and young daughter, accompanied by a memorable couple of gay hit men, Angel and Louis, who provide much of the books' black humour. More, perhaps, than any of his contemporaries, Connolly recognises the importance of the borderland to crime fiction. Maine is the most northerly of the continental United States, confined not only by Canada but also by the Atlantic Ocean, leaving its coast heavily indented – a feature of the landscape that also marks the compelling stand-alone novel, *Bad Men* (2003). Maine is border country in more ways than two, however, for its sparse population is gathered mainly in the coastal cities and towns, leaving the interior a frontier area, where nature and civilisation co-exist uneasily. Yet to describe Connolly's fiction only in these terms is to miss what is perhaps its most distinctive feature: its deployment of Gothic modes and tropes. Though books like *The White Road* (2002), partly set in the deep south, insistently recall William Faulkner's much quoted 'The past is never dead. It's not even past', Connolly's fiction could never simply be termed American Gothic. Rather, in its obsessive, murderous search for answers buried in competing religious and racial histories that the present seeks unsuccessfully to forget, his fiction reveals itself as inescapably linked to the much broader tradition of Irish writing in English, not least the displacement of Irish Gothic to other locations, seen in Sheridan Le Fanu. 'This is a honeycomb world': the opening words of *The Killing Kind* (2001) offer one metaphor for the interpenetration of different realities in Connolly's fiction. Here, as in his elision of past and present, of natural and supernatural, Connolly more particularly returns Irish crime writing to its early nineteenth-century origins, prompting readers to remember the often-forgotten Irish crime fiction of the past, which waits patiently in the shadows for its historian.

*

Ian Campbell Ross has written, edited and translated books on Irish, British and Italian literature and history. His course on Detective Fiction was the first taught in Ireland and introduced Popular Literature into the School of English, Trinity College Dublin, where he is Professor of Eighteenth-Century Studies. *www.tcd.ie/English/staff/academic-staff/ian-ross.php*

Part I:
Out of the Past

No Blacks, No Dogs, No Crime Writers: Ireland and the Mystery Genre

by John Connolly

When I was a boy, I spent my summers in my grandmother's house near Ballylongford, County Kerry, in the southwest of Ireland. My mother came from a family of girls, four of whom became schoolteachers, and houses that produce schoolteachers tend to be houses that value books. My grandmother's main room, where we ate and socialised, was dominated by a set of bookshelves just inside the door. Even now, a decade or more since that house was demolished, its contents dispersed or destroyed, I can still visualise some of the titles on those shelves. There was a single-volume encyclopedia, which was, in retrospect, not terribly encyclopedic, assuming as it did that the sum total of the world's knowledge could be crammed into about four hundred pages; a book of popular science, which probably included a great deal of science that has been superseded by more recent discoveries ('No Life On The Moon After All!' 'It's 1975. Still No Sign of Jet Packs and Flying Cars!'); a copy of *The Valley of the Squinting Windows* by Brinsley MacNamara that I wasn't allowed to read due to the suspect nature of its contents; a little hardback copy of Edgar Allan Poe's collected short stories, the only book from my grandmother's collection that I have retained; and various works of paperback fiction, including Ed McBain's *Let's Hear It For The Deaf Man*, the first crime novel that I ever read and, I suppose, the genesis of my interest in the genre.

It was a Catholic library, in every sense, but what was curious about it was the relative absence of Irish writing. There was the MacNamara novel, of course, and a John B. Keane book, I think, since John B. lived down the road in Listowel, although my grandmother might have considered his work slightly racy for the time given that it acknowledged the possibility of sexual activity between consenting adults. There might also have been a novel by Maurice Walsh, the author of *The Quiet Man*, as one of my aunts was interested in his work. After that, though, I'm struggling to recall much Irish literature at all on my grandmother's shelves, a collection to which assorted members of the family contributed by adding their holiday reading when they were done. There certainly wasn't any Irish crime fiction, of that I'm sure, mainly because there wasn't very much Irish crime fiction about, and certainly none that might have been regarded as popular or contemporary in the way that such fiction has become in recent years. The genre fiction that did find its way on to those shelves, whether crime or fantasy or romance, came from Britain and the United States. There was H. P. Lovecraft, but no Mervyn Wall; there was Stephen King, but no Bram Stoker; there was Ed McBain, and Agatha Christie, but no . . .

Well, there we have it. There were no equivalents of McBain and Christie in Ireland. A little later, novelists like Jim Lusby, Vincent Banville and John Brady would attempt to make inroads into a market dominated by British and American authors, but they were only partially successful and, to their credit, a little ahead of their time. Occasionally, some lost example of Irish genre fiction would be dragged blinking into the light, like those Japanese soldiers found living in caves on Pacific islands long after the end of the World War II but, like those confused combatants, they were anomalies. Such writers and their work simply didn't have a lasting impact upon their own national audience, regardless of impacting upon a larger readership beyond these shores. (One might add that this is still the case: Irish writers of crime fiction have yet to conquer the Irish bestseller lists in the same way that, say, their Scottish equivalents have on the other side of the Irish Sea. It is as if Irish readers are not yet entirely comfortable with the concept of Irish crime fiction, or of seeing Irish society examined in this way. That situation will undoubtedly change; in fact, it is changing, but more slowly than Irish crime writers might wish if the genre is to continue to grow here.)

Looking back, I wonder if my grandmother's library was actually very unusual for its time in the relative paucity of Irish titles on its shelves. I suspect that it was not. If it's not heretical to suggest it, I think that, for a very long time, Irish writing was more admired than read by the general populace. We took a certain pride in the achievements of our writers on the international stage, as long as they didn't get above themselves, but it's still depressing to recall that the greatest of them were forced into exile, and some of the best of those who stayed, including Patrick Kavanagh and Flann O'Brien, are remembered with greater fondness now that they're dead than they ever were when they were alive.

The argument that Irish fiction was, until recently, far from populist by nature is perhaps one for another day, and another volume, but it does impact upon the topic under discussion. After all, how could popular fiction of any kind be expected to thrive in an environment in which literary populism was regarded as suspect? Irish literature was not, of course, unique in this way, and the tension between popular, or genre, fiction – for the two terms are frequently interchangeable – and its literary counterparts has been played out to varying degrees in every society in which the two forms coexist, but it is interesting that during a period when crime fiction was becoming a major form of popular entertainment in the United Kingdom (in the form of the Golden Age mystery, and the writers who subsequently followed) and in the United States (in its more streetwise, hard-boiled incarnation), Irish writers largely ignored such developments, and continued to do so, with certain honourable exceptions, until the twenty-first century.

It is sometimes forgotten, in our understandable desire to emphasise our history and our heritage, how young a nation Ireland really is. As a modern state, the Irish Republic has been in existence for less than a century, and a young nation is compelled to engage in a period of questioning its identity, of coming to terms with the forces that created it in an effort to determine what shape it should take for the future. Writers as much as politicians, and economists, and historians, are involved in this act of interpretation, and a very serious business it is too, so serious, in fact, that any writing that is not actively contributing to this discussion may be disregarded entirely or at best relegated to a position of irrelevance. Such an environment actively discourages experimentation with genre, unless that experimentation is perceived to be commenting upon the process in hand.

It's worth noting, in this regard, that earlier Irish writers were not uncomfortable with genre fiction, and fantasy fiction in particular. In fact, it could be argued that Irish writers colonised gothic fiction and made it their own. After all, the great gothic novels of the nineteenth century – *Melmoth the Wanderer* (1820), *Uncle Silas* (1865), *The Picture of Dorian Gray* (1890), and *Dracula* (1897) – were all written by Irish writers: Charles Maturin, Sheridan Le Fanu, Oscar Wilde and Bram Stoker, respectively. Variously termed 'Protestant Magic' and 'Protestant Gothic', the Irish gothic novel finds itself underpinned by a very particular form of religious and social unease. In *Heathcliff and The Great Hunger* (1995), Terry Eagleton notes:

'. . . if Irish Gothic is a specifically Protestant phenomenon, it is because nothing lent itself more to the genre than the decaying gentry in their crumbling houses, isolated and sinisterly eccentric, haunted by the sins of the past. Gothic carries with it a freight of guilt and self-torment, and these are arguably more Protestant than Catholic obsessions . . .'*

By the early part of the twentieth century the Irish fantasy tradition has largely died out. It's still present in the work of Flann O'Brien, particularly in *At Swim-Two-Birds* (1939) and in Mervyn Wall's two underrated Fursey books,

---

* Speaking as someone who is both Catholic *and* freighted with guilt and self-torment, I'm not sure that I entirely agree with that last statement, but it does raise an interesting point in relation to crime fiction. If Eagleton is correct, then is crime fiction more likely to thrive in a Protestant society than a Catholic one, where the ultimate possibility of forgiveness and redemption is ingrained? Does that explain why England, Scotland and Scandanavia have such strong traditions of crime writing while Spain and Ireland do not?

Nevertheless, *The Butcher Boy* too owes a debt to its genre antecedents, and the larger argument can be made that all fiction has, at its heart, a seed of genre. After all, the novel

The Unfortunate Fursey (1946) and *The Return of Fursey* (1948), but there is no sense of a great desire among Irish writers to perpetuate the lineage. Like Sebastian Melmoth himself, the Irish fantasy novels of the mid-twentienth century appear to be less a part of their own time and more a holdover from another era, although in the manner in which they explore, and play upon, early Irish mythology and folklore, the Fursey books are as much a part of that ongoing exploration of national identity as the more celebrated products of the earlier Celtic Revival.

Wall's case, of course, is not helped by the presence of humour in his books which, as we shall see when we come to discuss the Northern Irish crime writer Colin Bateman, has always been confused with a lack of seriousness by a certain class of critic. One could argue, therefore, that the inability of crime fiction to make inroads into the Irish literary tradition at a time when its significance was being recognised elsewhere was part of a larger disengagement with genre on the part of Irish writers. To be mischievous about it, there might also have been a desire among Irish writers to become part of the new pantheon, to achieve a level of recognition among their peers, to join what we might subsequently term the 'Aosdána Brigade', and the surest way to avoid elevation to the ranks of the great and the good in the world of letters is to engage seriously and unironically with genre.

But there was also, I think, a certain expectation that Irish writers should write about the Irish experience, that it was somehow part of our patriotic duty to enter into an exploration of Irishness, and to do otherwise was to abdicate responsibility and risk opprobrium, or at best a dismissal of one's work as inconsequential. This links to the earlier observation about our comparative youth as a nation, but it's a view that seemed to persist until quite recently. In

was the first great populist art form and I might be prepared to make the argument that genre practitioners cleave closer to the original spirit of the novel that their brothers and sisters in letters who respond with a shudder to the mention of genre in connection with their work. To react in this way, either as a critic or a writer, represents a fundamental misunderstanding of the nature of fiction, and a wilful blindness to its past. The mistake that some genre enthusiasts make is to assume that the presence of genre seeds in a novel means that the novel in question becomes, *de facto*, a genre novel, which is like arguing that a novel with a cow in it is, to all intents and purposes, a book about cows.

his interesting introduction to *The Penguin Anthology of Irish Fiction* (1999), Colm Tóibín suggests that 'Irishness is not primarily a question of birth or blood or language: it is the condition of being involved in the Irish situation, and, if the candidate is a writer, often being crowned by it.'

As a young writer, I could think of few subjects with which I wanted to engage less than the nature of Irishness, or the Irish situation, and now, as a slightly older writer, that position has not changed. My decision to set my books anywhere but Ireland was as much a reaction to the worldview suggested, if not endorsed, by Tóibín as it was to the absence of any recognisable Irish models for the work that I wanted to do. For me, the choice was either to import genre conventions from the UK or the US to an Irish context, which I felt was neither appropriate nor, indeed, interesting; or to apply a European, outsider's perspective to those conventions, to try 'to change the system from within', to borrow a line from Leonard Cohen.

I admit that this decision may smack of a reluctance to engage with the issue at hand on a practical level. As I try to find reasons for the reluctance of Irish writers to engage with crime fiction, I might well be accused of being part of the problem by declining to write it when I had the chance. But I genuinely didn't want to be considered an 'Irish writer' in the very narrow sense in which I felt that description was being used. Had I set my first novel, *Every Dead Thing* (1999) in Dublin it would have become, by default, an Irish novel, not a crime novel. Setting it in the United States allowed me to escape that label to a degree.

If Ireland proved stony ground for the seeds of home-grown crime fiction for reasons that were as much political and social as cultural, there were other factors that may have compounded an already difficult situation.

THE RURAL DIVIDE

Despite the prevalence of a certain type of Golden Age-indebted crime fiction, largely British in origin, that uses rural landscapes as its backdrop, crime fiction functions best in urban settings. It was G. K. Chesterton who commented that crime fiction was unique in expressing 'some sense of the poetry of modern (which is to say urban) life'. For Chesterton, the city functioned as a text that required interpretation, a mystery in itself:

> 'There is no stone in the street and no brick in the wall that is not actually a deliberate symbol – a message from some man, as much as it were a telegram or postcard. The narrowest street possesses, in every crook and twist of its intention, the soul of the man who built it, perhaps long in the grave.' ('A Defence of Detective Stories', published in The Defendant, 1901).

For Chesterton, crime fiction is inextricable from, and actively concerned with, city life. It requires not only its architectural complexity and historical layering, but the energy that derives from the random collisions of people, the endless social interactions between both strangers and acquaintances. Even the village settings of Agatha Christie's novels (the 'Mayhem Parva school' of writing, as Colin Watson termed it in Snobbery With Violence (1971), his critical history of the genre) require an enormous degree of interconnectedness between individuals for the plots to function. Christie's villages are less microcosms and more enclosed spaces into which too many traumatised people have been crammed, like survivors of some dreadful natural disaster. Irish society, which was primarily rural by nature, was unlikely to accommodate the conventions of contemporary crime fiction without a struggle, despite its fascination with the secrets and foibles of others, itself the subject of the Brinsley MacNamara book that graced my grandmother's bookshelves, the hostile reaction to which led its author to leave his home county of Westmeath and not return.

In a sense, John B. Keane's play The Field (1965) is an example of the form that an Irish rural crime story might take, a study in which the core question is less 'who?' than 'why?', where the central mystery is the connection of a people to a landscape, so that land becomes not merely a convenient stage upon which to play out the drama but a thing inseparable from the nature of the protagonists.

Something of our national inferiority complex may well have played a part here too. Perhaps readers simply did not view Ireland as 'interesting' or 'kinetic' enough to comfortably accommodate the drama of crime fiction, however sedate the form. (A similar outlook bedevilled the development of our native film industry for many years, and it remains a battle to get Irish filmgoers to support home-grown product.) In this, we have a certain amount in common with Australia, another country that struggled to establish its own cultural identity in the aftermath of direct British rule, and suffered from a similar crisis of confidence as a consequence. It, too, now boasts a burgeoning homegrown crime tradition, and Australian crime authors, including Peter Temple and Michael Robotham, have begun to attract a readership beyond their own shores.

'HEY JOHNNY, WHAT ARE YOU REBELLING AGAINST?
WHAT HAVE YOU GOT?'

The Golden Age of crime fiction, generally taken as the period between the two world wars, produced two very different traditions: the British tradition, often referred to, somewhat unfairly, as 'cosy', and the American, referred to, somewhat less unfairly, as 'hard-boiled'. Each springs from a very distinct process of engagement with the concept of law and order and the perceived nature of society. The British tradition is motivated primarily by a trust in the Establishment; a belief that the propensity for criminal behaviour is a part of the human character but also, if acted upon, an aberration; and a desire for order as much as, if not more than, the rule of law, for the two are, of course, not the same. While there is an affection for the amateur eccentric as detective (Arthur Conan Doyle's Sherlock Holmes, Agatha Christie's Hercule Poirot and Miss Marple, Dorothy L. Sayers's Lord Peter Wimsey), such figures are only superficially outsiders while remaining essentially Establishment to their core. They may occasionally show up the police as well-meaning bumblers, but at heart they maintain a faith in those responsible for protecting society and enforcing the law. In the end, the criminal is handed over the tender care of the police in the certainty that justice, having prevailed, will now be seen to be done in a court of law.

The American tradition has no such faith. It's no coincidence that the spiritual home of the hard-boiled crime novel is California, a state mired in corruption during the period under discussion. With the police regarded, not without justification, as being bought and paid for by the wealthy and the privileged, the poor and the vulnerable had no recourse to the law in the event that they were victimised further. In that case they required someone standing outside the established forces of law and order to act on their behalf, and so begins the private eye novel. Actually the figure of the private eye is, in turn, indebted to the lone cowboy of the western tradition, facing down oppressors because to do otherwise would make him complicit in their crimes.

The point at which those two traditions finally begin to blend into each other is probably the publication of Dashiell Hammett's *Red Harvest* (1929), which is essentially a western in nice suits, although Hammett had earlier dabbled in the western with the neo-noir story 'Corkscrew' (1925). In *Red Harvest*, two rival gangs are set against each other by a lone, anonymous operative, until eventually they eliminate themselves. *Red Harvest* subsequently became one of the sources of inspiration for Kurosawa's *Yojimbo* (1961), along with Hammett's later novel *The Glass Key* (1931), which in turn influenced the Coen Brothers' 1990 gangster movie *Miller's Crossing*, Sergio Leone's *A Fistful of Dollars* (1964), and Walter Hill's *Last Man Standing* (1996), so *Red Harvest* has variously taken cinematic form as a samurai movie, a western, and a gangster film.

While police procedurals have since found purchase in the American tradition, most memorably in the form of Ed McBain's 87th Precinct series, albeit with something of the tolerance for the maverick that is a part of the private eye tradition, the private eye novel has struggled to make a successful case for itself in the UK. While that may be due, to some degree, to the sense that gun-toting PIs don't travel well across the Atlantic, I would suggest that it is also a consequence of a deeply held belief that the pursuit of justice is one best entrusted to the police, and an absence of the frontier spirit of the United States that places such a premium on independence and individual action. That belief may be shaken by reports of real life police corruption, brutality, and incompetence, but it seems such revelations may simply cause readers to turn to the more idealised police officers of crime fiction with renewed vigour. After all, crime fiction is less about the world as it is than the world as it should be. As William Gaddis wrote in his novel *JR* (1976): 'Justice? – you get justice in the next world, in this world, you have the law.' Crime fiction refuses to accept that this should be the case, and in doing so it reflects the desire of its readers for a more just society. Even at its darkest it is, essentially, hopeful by nature.

All of which brings us back to Ireland, and the question of which of these two opposing outlooks might best have suited an Irish crime novel. The answer, I think, is neither: the Irish police had yet to establish themselves in the mind of the populace, and after centuries of British rule our faith in the Establishment and its values was minimal. If we accept the view that crime fiction is not merely engaged with the society from which it comes but is representative of it, then the nascent Irish Republic – secretive, defensive, intensely parochial, and unforgiving of its critics – gave Irish crime fiction little with which to work. John Banville's twenty-first century crime novels, written under the pseudonym Benjamin Black, tackle the bleak Ireland of the 1950s but are informed by revelations that have only recently been formally examined: the cruelty of the Magdalene laundries and the collusion between Church and State that allowed the systematic physical and sexual abuse of children and young women to continue for decades. Such novels would have been difficult to write as contemporary fiction, and impossible to publish.

THE PROBLEM OF VIOLENCE, PT I

Irish society was not, until recent times, a very violent place, the elephant in the room that was/is terrorist violence excepted. Homicide, that staple of crime fiction, was not something that occupied the Irish people on a daily basis, and the most notorious cases were also usually solved quickly.

I can remember, as a teenager, the discovery of the battered body of nurse Bridie Gargan in July 1982, the first victim of the killer Malcolm MacArthur, who in turn provided the inspiration for John Banville's murderous dandy

Freddie Montgomery in *The Book of Evidence* (1989). Bridie Gargan was left dying in a lane not far from where I lived, one in which I sometimes played football. There was a business in the lane that manufactured trophies, and I often went there to pick up items for my mother, who was involved in all sorts of community events requiring the awarding of various medals and plaques. It was, I suppose, the first crime scene of which I had some personal awareness, one that I knew intimately. As the news bulletins spoke of the circumstances of Bridie Gargan's death, I could picture the lane, and for ever after it would have that young woman's body associated with it. Perhaps it might seem strange to some, but I rarely went back there in the years that followed. I didn't have any kind of ghoulish desire or curiosity to visit the scene of the crime. I wasn't fearful of it, or superstitious; it merely seemed wrong to linger there, even to a boy of fourteen.

MacArthur was subsequently arrested at the home of the Attorney General of the day, my semi-namesake Patrick Connolly, a development that led to a new phrase entering the Irish vernacular, 'GUBU', taken from the first letters of then Taoiseach Charlies Haughey's response to the matter: grotesque, unbelievable, bizarre, and unprecedented. It was the kind of end to the tale that would have seemed improbable in a work of fiction, but which Irish society seemed to throw up with bewildering regularity. After all, why read crime fiction when it could never match up to the sheer oddness of Irish life? Ireland has changed much since then, although our levels of homicide are still low compared to most countries. Gangland killings have skewed these figures, and the difficulty of securing convictions in such cases has given an impression of lawlessness in certain parts of Dublin and Limerick. From the point of view of the development of the genre in Ireland, it seems to me that plots revolving around such killings are a kind of literary dead end. I don't think that they have anything in themselves to say about the human condition or, indeed, shine any great light on Irish urban life. Books about our native gangsters sell well as non-fiction (while the relationship between fiction and real life murders has always been, as we shall see, particularly interesting in Ireland), just as headlines about them sell newspapers, but if such individuals are noteworthy it is only because of their blank viciousness. Expecting them to provide us with any kind of answers or material of substance for fiction is like expecting the protagonists of a dogfight to suddenly begin barking poetry. In fact, to take this argument a step further, it may be that a slavish adherence to contemporary relevance could be the undoing of Irish crime writers. Just as books set in the boom years of the Celtic Tiger now suddenly seem dated and largely irrelevant, even if some effort is made to contextualise those gold rush years, so too a stampede to use crime fiction as a means of interpreting recent changes may also lead Irish writers into an area that has only a narrow appeal and a limited lifespan. At the risk of sounding like a literary Luddite, it has always seemed to me that crime fiction is at its best when it recognises the role of the past in reaching an understanding of the present, and when it concerns itself with larger, universal themes rather than specific societal ills.

To take an example from America, the work of the great Californian crime novelists – and, in personal order of importance and novelistic excellence, I would list them as Ross Macdonald, Raymond Chandler, Dashiell Hammett, and James M. Cain – has survived not because of what they have to say about the Californian society of their day, but the way in which they used that society as a means of exploring the human condition. Macdonald in particular, with his fascination with the gothic, with old sins being passed down through generations of the same family, provides an interesting template for Irish crime fiction, one that Declan Hughes has adapted and developed to create his own fine novels.

Modern Irish crime novelists will have to balance their desire to write distinctive, native additions to the genre with a recognition of the need to appeal to a larger readership beyond Ireland if crime writing is to succeed here. That balance is difficult to achieve but, as with the recent boom in Scandinavian crime writing, all that it will take is for one writer to make significant inroads (in the case of the Scandinavians it was initially the rather overrated Henning Mankell) and others may then follow, although mention of the late Stieg Larsson in the company of Scandinavian crime writers, and Swedish ones in particular, does seem to provoke an interesting and not entirely positive response, perhaps because they have long tired of being asked about Stieg Larsson at the expense of questions about their own work. It is important, though, that Irish writers who achieve a foothold in the US, Britain, and Europe should use that position to spread the word about their peers. A certain generosity of spirit is required if the fledgling Irish crime family is to survive into maturity.

THE PROBLEM OF VIOLENCE, PT II

When it comes to the subject of violence in Irish society, and its relevance and impact upon the development of the crime genre, the Troubles in Northern Ireland inevitably loom large. If one were to include terrorist killings in the homicide rates for the island of Ireland as a whole during the three decades of conflict, a very different picture of homicide in our society would emerge. It's entirely possible that one of the reasons why native crime fiction remained the exception in Ireland was that the period of its greatest growth elsewhere coincided with the height of the Troubles.

It's difficult to write a novel about a common-or-garden murder, the stuff of mainstream mysteries, when, a couple of hours up the road from Dublin, soldiers, policemen, and civilians are being killed on a daily basis. Equally, given that so much criminal behaviour – drug-dealing, smuggling, the importation of pornography, protection rackets, bank raids – was linked to the ongoing carnage, writers who might have been tempted to create works of Irish crime fiction may instead have shied away from it for fear of becoming entangled in the larger political, social and religious questions surrounding the violence in Northern Ireland, or of being accused of trivialising it by using it as material for popular fiction. Simple common sense might also have played a significant part in the decision to shy away from the Troubles as a backdrop for crime fiction: after all, portraying either Loyalist or Republican terrorists as criminal protagonists in a work of popular fiction set in real cities and towns would have made the writers involved few friends. There were exceptions, though, the principal among them being the Bangor-based writer Colin Bateman, who recognised the tragic absurdity of what was taking place, with the emphasis on the absurd, and used that recognition to power his fiction. As with all satirists, there were times when the balance between rage and humour, between the need to confront the reality of violence and the satirist's desire to mock all involved in it, were less than perfect in Bateman's work, but it was brave and untypical nonetheless, and he has never received the critical acknowledgement that he deserves.

Other writers also made attempts to use the Troubles as a backdrop, among them Eugene McEldowney in *A Kind of Homecoming* (1994), and Eoin McNamee in *Resurrection Man* (1994), although the former is most definitely a crime novel, the latter is not, even if the definition in McNamee's case may be down to the intentions of the author rather than any divergence in structure or execution from crime fiction. Perhaps it could be argued that the work of such writers, possibly co-opting Bernard MacLaverty's *Cal* (1983) to swell their ranks, forms a kind of sub-genre: books that deal explicitly with terrorist crime and its effects on Irish society.

The end of terrorist violence, at least in the large scale, explicit form that had blighted this island for so long, seems to have freed Irish writers, both North and South, to write mainstream crime fiction, but also to use crime fiction to explore the aftermath of decades of low-level religious and political warfare. In the former camp, we might put the novels of Paul Charles, Brian McGilloway and others, and in the latter Stuart Neville's debut *The Twelve* (2009) and Declan Hughes's fourth novel, *All The Dead Voices* (2009).

Before leaving this subject, it would be untrue to say that murder has not left its mark on Irish fiction. It's not as though Irish writers have avoided murder entirely but the tendency has been to draw upon real life cases in order to fictionalise them. Thus, as I mentioned earlier, John Banville was inspired by the Malcolm MacArthur case to write *The Book of Evidence*; Carlo Gébler based *The Cure* (1994) on the 1895 trial of Martin Cleary for the murder of his wife (Cleary claimed that he was trying to exorcise a fairy possession by fire); *In The Forest* (2002) by Gébler's mother, Edna O'Brien, explored a thinly-disguised version of Brendan O'Donnell, who killed three people – Imelda Riney, her baby son Liam, and Fr Joe Walsh – in East Clare in 1994;

and, much earlier, *The Collegians* (1829) by Gerald Griffin took on the tale of fifteen-year-old Ellen Hanley, the 'Colleen Bawn', who was murdered on her husband's orders when he tired of her after six weeks of marriage. More recently, Eoin McNamee has used notorious murder cases in three of his novels: the activities of the Loyalist serial killers known as the Shankill Butchers in his debut, *Resurrection Man*; the murder of Patricia Curran, a judge's daughter, in Whiteabbey in 1952, in *The Blue Tango* (2001); and the 1977 killing of the British Army Officer Captain Robert Nairac by the IRA in *The Ultras* (2004).

Meanwhile, Patrick McCabe's novel *The Butcher Boy* (1992) follows another path. Francie Brady's killing of Mrs Nugent is not based on a real case but is no less disturbing for that. There is no great mystery to the actual murder of Mrs Nugent, and the book, narrated in a first person stream of consciousness, is largely concerned with the circumstances that created Francie. In other words, *The Butcher Boy* is a novel with a crime in it, but it is not a crime novel.

If there is a common trait to most of these novels, then I would suggest that it is acts of violence aimed at, or committed within, the family structure. Colm Tóibín identifies violence against women as a feature of Irish fiction but it seems to me that this, while true, might more accurately be described as a consequence of a fascination with intra-familial conflict rather than a theme in itself. This, in turn, is linked to the importance placed upon the family structure in Irish society, so that any act of violence against the family unit, in full in or in part, is viewed as an attack on Irish society as a whole. The murder cases that still attract the greatest coverage in Irish newspapers are those in which a husband has murdered his wife or, less frequently, in which a wife has taken, or attempted to take, the life of a husband. Such offences tend to resonate in the Irish psyche and inspire an appalled fascination but we remain less interested in the capacity of fiction to explore such crimes than in the 'facts' of the cases as revealed in newspapers and true crime books.

ON RATIONALSIM V ANTI-RATIONALISM

There is, I believe, a strong streak of anti-rationalism that runs, not just through Irish fiction, but through our character as a people and as a nation. It led, on one level, to a longstanding prioritising of the artistic over the scientific, of our acceptance of ourselves as an island of 'saints and scholars', as long as that scholarship was of a literary, religious or philosophical bent, a situation that, until recently, continued to undermine science education in this country.

The basis of crime fiction, though, is essentially rationalist: intellectual and deductive reasoning is the path to truth, either uniquely, to take an extremist view, or as a matter of precedent. Thus, we have Conan Doyle's Sherlock Holmes, and his predecessor, Edgar Allan Poe's Auguste Dupin (the progenitor of the modern series detective) applying the force of logic to apparently random events, and through that application coming to an understanding of the truth, even if that truth ultimately takes the shape of a luminous dog or a killer ape. This faith in the power of deductive reasoning underpins Golden Age crime fiction, even in the case of a novel such as Dorothy L. Sayers's The Nine Tailors (1934), where the death that powers the plot is attributed to a form of divine retribution, and continues in the modern police procedural and the forensic mysteries of such writers as Patricia Cornwell and Kathy Reichs. I'm not convinced that Irish writers ever shared that faith, and John Banville remains one of the few Irish novelists to have attempted to engage seriously with this tension between the artistic and the scientific in the novels of his Revolutions Trilogy: Doctor Copernicus (1976), Kepler (1981), and The Newton Letter (1982). The earlier fantasy tradition that produced the great nineteenth-century gothic novels was perhaps a more comfortable fit for Irish writers. In fact, one could argue that Flann O'Brien's The Third Policeman (1967) is essentially an anti-rationalist crime novel, manipulating genre conventions in much the same way that Nabokov, Borges and others in the postmodern tradition chose the form of the detective story as a way of disproving the rationalist belief that the mind can solve everything. By twisting one or two details of the classic mystery, they proved that the opposite could appear to be the case.

I accept that a degree of transference may be involved in my views on the streak of anti-rationalism in the Irish psyche and the importance of the Anglo-Irish gothic tradition in Irish literature. After all, the supernatural plays a part in most of my novels, an element that tends to attract a certain amount of ire from those critics and readers who are wedded to the rationalist tradition, and would like to see the genre set in aspic somewhere between the birth of Sherlock Holmes and the death of Poirot.

Almost as soon as I began writing *Every Dead Thing* back in 1994, the supernatural reared its troubling head. In part this was because, like most writers, I was writing what I read and the first genre fiction that I ever devoured was supernatural fiction, although, with the exception of Stephen King, all of the authors I read were part of an earlier dispensation. The most modern of them was probably the English writer M. R. James and he was, I believe, a nineteenth-century writer working in the twentieth century, a man fascinated by the past, both academically and stylistically. It seemed quite natural to me to attempt to combine some of the conventions of supernatural fiction with those of the mystery novel. In a way, I wanted to restore an older definition of 'mystery' to crime fiction, in the sense of secret rites and doctrines with a religious element or, indeed, as the creators of the English mystery plays, which were versions of Bible stories, would have understood it.

I also felt that a certain darker form of crime fiction shared its roots with supernatural fiction. Both were fascinated by intrusion, by the undermining of accepted mores. They constituted a warning about what might happen if one encountered someone – or something – who did not share one's own assumptions about the world. In supernatural fiction, this threat is non-human, or at least beyond human understanding; in mystery fiction it takes the form of another person, albeit one whose motivations may not be entirely explicable, depending upon how conventional an approach the author chooses to take to answering the question 'Why?' Both fictions play upon our deepest anxieties, our fears for ourselves and the stability of the society in which we live.

Ultimately, there is no simple explanation for why Irish writers should not, until recently, have felt compelled to explore the possibilities of crime fiction.

Rather, it's easier to explain why we are now experiencing a boom in crime writing comparable to the growth that occurred in Britain and the US in the 1980s.

Crime authors have cause to thank the writers of women's popular fiction for encouraging publishers to look at Irish writers not just as a source of literary fiction but also of genre fiction that can succeed commercially. Once female authors such as Maeve Binchy and Marian Keyes began to appeal to a readership in Britain and the US, they fundamentally altered the perception of Irish writing among international publishers and paved the way for explorations of other genre forms. Unfortunately they also forged a path that was followed by a lot of substandard Irish writers of increasingly homogenous, and desperately poor, women's books. While hardly unexpected – publishers and writers will seek to milk that which sells until eventually the teat runs dry – it's a potential hazard that Irish crime fiction, if it continues to grow, will ultimately have to negotiate.

Irish society has changed fundamentally and irrevocably in the last decade. Our faith in our politicians and the Catholic church, however compromised that faith might have been by an acceptance of a certain degree of corruption in the former, and a refusal to acknowledge the sins of the latter, has been significantly undermined by a series of tribunals and a steady stream of revelations about sexual abuse and clerical misconduct, and crime fiction relishes that disparity between the surface and the reality.

The ending of the Troubles has seen the emergence of a new type of criminality both north and south of the border, and with it a recognition that we live in a country where violence and criminal behaviour is not primarily motivated by politics or religion, but by the simple desire for money and power. True, the old enmities linger, and terrorist groups still exist, yet it is has been made clear to us, if such clarification was ever truly necessary, that thugs remain thugs. The removal of the flags of convenience beneath which the terrorists conducted their affairs has not significantly impaired their transition to purely criminal pursuits. This too crime fiction has begun to comment upon.

We enjoyed a sudden increase in our national wealth and are currently suffering an even more shocking decline in the same. The old certainties no longer apply. We are a society in which all the cracks and fissures have become visible and crime fiction is very comfortable with societies in which there are dark places to explore and a willingness to allow whatever may be discovered within them to be brought to light. The challenge facing Irish crime writing, if it is to find its place on the international stage, is how to create a uniquely Irish form of the genre without losing sight of the universal, how to explore all that is contemporary while remaining in touch with the past, and how to ensure that this is, at last, the start of a new and permanent tradition in Irish letters.

*

John Connolly is the author of thirteen books, including the Charlie Parker series of mystery novels; *The Book of Lost Things*; and *The Gates*, his first novel for younger readers. This year, *Hell's Bells* and *The Burning Soul* will join that list. He divides his time between Dublin and Maine. *www.johnconnollybooks.com*

The Informer: The Life and Art of Liam O'Flaherty

by Ruth Dudley Edwards

'I am going ahead with my Dublin story,' wrote our first and most distinguished thriller writer, Liam O'Flaherty, to his literary mentor, Edward Garnett, in 1924, a propos the extraordinary novel that would become *The Informer*. 'It should appeal as a shocker, thriller I mean, to the public that reads detective stories and murder stories.'

Writers of gritty thrillers are long bragged of their colourful lives as lumberjacks, bouncers, bartenders and so on, but who could match the young O'Flaherty for variety and richness of experience, breadth of intellectual exploration, and familiarity with real-life thrills and shocks? His is the kind of life history that makes the rest of us feel we never lived. And more than most writers, his experiences infused every aspect of his writing.

While we should note the caveat of Patrick Sheeran, O'Flaherty's literary biographer, that his memoirs are often contradictory, with 'a recurring tendency to dissolve the facts in wild fantasy, or to constrain them to fit a pose', they certainly tell us what O'Flaherty believes we need to know to understand him as a writer. And though allowances must be made for exaggeration, the basic facts are true enough. 'Man is a born liar,' was the opening line of his 1934 memoir, *Shame the Devil*. If he lied while attempting to tell the truth, he added, the reader should blame original sin rather than the deficiencies of his conscience. 'If not the truth, it will be at least the log of my folly, and as such, perhaps, useful to those of my species who are equally cursed with original sin.'

When he embarked on his first proper thriller, O'Flaherty was twenty seven. An Irish-speaker from the Aran Islands, eighth of the fourteen children of a smallholder, William (he became Liam in the early 1920s) O'Flaherty was born in 1896 and brought up in great poverty and insecurity in the miserable hamlet of Gort na gCapall, Inishmore, where the inhabitants lived in terror of famine, disease and eviction. It was as a creator of minutely-observed sketches of the beauty and cruelty of nature that O'Flaherty would first make his reputation.

His gentle mother came, wrote Liam's brother Tom, from the 'emotional, soft, witty, story-telling' Ganleys; their father was from 'the harsh, quarrelsome, haughty, 'ferocious O'Flaherties'. A natural rebel and sometime Fenian, who indulged in casual peasant brutality, Michael O'Flaherty once drove a landgrabber's cattle over a nearby cliff.

Liam wrote his first thriller before he was ten. A very brief tale of a peasant whose wife brought him cold tea to the field. 'He murdered her with a spade and then tried to bury her in the fosse, or furrow, between two ridges. The point of the story, I remember, was the man's difficulty in getting the woman, who was very large, to fit into the fosse. The schoolmaster was horrified and thrashed me.' He told the story to his mother as a fact, describing with relish how he had seen a neighbour strike his wife with his spade on the head many times, 'blaspheming joyously at each stroke, how she sank into a furrow, where she bled so profusely that the ensuing blows made her gore splash into her murderous husband's face'. This penchant for bloody, unsparing description would be a distinguishing feature of O'Flaherty's adult work.

Although his mother was a fine story-teller herself, when she discovered this was fiction, she begged O'Flaherty to cure his mind of this 'morbid leprosy' with the help of prayer. Henceforward, he had a dual personality:

'The one wept with my mother and felt ashamed of his secret mind. The other exulted in this mind and began to dream of greatness. And as my mind grew strong and defiant, I became timid and sensitive in my relationship with the people about me.'

Liam's cleverness was brought to attention of a visiting Holy Ghost priest who offered the thirteen-year-old a virtually free education if he became a postulant at Rockwell College in Tipperary, 'to be trained as a priest for the conversion of African negroes to the Roman Catholic religion'. It was, says Sheeran, 'a curious mixture of an English public school, a French lycée, and a monastery, all held together by reverence for Newman's ideal of the Catholic gentleman.' Four years later, when told to don the soutane, he refused: 'I had no interest in interfering with the negroes of Africa and I did not want to suffer the humiliation of wearing a priest's womanly rig.'

Transferring to Blackrock College in Dublin in 1913 as an ordinary boarder, in his spare time, O'Flaherty organised a corps of Irish Volunteers. In 1914, at eighteen, he won an entrance scholarship in Classics to University College, Dublin, but as priesthood was still an aspiration – at least for his mother – he became a seminarian at Clonliffe, whose denizens were marked out in UCD by their black suits, furled umbrellas and the bowler hats that were the butt of ridicule and practical jokes. Not only did the students have to walk in pairs for forty minutes through the Dublin streets every day, but on alternate Sundays, to the merriment of local urchins, they walked to the Pro-Cathedral in Marlborough Street to assist at High Mass, dressed in soutane and soprana (a black wool cloak lined with red silk) and with Roman hats with wide, circular brims lined with white silk. After a few weeks, 'I danced on my soutane, kicked my silk hat to pieces, spat on my religious books, made a fig at the whole rigmarole of Christianity and left that crazy den of superstitious ignorance.' Sheeran believes this account is embroidered, and that the virulent anti-clericalism came a bit later, but O'Flaherty hated being humiliated or patronised, so it would be in character to have resorted to some measure of sartorial violence.

For a few more months, now tarred with the dreaded Irish label of 'spoiled priest', O'Flaherty attended lectures in Classics and Philosophy, which at UCD was restricted to Thomism – the thought of St Thomas Aquinas – and which right up until the 1960s was taught exclusively by priests. A Jesuit professor's throwaway condemnation of Marxism as 'ridiculous nonsense' inspired a typically extreme reaction, causing O'Flaherty to read Marx intensively, with other such forbidden fruit as Engels, Proudhon and James Connolly thrown in for good measure. They convinced him that God – as understood by his mother – was dead, but they were too concerned with materialism then to attract his allegiance.

For leisure, he and other students often visited the enormous brothel quarter that had made Dublin the red-light capital of Europe. Bordered by Amiens Street, Talbot Street, Gardiner Street (down which he had paraded with fellow-seminarians) and what is now Seán McDermott Street, it was popularly known as Monto, after Montgomery (now Foley) Street: it would become famous again long after its heyday when in the 1960s the Dubliners recorded *Monto (Take her up to Monto)*.

The area, wrote O'Flaherty in his 1930 memoir, *Two Years*, 'was a disgustingly sordid place, and half the men that came there used it as a shebeen purely and simply.' While it was 'a merry place, with personality and a great demonish charm', there was 'no glitter, hardly any refinement, and a great deal of humanity and turmoil', and rather than awakening desire, 'unless a man was utterly drunk or foreign to the most primitive instinct of delicacy, its appearance aroused thoughts of hell and eternal damnation.' By nature, O'Flaherty found 'real pleasure only in thought and in the observation of life.' In time, all that thought and observation would make invaluable copy. Although Joyce immortalised Monto as Nighttown in *Ulysses*, it was O'Flaherty, who loved and hated it, who would bring it to life in all its gaiety and degradation in *The Informer*.

Early in 1916, infected by war fever, but despairing of the prospect of a revolution at home, and just a few months before the Easter Rising and Connolly's execution, O'Flaherty abandoned university. An adventurous youth, impelled 'not through idealism, but with the selfish desire to take part in a world drama', he joined the Irish Guards as William Ganley. His plan to desert to the Germans for the sake of the Irish republican cause was soon abandoned, not least because he warmed to the brotherhood of the ordinary soldiers. Although initially horrified by their coarseness, rigidity and foulness of language, he came to appreciate how men operate in extremis: 'If war had no further use than that of establishing a bond of friendship between those that fight side by side in it,' he wrote later, 'it would still be more attractive to warm-blooded men than the milk-oozing fruits of pacifism.'

Despatched to the trenches first in France and then to Flanders, O'Flaherty thoroughly learned the necessary survival technique of killing without remorse. As he wrote some years later to Garnett, ashamed of having broken off his engagement to a benefactor: 'To kill a man is nothing – that does not hurt. But to hurt some living thing that is kind is ugly. It's like murdering a dream.' In September 1917 he was seriously wounded in the head by an exploding shell which left him unconscious for three weeks and gave him shell-shock. Diagnosed with melancholia acuta, he was invalided out in May 1918 with a small pension. His memoirs speak of having 'to go through life with that shell bursting in your head': his fiction would draw on his terror of going mad.

After a few weeks convalescing in Aran, he went to Dublin under his assumed name, 'deciding to cut myself adrift from everybody I knew' and spent a fortnight failing to learn shorthand and typing. The £5 he had when he quit the business college went on a horse he had fancied for some time, won him another £15 and triggered his flight to London, where he arrived 'very excited, conscious that I was beginning the great adventure about which I had dreamt all my life, practically, my attempt to conquer the world'.

O'Flaherty had enough money to keep him independent for quite a while if he were frugal, or – and this would be an important theme of his Dublin novels – 'using my money as a bait, I could purchase the companionship of the poor.' Being the man he was, he spent the lot in forty eight hours: 'there are times when a debauch is as consoling to the weary spirit as its mother's milk is to a hungry child.' But this was no pointless debauch, for the war was reaching its climax, 'there was madness in the air' and O'Flaherty was undergoing a profound experience. He roamed London 'watching, listening, talking to people, frenzied with happiness because I was beginning an amazing adventure.' He 'was adrift on the face of the earth, walking about on the heart of civilisation, listening to its ponderous throbbing, watching the great veins of violent blood coursing towards the gigantic organs.' There were hosts of young men prowling about, recuperating from wounds or on leave from the front, 'trying to drown in wild enjoyment the horrors they had recently experienced and the pricking consciousness that life might hold for them only a few more hours.' He was soothed at finding himself 'among a host of men whom despair had made as callous as it had made me, laughing, drinking, scoffing at the black ghost that had taken possession of us all.'

Although much of this period was a blur, for O'Flaherty it was one of the most vital and influential of his life: 'Because I changed in its course as deliberately as if some preposterous devil had thrust his hand down my throat, gripped my gizzard and turned me inside out.' Until then, he had been terrified of life and shocked because God failed to reward good and punish evil. 'The lesson of the war, bringing cynicism and despair with it, had remained until then like a poisoning drug rushing through my system, which refused to assimilate it and was trying to expel it, still hoping that the idealistic dreams of youth had truth in them.' Now he surrendered to this drug and 'came to understand that 'experience was good and innocence evil'.

It was partly that perspective that would make many of his books so original and make it possible for him to identify with characters who appalled respectable readers. 'Perhaps I lack a moral sense, but I feel no fundamental repugnance against murderers, thieves, and scoundrels of all sorts, simply because they are beyond the law.' It was the same with prostitutes. 'The harlot retails what the respectable woman sells wholesale for a fixed annuity, and various other emoluments, personal and social.' It was society's hypocrisy that caused whores to rob and generally maltreat their customers, for it 'persecutes the harlot with one hand while it tolerates her with the other, thus making her skittish in her code of honour, and imbuing her with a stupid anger against those that traffic with her.' Yes, personally, he thought her 'a mean, scavenging, lying, thieving, filthy and odious being; but she attracts me as an artist, in the same way that criminals and other objectionable human types attract me, to arouse that remorse of conscience which is the necessary prelude to a bout of creative energy.' O'Flaherty was nothing if not conflicted.

It was from the perspective of innocence being evil that – now penniless and having to resort to pawning his overcoat – he set out to embrace what London could offer. Finding a job was easy for a good-looking discharged soldier. Despatched to a brewery, he was led into a 'monstrous, dark place', full of noise and an acrid stench. Discovering that that he was being trained to replace the terrified, sick-looking foreman so he could be called up, made him feel 'an utter scoundrel and an interloper'. There was no solace to be gained from contact with the deferential workmen, for the experience was second-hand: 'I am like a scientist watching bees. No matter how closely I watch I can only see the bees and write about them from the point of view of a person who may be a clever scientist but is not a bee. A bee of moderate intelligence could tell much more, if it could be persuaded to down honey and take to writing.' Like Jack London before him and George Orwell after him, O'Flaherty was to gain his greatest inspiration from living life at its most raw.

So he lost interest in learning the job, annoyed the manager, had a furious row and left. As a hotel night porter, he took instant objection to 'senseless drudgery' required of him, cleaned nothing, wiped the guests' shoes perfunctorily, fell out with the manageress, was briefly attracted by a buxom, dark-haired Irish waitress until she became possessive, and after two nights shouted at an expostulating resident that he was a 'red-faced ape' who should clean his own damn boots, threatened to thrash him and was fired amid a great tumult, avoiding arrest because the policeman charged with dealing with him had also been in the Irish Guards.

O'Flaherty was temperamentally even less equipped for his third job – as a clerk, 'a cipher, whose duty it is to be polite and to play with formulas of words and figures, to bow, to say sir, to be clean, to speak correctly, to efface his humanity . . . he must starve himself in order to keep his trousers pressed.'

Filing did not suit O'Flaherty, but others did it for him while he read newspapers and chatted, mainly with a charming Scotswoman who appalled him because she had brains but no originality and perfectly illustrated the deficiencies of civilisation, which 'murders individual thought', which is vital to progress: 'When a society becomes perfectly civilised it inevitably falls a prey to a more primitive society.' 'Don't you ever feel that you want to do something different,' he asked her, 'to stay in bed instead of coming to the office, to blow up the office, to poison the managing director, to rob the cashier, or even to arrive in the morning dressed in a suit of black silk pyjamas?' She almost fainted with horror. And then she said: 'You Irish people have an amazing sense of humour.'

O'Flaherty's contention that 'all good comes from unrest and dissatisfaction' led her to conclude he was a Bolshevik, an accusation he refuted on the grounds that Bolshevism would civilise the working class even more thoroughly than did capitalism and therefore further diminish them. 'If I want to find human companionship, gaiety, humour, I go to where the workers amuse themselves in taverns, dance hall, and at games,' he told her, for there could be heard 'laughter, song, jokes such as might be heard in Elizabethan times' and which were wholly lacking among the civilised.

Goaded into denouncing him as preposterous and illogical like all his compatriots, he accused her of envying the Irish. 'We are all where your working class is today, and where the whole English race was in Elizabeth's time. We are all violent, disorderly, inefficient, intemperate, and full of the poetry of life . . . I tell you that all this humbug about civilisation and cleanliness and contentment is rot preached by stupid mediocrities in order to justify themselves.'

When she again denounced him as a Bolshevik, he decided that a man needed a god and that without realising it, he had been coming to the conclusion that Bolshevism was the gospel of the new God: his place therefore lay in the army of the workers. 'I was a communist. I swore allegiance to my new god.' He had been in the job a fortnight when on 11 November, the night of the armistice, he tramped the streets among rejoicing crowds gazing around him with horror: 'That barren and inglorious war, whose record is mud and noise and obscene poison, ended in a common debauch of drunkenness, gluttony, and fornication.' So the following day he signed up as a trimmer on a tramp steamer to Rio de Janeiro, tending the three fires in the three enormous boilers. He enjoyed it as he hardened. 'I no longer minded the stifling heat, or the terrific work. I felt equal to my comrades, and could use oaths as foul as theirs. My habits became just as coarse.' On board he knocked out a thieving enemy; in a public fight with the man's mate, though knocked down twenty-seven times, he refused to surrender; and he went after an officer with a hammer, avoiding a severe punishment because he played the shell-shock card with the kindly captain.

Although sunshine and painted shutters made the brothel quarter in Rio look better than the Monto, at a deeper level it depressed O'Flaherty as much: he was repelled by its whores, the drunkenness and violence he encountered frightened him, and after abandoning his ship and finding himself a penniless vagrant, he spent a night weighing up the pro and cons of Jesus Christ, decided against him, and determined to conquer Brazil as a god of a different type, 'assuming the quality of Genghiz Khan, Julius Caesar, Alexander, Napoleon Bonaparte, men whose virtue lay in their brutality, courage, endurance, greed, and intelligence.' Instead, again as a trimmer, he joined a tramp steamer bound for Liverpool, as he ached to see if Europe was in revolt.

After three disappointing weeks in Cardiff submerging his consciousness into that of the mass of wage-slaves, he went to sea once again and then to Italy, Turkey, Greece and finally Montreal, from whence he wandered about Canada working for a day here, a few days here and the odd week as – yes, a lumberjack – and also as a maker of tinned milk (he briefly became an idio-syncratic worshipper of machines), then on the railroad, where his habit of beating up his colleagues in the evening caused some coolness, then as a copper miner, dock labourer and 'hobo carpenter'. From November 1919, travelling in the United States – which he had entered illegally – he was inter alia a farm labourer, pastry maker, telegraph messenger, house-porter, dishwasher, waiter in a boarding house, dynamite worker, shipyard worker, plumber's assistant, printer's assistant, tyre maker and a labourer in a biscuit factory, and – having linked up in Boston with his brother Tom, a socialist revolutionary in the James Connolly Club – he became briefly an activist for the Wobblies (the Industrial Workers of the World, who sought the violent destruction of capitalism) and tried and failed to be a commercial writer.

In the midst of all that, in New York, O'Flaherty broke his heart over a beautiful, brilliant émigré Russian anti-communist, in an affair unconsummated because 'I can only love a woman whom I can master', and when she had left him, signed on in Long Island as an oyster fisherman, where he promptly called a strike in outrage at being called a Bolshevik and was thrown off the boat. He left America in the grip of 'an inner madness', conscious that he was 'a wreck' not because of the war, but because of his nature. Physically fit, with his nerves 'in good order', he had a depression which caused his journey to Europe to become 'a debauch from port to port . . . So that when I arrived home I was like a ghoul, speechless, gloomy, a companion of the rough winds and of the breakers.'

After a period in Aran musing 'on the indefinability of the paregoric, the uncertainty of life, and the constant tribulation to be met in the world', in late 1921 he joined the febrile left in Dublin, editing and selling the *Workers' Republic* on the streets, trying vainly to persuade the party to back workers who were seizing workplaces and setting up soviets, and organising the Dublin unemployed – many of whom were ex-servicemen. In January, after the Treaty was ratified by the Dáil, O'Flaherty – now Liam – the Chairman of the Council of the Unemployed, seized the Rotunda Concert Hall with two hundred followers and raised the red flag. After three days, threatened with violent ejection by the authorities, and having no taste for pointless bloodletting, he ordered the men to evacuate the building and fled south. He was back in Dublin after the outbreak of the Civil War in June, in a unit of the Irish Citizens' Army in Vaughan's Hotel on the corner of Parnell Square. The unit was disbanded as the Free State gained control and on 5 July he stood south of O'Connell Bridge watching the capture of the republican headquarters and heard an old woman thanking God that 'that bloody murderer, Liam O'Flaherty, is killed'.

Later he would have a vision of himself in flight, 'a lean man with terrified, furtive eyes, wearing a shabby trench coat, with a revolver strapped between his shoulder-blades, arriving in Liverpool on a cargo-boat'. Strangers took him in and encouraged him to write, and after rejection slips for a 'trashy' novel and equally unsuccessful short stories set in London, he realised he should write of what he knew. *Thy Neighbour's Wife* was a melodramatic exploration of the conflict between sex and religion, but led Edward Garnett, publishers' literary adviser, to take O'Flaherty in hand and help him write *The Black Soul*, which achieved critical acclaim in Ireland.

Another Garnett protégé, H .E. Bates, recalled decades later this 'virile and impassioned Irishman' with 'a firebrand swagger, a fine talent and a headful of rebellious fury about the English, and 'who, rather like me, had this facile demon in him . . . true Irish, he could talk a donkey's hind-leg off and with fierce, blue unstable eyes would stand up in the middle of the room and begin reciting flowing nonsense from some as yet unwritten book, about women pressin' their thoighs into the warm flanks of the horses, until he codded you that it really happened and was really true.' It was Garnett who inspired him to write the delicate, brilliant sketches about nature that Bates said 'few, even among the Irish, have equalled'.

O'Flaherty settled in Dublin and in 1924, eloped with the beautiful wife of a Trinity medieval historian, and along with a group of young radicals like Austin Clarke and Francis Stuart engaged in fierce literary assaults on W. B. Yeats, Oliver St John Gogarty, AE, and anyone else O'Flaherty considered one of the 'old fogies'. His attempt to recruit Sean O'Casey failed, for O'Casey considered that quite apart from being a lesser talent than Yeats, 'O'Flaherty, in a way of arrogance and sense of being a superior being, was worse than Yeats, without the elder man's grace and goodwill'.

It was Yeats who in 1926 took on the Abbey audience who became violent over *The Plough and the Stars*: in an allusion to the scenes twenty years earlier over Synge's *Playboy of the Western World*, he said, 'You have disgraced yourself again, is this to be the recurring celebration of the arrival of Irish genius?' 'One of the strongest attacks (if not an entirely coherent one) came from the novelist Liam O'Flaherty,' wrote Roy Foster in his biography of Yeats, 'himself an avant-garde socialist-realist whose work was considered offensive to conventional opinion.' Considering O'Casey's play concerned the sufferings of tenement-dwellers caught up in the Easter Rising, O'Flaherty's denunciation in a letter to AE's *The Irish Statesman*, that 'Yeats's protest against the protest of the audience was an insult to the people of this country', might have seemed baffling – not least because it lined him up with such forces of reaction as the *Catholic Bulletin* – but it was not quite contrariness for contrariness's sake. After all, while O'Casey was on the side of the little people whose lives were ruined by ideologues, O'Flaherty, as he explained in his letter, admired anyone who died for an ideal, however impractical. He had been 'cut to the bone' by this 'bad play', because it did not do justice to those who deserved credit for 'the most glorious gesture in the history of our country'.

Of course, there would also have been jealousy, for at the time O'Flaherty was increasingly debt-ridden, his mistress was pregnant, he had more enemies than he could cope with and was 'violently oppressed' because he felt his first thriller, *The Informer*, had been a commercial failure, not least because – contrary to his pleas – his publisher had insisted on publishing it as a literary novel. His inspiration for the form had been J. B. Priestley, who advised him that there was such competition for contemporary writers that 'spectacular conduct of some sort is necessary to draw attention to one's talent'.

O'Flaherty had worked out the plan of *The Informer*, 'determined that it should be a sort of high-brow detective story and its style based on the technique of the cinema. It should have all the appearance of a realistic novel and yet the material should have hardly any connection with real life. I would treat my readers as a mob orator treats his audience and toy with their emotions, making them finally pity a character whom they began by considering a monster.' And so Gypo Nolan, the enormous, grotesque, brainless brute was born, for £20 betrayed his fellow revolutionary in the (presumably Communist) 'Revolutionary Organisation', was tracked by the pitiless intellectual Commandant Dan Gallagher, who sought 'the satisfaction of one lust, the lust for the achievement of my mission, for power maybe, but I haven't worked that out yet.' During the hours before he was killed, Gypo rampaged around Monto, squandering his blood-money on the company of the poor, and engaged in several violent encounters with his enemies.

'The literary critics,' wrote O'Flaherty sneeringly in a memoir, 'almost to a man, hailed it as a brilliant piece of work and talked pompously about having at last been given inside knowledge of the Irish revolution and the secret organisations that had brought it about.' Yet there was much to admire, including the shocking exposure of the dreadful condition of the Dublin poor that the authorities kept well hidden and O'Flaherty's uncompromising depictions of squalid places and the desolation and cruelty of lost people: 'It was only a ragged old woman of ill fame, with a debauched face and melancholy eyes. She paused drunkenly in front of him, muttering something unintelligible. Then she bared her ragged teeth. She spat and passed on without speaking.' It would win the 1926 James Tait Black Memorial Prize for fiction, be translated into several languages and there would be four film and several stage versions. To O'Flaherty's fury, it is for this flawed melodrama that he is best remembered when better novels and his magnificent short stories are largely forgotten.

Not that his other Dublin novels were his best, though like *The Informer*, they all benefited from his passion for Conrad and Dostoyevsky – who could well also be classified as writers of psychological thrillers – as, of course, from the understanding of degradation, passion and ruthlessness that O'Flaherty had learned about at first-hand during his extraordinary youth. Like Joyce and O'Casey, O'Flaherty was exploring a Dublin that shocked the reading public. Mr Gilhooley, the eponymous anti-hero of what actually marketed as a 'thriller', was a retired engineer who had returned home from South America: a 'lonely voluptuary', his misery was worse than that of the hungry, the diseased or the homeless, for he had neither 'hope nor a sense of righteousness'.

Wandering around the hostelries, Mr Gilhooley moved among post-Civil War moral ugliness, where hatred, corruption and poverty reigned and opportunist priests were taking over. Obsessed by the waif Nelly, whom he loves and hates, and who in turn is obsessed by her lost lover, he experiences sexual shame, goes mad and ultimately commits murder and suicide. It was often brilliant and sometimes absurd, but always powerful. The generous Yeats referred to *The Informer* and *Mr Gilhooley* as 'great novels and too full of abounding life to be terrible, despite their subjects'.

The Assassin (1928) was inspired not just by the murder in 1927 of Kevin O'Higgins, Minister for Justice, but also by O'Flaherty's creditors, to whom the book was dedicated. With the help of disappointed republican dissidents, Michael McDara – who had been born a peasant, shell-shocked in the war and travelled the world as a seaman – sets out to murder a republican strong man known as 'HIM', mainly on the grounds that strong men in power were to be struck down by true revolutionaries before they made slaves of the masses. Filled with the 'intoxicated consciousness of the romance of his intended act', he found his appetite whetted by the slums: 'Everything here excited a savage hatred of society in him: barefooted children with a hectic flush on their pale, starved faces, tottering old people with all manner of disease scarring their wasted features, offal in the streets, houses without doors and with broken windows, a horrifying and monotonous spectacle of degrading poverty and misery everywhere. The foetid air reeked with disease.' There was much tedious Nietzchean philosophising about the duty of the revolutionary to create a 'superior type of human being', as well as a brilliant assassination scene, but essentially the book is about aspects of O'Flaherty's life and intellectual torments, right down to his 1922 flight to Liverpool.

The Puritan (1932) had fascinating insight into the hypocrisy and zealotry that had taken control of post-revolutionary Ireland, but Francis Ferriter, the psychopath at its centre who murders a prostitute, is too one-dimensional and alienating a character to carry the book and the violence and debauchery seems more of the same. And in any case, O'Flaherty's satirical *A Tourist's Guide to Ireland* (1929), was much more effective in his castigation of priests and politicians. Yet Yeats, who was fighting valiantly against authoritarianism and repression, thought it a masterpiece: 'I must make a fight for this book,' he said publicly, when it was banned by the Censorship Board. His friend Desmond FitzGerald (father of Garret) disagreed profoundly: 'if you eliminate Bolshevism and muck-racking from Liam O'Flaherty you have a very unimportant writer left.'

O'Flaherty was an uneven writer, but never unimportant. His Dublin thrillers would probably not work for many modern readers, but they are still of interest to those who want to smell the Dublin underworld as it was in the 1920s or gain insights into the unintended consequences of revolution. Like such writers as Gene Kerrigan and Declan Hughes, who peer under the stones of contemporary Dublin, O'Flaherty used a new but unfashionable vehicle to go where respectable novelists feared to tread. He deserves respect as the father of the Irish psychological thriller. Irish crime writers should find some way of honouring him.

*

Ruth Dudley Edwards is a Dubliner who lives in London. A prize-winning historian and satirical crime novelist, she is also a journalist and broadcaster. Her latest book is *Aftermath: The Omagh Bombing and the Families' Pursuit of Justice*, for which she won the Crime Writers Association Gold Dagger for Non-Fiction.

Twenty-Five and Out

by Kevin McCarthy

3 March 1922. Victoria Barracks, 6th Division HQ, Cork.

'They could've left us where we were,' O'Keefe said, laying down a five of hearts on the upturned crate placed between two bunks. 'Five points.' He added his five to the five he had earned in the previous round on a page torn from a patrol diary they were using to keep score.

Sergeant Jim Daly smiled around his pipe stem, as if indulging one of his many children. 'That would have made sense, leaving us where we were and where we might do some good. And brass can't start going on like that at this late stage. Making sense. It wouldn't make any fucking sense at all, at all, for the bastards to start making it now, sure.'

O'Keefe realised late why Daly was smiling. The big man – with a brutish, culchie copper's bulk and country slyness belied by doe-like, almost sad eyes– placed an ace of hearts down to take the trick and the game. 'Fifteen, makes twenty and five. Twenty-five and out, my china, and you owe me six bob to be paid at your best convenience. You played that five early enough, you did.'

O'Keefe tossed down his remaining cards. 'Cute bastard, Daly, you are,' he said, stretching his legs, rubbing at the ragged scar left by a Turkish bayonet on his face.

Though it had been little more than a month, it seemed a lifetime to the men since they had handed over Bandon RIC barracks to the amateurs in green armbands calling themselves the Republican Police and pitched up in the disbandment depot in Victoria army barracks, bringing to an end nearly two years spent policing a war.

Daly puffed at his pipe. 'You sure you don't want to head down and play Pontoon with the Tans, there, Séan? It's an easier game, so it is . . .'

'Fuck off. I'll beat you if I put my mind to it.' O'Keefe gathered up and shuffled the cards.

Over the past three weeks he had played more cards than he could ever remember playing, his time in the army included. Like thousands of his fellow RIC men and Black and Tans, in depots all over Ireland, he was a virtual prisoner in the barracks. Cooling boots while Dublin and London processed the paperwork that would make him, make all eight odd thousand of them at once, redundant.

And who would take the place of this Royal Irish Constabulary that, for all its faults, had served the people – and the Crown, no denying it – of Ireland for more than ninety years with a degree of professionalism and discipline envied by police forces the world over? Who would keep order in a nation where order had come, for the past number of years, from a gun barrel rather than courts of law? The IRA? O'Keefe scoffed at the idea. They were wily, disciplined fighters, some of them. Particularly ones he had himself faced and even worked unwittingly alongside in West Cork. But fighting and policing were different skills altogether. The introduction of the Black and Tans and the Auxiliaries into the bloody mix of the Troubles had proven that in spades. Who else then? The Provisional or Republican Police? Local bullies in green armbands, was the opinion shared by O'Keefe and his constabulary colleagues. Even Michael Collins himself recognised he couldn't police a state with the likes of that shower and had intimated there would be a new force of some kind in the future. But whoever it was, O'Keefe knew, it wouldn't be the RIC.

So now they played cards and waited for word that their paperwork was in order and they could finally be escorted by army or fellow RIC to the train or ship that would deliver them to new lives as ex-coppers.

The Black and Tans were easiest to process. They had no pension rights unless they had been severely injured. Also, there was little difficulty in their returning home. They simply boarded a troop train to Dublin or a ship back to Blighty. The majority of them had already been discharged and sent home.

Many of the Irish cons – constables – however, could never go home. Their families had been warned by the IRA. Threatened harm if their men returned to their villages or farms. Some had disregarded warnings and returned of their own accord and some of these had been killed, their homes put to the torch. The wiser among these waited for relocation, hoping it was a place where they could find work. There was talk of jobs in the Palestine Police and that Greater Manchester was looking for experienced lads. The wise waited for the safety of exile from Ireland.

O'Keefe did not need to seek the refuge of empire, and he thanked God for it. He had no wife or children and had been raised in Dublin, the capital city being anonymous enough for all but the most rabidly anti-Sinn copper to return to, but still no word of his discharge had come through.

And Daly, after some anxious weeks awaiting word, had been given leave by the IRA to join his wife and children in his wife's home county of Kerry, where they had moved after the burning of Cork in December 1920. His wife had a first cousin who was ranking member of the IRA in Tralee. This had no doubt helped his cause, as had his reputation for looking the other way when confronted with all but the most violent assaults by republicans.

'Your deal,' Daly said, scratching his score onto the torn sheet. 'Be fair to yourself, Seán. Deal the cards you deserve.'

'I'm not arsed.'

'Of course you aren't. Try to think of your losses as a charitable contribution to my retirement.'

And while they all waited, RIC brass had impressed upon the men that they were still constabulary until they had signed their discharge papers and that constabulary discipline was to be maintained. Pay packets could be docked for breaches, demotions of rank affecting pensions could still be incurred in the depot. To this end, sergeants barracked with the men – O'Keefe and Daly among others – and woke them each morning to march drill, clean weapons and sit through 'school' – memorising and answering estions on acts of common and criminal law. But it was a façade and the men knew it. Their feet scuffed the stone of the parade ground without any of the crisp, syncopated rigour of days gone. Weapons – in peace time, as one con had remarked to O'Keefe, being roughly as useful as tits on a bull – were given a cursory, almost friendly oiling and wipe down. Laws and acts were recited amidst banter and innuendo and comical stories of policing brought to mind by points of law being studied.

Sergeants O'Keefe and Daly let the jokes and stories run. Like the men, their days as policemen were over. The job of work they had thought they would have for life declared null and void overnight. Even the laws they had sat and studied and recited from rote to scolding sergeants and head cons – laws they knew better than most barristers, it was said – might cease to exist in the new Free State of Ireland. No one quite knew what would change and what would stay the same. And so the jokes and stories punctuated study of potentially archaic law. Stories, O'Keefe thought, of better days. Back when being a copper meant more than being a slow moving target for snipers in the hedge.

'I'm sick to my back teeth of this place, to fuck,' O'Keefe said, lifting his mug of cold tea from the crate. He sipped it and winced.

'Jesus, man, can you not just enjoy collecting a wage for sitting on your arse? This is a paid fucking holiday, Seán. And you've had it coming, you have. We all have, by Jesus, and I mean to enjoy it. Here, shuffle the cards and we'll start another game.'

As well as cards, the men drank. They were not supposed to. They were still technically on duty and confined to the grounds of Victoria barracks, but there were ways and means of obtaining a bottle or ten and most of these had been discovered within the first few hours of arrival in depot. There were sports as well: a boxing match had been staged, and some young constables hefted dumbbells on a corner of the parade ground or played handball against the rear stable walls. A table tennis table had been rigged up in the enlisted mess and even during meals one heard the metronomic tock of celluloid ball on bat. But most of the men had little heart for these pursuits. Even for drinking. There was only occasional open drunkenness or revelry. Rather, men were content to play cards, sip whisky, read tattered and much handled cowboy novels, often falling into dozing in the afternoon. It was as if they were all convalescing from some outbreak of illness, which, O'Keefe thought, in some ways they were. He had more than once thought to himself how Crown control of his country had been a disease of sorts, and that the country had required treatment, but that the treatment prescribed by the IRA had been too radical by half. Amputation of the soul to save the heart? Something like that, he thought, but couldn't be bothered to follow the analogy to its logical conclusion. He was as much a victim of the slothful daze of waiting as the rest of the men. He listlessly dealt the cards then lit a Player Navy Cut.

Daly said, 'Sure, scut has it they're sending a rake of Tans and regular cons on the train with the Essex regiment tomorrow or the next day. Not sure who'll be escorting who on that train.'

O'Keefe looked at his cards and mentally conceded the game to Daly. He would never learn the game of Twenty-five properly. It was a country game, and though he had learned it years before as a young constable at his first posting in Navan, he was now more convinced than ever that a fella needed to learn it at his mother's breast like every country copper he knew, to be any good at it. The rules seemed as arbitrary, as contradictory as life. In Twenty-five, low cards had high value and high cards low. Except when they didn't.

'I'd sooner walk to Dublin than ride with that rabble,' O'Keefe said, thinking back on the brutality the Essexes had lowered on the people of West Cork in the name of the Crown.

'And miss the waving, cheering masses as you roll through stations of the sovereign nation?'

'Waving Webleys and slash hooks.' O'Keefe led with an ace of spades, a relatively potent card with spades as trumps.

'Ah now,' Daly said, dumping a nine of clubs to rob the face-up queen of trumps, 'that would be contrary to the terms of the truce, Séan. Acting with malicious intent towards departing servants of the Crown.'

O'Keefe laughed bitterly through his nose. 'Like reefing Kenny Synott off the train and stopping his clock isn't contrary to terms of the ceasefire?'

Daly took another trick with a trump four. 'There's none of us know that Synott didn't just step off that train to share a few homely jars with auld pals. He may well surface yet.'

'Surface face down in a bog hole,' O'Keefe replied and instantly regretted it. He had known Kenny Synott; not well, but he had liked the man, the times he had met him at Bandon courts or carting lags to Cork prison. Synott was – he was already thinking of him in the past tense, was – a tough, fair copper who had worked his way up from the shop floor to head constable of Mallow RIC barracks. He was a Protestant from Bangor, County Down and maybe, O'Keefe thought, he had been too tough, too proficient in his attempts to stop the men who murdered in the name of liberty. You could disappear these days, for having done your job too well. Not, O'Keefe reflected with a low burning anger, that you would read a word about it in the papers. The truce would hold, peace would prevail in the land, and no news of any murdered RIC man would interfere with this.

'Out for . . .' Daly dropped his cards and made a dumbshow of totalling his points. '. . . twenty.' An almost insurmountable lead.

'For fuck sake.' O'Keefe tossed down his meagre haul of five points. 'You need to smell of cow shite and bog to be any good at this game.'

Lean and wiry, with a face and walk like a welter-weight fighter or a pimp, Black and Tan constable Jack Finch entered the barracks and made his way over to them, rubbing his hands together and trailing March cold in his wake. 'Swearing like a right Tan,' he said, sitting down on the bunk next to O'Keefe. 'You should play Pontoon with the lads down the end bunk, Sar'nt. Much easier game and not as pricey by 'alf.'

'My sentiments exactly, Mr Finch,' Daly said.

'Were you invited into this country, Finch? Have you done anyone in it an ounce of poxy good?'

'I answered the call, Sar'nt. Only go where I'm needed, me.' He took a quart bottle of Powers whiskey from his uniform trouser pocket. 'Gentlemen?'

'You're needed right here, Finch,' Daly said, tapping his pipe against the side of the crate table, blowing in the bowl and rummaging in his jacket for his tobacco. 'I always said you Tans were a fine body of men. Didn't I, Séan?'

'I wouldn't want to scorch poor Fincheen's heart, telling him what you really said.'

'Now lads,' Finch said, uncorking the bottle with his teeth and passing it to Daly. 'You won't 'ave poor old Finchy round to rag with for much longer.'

Daly drank and passed the bottle to O'Keefe. 'And why's that, Finch?'

'Cause I got my fucking demob orders is why!' He smiled and took a set of official discharge papers, including a letter of safe passage as provided by the provisional government of Ireland and approved by the IRA. A guarantee of safety proffered by its leadership but ignored by many of its members. Just ask Head Constable Synott, O'Keefe thought, how much use his letter of safe passage proved to be.

'Well done, Finch,' O'Keefe said, shaking the Tan's hand.

Daly shook Finch's hand as well and began to pack his pipe. He had always kept a professional, if not disdainful distance from the Tan constables – as much from an atavistic dislike of the outsider as from the fact that they were generally more of a danger than a help to have around a police barracks – but he had taken to Finch. 'So,' Daly said, 'when are you off, then?'

'Tomorrow. Troop ship out of Queenstown. Just my bloody luck, mate. I 'ate boats. Chucked up over the rail the 'ole way over when I came out. Same when I shipped out to France in the war.'

'How else were you planning on getting home, Finch? Plane?'

Finch laughed. 'Only pigs fly, Sar'nt Daly, and Jack Finch is no pig. See, my thinking is,' he said, taking the bottle from Daly and drinking, 'I might as well get myself well olivered tonight as I'll hardly feel any worse off tomorrow either way.'

O'Keefe took the bottle back off Finch and raised it. 'Here's to you, Finch. Ireland thanks you for your contribution to law and order in the land.'

'Only a pleasure, Sar'nt, only a pleasure. And if you boys are ever in London town, look up old Finchy and I'll show you a time that'll turn the hair on your 'ead curly and the hair elsewhere straight. Now drink up, lads, there's more where that came from.'

*

The next morning heads were sore and the faint odour of sweated whiskey rose in the damp air as Finch and the nine men who were departing with him that day mustered on the parade ground in their civilian clothes.

Finch, despite the death-pale pallor of his skin, was resplendent in a suit of worsted wool he had stolen from his older and reputedly criminal brother upon leaving London for Ireland to serve as a Black and Tan. To the suit he had added a beige cashmere overcoat with red silk lining, and a Trilby with a razor sharp brim. To O'Keefe, Finch looked like an aging pickpocket who had lucked upon a gentleman's suit of clothes. You could take the lad out of Shoreditch . . . Still, apart from Jim Daly, whom he had known and served with for seven years, O'Keefe considered Finch his closest friend in Ireland. They shared an understanding of the horrors of a pointless war – Finch in the trenches of France and Belgium, O'Keefe under the bone bleaching sun of Gallipoli – and they had fought together here in Ireland. The strange bed-fellows of war. He would miss Finch.

'Fuckin 'ell, we'd better not miss this bloody boat,' one of the departing Tans griped. 'Where's the bloody escort?'

As he said it, a young cadet constable came jogging across the parade ground. 'Sorry, men. Look,' he said, 'there's been a balls up. We're going to have to raise an escort ourselves. Tommy doesn't want to know. They're ship-ping the Liverpools out today.'

Another of the Tans spoke up. 'Fuck them Scouse bastards. How we sup-posed to get through town with packs of Shinner boys on every fucking corner waiting to hammer shite out of us?'

A different man, his skin more green than pink, said: 'We'd best not miss this pox-ridden boat. My missus is up the duff. Due any day now. . .'

Another said, 'Don't fret, mate, the lad who put her up it will mind her for you.'

'Fuck off.'

O'Keefe, who had come out to see off Finch, found himself speaking. 'I'll raise the escort,' he said to the cadet constable. 'You find transport.'

The cadet constable looked at O'Keefe, unsure whether or not to take offence. The cadet constable was a member of the county inspector's entourage and, though of a lower rank than O'Keefe, was unused to taking orders from any but the highest of brass.

'You know you're to be unarmed, Sergeant,' he said. 'Under the terms of the Truce.'

O'Keefe ignored him and went into the barracks to gather men for escort duty, drumming up six of the largest, most sober cons he could find – Sergeant Daly not among them, as he was heavy at cards with three demobbing brothers from Leitrim.

Fifteen minutes later, the cadet constable returned. 'Umm, Sergeant,' he said to O'Keefe, his voice low so the men could not hear him, a sheepish cast to his face. 'There's nothing in the motor pool, Sergeant. There's a Bedford but it dropped its transmission last week. They're having difficulty accessing parts, apparently, as no one is sure who's paying, us or the new Irish government. Tommy's got the rest out to bring the Liverpools to the ship and the Essexes to the train—'

'How are these men supposed to get to Queenstown harbour then, Constable?'

The cadet constable looked away. 'The tram?'

O'Keefe stared at the man for a long moment before deciding that the cadet constable was not joking. He turned then to the departing Tans and explained the predicament, their choice between the potential gauntlet of corner boys and angry IRA men on the streets of Cork city or waiting another day, another week possibly, for a different ship.

Finch spoke for the demobs. 'Fuck my brass buttons, Sar'nt, but I've 'ad just a-bloody-bout enough of this country, no offence. Let's hop the tram, lads.'

They marched double time to Patrick Street where they boarded a Cobh-bound tram, taking up the entire lower deck and half of the upper. One of the demobs pulled a bottle from his trench coat pocket and drank deeply. He passed the bottle to his mate and started to sing as the tram pulled away.

'We are the boys of the RIC / As happy as can be . . .'

They were halfway down Patrick Street and the song had changed to an obscene ballad about a Peeler arresting a nanny goat – subsequently abusing the goat in a most unnatural manner – when O'Keefe noticed the two teenaged boys jogging at pace with the tram. O'Keefe smiled as the men sang, the Peeler now mounting the nanny goat to the horror of the tram driver and remaining passengers on the upper deck. The hair of the dog had brought some colour back to Finch's cheeks and he slapped O'Keefe on the arm.

'Survived my second war, Sar'nt. Who'd 'ave fucking thought?'

O'Keefe ignored him for the moment, continuing to track the progress of the two youths as they wove their way along the crowded footpath, watching them shout to other young men as they passed them, pointing at the tram. He said, 'The war might not be over just yet, Finch.'

But Finch had turned back to his Tan mates, bellowing himself now. 'The Peeler pinched a nanny goat and took her as his wife / Alas said the nanny goat, what's happened to my life . . .'

At the intersection of Patrick and Maylor Streets the tram stopped and O'Keefe's suspicions were proved correct. The first chunk of paving stone shattered one of the tram windows to O'Keefe's left, showering him with glass and smashing the jaw of one of the singing Tans. He brushed the glass from his coat and shouted at the driver to move the tram.

'I can't move the bloody thing, boy, there's a motor car blocking the tracks,' the driver shouted back as he locked the tram's brake and jumped from his seat, abandoning the tram, leaving the men and the few passengers on the upper deck at sea on a crowded street, more missiles now beginning to fly from the growing mob of men and boys on the footpath.

O'Keefe moved to the man who had been struck by the brick, helping him to his feet, dazed and bleeding from the mouth but blinking himself back to enraged awareness. Turning, O'Keefe realised that the cohort of demobs were spilling out from the relative sanctuary of the tram and into the surging throng on the footpath. Their last scrap in Ireland. Couldn't even leave the country in peace, O'Keefe thought, before stepping down from the tram himself. They wouldn't be let.

A few of the demob men went down under a barrage of more paving stones but most made it into the scrum of capped young Corkmen unscathed, swinging fists wildly, some of them smiling with a savage joy as bone and flesh connected, as makeshift weapons scavenged from shopfronts clashed with the hurls and walking sticks carried by the cornerboys. The Tans, distinguishable to each other by their trench coats and Trilbys, took the fight to the cornerboys and O'Keefe joined them with his small consort of uniformed RIC men, leaving his baton in its hook on his belt, clenching his fists, gritting his teeth.

He picked a man without a weapon, a big fella in white shirtsleeves and waistcoat. A docker or a carter. O'Keefe roared as he moved on him, a smile breaking on his face unbidden. He couldn't help himself. Two months of sitting around a barracks playing cards while men in offices sifted through his future. This was wrong, O'Keefe knew. And it felt grand. He swung a wild punch, the capped man seeing it late but sensing it, ducking, O'Keefe's fist crashing into the man's neck instead of his jaw. A grunt of pain and a heavy, professionally delivered uppercut later and O'Keefe was vomiting up his breakfast, his breath gone but still swinging, kicking, catching the capped man a blow on the left ear that hurt him, dazed him. O'Keefe brought his knee up into the big man's ribs, his breath returning. Laughing as he fought. Laughing. Release. Grunting men and spewing curses, half-barked, cut short by landing blows. Scuffling feet, furious milling fists. Someone swung an advertising board. A full crate of apples buckled over the head of an already bleeding Tan. Finch was punching a small man in the testicles as the small man pounded close-fisted on Finch's back and head. Some fucking truce! The thought banged through O'Keefe's skull as he focused on another adversary. He swung wild. He lost his hat. Laughing. Swinging mad. Laughing.

*

Most of the demobbing Tans missed the boat that day and returned, singly or in small groups, by various routes, via various pubs and brothels, to barracks. They were driven in tarpaulin-covered Bedford lorries under army escort to Queenstown harbour three days later.

O'Keefe had bruised ribs and a black eye and cut knuckles he cleaned with whiskey. He never saw Finch again and it was rumoured that the Shoreditch Tan had stayed behind in Ireland, for some months after his demob, robbing banks with a gang of former Tan and Auxiliary police constables in a country which, for several years after disbandment, remained essentially un-policed. For his part, Daly was sorry he had missed the battle of Patrick Street, but he had won two pound eight playing Twenty-five and sure, a man could always find a fight if he wanted one whereas two pound eight was more than a day's wages and a harder thing by far to come by.

A month later O'Keefe said goodbye to Sergeant Jim Daly and the few remaining lads he was friendly with in Victoria barracks, and caught a troop transport train to Dublin with the last departing members of the King's Liverpool regiment. On April 4, 1922, he marched in the last RIC parade in Phoenix Park Depot and two days later, he walked through the gates of that depot, past the zoological gardens, and rode a tram down the North Circular Road. He was dressed in his one grey suit of worsted wool – sporting a claret-coloured tie and a tan trench coat, his Trilby tilted at a rakish, civilian angle – and no one paid him a second look.

*

Kevin McCarthy was born in Suffolk, UK, where his father was stationed with the US Air Force. He served in the Air Force himself before studying at Boston College and University College Dublin. In 2005 he was awarded the Fingal County Council Arts Bursary for Fiction Writing. He lives in North County Dublin with his wife and two children. *Peeler* is his first novel.

Irish Ways and Irish Laws

by Cora Harrison

It is a truth universally acknowledged, as Jane Austen would say, that no one writes crime/detective stories unless they enjoy reading them.

It follows, therefore, that an author will write a crime/detective story in the style of one which they enjoy reading.

I suppose I am hopelessly old-fashioned and out of touch with the times when I say that I hate having my nose rubbed in rape and gore, am bored by police procedurals and find all those drunken, neurotic policemen unpleasant and improbable. My favourite crime novels are by Ellis Peters (The Brother Cadfael Series), Agatha Christie, Dorothy Sayers, and Patricia Wentworth – in that order.

So when I decided to try out the detective story format, it was inevitable that I should go for a pleasant main character and an agreeable and evocative background.

But in order to get published it probably needed something extra.

In my case this something extra was to use a different system of laws – the Brehon laws. No unpleasant hanging or life-imprisonment at the end of the book, just a public admittance of guilt and a fine to be paid to the family of the victim . . .

I'm trying to think which came first – my desire to write a detective story or my deep interest in Brehon law. I think it was probably the Brehon law because once having read a book about these early Irish laws I seemed to be imbued with a crusading zeal to tell the world about their humanity, their richness and their uniqueness.

The Brehon Laws are known as early Irish laws – St Patrick of fifth-century fame was supposed to have looked through them and substituted a few of his own, such as capital punishment for murder. However, this wise and humanitarian law system outlived St Patrick by more than a thousand years in the north and west of Ireland – and in other places, also – and only died eventually in the hands of Queen Elizabeth in the sixteenth century. These laws were community-based laws, administered by the king's representative, the Brehon, but enforced by the consensus of the people in the kingdom. In the case of an injury, or even of murder, the Brehon, or judge, of the area would hear the case (always in the open air, so that the whole kingdom could come to listen, usually near some landmark like an ancient dolmen or a cairn or mound), then allocate a fine according to the extent of the injury and the status (honour price) of the victim. When the fine was too large for the individual to pay, then the family or even the whole clan had to find the cows or silver to pay it. This had significant consequences, in that relatives closely monitored the culprit's behaviour from then on.

For me the fines make fascinating reading. Murder, of course, was the most serious crime and the punishment was not death, but the payment of twenty-one milch cows, or twenty-one ounces of silver and the victim's honour price. An honour price was determined by your status in the community. So, if someone as important as a Brehon was murdered, the guilty person had to pay eight extra cows in addition to the basic fine – two or three cows would suffice for a farmer. The fines for injuries are detailed and take in every part of the body, even distinguishing between injury to a front tooth and to a back tooth. Interestingly enough, the fines for any injury or insult to a woman are quite severe – in an era when maid servants and workers could be raped with impunity in England, in Ireland, under Brehon law, the fine for the rape of a 'girl in plaits' was the same as for a murder and the fine for raising a woman's dress against her will was ten milch cows or ten ounces of silver.

Marriage contracts were an important part of Brehon law and, again, women's rights were safeguarded in a way that was unknown in medieval Europe. If the marriage broke down through the fault of the husband then divorce was granted, the property halved and the 'bride price' retained by the woman. These were the grounds for a woman to obtain a divorce with retention of the 'bride price':

- If the man leaves her for another woman
- If the man is impotent or homosexual
- If he is so fat as to be incapable of intercourse
- If the man relates secrets of the marriage bed in the alehouse

The laws of trespass were so detailed that it is obvious that keeping peace in a neighbourhood was an important part of Brehon law. They even take in something as trivial as apportioning a fine if a dog defecates on your land – in this case the owner must remove the offence and compensate by giving an equivalent weight in curds or butter. If bees trespass, then compensation must be paid in the form of a jar of honey for a person with a garden, and a hive for a person with a whole farm.

I think that even these few examples will show how one can get fascinated by the Brehon Laws and how it is almost irresistible to communicate the knowledge of them to a wider audience. Soon I began to consider how I could weave them into a detective story series.

I had always wanted to do a 'Miss Marple'-type detective story where intuition and a knowledge of human beings would come into the solution of the mystery, but I had to accept that the era of the gifted amateur was over – it was no longer credible for an elderly spinster in an English village, not only to solve murder after murder, and with full co-operation from the police, but to actually encounter the sheer numbers of crimes in these places.

However, by going back into an era where there were no police and into a land with its own system of laws, I had a chance to produce a 'Miss Marple' of early sixteenth century in Gaelic Ireland.

And so I created Mara, Brehon of the Burren, a woman who held the responsibility for law and order in this tiny one-hundred-mile square kingdom on the western Atlantic coast of Ireland.

A Brehon (and this is an anglicisation and a corruption of a Gaelic word) is translated as 'judge', but when Brehon law reigned (up to the later years of the sixteenth century in some parts of Ireland) their function was wider than that of mere arbiter. A Brehon carried out the function of a detective also, something a little like an investigating magistrate or a procurator fiscal in Scotland. Therefore, since the Brehon of an area did carry out the function of a detective as well as that of a judge, Mara was not going to be a gifted amateur, but a professional woman carrying out her work with skill and intelligence.

Initially I was planning to have my main character be a man, but that didn't work out so well for me – perhaps it's more difficult for a woman to write about a man, or perhaps it's just me – but once I restarted with a woman Brehon, everything flowed very quickly. Since Brehon law was administered without use of police or of prison, it has to be enacted through the consensus of the community – through the clan system – where the ultimate punishment is banishment from the clan, and I felt that many of the problems encountered by a Brehon would be best handled by a woman, as qualities of tact and insight into human relationships would be very much needed when enforcing laws without that underlying threat of prison or capital punishment. This is per-haps a rather sexist point of view, but my own experience in the world of work tells me that women are much better at enforcing rules without aggression.

I chose 1509 as the date for the opening book, *My Lady Judge*, for many reasons. One is that it is the first year of the reign of Henry VIII, a king whose reign had enormous consequences for history, and a king that would allow most readers to immediately orientate themselves within the period. Secondly, those early years of his reign were characterised by extraordinarily good sum-mers that lasted well into autumn, and I must confess that the Burren does always look a lot better in warm sunny weather. My third reason was that this was a turning point in Irish history. English kings, though nominally consid-ering Ireland to be their own property since the twelfth century, had, in fact, seen their power shrink to a narrow strip of land on the east coast of Ireland.

Henry VIII (and his daughter, Elizabeth) changed all this. So what I am writing about here is, in a way, a *fin de siècle* piece of nostalgia, an evocation of a time when the clans led their lives under the humane and advanced system of laws, known as Brehon laws.

One of the big problems in any historical novel is how to keep the characters true to their period. This is especially true if you are writing about Gaelic Ireland up to the middle or end of the sixteenth century. Very little has survived in written form – we have to wait for the middle of the reign of Queen Elizabeth I for the voluminous state papers about Ireland and even these are not enlightening about the motivation behind the actions of the Gaelic chiefs.

So writing on the subject of the era of 1509 is quite difficult. There are no letters or journals from the place and period to help me. I made a decision not to try to second-guess anything, just to feel my way into the character and to keep on asking myself the question: what would Mara have done, or said on this occasion – in other words, to keep in mind her historical background, but not to try and make her different to a twentieth-century woman in her thoughts and emotions. One other decision that I made was to write the books in standard English – with the odd, self-explanatory Gaelic word thrown in for atmosphere. As Mara would have spoken Gaelic, there was no point in heavy-handed Tudorisms, or any of those rather off-putting 'thee's or 'thou's or 'ye olde's.

When it comes to how Mara would have acted – and she has been criticised for being too 'modern' – it has to be said that the Celtic society was very different to the Anglo-Saxon, or Norman societies. The women of the Celts were always fairly liberated (look at Boudicea, the warrior woman of the British Celts). There were women lawyers, women doctors and even women blacksmiths in early and late medieval Ireland – the evidence for this comes from the Brehon laws.

The nearest historical female example of a liberated woman of the place and time was Grace O'Malley. She was also from the west of Ireland, and was born in the same year as Queen Elizabeth I, about sixty years later than my Mara. Though there is nothing in Irish historical records about Grace, she does appear in the Elizabethan papers. Despite having at least one brother, she was the one who inherited her father's position as chief of the clan, his main castle, and also his shipping interests (which, like those of Drake and Raleigh, included quite a bit of piracy). She had three husbands, two of whom she divorced. She was a thorn in the side of the English, who by the end of her life were gaining control over the west of Ireland. Grace harassed their shipping and was considered a great obstacle to law and order in the region of Galway and the west coast in general. When in her sixties, she sailed to London, where she visited Queen Elizabeth at Whitehall to complain about the English Administrators. She managed to gain an audience with Elizabeth – they, apparently, conversed in Latin, and Grace gained quite a few concessions.

I think an example such as this justifies having a female Brehon. I read, also, of a famous female Brehon, who was able to put male judges right, in many of the books on Brehon law, but I think my real inspiration for Mara came from standing outside the ruins of the sixteenth-century law school at Cahermacnaghten – now a ruin in the Burren. It seemed more than likely that the Brehon of such a small kingdom as the Burren would also have been the professor at the law school.

Cahermacnaghten, an Iron Age fort in origin, was probably built about two thousand years ago, but was occupied certainly until the mid-seventeenth century – perhaps beyond that. There was a law school here certainly in the fifteenth, sixteenth and seventeenth centuries, and some of the documents, copying out the Brehon laws, were written here by Domhnall O'Davoren and his students in the middle of the sixteenth century. I actually saw and handled this book, named Egerton 88, in the British Museum.

When I was tentatively considering the series I spent quite some time wandering around these ruins. The law school was set within the walls of the ancient fort, with its immensely thick walls. As you walk over the grass you can see the remains of the houses within the walls, and there is a will, written in the seventeenth century, that mentions the kitchen house, and three other houses – probably there would have been a school house and a house to lodge the scholars, and I imagined also that there would have been a house for the farm manager and his wife.

There are the ruins of a house standing about a hundred yards away from the law school (part of the Cahermacnaghten property) and I imagined that that was the Brehon's residence. As I love plants, I visualised her as a gardener, and so I opened *My Lady Judge* with a scene that sets her in the garden. Once she began to speak to her neighbour Diarmuid and solve his problem of the missing brown cow, I found her personality. I'm not someone who maps out a character beforehand – though I am a meticulous plotter of the bones of the story – but when it comes to character I usually start with dialogue and the personality grows from there and this worked for me with Mara, Brehon of the Burren.

I like to think that my Mara solves her crimes by a mixture of sharp intelligence, intuition and reasoning power, but above all by a deep understanding of people, which arises from her interest in their personalities and their lives.

I decided to make her a woman of a certain age – I fixed on thirty six – as her position as professor, as well as judge and law-enforcer for the hundred-square-mile kingdom of the Burren, would suggest a certain maturity and experience. I gave her a 'back story' of having a slightly scandalous past, a woman famous for having successfully conducted her own divorce case as a young lawyer aged sixteen. Mara is already a grandmother, but the object of the romantic interest of King Turlough Donn, lord of the three kingdoms of Thomond, Corcomroe and Burren, who is a real character in Irish history and the last of the old kings of medieval Ireland – his son, Murrough, known as Murrough the Tánaiste (heir), sold his birthright for a mess of pottage and was dubbed Earl of Inchiquin by King Henry VIII.

I'm slightly amused now when I look back through my notes about King Turlough Donn and see how little I knew about him and how much I have invented about him. My readings through as many Irish history books as I could find seemed to have only turned up the facts that he was born in 1459, crowned king in 1499, fought against the anglicised Earl of Kildare in 1504, was described by that same Earl to Henry VII as 'a mortal enemy to all Englishmen and the most maliciously disposed of any that I heard speak of'. I knew, also, that he built a bridge across the Shannon in 1506, that he defeated the Earl of Kildare in 1510 and that he died in 1529. From that I wove a character of a man, perhaps out of his time, a man who clung to the romantic past of his people, to whom the Gaelic customs, laws and ties of clan and family were of huge importance, to be guarded at all costs against the new ways that were seeping in through the anglicised east of Ireland and the chartered city of Galway. My King Turlough Donn I imagined as a medieval Gaelic warrior who feared that he might be the last of his kind.

One of the fascinating things that I found out when researching the historical background for kingship at that late medieval time was about the difference between the English ceremony of crowning and the inauguration of a Gaelic chief such as Turlough Donn or his fellow clansmen the MacNamara clan. I describe the ceremony at the beginning of *Michaelmas Tribute*, the second book of the series:

Garrett MacNamara, dressed in a white léine and a mantle made from pure white lamb's wool, was led in procession to the cairn, a burial mound covered with small white quartz pebbles and a sacred place to the MacNamara clan. At the foot of the cairn, King Turlough Donn touched him on the head with a newly peeled white rod from the ancient ash tree that grew nearby. In a loud, steady voice, Garrett swore to be the king's vassal in accordance with the ancient Brehon laws, to maintain his lord's boundaries, to escort his lord to public assemblies, to bring his own warriors to each *slógad*, and, in the last hour of his lord, to assist in digging the gravemound and to contribute to the death feast. And then his people acclaimed him in a loud voice as the MacNamara.

So my Mara has her romantic interest when the noble King Turlough Donn proposes marriage to her. This proposal, I felt, might pose a dilemma, which could be worked out as the series progressed. After all, she was a professional woman with two careers, that of being Brehon and also that of being *ollamh*, or professor to the scholars of the law school. Could she fit being a royal consort into that busy schedule?

*

And now I come back to my original vision of a detective series which I personally would enjoy reading. I love the Devon villages in Agatha Christie, the medieval town of Shrewsbury and the beautiful Welsh countryside in the Ellis Peters books, but in choosing the Burren I knew that I had a setting to rival any of these – if I had the skill to do it justice.

To my mind, the Burren, with its unique limestone pavements, terraced mountains and collection of rare wild flowers, is the most beautiful place in Ireland and probably one of the least known. I wanted everyone possible to share in my love for the place and in my delight in its beauties. It has been described as lunar, but I think this is a rather cold picture; when I think of the Burren I think of it as symphony of colour and of light. I tried to give an idea of this in my opening paragraph to the first book:

> Early summer in the Burren has a glory about it: in the valleys a glory of soft greens, creamy hawthorn blossom and purple foxgloves; on the sparkling limestone of the uplands tiny jewel-like flowers of purple, yellow and blue sprinkled in the grykes between the flat shining slabs of stone. Orange tip butterflies swoop among the cuckoo flowers, vibrant blue-green dragonflies haunt the crystal waters of the spring wells and larks soar high above the contented cattle.

I have a theory that environment influences character immensely. When I read C. S. Sansom's historical trilogy set in the time of Henry VIII, I must say that I found the number of savagely cruel people described there, especially in the second book, to be quite disturbing. They are not books that I would reread. However, the London of that time was probably a fairly appalling place to live in. Before the days of proper sewage disposal, social welfare and policing, London would have been full of disease, smells, poverty, prostitution, open crime and savage punishments. This was bound to have an effect on its population and I am sure that Sansom, a writer that I respect hugely, is correct in his recreation of the people of sixteenth-century London.

The Burren in the sixteenth century, on the other hand, was not at all like that. The climate is, and was, relatively mild. With industry, and help from family and neighbours, a man could build a solid house for himself, his wife and his children in the space of a few weeks, as the stone was literally lying around ready to be picked up, and oat straw or reed, or even rushes, could be used to thatch it. Animal husbandry, with the big stretches of common land on the High Burren and on the mountainsides, encouraged a neighbourly way of life (still to be seen here, even in this twenty-first century). More importantly, the population in the hundred square miles was very small in the sixteenth century and there was little tradition of village life, so people lived on well-spaced farms. This meant that there would have been no smells, no pollution, and probably far less disease and far longer life-spans. In addition, since the limestone was freely available, it could be burned to make lime which seems to have been the traditional way of keeping the walls, inside and outside, of houses and sheds clean and, we all know now, free of germs.

*

It is, of course, part of the format of the detective story that each sleuth must have his or her Dr Watson. In the case of Mara, I used the six scholars of the law school in that role. It meant that the explanations about the complexities of Brehon law could come without any sense of lecturing to the reader and since they are a crowd of adolescent boys with the usual high spirits and growing-up problems of that age group, it added another dimension to the story.

The history of the law schools was harder to research than the Brehon laws, where various lawyers and scholars such as Daniel Binchy and Fergus Kelly have been outstanding in their published works. Fergus Kelly lists some of the late medieval law schools in the west and north of Ireland – mostly run by the MacEgan family, but one by the Davoren family in the Burren. However, when it comes to the content of the curriculum, it is an Englishman, Edmund Campion, sent over to Ireland by Queen Elizabeth I, who remarks on the excellence of their Latin and how they studied the laws for as long as fifteen or sixteen years. He describes the sitting of the court thus:

> 'The Breighon (so they call this kynde of lawyer) sittethe him downe on a bancke, the lordes and gentlemen at variaunce rounde about hym and then they proceede.'

At the time of writing, five books in the series have been published: *My Lady Judge, Michaelmas Tribute, Sting of Justice, Writ in Stone, Eye of the Law, Scales of Retribution* – and after that I'm not sure, though I have other books planned. I hope it does continue because I enjoy writing them so much and I think that Mara and King Turlough Donn, and her law students, can go on growing and developing as time goes on.

I had written a couple of books about the law school when I got the opportunity to see that very precious book, Egerton 88, the book written in this Burren law school in the mid-sixteenth century and now preserved in the British Museum Library. When I was looking through it, I could see the different scripts, some neat, some slapdash, one obviously left-handed, and I found myself speculating on the varying personalities of the scholars. It was great to read the scholars' comments in the margins, wishing they were out making the hay, complaining of the bad food, commenting that the week felt so long that it seemed as if it had two Thursdays in it, and making jokes about Sémus and the drink! I felt as though the law school that I had created in my books had suddenly become real.

I was amused to find that each scholar signed off the contribution in a very exuberant style, which showed an easy, affectionate relationship with the teacher. One of them – and this was quite extraordinary – was signed Síle (it must be a girl's name), giving her felicitations.

So there was a girl scholar! I had already written two of the Mara books and here was proof that I had been right to go with my instincts and to say, Well, why *not* a woman Brehon?

*

Cora Harrison lives near the Burren in the west of Ireland, an area whose landscape and history form the background to her medieval crime series for adults, the Burren Mysteries. The latest Burren Mystery, *Deed of Murder*, will be published in 2011. She has also published thirty-three books for children and young adults. *www.coraharrison.com*

Odd Men Out

by Adrian McKinty

Even before the creation of the artificial 1921 border that separated Northern Ireland from the Free State, the north of Ireland had always had a somewhat different atmosphere than the south. For centuries Ulstermen and women had been blessed with a unique accent, a darker sense of humour and a taciturnity unshared by their countrymen in the more salubrious portion of the island.

By the time of partition, these cultural incongruities had been given a physical dimension, as most of Ireland's heavy industry, particularly ship building, linen manufacture and engineering, had been established in and around Belfast.

Attempts have been made to the explain the province of Ulster's singularity by laying the blame on the thousands of dour Scottish planters who began arriving in the northeast of Ireland in the 1590s, but well before the Plantation, the land north of the Mournes had always revelled in its exceptionalism. Ulster was the most Gaelic and least English province of Ireland in the time of Aodh Mór Ó Néill (known as the Great O'Neill) and, further back into the mists of pre-history, the story of the Táin Bó Cúailnge is that of Cuchulainn, champion of Ulster, battling the forces of the rest of Ireland.

But be that as it may, post-partition Northern Ireland suffered from an inferiority complex. It had been in no one's plan during the Home Rule crises of the nineteenth century that a six-county statelet be formed in the north with

Belfast as its capital. Northern Ireland struggled to find any identity to speak of and, cut off from cultural developments in Dublin and London, it became something of a provincial backwater. Queen's University and the Progressive Bookshop in Belfast's Union Street were intellectual hubs but international literary trends tended to pass Ulster by, and Northern Irish fiction itself went through a lean period until after the end of World War II.

One of the earliest and most interesting post-war Northern Irish crime novels was *Odd Man Out* (1945), written by English-born novelist F. L. (Frederick Lawrence) Green, who had been living in Belfast since the 1930s. In unadorned straightforward prose, Green tells the story of an IRA fugitive from a failed robbery trying to find allies in Belfast who may be able to hide him before the police close in. Even back then the 'caper gone wrong' was an old trope of crime fiction but Green's spin on the idea was to have us identify with the outlaw as, seething with pent-up fury, he moves through an expressionist nightmare of a city surrounded at every turn by informers and betrayal. This is a Belfast of uncertain alliances, where the currency of trust has been devalued to junk status and where the status quo is so ingrained that it seems foolhardy to do anything but cooperate with the Stormont government and their operatives in the police. The main action of the book takes place over a few hours and during this time we are driven through a Belfast of narrow alleys, choked pavements, men-only bars clogged with pipe and cigarette smoke, a city where the clank of street cars competes with the hammering of rivet guns at the busy shipyards of Harland and Wolff.

F. L. Green's screenplay for the Carol Reed film adaptation of *Odd Man Out* (1947) is in some ways an even more impressive achievement. Co-written with British playwright R. C. Sherriff, Green takes Johnny McQueen (played by James Mason in the film) deeper into a surrealist hell until, past the point of caring, McQueen accepts his fate as Dante, struggling through Belfast's night-time warren of streets and circles of madmen, liars and that most hated agent of the Castle – the informer. Ignored by confederates, let down by his allies, exploited by money grubbers, McQueen is finally hunted down like a dog near the city's iconic Albert Clock, where he and his girlfriend are both brutally killed in an early example of suicide by cop.

Carol Reed's impeccable direction and a stellar Abbey Theatre cast set the bar very high for a northern Irish crime movie, and although Reed himself went one better with *The Third Man* (1949), no Belfast-set film has yet surpassed *Odd Man Out* in this genre.

Exile has been a theme throughout this book and it was perhaps not surprising that the first truly great Northern Irish novel to appear, *The Lonely Passion of Judith Hearne* (1957), was written by Belfast-born Canadian exile Brian Moore. Hearne is a beautifully observed novel of a schizophrenic society and its effect on ordinary people. Moore returned to his Irish roots more than once, and he is represented here by his wonderful, complex crime story *Lies of Silence* (1989), which we will discuss later.

Northern Ireland's leading literary figures Moore, C. S. Lewis and Louis MacNeice all left Northern Ireland to ply their trade under brighter lights and Belfast languished until the early 1970s, when in the midst of the Troubles the city became the focus of an extraordinary group of poets who all went on to attain world renown: Seamus Heaney, Paul Muldoon, Derek Mahon, Ciaran Carson, Michael Longley and Tom Paulin, among others. These young poets loosely based around Queens University Belfast between them produced the greatest body of Irish literary work since the Gaelic Revival.

And as the violence worsened, ironically, Belfast grew in cultural confidence, kick-started by its incendiary poetry, which in turn provided the kerosene for the other arts. By the mid-1970s, Northern Ireland saw a boom in play-writing, screenwriting and finally in novel writing.

The situation on the ground could not have been worse. The Stormont government collapsed, British troops were sent to attempt to impose order, paramilitary organisations sprang up on both sides of the sectarian divide. Northern Ireland was in the midst of what some called a 'low-level civil war' and what most of us recognised as the darkest period of the Troubles.

Northern Ireland's Catholics had never bought into rule by the parliament in Stormont, the border of the six counties having been deliberately gerrymandered to assure a Protestant majority, and after the Official IRA announced a unilateral ceasefire, a more virulent group known as the Provisional IRA began its campaign of violence.

In reaction to the IRA bombings and shootings, successive British governments panicked: interring IRA suspects without trial, flooding Northern Ireland with yet more soldiers and strengthening the local police, the Royal Ulster Constabulary. And of course violence spiralled into violence. The UVF re-formed to counter the PIRA and the UDA became an umbrella group for various Protestant factions. Of course, the majority of those killed were innocent civilians on both sides.

Perhaps prose was seen as too direct a form to deal with the horror all around and certainly poetry was the medium of choice for a long time, but eventually fiction writers did come out of the woodwork. The crime novel really began to take off with the publication of Bernard MacLaverty's *Cal* in 1983.

Cal McCluskey is a Catholic living on a predominantly Protestant housing estate in the bleak rural wastes of mid-Ulster. Cajoled by an IRA handler into becoming a getaway driver in a sectarian killing, Cal falls for the dead man's wife and sets up the tragedy which everyone, including Cal, knows is coming. Cal is sickened by his part in the murder and he wants to be caught, but more than that he wants to be punished.

The pace of the novel is leisurely and MacLaverty takes his time to attempt a portrayal of the people who live in these bleak townlands. Rural Protestants and Catholics who, like characters in a Sartre play, must share together the rain-soaked tedium of unemployment in a boggy Nowhereland within the greater Nowhereland that was '70s Northern Ireland. Barnyards, abattoirs, grungy pubs, dirty cafes and newsagents are Cal's world, and his attempts to break out through music and, ultimately, love, are doomed. Perhaps the only answer is to escape Northern Ireland, as MacLaverty himself did by moving to Scotland. But Cal does not have the motivation even to get the ferry to Stranraer. This is a world of pessimism and apathy, punctuated by random inexplicable violence.

One day Cal attempts to earn some money potato picking:

'Suddenly a police Land Rover with its hee-haw siren blaring swung into the main road behind them with a squeal of tyres. It roared along and overtook them so fast its body tilted at an angle to the chassis. Someone said, 'Jesus, they'll sell no ice-cream going at that speed.' But as the day wore on the laughter died. A fine drizzle of rain came on turning the ground soil to muck. It clogged behind Cal's guitar nails and continually he had to sweep his dirty hands so that it and his forehead became dirty too. After a time his fingers became like sausages with the cold. The tractor, driven by Cyril Dunlop, came round wheeling up the soil and potatoes with an inevitability he hated. The only colour in the landscape was the red and blue of the plastic baskets.'

Bernard MacLaverty went onto write several short story collections as well as the novel *Lamb*, which was short-listed for the *Guardian* fiction prize, and *Grace Notes*, which was short-listed for the 1997 Booker Prize. He also wrote the screenplay for a fine film adaptation of *Cal* (1985), starring John Lynch and Helen Mirren.

Hollywood made several forgettable Northern Ireland-themed films in the years to come but one of the better ones was *Resurrection Man*, based on the novel of the same name by Kilkeel-born Sligo resident, Eoin McNamee. The novel's title comes from the ancient practice of corpse stealing – grave robbers taking the recently deceased and selling them on to doctors and anatomists, although in McNamee's book it is someone who takes the still living and tortures them lovingly and long until they beg for death and their personal belief (or not) in resurrection.

Resurrection Man (1994) is based on the true story of the Shankill Butchers, serial killers from the Protestant Shankill Road, who kidnapped Catholics off the street, beat them, shot them and murdered them. The book is dark and uncompromising and the protagonists thoroughly believable, hard-drinking sociopaths with such names as Onionhead Graham and Hacksaw McGrath. It is hard to feel any sympathy at all for these people who are so off the deep end that they have even accrued the wrath of

OUT OF THE PAST

their more moderate paramilitary brethren.

Resurrection Man, however, is a wonderfully written novel, both lyrical and also strangely funny (though perhaps only Belfast people will get this blackest of black humour). McNamee does not pull his punches, levelling an intelligent and indignant eye on the Shankill Butchers themselves but also on the wider system that allowed the perpetrators of these horrors to get away with it for so long.

McNamee, who writes more conventional thrillers under the pseudonym John Creed, has gone on to write several more extraordinary novels, novellas and screenplays, and has been short-listed for the *Irish Times*/Aer Lingus Award for Irish Literature.

Brian Moore's *Lies of Silence* (1990) is perhaps the most objective of the crime novels that were produced in this era of Northern Irish fiction. From Northern Ireland, but not of it, Moore used his years in Canada to gain an Archimedean distance from the conflict. But do not mistake distance for indifference. Moore too burns with rage about what has happened in the intervening decades to the city where he grew up, and this anger permeates the text even as it adds kindling to the motivations of his characters.

Lies of Silence is a pacy thriller, evocative and literary even as it acknowledges the conventions of the genre:

'When he turned on to the Antrim Road, the white Ford was following him. His route would take him from North to South Belfast, through streets little changed since his childhood. He would skirt the boundaries of poor working-class areas and drive past the large monuments and buildings at the city's centre. It was a route which on a normal day was far too familiar to evoke in him any thought of what he was passing. But this morning, in a car which was a moving bomb, followed by terrorists who could radio in an order to kill his wife, he was driving what might be the last time through this ugly, troubled place.'

Moore's compassion for both sides of the zero sum equation in Northern Ireland means that there are few stereotypes in his fiction. All of Moore's characters have fully-fledged back stories and motivations and no one does anything until after they have recapitulated their well thought out – if morally dubious – reasons.

Lies of Silence is the story of Martin Dillon, whose marriage to the beautiful Moira has fallen apart into melodramatic arguments, petty bickering and psychological cruelty. On the verge of leaving her, he is forced into becoming an accomplice for the IRA and from there on in there are no easy ways out for Dillon or his family, or indeed his confederates, who are all riding the bus to hell together.

Like many of these Troubles fictions, *Lies of Silence* is the story of a flawed protagonist and takes its cue from the modernist anti-heroes of Graham Greene or Albert Camus. You or I would probably act in very similar ways to Martin Dillon and we feel as a trapped as he is by his circumstances and the history and geography of Belfast.

From his outsider/insider perspective, Moore is able to explore the notions of identity in some depth. What does it mean to be a minority Catholic in a British-ruled statelet? What is like to be an unloved Protestant, alienated from Brits over the water and despised by fellow Irishmen south of the border? Perhaps, Moore suggests, the ideal solution to these questions of identity is to turn them on their head. How easy it is to be a Catholic living in the Republic of Ireland surrounded by confirmations of one's identity in church, in government, even in the colour of the post boxes? How much more interesting to be in the north where identities are confused, muddled occasions for angst? And what exactly is this bastard type – the Northern Irish Protestant? Who are you? English, Scottish, Irish, Northern Irish, British? Why do you feel that you stand apart from your fellow Irishmen and why do you wish to pledge fealty to a Queen and country who so obviously despise you?

Moore enjoys taking his characters on the inward journey and trying to understand where they are going. And unlike many novelists who wring their hands in despair, Moore actually tries to give us some answers. The solution to this question of loyalty and provenance is that identities nest themselves and ultimately blur. You are neither one thing nor another, you have no easy standpoint from which to survey your life, and every day you must reinvent yourself, unlike the comfortable residents of Dublin or London, and this is what makes life in Northern Ireland very complex, very Modern(with a capital M) and very interesting indeed.

Eugene McEldowney is a novelist who grew up in the crucible of 1940s and 1950s West Belfast and who now lives in Dublin. He has written a series of four mystery novels featuring Superintendent Cecil Megarry: *A Kind of Homecoming* (1994), *A Stone of the Heart* (1995), *The Sad Case of Harpo Higgins* (1996) and *Murder at Piper's Gut* (1997).

The whole series and especially the first of the novels, *A Kind of Homecoming*, is a brave attempt to impose order on the disorder of a troubled city by giving Belfast something every other place in the world is allowed to have – a straightforward mystery novel with a sympathetic but dysfunctional detective, red herrings, a taut plot, and a classic well-crafted denouement.

Borges said that the detective novel was an important bastion of culture, a candle against the dark, for 'in this chaotic era of ours it is the one thing that has maintained the classic virtues of the novel and detective fiction cannot be understood without a beginning, middle and end.'

The story of *A Kind of Homecoming* inevitably involves those lords of Belfast crime – the paramilitaries. Two bodies are found in and beside a Ford Cortina on waste ground. One of them is an IRA informer and thus an excellent candidate for death, but he was shot with a different weapon and several hours earlier than the man beside him, who had a history of child molestation and a lot of money in the bank.

Superintendent Cecil Megarry is put on the case and he battles his own demons as he tries to unravel the complex history of what exactly happened. On our journey towards truth we encounter corruption, decadence, cowardice and paramilitaries more interested in making money than in making revolution. What makes *A Kind of Homecoming* so fascinating and so different is how ordinary everything is. We have a harassed policeman, complicated forensic evidence, plot twists, familial discontent – this could be any copper in any city in the world, but the fact this novel takes place in the insanity of Troubles

Belfast makes it a kind of miracle, a little rhymed couplet of civilisation in a free-verse madhouse. We want Megarry to succeed not just to save himself but to save the whole city too; God would have spared Sodom if Lot had found ten righteous men, and perhaps God would spare Belfast if he could find ten good coppers.

Although it was hard to see it at the time, the Troubles were winding down when the first Megarry novel was published in 1994. Unknown to everyone, the Provisional IRA and the British government had been in secret negotiations over the terms of a permanent cease-fire. On August 31, 1994, the IRA announced a complete cessation of hostilities and although this shaky truce faced several stumbling blocks and setbacks, before anyone really knew what was happening the Troubles were over and a new era in Northern Irish history (and literary history) had begun.

It is difficult to draw any conclusions about so diverse a group of writers as I've covered in this chapter. The novelists I looked at share almost no stylistic or metaphoric traits but perhaps it is significant that none of them currently live in Northern Ireland (Green died in 1953 and Moore in 2001). One wonders if that makes it easier or more difficult to write about the Province, and whether one's attitude changes or becomes more rigid as the years of self-imposed exile roll on. It's also sad that none of the novelists within my purview were female, (with the possible exception of Michele McMullan, who wrote action thrillers under the name of S. J. Michaels, including *Summary Justice, Dieback* and *The Heir*). Perhaps one thing that Protestants and Catholics do share in Northern Ireland are retrograde attitudes towards women; female crime novelists of the Troubles era will emerge and when they do they will give us a whole new layer of understanding that will undoubtedly show the macho posturing of the '70s and '80s for the empty rhetoric it certainly was.

Northern Ireland during the Troubles was a grim, scary place of bombings and bomb threats, sectarian killings and riots, where you were physically searched going into the centre of Belfast and where normal life was anything but normal. But it was also a place of scalding black humour, grim ironies and uncommon courage that left a mark for good and ill on everyone who went through it.

There is a certainly a difference in accent and in attitude but perhaps climate is as good a metaphor as any to delineate the difference between Belfast and Dublin, between northern and southern Ireland: northern autumns are harsher and colder than those of the slightly more temperate south, northern summers are wetter and distinctly chillier, and in the winter no one would dispute the fact that in Ulster, the darkness lasts a little longer.

*

Adrian McKinty was born and grew up in Carrickfergus, Northern Ireland. He emigrated to the United States in 1993 and worked as a bartender and construction worker in New York before becoming a high school English teacher in Denver, Colorado. His first crime novel, *Dead I Well May Be*, was published in 2004. His most recent book, *Falling Glass*, was published by Serpent's Tail in 2011.

The Dead Generations

by Cormac Millar

As an international genre, crime fiction gets imported into many countries. At first it may be a hybrid product, sitting awkwardly in its new setting, but it can win its naturalisation papers if it is seen to respond to local conditions, reaching the parts that other forms can't reach. Many of us have drawn inspiration from external sources. Long before becoming a published mystery author, I had been an admirer of Californian writers like Raymond Chandler, Ross Macdonald and Joseph Hansen, and of films like *Chinatown*, *The Big Sleep*, *LA Confidential* and the strangely underrated *Twilight*.

I was dazzled by Macdonald's direct access to myth and tragedy, his fluid handling of shifting family structures. I admired Chandler's creation of Marlowe, iconic dispenser of imperfect justice, and Hansen's brilliant exploration of the parallel life of gay characters, throwing a different light on society's hidden networks. Most of all I loved the episodic structure of their work, where the detective travels through layered cycles of complexity, often encountering the same people several times as if in a dream, until the pattern tumbles into place and the truth becomes plain. But that complex and mysterious structure is hard to import into the Irish context. Especially in the decades before the Celtic Tiger, Ireland was a rather predictable country where everyone knew everyone, people were who they said they were, distances were short and social relations were intimate and sclerotic. Even today, the roving private eye cannot avoid a hint of parody as he explores our miniature universe. All the more reason to celebrate the achievement of writers like Declan Hughes, Ken Bruen and Vincent Banville, who in their different ways have managed to create freewheeling heroes within Ireland's little room.

My own first creation, Séamus Joyce, was deliberately unheroic. Cautious and gullible, Séamus has little to recommend him other than occasional moments of integrity and rare flashes of intelligence. He was not Philip Marlowe, nor was he meant to be. His closest literary cousin might well be Dr Pereira, the timid Portuguese journalist coaxed into anti-fascist resistance in Antonio Tabucchi's 1994 novel, *Pereira Maintains*. A drab civil servant conceived under a Catholic clerical blanket, Séamus Joyce was ill-suited to life inside the Celtic Tiger, up whose gentrified streets he had to go as a man who was quite nervous, uneasy and out of sorts.

I put Séamus through his reluctant paces in two novels, and he may get another outing one day. His very name – James Joyce with the first name translated into Gaelic for reasons of nationalist piety – is a tribute to the unoriginal and the secondhand in us, our facile claims to culture, our distance from authentic heroism. Séamus is a man whom life has passed by, a besuited functionary; his middle name is disenchantment. Ironically, he does succeed in enacting one of the canons of crime fiction, when he reluctantly exposes something rotten in the state.

My model in this particular line of mystery writing is Leonardo Sciascia, the Sicilian author whose magisterial depiction of organised crime takes in many of the social and political failings of Italy. But we in Ireland are not governed by the Mafia, even if it now turns out that for the past few decades the country has largely been run by complacent fools and incompetent crooks. We do have some small pockets of organised crime, a fashion for drunken stabbings, and a thirty-year carnival of paramilitary murder, which we are busily forgetting even though it claimed three thousand victims (my first novel is dedicated to the memory of one of these forgotten deaths). In short, despite many advances in recent decades, there's still plenty wrong with Ireland, and that can only be good news for the crime writer.

Having set up in the field, I thought I would list some fellow-authors and predecessors on my website. I thought there might be as many as two or three dozen of them. In fact they are more than a hundred strong and reach back more than a century: a fine set of virtual ancestors. The 1916 Proclamation launched a new war of independence 'in the name of God and of the dead generations': can Ireland's contemporary crime writers also claim to be continuing a glorious national tradition?

Some of the illustrious dead I knew already. My mother, Eilís Dillon, had published three moderately successful detective stories in the 1950s (these have recently been reissued by Rue Morgue Press in America). I had read a few crude tales of gangsterism by Liam O'Flaherty, and a somewhat weird novel from 1943, *Murder and Music,* by Gerald Lee, in which the evil musician Luke Bloggs augments his income by forcing his blackmail victims to sign up for piano lessons, and is very properly murdered by his butler (another blackmail victim). I had admired John Banville's polished true-crime retelling of the Malcolm McArthur murder story in *The Book of Evidence,* and enjoyed the criminal elements in some relatively mainstream Irish writers. Crime is in fact endemic in respectable Irish literature, which has had a long dalliance with mystery and downright violence. To mention a few examples: Old Mahon got his head bashed with a spade in J. M. Synge's *Playboy of the Western World* (1907), old Mathers suffered the same fate in Flann O'Brien's *The Third Policeman* (1939-40), and Eamonn Eales was wiped out by a volume of the *Encyclopedia Britannica* in Patrick McGlinchey's *Bogmail* (1978), a comic crime novel of remarkable indecency. In a more sombre key, Mervyn Wall's *Hermitage* (1982) shows Tony Langton, an elderly civil servant, killing his girlfriend with an old-fashioned clothes brush. Roddy Doyle's *The Woman Who Walked Into Doors* (1996) provides a powerful account of marital abuse, framed by the more conventional crime of armed robbery. Patrick McCabe's cult novel *The Butcher Boy* (1992) is narrated by a psychotic killer. John Banville's *Athena* (1995) and Claire Kilroy's *All Summer* (2003) hinge on stolen paintings. But when literary authors stoop to crime, heavyweight reviewers are usually quick to reassure them that they have transcended the thriller genre by virtue of the artistic beauty of their prose. Unlike the rest of us.

Ireland is, then, a reasonably problematic space, with a decent sprinkling of criminal elements within its established literary tradition. But what of the honest average crime writer who seeks not to transcend the genre but to meet its exacting standards (even at the cost of having to write better than some literary novelists)? What can simple folk like us do for our country, presuming that we would want to do such a thing?

One valid response to the question of national identity is to go international. Some Irish crime writers have done this successfully: you can read their books without suspecting their nationality. The most celebrated example today is John Connolly, whose predecessors include J. B. O'Sullivan, author of such titles as *Don't Hang Me Too High*, set in a nameless American city replete with dames, Chevrolets and police lieutenants, and Brian Moore, whose international pulp thrillers started out under the pseudonyms of Bernard Mara and Michael Bryan. Like Graham Greene, Moore could move between crime fiction and the literary novel, or combine the two within a single book; he could also shift effortlessly between Irish and international settings. Rather than 'transcending' the thriller genre, Moore brought it to a high level by realising its potential as an art form that reveals hard truths.

Other Irish, or Irish-born, crime novelists also wrote for the international market (in this context, 'international' can often mean little more than British or American). Robert Brennan (1881-1964), father of the *New Yorker* writer Maeve Brennan (currently enjoying a posthumous revival), wrote several crime stories in the intervals of an eventful life as revolutionary, political organiser, newspaperman, Irish ambassador to Washington and head of the Irish national broadcasting service. Maeve Brennan's biographer, Angela Bourke, has pointed out the non-Irish character of Robert Brennan's novels: 'throughout Bob's writing life, he embraced the conventions of English popular fiction. The stories he wrote were always literate and well crafted, but none of them attempted to explore motivation or emotion [. . .]. For all his allegiance to the idea of a deanglicised Ireland, he gave many of his characters quintessentially English names, and placed them in different settings that were English by default.' This is certainly true of some of his books, including *The Toledo Dagger* (1926), which has a French setting and is liberally peppered with people called Monsieur and Mademoiselle but is for all that as English as Agatha Christie. This typifies the mystery novel's status as an international import. Much more interesting, though, is Brennan's 1921 novel, *The False Finger Tip*, written under the pseudonym Selskar Kearney while the author was a prisoner in an English jail. *The False Finger Tip* tells of a villainous innkeeper named Sealy who is perfectly prepared to murder people, dropping their bodies into the River Liffey, in his relentless pursuit of a safe full of money which had got buried in the rubble of a house destroyed by shelling during the 1916 Easter Rising – the same revolutionary event following which the author had been imprisoned by the British authorities. In the novel the names are as Irish as one could desire: Christy Kirwan, Sam Lanigan (a horribly garrulous fellow apparently modelled on the author's cellmate), Paddy Byrne, Jemmy and Cissie Delaney. The farfetched tale is told mostly in luridly colourful demotic Hiberno-English strongly reminiscent of Flann O'Brien (the opening scenes could have come out of O'Brien's 1939 masterpiece *At Swim-Two-Birds*). Veering between subversive wit and patriotic piety, *The False Finger Tip* remains – despite its faults or because of them – an entertaining and appealing document of its time.

Following the 1916 Rising and the War of Independence, the Irish Free State emerged. Comprising twenty six of Ireland's thirty two counties (the rest formed Northern Ireland), the Free State drew its authority from a tradition of self-dramatising physical force which occasionally threatened to overwhelm it. Deeply protectionist, isolationist, sectarian and backward, the new state was mostly run by religious bigots whose control-freak morality generally ignored issues of business ethics and countenanced a high level of self-righteous corruption. This problem has tended not to be addressed by Irish crime writers. The systematic abuse of women and children in religious-controlled orphanages and reformatories is another issue, which up to recently was underrepresented in our literary system, although there were honourable exceptions.

The official version of the fight for Irish freedom glorified physical force so long as it was safely in the past and had been exercised purely against the

British; patriotic novels of the War of Independence thus tend to be morally simple, lacking the complexity and sense of personal responsibility usually associated with crime fiction. The problem, for the authorities, was that not all revolutionaries were satisfied with the Irish Free State (later rebadged as the Irish Republic), which was run almost entirely by former subversives who still sympathised with revolutionary ideas at some abstract level, while rigorously enforcing authoritarian and pseudo-Victorian norms in everyday life. An unreconciled physical violence tradition, changing its aims and its allies from time to time, remained as an undercurrent in the national consciousness, periodically disturbing the security of the state and incidentally providing grist to the mill of thriller writers. The actions of guerrilla fighters, even during the war against the British, came to be questioned in literature, most famously in Frank O'Connor's great short story 'Guests of the Nation'. A young man calling himself Rearden Conner (a variant of his real name) made a considerable hit with his first book, *Shake Hands With The Devil* (1933), which criticised the motives of an embittered underground leader; the book was later filmed, starring James Cagney. A similar vein is mined by Liam Redmond in his 1959 novel *Death Is So Kind*, and has continued up to the present day, aided by the renewed terrorist wars, with attendant gangsterism, that disfigured Northern Ireland from the 1970s to the 1990s. A stunning recent example, compulsive and unflinching, is Stuart Neville's debut novel, *The Twelve* (titled *The Ghosts of Belfast* in the US).

Having abandoned his landscape gardening trade in favour of the literary life, Rearden Conner went on to write other stories of Irish criminality, with diminishing success. Several of his books were banned by the Irish Censorship Board, which at the time was usually a token of literary distinction. After his death in 1991 his literary papers were acquired by the British Library. In his precocious autobiography, *A Plain Tale from the Bogs* (1937), he complains about the censoriousness of his own culture: 'a section of the Irish and Irish-American reviewers demand that Irish novelists depict Irishmen as models of virtue, and Irishwomen as models of chastity. God help the Irish writer who, in the genuineness of his heart, thinks fit to depict an Irish villain! God doubly help him if he dares to suggest that such a creature as a prostitute exists in Ireland! I have seen it suggested that this attitude is responsible for the absence of detective fiction from Irish letters.' Apart from censorship, Conner cites the inferiority complex of his countrymen as a major obstacle to the reception of his writing. 'Irishmen in all parts of the world accuse a fellow countryman of "showing them up" if he merely presents one or two of his characters as they exist, in Ireland and elsewhere'. He complains that he was considered a traitor in writing about the War of Independence 'because I have noted the fact that there were brave men on both sides, and cruel sadists on both sides. The gunmen who later joined the gangsters and racketeers in the United States were no more angels than the Black-and-Tans'. Not for Conner the idyllic ethos of the mystery story as described by W. H. Auden in 'The Guilty Vicarage', his celebrated essay on crime fiction, whereby a crime disrupts a place of pastoral peace, and its solution restores the perfect setting. Conner is out to show that even the greenest garden is not without its snakes.

Crime writing today falls along a continuum that ranges from cosy to hard-edged. Of course the hard-edged stuff can often serve as pure escapism and hence prove even more predictably comforting than the cosy end, but these are inevitable paradoxes of reading. What is odd is that, for much of the twentieth century, describing Ireland in cosy or comical terms, in effect presenting it from the sentimentalised English point of view, was the preferred strategy of patriotic Irish writers. My mother's three Irish detective stories give no hint of her family's involvement in the physical force tradition of Irish politics. Her uncle Joe, one of the seven signatories of the 1916 Proclamation of Independence, had been executed at the end of the Easter Rising. Her family was traumatised by this for many years. In 1940, she married my father, a much older man who had fought against the Black and Tans and in the Civil War, but the wedding was a quiet affair because another uncle, Jack Plunkett, was on hunger strike, having been interned for broadcasting illegally to Germany (perhaps a slight lapse of political judgment, but he was only obeying orders). Jack's mother, Countess Plunkett, was unsympathetic; my grandmother records in her memoirs that when Jack came home from the internment camp, ill and depressed, 'he found that Ma had taken over his bedroom and thrown out his stuff as though he were already dead'. Yet, apart from the occasional murder, there is little sense of personal, family or national trauma in my mother's three detective stories, which present an urbane, lightly comic view of life, sometimes poking gentle fun at the foibles and aspirations of Irish people as if from the viewpoint of a superior stranger. Although a straight novel of hers provoked an outraged reaction by suggesting that a doctor in the west of Ireland might be addicted to cocaine, reviewers voiced no objection to her slightly comic portrayal of Irish people in crime fiction. 'Miss Dillon writes with a charmingly light touch', said the *Irish Independent* reviewer of *Death in the Quadrangle*, while the *Montreal Star* commented, 'They'll hate this in Dublin, but this is a fine example of the English detective novel.' Strange praise for an Irish nationalist, and yet there is a long history of writers borrowing a foreign viewpoint – or even a foreign genre – in order to 'see ourselves as others see us' – and native readers understand the game well enough.

Other writers had laid on the cosy and comforting elements rather more heavily. In *Murder and Music*, already mentioned, Gerald Lee is anxious to reassure his readers as to the sensitive paternalistic qualities of the Irish police force. A nice young man is concerned that some embarrassing family secrets, uncovered during the investigation into the murder of Luke Bloggs the blackmailer, might be revealed by the police. The detective sets his mind at rest:

> 'No, Mr Fitzgerald. Have no fear that the police will reveal anything you have told us. As a matter of fact we knew most of it already. [. . .] Why do you people insist on regarding us policemen as your enemies? I suppose it is a heritage from the days of alien rule; but those unhappy times are gone forever. I can assure you we are ordinary decent Irishmen like the rest of you. We know thousands of things that we would never dream of letting the public hear of.'

Murder and Music manages to work in some other items of uplifting national information, too, sometimes adding international comparisons for good measure. Suicide, we learn, is almost unknown in Ireland, running at less than one percent of the English *per capita* figures. Dublin Castle houses the Detective Branch of the Irish Civic Guards, 'the Sûreté of Éire', and given that Ireland supplies 'no small portion of the brains and stamina of the police forces of New York, London, and other cities throughout the English-speaking world, one is not surprised to learn that many a brilliant bit of police work has been carried out in that quiet corner of the Castle Yard.' The reader is offered, from time to time, the sort of informational travelogue that might appeal to those readers of crime fiction for whom a sense of place is paramount:

'It was now much later in the morning. The traffic had increased from the occasional bus to a stream of motor-cars. Cyclists, of whom Dublin has a greater *per capita* population than any city in the world, were steadily pedalling by in droves. Two distinct classes were noticeable, both amongst the cyclists and the pedestrians. They were those going to early work and those going or coming from Mass in the hundreds of city churches whose bells had from time to time chimed in harmony with his thoughts. Dublin easily holds the world's record for those who attend daily Mass.'

Religion and crime fiction often go together, but the Irish have a slightly different take on the question. When I worked in publishing at the end of the 1970s, we issued T. P. O'Mahony's *The Vatican Caper*, in which the first Irish Pope in history is elected, takes the name of Patrick the First, and is promptly murdered by terrorists, for reasons connected with Irish politics. No sooner had we agreed to issue this book when we received a coincidental book proposal for a thriller outlining the mysterious death of another Pope Patrick the First.

The terrorist wars, already mentioned, can be a viable component in genuine crime fiction, as was most brilliantly demonstrated in comic vein by Colin Bateman, but they can also turn into boys' adventure stories. Eugene McEldowney deserves all the more credit, then, for four novels published in the 1990s in which he created the sympathetic figure of a Northern Irish policeman, Inspector Cecil Megarry, who maintains a semblance of decency even in the midst of the Troubles. This author makes you care about the fate of individuals rather than the outcomes of campaigns. Among Megarry's successors are the dangerously complicated Dublin Garda Pat Coyne, given two outings by Hugo Hamilton in 1995 and 1998, and the latest police-procedural icon, Brian McGilloway's Inspector Benedict Devlin.

No crime writer gets everything right, and the most enduring creation is often the series character rather than the individual plot. Having had some fun at the expense of Gerald Lee's *Murder and Music*, let me record that its principal investigator, Detective-Inspector Terence Crowley, is an attractive and credible character. Likewise Vincent Banville's John Blaine, although his narrative voice is distractingly exuberant, has some intriguing quirks of character that keep the story moving on the page, and would seem even better suited to the screen. In fact Irish crime writing offers a number of leading characters ripe for cinematic development, although it must be admitted that some of the best books would lose their unique qualities in the transfer. This is probably true of my final example.

All writers create their own precursors, and most are vain enough to look for shelf-space among the best authors of the past. Personally, I wouldn't mind being seen on the same shelf, or at least in the same bookcase, as John M. Kelly, classicist, legal scholar, parliamentarian and writer. His brilliant early pseudonymous novel, *Matters of Honour*, dealt with student life in Heidelberg where he had studied; it was whispered of as a scandalous book involving a sexual affair (which was a bit of an exaggeration), and was never reissued. After his death another typescript was discovered and published by a Dublin publisher, Moytura Press, in 1993. This novel, *The Polling of the Dead*, evokes something of the murky atmosphere of the Arms Trial of 1970, when two Irish government ministers were dismissed and charged with smuggling weapons to the IRA in Northern Ireland. One of their co-defendants was a Flemish gentleman named Albert Luykx, a successful asylum-seeker who had moved to Ireland after World War II, as Belgium was becoming uncomfortable for people who were believed to have collaborated with the German army of occupation. (Ireland, which had remained neutral during World War II, acquired quite an interesting menagerie of former Nazi warriors and hangers-on during the post-war period.) The narrator of Kelly's subtle and beautiful novel is a hard-drink-ing, soft-living lawyer who investigates the disappearance and, as it turns out, death of his friend, an opposition politician who had unearthed an ancient murder, perpetrated by a German businessman now associated with corrupt members of the government party. It doesn't help that the narrator is in love with the victim's girlfriend. The story proceeds in an aimless and moody man-ner which turns out to conceal a pretty well-oiled clockwork plot. Several of the leitmotifs of modern Ireland – crooked investors, slippery politicians, nerv-ous policemen, disaffected misfits, puritanism, alcoholism, even the occasional outbreak of independent thought – flit beguilingly across the surface of the book. The whole thing is done in a sketchy and gappy manner, yet works in the most affecting way. Kelly, a born satirist, commits the ultimate joke of tak-ing Ireland seriously, and situates its moral mess in relation to the history of twentieth-century Europe, where indeed it belongs. If Irish crime writers, or Irish writers in general, can occasionally match the quality of John Kelly's work, we may not be doing too badly.

*

Cormac Millar, from Cork, teaches Italian at Trinity College Dublin under the name of Ó Cuilleanáin. His crime novels are *An Irish Solution* and *The Grounds* (Penguin, 2004, 2006); an Italian translation by Alessandra Di Luzio was published in 2010 as *Una soluzione irlandese. www.cormacmillar.com*

Murder in Mind:
The Irish Literary Crime Novel

by Alan Glynn

'Not everybody knows how I killed old Phillip Mathers, smashing his jaw in with my spade . . .'

Flann O'Brien, *The Third Policeman*

'My Lord, when you ask me to tell the court in my own words, this is what I shall say. I am kept locked up here like some exotic animal, last survivor of a species they had thought extinct.'

John Banville, *The Book of Evidence*

'When I was a young lad twenty or thirty or forty years ago I lived in a small town where they were all after me on account of what I done on Mrs Nugent.'

Patrick McCabe, *The Butcher Boy*

As Dory says in *Finding Nemo*, at the point where Marlin starts telling his story, 'Oh boy, this is gonna be good, I can tell.' When I first started reading *The Third Policeman*, in the mid-1970s – the Picador edition with that haunting cover art by Nick Bantock, an eerily smiling face superimposed on itself as it turns to look in our direction – I could tell it was going to be good. Other, recent books that had been 'good' included *Catch-22*, *The Long Goodbye*, *High-Rise* and *Brighton Rock*. There's a quality to your reading at that age (this also applies to love, of course) that can only be described as 'magical', and that you can easily spend the rest of your life trying to recapture. You give yourself up to it unconditionally, you let it wash over you, and not only does it feed your imagination, in some sense it activates it, defines it, shapes it.

The Third Policeman had that kind of power. First of all, it was funny – and back then (mid-'70s, mid-teens) funny was important, funny was currency, funny was the *lingua franca* of the schoolyard. It's hard to appreciate now just how revolutionary and mind-blowing the comedy of that time was, particularly Monty Python and the early, funny Woody Allen movies, where the main response tended to be, 'I didn't know you could do that. I didn't know you were allowed.' And with *The Third Policeman*, here was a novel breaking all the rules as well, that had not only been published a decade before but had been written almost three decades before that again. *The Third Policeman* was playful and deliriously post-modern. It had the de Selby footnotes, the interpolations of Joe, the narrator's soul, and, of course, the bicycles. (The temptation here, to be resisted at all costs – as it never was in the schoolyard – is simply to repeat the jokes).

But funny as it was, a good deal of *The Third Policeman's* power lay elsewhere. Its opening sentence, for example, isn't terribly funny. Nor is its relentless portrayal of psychological torment, its clinical dissection of human guilt. Of course it is easy to forget this, but what lies at the heart of *The Third Policeman* is an act of violence, a brutal murder – a crime, if you will. This aspect of the book forms an essential part of its lingering appeal, and whereas an episode of Monty Python or an early, funny Woody Allen movie can seem curiously alien today and leave one feeling a little lost, I find that *The Third Policeman* easily retains its grip on the imagination. Flann O'Brien himself was well aware of the book's duality. In a letter to William Saroyan he famously wrote, 'When you are writing about the world of the dead – and the damned – where none of the rules and laws (not even the law of gravity) holds good, there is any amount of scope for back-chat and funny cracks.' But it could just as easily have been the other way around: limitless scope for back-chat and funny cracks shouldn't preclude a writer from dealing with the darkest, most macabre of subject matters.

This is not by way of preamble to some elaborate theory that the book is secretly a crime novel, or even a proto-crime novel. Life is too short for that kind of engagement. But what I do think is interesting is that *The Third Policeman* contains elements of the crime novel which contribute significantly to its power and lasting appeal.

Narrated in the first person, it is a disturbingly intimate and claustro-phobic portrait of the contorted mind of a murderer – and we are given access to its darkest corners, to its slipperiest rationalisations, to its most grandiose self-delusions. In addition, we are forced to watch as the narrator commits his crime. We are forced to help him tidy up afterwards. We are forced to sweat along in a fever of terror and guilt as he transmogrifies the external world and reshapes it to mirror his own crumbling sanity. But perhaps the most curious thing here is that Flann O'Brien is not the only major Irish literary writer to do this. In different forms, and within fairly broad parameters, several others have done something very similar – John Banville in *The Book of Evidence*, for example, and Patrick McCabe in both *The Butcher Boy* and *Winterwood*. There are also strong elements of it in Edna O'Brien's *In the Forest* and in William Trevor's *Felicia's Journey*. For these authors the principal concern is not the pro-cedural but the psychological, not the 'who' or 'how' but the 'why', so whether it be due to greed, ennui, neglect, psychosis or abuse, what we get is a widely diverse series of widescreen POVs of the sick-fuck Mick in action.

However, because these book are so diverse – and mostly predate the recent surge in Irish crime fiction – there is no point (and I have no interest) in trying to claim them as some kind of sub-genre, much less in trying to shoehorn them onto the genre shelves.

What would be the point?

Genre classification is useful, but only in this sense: if you went into a Waterstone's or a Barnes & Noble and found that they employed no sorting mechanism other than the alphabet, it'd be pretty inconvenient. Classification saves time and makes thing easy. But that's about it. It doesn't tell you if a book is good or bad – and there's plenty of both on whatever shelves you might hap-pen to be browsing at. (An interesting case here for students – or combatants – of the genre wars is Brian Moore, a writer who achieved the neat trick of being classified as a literary novelist, but many of whose novels are routinely described as thrillers, and whose first five books, avowedly genre thrillers, are airbrushed out of existence whenever his first 'novel' is declared to be *The Lonely Passion of Judith Hearne*). The books mentioned above, however, share a common concern. They are all interested in what leads up to the act of murder and they are all interested in what happens afterwards, in the psychological fallout. They are all interested in the universal truth that murder leaves a stain that can never be eradicated.

And, for the record, they are all 'good'.

*

In a letter to his publisher, written in 1937, Flann O'Brien explicitly referred to *The Third Policeman* as starting out like 'an orthodox murder mystery'. While it's not clear to us today what exactly that might have meant to him – or what murder mysteries he was reading at the time – it's very clear that O'Brien wasn't reined in by notions of form or convention, and he certainly wasn't writing within any confines we would recognise today as genre. But if we go ahead and relieve O'Brien of all responsibility in this area, it's still hard not to suspect that, had he been tempted, he might actually have enjoyed writing some form of genre fiction. And, indeed, he may well have been tempted, because several times in his life O'Brien claimed to have written short novels for the popular Sexton Blake detective series – pseudonymously of course. Anthony Cronin, in his biography of O'Brien (*No Laughing Matter: The Life and Times of Flann O'Brien*), investigates this matter thoroughly and it seems O'Brien may not actually have written the stories as claimed – but it is also clear that even if he had he would have been doing so exclusively for the dough. Still, the notion is intriguing, and what one wouldn't give to read O'Brien's take on the so-called 'prince of the penny dreadfuls' – and from a time in the series (the early 1950s) that was offering up such titles as *The Mystery of the Red Tower*, *The Riddle of the Body on the Road*, *Dark Mambo*, *Devil's Can-Can* and *Requiem for Redheads*. It's the stuff that de Selby-like cults are made of, and has even resulted in an obscure 1992 movie called *The

Cardinal and the Corpse, which deals with the search for a long-lost Flann O'Brien Sexton Blake text of the same name.

But – coming back to earth – one story we know that O'Brien did write in the early 1950s is called 'Two in One' (later adapted for television as *The Dead Spit of Kelly*). Short, slight and decidedly non-comedic, it gives us a glimpse of O'Brien's continuing interest in the macabre. The story tells of Murphy, a taxidermist who murders his boss, Kelly, and gruesomely disposes of the body parts, retaining only the skin, which he then inhabits. In effect, he 'becomes' Kelly and proceeds to live Kelly's life. Eventually, however, he is arrested and found guilty of murdering himself. In his one-man show *The Brother*, Eamon Morrissey narrates the story from the setting of a prison cell. He tells it straight – in contrast to the rest of the show, which is hilarious – and the effect is very chilling. I remember seeing the original production in the Peacock and being mesmerised by this section of it. The story itself predates TV programmes such as *Alfred Hitchcock Presents* and *The Twilight Zone*, but it displays some of the qualities that made those shows so popular and is further evidence of a certain thriller-ish strain in O'Brien's writing.

And although it would be a mistake to make too much of this – because let's face it, Flann O'Brien didn't write thrillers or mysteries or SF (or bodice rippers, something else he laid claim to), he wasn't genre, he was *sui generis* – it is still in *The Third Policeman* that we find this strain of his writing at its most developed and most interesting.

The book's original title was to be *Hell Goes Round and Round*. Mercifully, this was dropped (not only is it an awful title, it contains a pretty big example of what we would now call a 'spoiler'), but it does give us a pretty succinct formulation of what O'Brien was trying to do in the book. The protagonist commits a murder; he pays for this heinous act with his soul, and goes on paying for it until the end of eternity. The structure of the novel is one revolution of hell, with the shocking promise in its tail of all the others to come. The opening chapter is probably the straightest, most deliberately unfunny thing O'Brien ever wrote. In curiously detached language, the narrator introduces himself, sets out the depressingly venal reasons for the murder – he could use the money old Mathers keeps in his black cash-box – and then he and his accomplice John Divney carry out the deed:

> 'I went forward mechanically, swung the spade over my shoulder and smashed the blade of it with all my strength against the protruding chin. I felt and almost heard the fabric of his skull crumple up crisply like an empty eggshell. I do not know how often I struck him after that but I did not stop until I was tired.'

Despite the cold, mechanical nature of this act, the narrator is soon stewing in fear and guilt, and it is not long either before he invokes the spectre of the gallows. After a lengthy period of time, he manages to get back to old Mathers's house to try and retrieve the black cash-box, but there – unbeknownst to himself, of course – he meets his own violent end. Thus begins a most eerie ghost story, as the narrator's consciousness sets out on its hallucinatory journey into the great circular void.

This middle section of the book is a long, agonising recalibration of what the narrator still assumes to be reality. Here O'Brien indulges his interest in physics and philosophy and new scientific concepts that were current in the late thirties (and let's remember that O'Brien, who we tend to think of as a razor-witted but curmudgeonly old bollocks – thanks in large part to that amazing footage of the first Bloomsday in 1954 – was only twenty-eight at the time). Sources he cited include A. N. Whitehead's *Science and the Modern World* and J. W. Dunne's *An Experiment with Time* and *The Serial Universe*. (There is a full study of O'Brien's use of these sources in Anne Clissman's *Flann O'Brien: A Critical Introduction to his Writings*).

What we find in this middle section of the book is a nightmarish, looking-glass world where the laws of physics are casually turned on their head and where the narrator is constantly struggling to corral his experience into language that is rational and familiar. There is then a marked shift in pace and tension as the narrator becomes increasingly concerned about the building of the gallows. There is also a resurgence of his venality as reflected in his renewed attempts to get at the contents of the black cash-box, which are always just out of his reach. When he is leaving 'eternity' with the Sergeant and MacCruiskeen he also believes he can take his new-found treasure with him, a bag stuffed with precious stones, cash, a bottle of whiskey and a lethal weapon he clearly intends to use on his captors. But this, frustratingly, turns out not to be possible. Later, he indulges in a wild flight of Faustian fancy, imagining the incredible things he'll be able to achieve with his four ounces of omnium, but any hope of realising these dreams slips all too easily from his grasp as well . . .

The closing of the book is heart-stopping in its psychological horror. There is that awful scene in the kitchen of the narrator's old house where we realise that he has been away, not for a few days, but for sixteen years, and that John Divney is about to join him – and, for as long as we go on reading the book, us – in the befuddlement and tedium of eternal damnation.

But for all that *The Third Policeman* is thematically adventurous, with its philosophical investigations into absurdity and negation, and for all that it is a treasure-trove of comic inventiveness, it is the novel's dramatic structure, this unfolding of the mystery at its heart, that is one of its most satisfying and memorable aspects. What stays with the reader is the novel's portrayal of a murderous mind in the perpetual motion of perpetual anxiety.

The book was rejected by Longman's in 1940 and this dealt a severe blow to O'Brien's confidence. He put the book away and even grew to dislike it. *The Third Policeman* was a risky and courageous work and if it had received the attention it deserved at the time – when O'Brien was still young – who knows in what direction he might subsequently have ventured.

*

We enter the mind of a very different murderer in John Banville's *The Book of Evidence*.

The narrator of *The Third Policeman* remains nameless and is generally reluctant to reveal any personal details – considering it desirable that nothing should be known about him but even better if several things are known about him which are quite wrong. The narrator of *The Book of Evidence*, by considerable contrast, has a name – Frederick Charles St John Vanderveld

Montgomery, and is quite happy for us to know absolutely everything about him. And while the narrator of *The Third Policeman* often seems unaware of himself, even uninterested, Freddie Montgomery is almost pathologically self-aware and interested in nothing but himself.

The atmosphere inside this murderer's mind is airless and claustrophobic. He views the world with 'grand detachment' while at the same time viewing himself with a sort of queasy incredulity. He has no sense of being real or authentic. He is 'something without weight . . . a floating phantom' who is also condemned to endure the endless, petty humiliations of living in the physical world. Despite his ability for rigorous self-analysis – and in language that is precise and often very beautiful – Freddy is an unreliable narrator, and his 'confession' is full of internal contradictions.

Of course, none of this would be of any consequence if the man could manage to stay out of trouble. But he can't. He commits murder. And again, it is this extreme act of transgression which throws everything into relief and heightens, defines even, our interest in his behaviour and in his mindset.

Freddie blackmails a small-time drug dealer on a Mediterranean island, spends the loot and then finds out that he must repay it or his wife and son will come to harm. Unable to raise the money, he returns to Ireland with the intention of liquidating his late father's art collection only to discover that his mother has already sold it to family friend Binkie Behrens for a paltry sum, which she then proceeds to blow on 'a string of plug-ugly ponies'. In anger and desperation, Freddie steals a seventeenth-century Dutch portrait and ends up kidnapping and killing a servant girl in the process – a murder which is quite startling in its graphic horror.

'I pushed her away from me and swung the hammer in a wide, backhand sweep. The force of the blow flung her against the door, and her head struck the window, and a fine thread of blood ran out of her nostril and across her cheek.'

In some respects Freddie is not unlike Patricia Highsmith's Tom Ripley. He is cultured, has a taste for the finer things in life and is motivated by nothing more complex than a desire for creature comforts. But in certain other respects

OUT OF THE PAST

he is the anti-Tom Ripley, because whereas Tom kills for practical reasons and is very efficient at covering his tracks, Freddie is a victim of the 'ceaseless, slow, demented drift of things' and acts with such abandon that his eventual capture and conviction for murder are inevitable and arrive with little or no tension.

Banville based his novel on the Malcolm MacArthur case from the early 1980s. He follows the story closely, though there are differences – the most significant one being that MacArthur killed twice. In an interview a few years ago, Banville said – and defensively, almost tenderly – that Freddie Montgomery would never have killed a second time.

This is fine, of course, and entirely legitimate, but there are dangers inherent in writing about 'true' crimes. For those familiar with the facts of the original case, MacArthur hiding out in the Attorney General's apartment, during which sitting Taoiseach, Charles Haughey, may or may not have paid a visit, is tantalising stuff indeed and certainly a lot more grotesque, unbelievable, bizarre and unprecedented than the curiously muted version in the book. It is hard to say, but for those not familiar with the source material, Max Molyneaux may just prove to be an unnecessarily puzzling figure.

Freddie Montgomery, in any case, is a wonderful creation, a sort of late-twentieth-century poster-boy for good old-fashioned existentialism. Rubbing shoulders with the likes of Camus's Meursault and Dostoyevsky's Raskolnikov, Freddie stumbles through a meaningless universe. Like them, too, he stumbles into a moral black hole.

But something you can't help wondering here – if it weren't for murder, would we ever have heard from these tortured souls in the first place? And if we had, would we have been interested in their stories?

It seems unlikely.

*

While it may be hard to drum up any sympathy for either of our first two killers, the next one in line is a different kettle of fish altogether. Francie Brady, the hero of Patrick McCabe's magnificent *The Butcher Boy*, wins our vote from the get-go – though he certainly does commit a vile and unspeakable crime, to wit:

'I smacked her against the wall a few times there was a smear of blood at the corner of her mouth and her hand was reaching out trying to touch me when I cocked the captive bolt. I lifted her off the floor with one hand and shot the bolt right into her head thlok was the sound it made, like a goldfish dropping into a bowl. If you ask anyone how you kill a pig they will tell you cut its throat across but don't do it longways. Then she just lay there with her chin sticking up and I opened her then I stuck my hand in her stomach and wrote PIGS all over the walls of the upstairs room.'

The difference here is that rather than drifting into murder through greed or venality, Francie is pushed into it. Slowly, incrementally, he is tipped over the edge by the relentless neglect and abuse he suffers as a child. Denied even the least shred of love or security, he learns to insulate himself from pain, and even from awareness. And whereas the other killings happen easily enough, even casually, and spark the events of their respective stories, the murder that Francie commits is a slow-burn affair, and is the endpoint of his story, its inevitable and logical conclusion.

The thing is, Francie Brady isn't adrift in a meaningless, dysfunctional universe, he *is* a meaningless, dysfunctional universe. And it's a seductive one at first – funny, engaging, subversive, iconoclastic. Francie has all the attractive energies of a young boy, the boundless imagination, the generosity of spirit, the ingenuity, the playfulness. But what happens to these attributes when they are denied the oxygen of real and meaningful human interaction? They shrivel up is what, they become bent and twisted out of shape, and ultimately, in their new form, they become lethal.

It is a process which is deceptive in its simplicity, because again, through expert use of first person narration – and, in this case, a glorious supernova of linguistic brilliance – we are seduced, cajoled and distracted from what is really happening. Francie's voice constantly slides from a sing-song intimacy, rich with humour and popular culture references, to a sort of demented, hallucinogenic white noise. And what he's telling us often feels like the tip of a very large iceberg, with the tip a distraction, a coping mechanism, and what lies beneath the gradual descent of a human mind into homicidal madness.

We get something similar with another of Patrick McCabe's heroes. Initially, Redmond Hatch in *Winterwood* comes across as more together – more self-aware and more articulate – than Francie Brady, but we are slowly led to suspect that he may well be just as unhinged as the butcher boy. There is no explicit murder scene here to parade before your eyes, only suggestion and oblique hints, talk of maggots and the hellish sanctuary of Winterwood itself. The narrative is fragmented, a jigsaw of abuse, pain and damage. It is a folk epic, but one in which the transformative power of song and storytelling can only go so far – because behind all the phantasmagoria lies a simple truth, and a simple dynamic: the damage caused by violating innocence cannot be contained or expunged, it is a malevolent force that filters down from generation to generation.

Redmond Hatch's ultimate fate is not unlike that of the narrator's in *The Third Policeman*. The price he must pay for murdering his wife and daughter is eternal damnation, and the final paragraphs of *Winterwood* are among the most horrific, bleak and devastating you will ever read.

Another victim of neglect and abuse who ends up committing murder is Michen O'Kane in Edna O'Brien's novel *In The Forest*. The book is based on the 1994 case of Brendan O'Donnell, who murdered Imelda Riney, her three-year-old son Liam, and a priest, Fr Joe Walshe, in Cregg Wood, County Clare. The book explores not just the mind of a single deranged killer but also seeks to explore the impact of his crime on a whole community. Like Patrick McCabe, Edna O'Brien mythologises her protagonist. He is the kinderschreck, the bugbear and, at some level, the scapegoat – the one fated to channel the community's fears and weaknesses, its darkest impulses and desires. We never identify with O'Kane, or even sympathise with him, and this is probably because *In the Forest* also gets inside the heads of his victims, Eily Ryan, young Maddie and Fr John. Significantly, too, O'Kane lacks the macabre charms and manic energy of a Francie Brady. This isn't necessarily a problem, though – because while O'Kane remains a terrifying and tragic figure, there is at the same time something very grounded and realistic about the way O'Brien portrays him. There is a clinical as well as a mythic strain to the language, and this seems appropriate as it implies O'Kane is not just a product of some collective communal unconscious but also that he is a product of our seriously deficient mental healthcare services.

Not all killers in Irish literary fiction, however, are wild and out of control. Take the case of Mr Hilditch in William Trevor's *Felicia's Journey*, for example. Here is a quiet killer, fastidious and middle-class, someone who keeps bound volumes of *Railway and Travel Monthly* on his bookshelves. OK, so he's English. But William Trevor isn't. He's from Cork. And in *Felicia's Journey* he gives us one of the most memorable, most masterfully drawn characters in recent modern fiction. Mr Hilditch is a catering manager in a factory not far from Birmingham, he lives alone in a house built by a tea merchant in 1867 – Number 3, Duke of Wellington Road. He is over nineteen stone in weight and, not surprisingly, likes his food – turkey pies, liver and onions, steamed puddings, packets of crisps, Bounty bars, anything that is to hand. Occasionally, he befriends distressed or lost young women, derives pleasure and some form of validation from being observed in their company, and then, when they withdraw, when they turn, he murders them. This is all conveyed in the subtlest way, there is no act of violence described or even alluded to. We infer everything and information is meted out one carefully placed crumb at a time. As with *In the Forest*, we also get the perspective of the victim – or, in this case, let us say, his latest potential victim, Felicia, a pregnant young girl from Ireland who has come over in search of her boyfriend. Mr Hilditch is a monster, a serial killer by way of Dickens, and while we don't quite sympathise with him, we are nevertheless drawn into his world and are given sufficient glimmers from his childhood to understand, once again, that serious psychic damage leaves its mark, it incubates and one day it will hatch. This superbly controlled novel dramatises the random intersection of two lives, Mr Hilditch's and Felicia's, and its account of their respective fates is both uncompromisingly bleak and heartrending.

Central to each of these books, then – most foul or otherwise – is murder. They may not be crime fiction in the popularly accepted sense, but in each case it is the primordial act of homicide which gives the story focus and definition. Without the murders these might be interesting psychological case studies of damaged people, but they would lack a certain inexorable narrative logic – not to mention very welcome doses of pacing and tension. In the end, they wouldn't be as interesting or anywhere near as appealing as they clearly still are. Irish crime fiction has come a long way in a short time, but writers here have always been fascinated by violence, by the psychological states that can lead to it and by the lasting damage that inevitably flows from it. This fascination – which can also be found in the theatre, most obviously in *The Playboy of the Western World* and *The Field* – has found a natural home in the various forms, voices and tropes of crime fiction. But that's not the whole story. Just as the Irish literary novels discussed above contain significant elements of crime fiction, many of the finest examples of recent Irish crime fiction contain what might be considered significant elements of literary fiction – depth of characterisation, subtle and poetic use of language, and a keen willingness to explore the darker corners of human nature. So it seems to work both ways now. Lines are blurring, parameters broadening, and there's a whole lot of cross-fertilisation going on. Which either complicates matters or simplifies them. I go with simplifies. Because back in the mid-1970s when I was browsing around the Dublin bookshops – the old Eblana, the Paperback Centre, the APCK – I was just as excited by *The Third Policeman* as I was by *The Long Goodbye*, by the Nick Bantock jacket as by the updated 'green' Penguin with (curiously) Bogie and Bacall on the cover. I wasn't going around the place worried about what was probably still being referred to – though not by me, or by anyone I knew – as 'high art' and 'low art'. In those prelapsarian times, long before the sales and marketing folk took over the asylum, I certainly wasn't fretting about such stuff. And I don't see why I should be now.

*

Alan Glynn is the author of *The Dark Fields* (just filmed as *Limitless* with Bradley Cooper and Robert De Niro) and *Winterland*. His new novel, *Bloodland*, will be published by Faber in September 2011.

The Judge

by Eoin McNamee

At 2.20 AM on the morning of 13 November 1952, the body of nineteen-year-old Patricia Curran was carried into the family doctor's surgery. She had been stabbed thirty-seven times. The Curran family were tainted by scandal. Patricia's father, Judge Lance Curran, was weighed down by gambling debt, her brother Desmond lost in religious zealotry. There were rumours of savage disagreements between Patricia and her mother.

The case became a cause célèbre, and a miscarriage of justice. The young man convicted of the crime had his conviction overturned. The murderer has never been found.

It's a case that has all the attributes of classic noir. There are themes of corruption and deceit. There are political undercurrents. There is the beautiful doomed victim, and the brooding powerful figure of her father the judge.

It is easy to imagine the whole affair transposed to Los Angeles in the fifties, Black Dahlia territory, to haul in W. R. Burnett or Cain into the ghost-written terrain. Set the Curran house, the Glen, in Laurel Canyon, give it to Ross MacDonald and let him track back into the family, the taint of incest hanging in the air. The cast of supporting characters like something from Jim Thompson, awash with bad faith.

Such a crime could have taken place in Foxrock or Glenageary, but it's hard to see it perceived in the same way. The atmosphere isn't there. The streets aren't haunted in the same way, the characters aren't shadowed. There are provinces of noir in France and England but not in Ireland.

The difference is in the judge. Not in the personality of the man, although there's plenty to go on there. Curran was a high flyer – Attorney General in his early thirties, he went on to be a privy counsellor. He was reputed to be a heavy gambler. And, if you believe the evidence, he at the least covered-up the identity of the murderer of his daughter, and perhaps was responsible for leaving an innocent man in the shadow of the gallows.

Leaving all that aside, the judge is the key because of his office. What we understand to be noir has the mark of John Calvin on it. The universe is a cold and pre-determined place. Your fate is decided before you set yourself to defraud your employer or catch a faithless eye across a downtown cocktail bar.

It is the essence of the noir hero to go among the damned, to relate to them, to be one of the damned himself. He sets himself (it is always a man) against the judge, knowing that the verdict has already been reached.

It's hard to find an Irish murder that you can fit into the noir mould. You have the strange, such as Malcolm McArthur, half existential fiend and half bow-tied nutter. You have the bizarre, such as the Green Tureen murder, where Shan Mohanji set about his victim with Fred West-type relish but was seen as a aberration. Brendan O'Donnell. The case of Geoffrey Evans and John Shaw seems to bring a slice of English across the Irish Sea (English being a sub-genre of the main body with a bleak style all of its own). The two petty criminals took a ferry across from England. Murdered Elizabeth Plunkett outside Dublin. At Ballynahinch, near Maam Cross, they kidnapped and abused Mary Duffy over a three day period before murdering her. Shaw and Evans, brutes that could have been ripped from the Red Riding Quartet, had decided that they would kidnap one girl a week until they were caught.

But their role as agents of an amoral fate was undermined by the ending of their tainted little enterprise. They were caught and brought to Dublin where they were interrogated by Detective Inspector Gerry O'Carroll. O'Carroll wasn't having any luck in getting admission out of either of them, until, at two o'clock in the morning, O'Carroll brought Burke into a separate room where, in O'Carroll's description, they prayed together. Following an impromptu novena, Burke confessed and dragged his partner down with him.

It's strange, but it's not noir. It seems to happen with Irish murders. A folkloric element leaks into the pure air of noir, the Ireland of rag trees and holy wells and roadside virgin Marys.

The late Gordon Burn, on a visit to Kilkenny a few years ago, told about covering the Fred and Rosemarie West trial, which he later wrote as *Happy Like Murderers*. He said that he had never believed in the existence of pure evil until he had sat in that courtroom. It shook him to the extent that it finished him with the true crime genre, for want of a better term, for ever.

Maybe noir could better be described as a style, or a way of seeing, for you get the feeling that its conventions buckled in the face of the unrelenting perversions of the West.

About fifteen years ago I was at a Presbyterian funeral outside Lurgan. It was a freezing Sunday afternoon in November. I watched the cortege of men (the women stay in the house – the men form the funeral). There were dark clouds over the lough, lines of sleet sweeping in horizontally across the pewter-coloured water as the small cortège made its way to the lough shore.

The graveyard was on a small treeless rise overlooking the lough. A black-robed preacher stood beside the opened grave, silhouetted against the lough sky, his book of laws open in his hand. The cortège halted at the graveside and the coffin was lowered. The preacher opened his book, the wind plucking at his robes, the darkening sky behind him seemed weighed down with judgement. The preacher's voice was carried towards me on the wind.

'Men, will ye be saved or will ye be damned?'

If the writing is high-flown, it is because the moment seemed self-conscious in its bleak lyricism, the stylised outworking of the Calvinist ideal.

Lancelot Curran was born in Antrim in 1907, one of seven children to Edith and Myles Curran. There have been persistent rumours of Catholicism in Curran's background and you have to wonder about the father's name. Myles is an unlikely Christian name for an Irish Protestant – was Lance Curran's father a Catholic? This fault-line runs throughout the Curran story and echoes some of the primal undercurrents of American noir – the crossing of racial lines, the horror of sexual relations between the races – all the tales of negro coupling with white women leading back not to fears of sexual inadequacy but to the soul-taint of Calvinism, the raising of a fist against what is already written in the book.

(Echoes of lurid accounts of sexual relations between black men and white women are seen in the seventeenth-century accounts of massacres of Protestants in Ulster, the delicate flesh of Protestant women rent asunder, the pitchforks of fiendish Gaels steeped in their gore.)

In Lance Curran's world, to be the product of a mixed marriage would have been seen as going against nature, the natural God-given order of things. Defying, in the great sin of noir, your pre-ordained fate. Product of sectarian miscegenation. It's another noir theme. The lie of origins, of not being who you say you are, of something tainted at the core.

It doesn't end there. Desmond Curran, Patricia's brother, was twenty six at the time of the murder. He was a junior barrister at the Belfast bar, full-time lawyer and part-time proselytiser for the Moral Rearmament campaign founded by Frank Buchman. A forerunner of AA, Moral Rearmament was vehement to the point of cultishness and souls were pursued with 'loving relentlessness'. Following the murder, Desmond Curran left the bar and studied to become a Catholic priest. He was ordained in Rome in 1960 (the ceremony attended by his father) and still serves in a township parish in South Africa, where he was known for his courage in resisting apartheid. He acquired an Xhosa nickname in these years – Isibane. The Lamp.

What was Lance Curran doing at his renegade son's ordination in Rome? He had been an Orangeman all his life, a bigot to the core. Or was that fake too? Had he hearkened to the Roman whore, abandoned the delicate milk-white flesh of the protestant woman-folk to their fate?

Lance Curran knew the rules of the toxic Ulster game and was well able to play them. Attorney-General at thirty six, High Court judge, clambering relentlessly and ruthlessly towards the ermine collar that was eventually placed around his neck in the House of Lords. There were rumours about his background – no-one seemed to know where he had come from. The lack of detail implying that Lance had been busy erasing the traces of his passage.

There's a made-up feel to the Currans, as if they'd been sprung on the world from a lurid dime-store fiction. Doris Curran, Patricia's mother, was consigned to a mental hospital after her daughter's murder and remained there to her death. For want of a better candidate, the finger of suspicion for her daughter's murder has been pointed at her. And there is a detail of Doris Curran's life which adds substance of a sort to the claim that she was involved, or at least deepens the corpse-murk around the killing of Patricia Curran. Doris Curran had been brought up in Broadmoor Prison for the Criminally Insane.

It's hard to bring up the fact without peppering the page with gothic imagery, turrets emerging out of swirling moorland fogs and the like. Doris Curran's father was the superintendent of the hospital, and you'd like to think she was raised well away from the inmates, the fiendish and the damned. But there's a symmetry in her passage from the bedlam of Broadmoor through the murder of a daughter to the silence of a Belfast mental hospital, the symmetry of a fiction where you feel that the author is pushing it a bit, stretching the synchronicity.

There aren't many photographs of Lance Curran. One taken at his elevation to the Bench shows a cold-eyed man, high cheek-boned with a long nose. It's the mouth that stands out, the same mouth as his daughter Patricia, turned down at the corners. In Patricia the mouth is sulky and sensuous, but her father's mouth shows hauteur and petulance.

The other photograph shows Judge Curran inspecting a guard of honour of the Royal Sussex regiment outside the opening of the Downpatrick Assize in 1961. A hanging assize.

On the morning of Sunday 29 January 1961, a young Newry woman, Pearl Gamble, was found stripped and murdered half a mile away from her house at Damolly. She had been beaten, strangled and stabbed, her clothing scattered in the approaches to the stubble field where she had been found. The police focused their attention on a twenty-six-year-old local man, Robert

McGladdery, who had danced with the dead girl at a hop in a Newry Orange Hall the previous night. According to McGladdery's solicitor, at the time the RUC were convinced, on thin enough evidence, that they had their man and did not investigate any other possibility. When the dust settled and McGladdery was charged, it emerged that Judge Lancelot Curran was to sit on the bench at his trial for capital murder.

If it weren't for the McGladdery case, it might be possible to see Lance Curran as a clever opportunist who played a bad hand well. An ermined chancer, who, when his mad wife allegedly murdered his daughter, steered his family out of trouble with an amoral deftness, and resumed his career as before, leaving a casualty or two behind admittedly, but the likes of Iain Hay Gordon should have known the rules of the game before they sat down at Lance Curran's table.

The McGladdery case casts another light on Lance Curran. For a start, a man whose nineteen-year-old daughter has been murdered in a crime with sexual overtones should never have offered to, or been permitted to, sit in judgement over the trial of a man accused in the sex murder of another nineteen-year-old girl nine years later. The Patricia Curran case could not have failed to have been in the mind of the jury when Lance Curran took the bench.

I'd had a book on the McGladdery case in mind for twenty years and had been working on it for over a year and still hadn't got to the core of it. I went back to the source material, started reading through the case again in the newspaper archive of the *Belfast Telegraph* in the Central Library. 1961. Year of Yuri Gagarin and the Bikini Atoll. I realised that I hadn't read Judge Curran's charge to the jury all the way through, so I went to the case report and started to read.

The evidence against McGladdery was all circumstantial and he denied the charge vehemently. The case hinged on two issues. Had McGladdery lied about what he had been wearing that night (a short fawn overcoat, a light-coloured suit later found concealed)? And had he been abducted and aggressively interrogated in relays by Newry police for fourteen hours, as he had claimed? (If he had, then the police would have been shown to be liars.)

You read through the charge to the jury. It is a reasonable summary of the evidence, clear, unambiguous and incidentally closing off all avenues of appeal on the grounds of misdirection if McGladdery was found guilty. Then, when you get to the final page, you feel the hair on the back of your neck stand up.

'Thirteen witnesses said that McGladdery wore a light blue suit. You will be very slow to say they were all mistaken.

'Before you would agree there is any knavery on the part of the police force you will want strong evidence and not merely the say-so of a man charged by this court.'

In cop argot, it's a steer to the jury, about as clear as you're likely to get. Don't believe this man. Curran might as well have winked at them while he was at it. In a case which raised many complex issues and in which the accused, in jeopardy for his life and knowing that clemency might lie in a guilty plea, protested his innocence to the end, the jury were out for forty minutes, enough time for a cup of tea and a smoke, before they came back with a guilty verdict. Robert McGladdery was hanged on 20 December 1961.

(McGladdery's QC Jimmy Brown went to his grave believing his client to be innocent. When I brought this up with a member of the current Belfast bar he told me that the word in the bar library was that Brown had become 'obsessed' with the McGladdery case. When I asked another barrister about the peculiar legal shenanigans that went on around Iain Hay Gordon's trial for the murder of Patricia Curran, I was told of the rumour that Gordon (later proved innocent) had 'confessed' to his first legal team that he had murdered her, prompting their refusal to represent him. The lawyers burying their own sins under self-serving innuendo. The info on Jimmy Brown came from David Torrans from No Alibis in Belfast. Shotgun synchronicities going on.)

It's easy to get caught up in the faux celluloid allure of the Currans, the slightly over-written feel of the whole story, the lurid asides of Broadmoor and Isibane, the hints of white mischief in provincial outposts. But it's the Gordon Burn moment in the Central Library that catches you out and fixes the whole affair. The newspaper archive. The dusty back-office feel to the place, the smell of warm plastic and the clattery edge-of-reason whirr from the microfiche machines. You can hear the malice in Curran's voice as you turn the pages, the rendering of himself as agent of fate. The matter of the soul is weighed and judgement is meted. Damnation dealt to the condemned man in the dock. There's a shift in the Calvinist position. Not only is the universe indifferent. It is weighted against you. There is a hand on the scales.

Backtrack to the night of 13 November 1952. Patricia Curran steps off the Whiteabbey bus and disappears into the dark avenue leading to the Glen. Backtrack to the independent nature, the reputed promiscuity. In the single photograph of Patricia used repeatedly through the years she is wearing pearls and a formal cowl-neck dress. The photograph is badly lit. Her cheeks are slightly dimpled and the mouth down-turned at the corners, but it is the eyes that hold you. Her face is dominated by the shadow of them. You are drawn to their mesmeric void. She is the judge's daughter. She is the classic noir heroine. She knows how it works. Patricia knows that once the judge fixes his eye on you the game is up. You can see it in the mouth, the wry downturn. It is what is expected of her, and she shares it with all the other girls trading come-hithers in on-the-slide cocktail bars. The good-time girls and the other side of the tracks girls, the gone to the bad and the born to be bad. You only get one chance so you'd better take it. Besides, the judge has you tried and condemned before you ever put yourself in the way of temptation.

If the rumours are to be believed (and there's no proof of it one way or another), Patricia Curran was stabbed to death by her mother, and then her father orchestrated a cover-up of the murder. You'd wonder that a mother could stab a daughter thirty seven times, but a paranoid schizophrenic would be capable of it, the symptoms reading like a lunatic's charter – delusions of persecution, of exalted birth or special mission, bodily changes, hallucinatory voices that threaten or give commands, auditory hallucinations. Hallucinations of smell or taste or of sexual or other bodily sensations. Who did Doris Curran think she was? Who did she think Patricia was?

And you'd wonder that a father could cover it up. Unless he believed his own fate sealed and then a bit. If the heroes of noir know that their fate is sealed but turn and shake a fist it at in the name of humanity, then the villains are guilty of the negative. Like Judge Curran they become the agent of fate, and are capable of giving events a dire twist of their own. The French talk about *noir et maudit*. Dark and accursed. A girl's voice calls out in the provincial night. McGladdery proclaims his innocence then submits to his fate. There's always wriggle room on the other side of the house, the chance of redemption, the fat being pulled from the fire, but once the judge's gavel falls, hope is abandoned.

*

Eoin McNamee was born in Kilkeel, County Down in 1961. His novels include *Resurrection Man*, *The Blue Tango* and *12 23*. His latest novel is *Orchid Blue*, based on the execution of Robert McGladdery for the murder of Pearl Gamble.

Inheritance

by Jane Casey

From the road, you couldn't see that there was a house there at all. The granite gateposts still stood but the gates themselves were long gone, and the lodge beside them was dark and shuttered, derelict.

But there was a house, and Anthony Gallagher knew it. He knew a lot about it, in fact. He had done his research. And he had chosen a moonless night, a night when the rain was relentless – a night when you wouldn't turn a dog away from the door, no matter who you were – to make his move. He stood just inside the gate, tapping his fingers against his thighs like a foot-baller preparing to take a penalty. This was the worst bit. It was always the same. Once he got started, he'd be all right. But before, the nerves got to him. Every time.

The rain fell steadily, collecting in the potholes that pitted the gravel drive. He flipped up the collar on his jacket and started walking. A good half mile in the dark, on a surface that promised a broken ankle or worse with one false step. He was swearing blue murder before he'd gone halfway, wishing he had his torch handy, but it was somewhere at the bottom of his bag. Besides, it would look suspicious to turn up with a torch. It wasn't the sort of thing a casual traveller would carry, probably, and he wanted to look like nothing more than a casual traveller.

The bag kept knocking against his legs no matter which hand he carried it in. It was light enough. Just a change of shirt, a toothbrush, a razor and shaving foam, the torch and some odds and ends for later on. He needed to be present-able. Part of the game was looking smart. It was all about setting them at their ease. Making them trust him. Gaining their confidence.

Taking advantage.

There was a light on, he was glad to see as he rounded the last corner of the drive. It wasn't late, he knew. Half past eight. Too late to send him away, not so late that the occupant would refuse to answer the door on principle. But there was always the danger they would have gone to bed early. Old people did. Especially in houses where central heating was an unfamiliar concept.

Framed between two straggling yew trees, the house looked grander than he had expected. It was a foursquare Georgian box, grey stone like the gateposts. Five windows ran across the top. On the ground floor, soft golden lamplight shone through the two windows to the left of the porch. He moved towards the rectangle of brightness nearest him, careful to stay in the shadows, treading softly on the loose gravel that gave under him with every step. A lovely room: small, but elegant, with grey silk walls, a marble fireplace carved with sleek, well-fed figures and Doric columns, and a ceiling ornate with swags and garlands of plasterwork. On the walls, landscapes, portraits, miniatures and hunting scenes hung three and four deep, as if there wasn't enough wall for all of them, and pairs of gold-framed mirrors with dim old glass in them softened the room's reflection to a dream. And the furniture. He didn't know a lot about it – small items were his bag – but he'd spent enough time looking in windows on Francis Street to recognise the living glow of top quality mahogany and the arrogant, springing sweep of an Irish Georgian table-leg. A fine breakfront bookcase filled most of one wall, and a pair of brassbound peat buckets flanked the fire. He was looking at wealth, generations of it, there for the taking by anyone who chose to walk up the dark drive.

She was alone, anyway. There was a decent fire lighting and she had a chair pulled up to it, a sagging armchair that looked comfortable. Her back was to the window, but he could see her head was bent over something. A book, maybe, or some sewing he thought, stretching his imagination to the utmost. He had very little idea what an elderly woman might do on a winter's evening to entertain herself. No TV that he could see. No music playing. She wasn't asleep; he could see her head turning as she concentrated on whatever it was. A movement by the door set his heart thumping but it was nothing, it was just a dog walking over to her, a black yoke that looked like four bits of different dogs stuck together. The great lantern jaw belonged on a mastiff; the body was fat and barrel-shaped, like a Labrador succumbing to middle-aged spread. Short little legs and a flailing tail that threatened to knock over the table beside her completed the picture. At a word from her it collapsed to the ground as if shot, the two stumpy legs that were uppermost paddling the air beseechingly until she leaned over and rubbed its stomach.

It wasn't much of a dog, he thought, but a dog nonetheless. It might hear him, or smell him. Better to knock on the door before he was discovered lurking outside. Peering in through the window would be hard to explain. He moved away. Trust was the key, he'd often thought. Establish that and they're yours. And they *want* to like you. He pressed the bell by the front door, hearing it jangle deep in the house. They want you to be nice and honest and decent. They want you to be like they are themselves. He took a couple of paces back so as not to crowd her when she opened the door. It had the effect of taking him out of the shelter of the portico, exposing him to the rain, flattening his hair to his head. The light went on in the hall. He assumed a doubtful expression, a wistful look that had worked like a charm many times before. The door opened – not wide, but enough.

'You'll have to forgive me for knocking on your door at this late hour,' he began. Word perfect. Practised. All the consonants where they should be. A little too mannered to be credible, did he but know it, but a fair attempt at sounding well-spoken. 'My car broke down, I'm afraid. Just down the road. There isn't anywhere else around here – I was hoping I might get some shelter for the night.'

'How unfortunate.' Her voice was unexpectedly deep for such an elderly lady, such a slight frame. She had her back to the light and he couldn't see the expression on her face. 'Have you no mobile telephone?'

'Out of battery,' he improvised. 'I would have asked to use your phone, but

I don't know who to call at this time of night.'

'A garage would seem to be the obvious choice.'

He tried a laugh, spluttering a little on the rain running down his face. Jesus, he was getting drenched. 'You're right there. But there's none of them at work at this hour.'

'There is always the Automobile Association.'

It took him a second. 'Oh – the AA. I'm not a member. I should be, but I'm not.' He sniffed. Time to turn it up a notch. 'I don't want to put you to any trouble. If there was a barn, or an outbuilding of some kind . . .'

'This isn't Bethlehem, young man.' A gravelly note of amusement in the throaty voice. 'You may come in. But you must take the place as you find it. I can't promise you comfort.'

'A roof over my head is all I ask.'

'Well, I have one of those. Of a sort.'

She stepped back, holding the door open, and he ducked his head as he passed her in an awkward kind of bow. He took up a position a few paces away from her on the stone-flagged floor, trying to appear unthreatening, but his mind was working at top speed. The air in the hall was freezing and damp, a damp that had nothing to do with the weather and everything to do with a couple of centuries of decline. Overhead, a brass hall lantern was blazing, shining brightly enough that he could see the wavering cracks in the floor, the worn treads of the carpet on the stairs, his breath misting in front of his face. Indoors. Jesus.

He was able to see his hostess properly too, and she him. She was old – of course, he had known that, but so old now that he looked at her skin, folded in hundreds of tiny wrinkles that looked powdery soft and delicate. She had high, slender eyebrows that she had drawn herself in an unlikely brown-pencil arc, and the remains of bright pink lipstick feathered the edges of her mouth. So she still cared about her appearance. You wouldn't have known it from the dress she wore – a shocking thing it was, black but you could still see the stains of food and God knows what down the front. A few inches of hem hung down at the side. She had a shawl around her shoulders pinned carelessly with a crescent brooch that had the yellowish, muted dazzle of filthy diamonds. No rings on the hands that still looked strong despite the veins that wormed across their backs, the loose skin dappled with age spots. That made sense. She hadn't ever married. He could smell cigarettes off her from where he stood. The front of her hair was yellow-grey with nicotine staining, and her teeth were as brown as if they'd been carved out of wood. Unconsciously he ran his tongue over his own set: capped as soon as he could afford it, Persil-white and even. He was twenty-seven – almost thirty, which he couldn't believe personally, but at least he looked younger. Baby-faced was what they'd always said. He played up to it, with the big blue eyes and a smile he practised every time he was alone with a mirror. The smile said, trust me. The smile said, I'm only a young fella. The smile said, I'm harmless. He kept his hair short and his clothes neutral, dark, unmemorable.

He had a story prepared about being a pharmaceutical salesman but there was no need for it; she went past him to the door of the room where he'd seen her sitting.

'You'll be warmer in here.' The handle was loose and rattled as she turned it – a bad noise, distinctive and hard to muffle. The dog had its nose up against the door, desperate to get out. He hadn't heard it bark but it was on to him all right. It pushed out past her, lunging towards him, wheezing aggressively. Without meaning to, he stepped back, away.

'Don't be frightened. He won't harm you.'

'Good boy,' Anthony said feebly.

'He's deaf. Getting old.' She stood holding the door, too polite to tap her foot but impatience in every angle of her body. 'You're letting the heat out.'

'Sorry, I—' He gestured helplessly. The dog was standing between him and the door. He itched to kick it. A good punt in the ribcage. If she wasn't looking, maybe.

'Oscar.' There was a whipcrack of command in her voice and the dog squinted back at her, reluctant to obey. She tapped her thigh and it moved at last, stomping past her on its short little legs, heading for the rug in front of the fire. He slunk after it, looking around with frank admiration once he had gone through the door.

'Beautiful room.'

'It was once.' She sat down in her chair and picked up the book that she had left on the floor. She was going to start reading again, he realised, wondering with a flare of panic what she expected him to do with himself.

'I suppose I should introduce myself. Graham Field.' A nice Proddy name.

She looked up briefly. 'My name is Hardington. Clementine Hardington.'

Clementine Lavinia Hardington, daughter of Colonel Greville Hardington (d. 1963) and Audrey De Courcy Hardington (d. 1960). Last of her line.

'Pleased to meet you, Miss Hardington.' *Shit.* 'Or is it Mrs Hardington?'

'Miss.'

No 'call me Clemmie', he noted, sitting down opposite her and stretching his hands out to the fire. *Know your place, young man.*

She had gone back to her book. He scanned the room, seeing signs of neglect everywhere now that he was inside. The plaster ceiling was missing chunks of its frieze and had a huge water stain over most of it. The upholstery was frayed on every chair, the stuffing spilling out. The silk on the walls was in tatters. Long curtains at the window were two-tone from years of exposure to sunlight. They were threadbare along their folds, torn in places, probably riddled with moths. The rug was worn to its backing in places and the pattern was hard to distinguish, coated as it was in a thick layer of dog hair. And why was it that all dogs, no matter what colour their coat, seemed to shed grey hair?

'Have you lived here long?' He'd got the tone exactly right. Innocent curiosity.

'I was born in this house.'

'Very good,' he said, as if she had done something impressive. Pure chance was all it was. Pure chance had left her sitting in her big house with the grand paintings and the high ceilings. You couldn't respect that.

But you could respect the collection of eighteenth-century miniatures on both sides of the fireplace. And you could respect the collection of Japanese figurines on the table beside him: topsy-turvy animals, twisted people, weird things like a plum being eaten by a wasp, a mouse fighting with a lizard. He

144

itched to pick them up for a closer look but didn't dare. He looked around stealthily. What else? A pair of silver-mounted horns caught his eye but he could see the inscription engraved on the base: too identifiable. Blue-and-white china in various shapes and sizes, fragile and faded. Matching vases that were probably Meissen, but one was chipped. Forget it. The paintings now: they were worth a second look. Not on this trip, though. Too big, too awkward.

He turned his attention to the other side of the fireplace and choked despite himself. A pair of shotguns, the real deal, fine engraving on the silver side plates and polished walnut stocks.

She looked up at the noise and saw where he was staring.

'The guns? They were my father's. Purdeys. Quite the best game gun there is. They were made for him in 1936.'

And nowadays they were worth about a hundred grand, easy. 'Do they still work?'

'Of course.'

'Can you shoot?'

'Of course,' she said again, turning the page. 'My father taught me.' My *faw*-ther. And that would be him in the silver photograph frame on the table beneath the guns, he presumed. Big moustache. Heavy jaw. Small eyes.

He looked at the guns again, longingly. No point in trying to take them. Twenty-eight inches long; he'd never get them out without being spotted. Another time.

She had lit a cigarette and now, without looking, she tilted her hand to tap the ash into a vast cut-glass ashtray at her elbow. She missed and a shower of grey flecks drifted down onto the floor. Easy to see why the carpet was in a jocker. It would be a long time before anyone pushed a hoover around it either.

She must have noticed him watching her. 'I didn't offer you a cigarette.'

'I'm grand.' He was gasping for one, but Graham Field was a clean-living non-smoker. He wouldn't have taken a drink if she'd asked him to. Not an issue so far, it had to be said. But he was obviously making progress, because she put down the book.

'Are you hungry?'

A polite answer was no. He hesitated for long enough that he was sure she got the message he was lying. 'No. Not at all.'

'Did you have your dinner?'

'No,' he said again. 'No. I don't need anything, though.'

'You can't go to bed hungry.' She stood up. 'I can make you something. An omelette.'

He couldn't stand egg in any shape or form. 'Lovely. But I don't want to put you to any trouble.'

She didn't bother to say it wasn't any trouble, but she didn't sit down again either. Bending with a sigh, she tweaked the fireguard across the hearth, then switched off the lamp beside her, leaving only the dying fire to light the room. Anthony got the message and stood too, letting the dog have a head start in the race to join her.

There was a pile of fur on a chair by the door. When she picked it up and shook it out, it resolved itself into a full-length coat that must once have been beautiful. It stank of mothballs, but by the looks of things they hadn't worked. Slinging it around her shoulders, she turned and gave him a sidelong smile. 'Brace yourself.'

It was good advice. After the heat of the drawing room, the cold in the hall struck into his very bones. His clothes had dried on him, more or less, but the chill found out the patches of damp behind his knees, along his shoulders, down his back. He would catch his death, he thought, not quite closing the drawing room door before following Miss Hardington to the back of the hall, Oscar shambling between them with an occasional wary look in his direction. There was an archway leading to a short flight of stairs that twisted into a passageway dimly lit with a weak bulb. He thought at first that the walls were decorated with more pictures, frame upon frame jostling for space, but when he looked he saw beetles and butterflies and moths lovingly mounted on rubbed green velvet.

'Who likes the bugs?'

'My grandfather was a keen naturalist.' Disapproval in her voice. A warning to him to watch himself and a timely one at that. It had been an Anthony question, not a Graham one. He, Anthony, wouldn't fancy looking at a load of insects on his way to the kitchen, but Graham might see the point.

'Very interesting.'

She didn't respond. She was grappling with the door handle, another brute that screeched with a nerve-shredding sound of metal on metal when it finally gave way. The door opened and he peered into the kitchen, which proved to be smaller than he had imagined and disappointingly prosaic – sterile white cupboards and a too-bright fluorescent light. No big Aga keeping the place warm, either. It was arctic. Nothing to interest him here. The gas cooker looked to date from the 1960s at the latest, but that didn't make it an antique – just a health hazard.

'Sit down there.'

'There' was a plain wooden table with rotting feet from years of standing on a much-washed tile floor. He sat gingerly on a chair that threatened to give way under him, wondering if woodworm ever turned on humans. The table and chairs were riddled.

'Water?'

If that was all that was on offer. 'Yes, please.'

A glass landed on the table in front of him, a cheap tumbler. 'There's a tap in the scullery.'

And you can get it yourself, he filled in silently, taking it and going through to the next room where he found a sink and shelves weighed down with old Waterford glass: bowls, decanters, glasses, vases. They were dusty, untouched for years at a guess, and as he washed out his own glass fastidiously and waited for the water to run cold again, he found himself eyeballing a dead fly in the wineglass directly in front of his face. *One that my grand-*faw-*ther missed*, he thought, allowing himself a small chuckle.

She had been busy; the omelette was almost done when he got back, and there was a fork and a folded napkin on the table. The napkin was starched linen, at least two foot by two foot when he unfolded it, and the folds were so stiff that it stood up in his lap as if he had an erection, which was far from being the case. The omelette was heavy on bits of eggshell and light on filling. He had an awful suspicion that the flecks in it were not black pepper but cigarette ash.

She sat opposite him, sideways to the table, smoking, and didn't seem to notice when he slipped the guts of the omelette into the napkin and flicked it under the table to the dog.

'That was very nice. Thank you very much. Were the eggs from your own hens?'

A blue glare. 'I bought them in SuperValu.'

Right. Enough of trying to make friends. Fuck it. He was only going to rob her anyway. 'It's getting late. I don't want to keep you up. I can tidy up here if you just point me to where I'm to sleep.'

'There's no need to tidy up. It can wait.' The dog had dealt with his leftovers and was now investigating the frying pan. She had left it on the floor for him. Anthony felt his stomach heave. No cooked breakfast for him in the morning, thank you. She stood and it still came as a surprise to him that her posture was better than his, perfectly straight, not hunched over like the doddering old lady he'd expected. She should have looked ridiculous in the fur coat but she wore it as if it was the obvious thing, and so it was for the conditions. He'd have dressed like a fucking Eskimo if he'd lived in that house.

He'd expected to go back to the main hall so he could get his bearings, but there was another staircase, a wooden one that climbed up the back of the house. The creaks from it were chronic.

'I'll put you in the guest room. The bed isn't made up but the sheets and blankets are on the end of it.'

'No problem.'

'It may be a little cold.'

'I'll be grand.' *I'll be keeping busy* . . .

'The bathroom is here.' She indicated a room off the half-landing where they had paused. It reeked of Dettol, which was better than he might have hoped even if not exactly inviting. Anyway, he wouldn't be committing himself there. Face and hands only. Stripping for a bath was out of the question.

The bedrooms opened off a narrow central hall. His, she indicated, was at the very end of the house, and he went down the hallway counting doors, noting creaking floorboards, marking out his route. Opening the door, he recoiled as if someone had punched him. He would not have thought it was possible for the air temperature to be so low in what was technically a sound structure. The bed was a few inches shy of being a double and looked as if its last occupant had died in it. The curtains on the window didn't meet in the middle when he pulled them. The bow-fronted chest of drawers listed to one side. The pictures were dismal flower studies, definitely the work of an amateur. This was not a house that welcomed visitors.

He made some attempt to make the bed, laying the sheets and blankets over it. One blanket to protect him from the mattress which was probably jumping with vermin. Two to go over him. And his damp coat over that. He would still freeze. He huddled under them, smoking, reckless of being caught as she would never be able to tell it wasn't the smell of her own smokes. Usually he would have been worried about falling asleep, but there was no chance of that. He was shaking too much. At least it was no longer raining. He hoped it would stay that way. He had to drive back to Dublin the following day and it would be quicker if the roads were dry. He would boot it the whole way, with the car's heater knocked up to the max, he promised himself.

When he finally uncoiled himself and slid out from under the blankets, he was stiff. He stretched, rolling his head from one shoulder to the other, shaking out his arms, breathing deeply the way he'd seen runners prepare before fitting themselves into the starting blocks.

'Off we go.' He slipped through the bedroom door into the hallway. It was pitch dark. No streetlights. No moonlight. Just him and his trusty torch, hooded so it only cast a speck of light. He drifted down the hall, silent in his socks, holding his breath as he went past the door of your woman's room. The stairs were an unknown quantity which he didn't like, he didn't like at all, and he took his time going down them, testing each tread before he put his weight on it. Then the hallway, the stone floor cold under his feet but solid, reliable, and he could pick up the pace.

He started in the dining room, playing his torch over the paintings on the walls, the long table, the fine chandelier and the twenty-four matching chairs, before he got down to business. Most conveniently, there was plenty on display that he liked the look of: silver, mainly. Serving spoons engraved with what had to be the family crest, a sauce boat standing proudly on tiny clawed feet, a pair of oval salt cellars with blue glass liners, a silver dish ring decorated with leaves and bunches of grapes. It was hard to stop himself from taking too much. He couldn't go mad. He had to take enough to make it worth his while but not so much that she'd notice straightaway. He wrapped everything that he took in strips of dusters, brand-new and soft, to cushion them from damage and keep them from banging together when he carried them upstairs. It was a matter of pride to make neat bundles, folding the material intricately. He should have been hurrying but he took his time over it.

In the drawing room he hesitated, suddenly struck by what he was doing, unsettled by the looks he was getting from the family portraits on the walls. Her ashtray was still there, her book over the arm of her chair. She sat there day in, day out, surrounded by the things that had been passed down to her by her family. Who was he to take them?

Except, why shouldn't he? She and her family had had the best of everything through at least two Irelands: the one where they were top of the heap and the ordinary peasants were just there to admire them and pay them rent, and the one where the proles suddenly had the power, riding the crest of a wave of prosperity, buying up the old houses and furniture and art as if there would always be money, as if there was nothing but. She had held on to what was hers, even then. And in the third Ireland, the new one, the one where no one had a euro to their name, it was time to share out what there was. Specifically, with him. Why should she keep it anyway? She wasn't really Irish, Anthony thought, conveniently forgetting the generations of Hardingtons who had lived and died in the house. This was practically his duty as a proud Irishman.

He bagged a handful of snuffboxes, silver and gold, a pair of blue-and-white plates, a Dresden shepherdess of exquisite frailty accompanied by her would-be suitor plucking a lyre, and three of the little Japanese curios. God knows if anyone else would like them but he did, he thought, deliberating over which ones to take. He settled on a dormouse dozing inside one half of a walnut shell, a snake coiled into an evil-looking pyramid and an ivory samurai in full armour, his hands by his sides, his chest puffed out nobly. Six of the miniatures came with him as well: pretty girls in low-cut dresses, the sort of thing that appealed to collectors. They were easy to package up.

On his way out, he stopped by the shotguns. Putting his bag down, he lifted one of them off its hooks, feeling the heft of it, the lethal snugness of it against his shoulder, the *willingness* of the trigger. A thing of beauty. He put it back on the wall slowly, longingly, and winked at the black-and-white photo.

'Fair play, Greville.'

There had been nothing in the kitchen for him – he didn't touch glass, too fragile – and although he looked into the library, he didn't fancy it. Dustsheets covered the furniture and the books were locked behind elaborate grating. He didn't know what he was supposed to be looking for, anyway. And he had a fair bit, he thought, hefting the shoulder bag that contained his night's work. Time to quit. He ghosted back into the hall and up the stairs, counting them under his breath and skipping the fourth, the ninth, the seventeenth . . .

Where he came a cropper was halfway down the landing. Seduced by the dim light from the window at the end that guided him towards his room, he had decided he knew his way well enough to dispense with the torch. He had no warning when he collided with something solid, something heavy, something that uttered a long-drawn-out howl as he nosedived into the ancient carpet, tasting the dust of ages and his own very modern blood.

It was as if she had been waiting behind her door. It slammed back against the wall, light spilling out into the hall so he had to shield his eyes for a second. She was still wearing the coat, he noticed, blinking up at her.

'Mr Field. What happened?'

'It was the fu— it was the dog. It was Oscar. I just – I needed the toilet. I was just looking for it. I got confused.' *Stop talking. Start thinking.* He couldn't hit her. Not an old woman. But if he ran downstairs . . . an image flashed into his mind. The shotguns. He curved his hand around an imaginary stock, practically feeling it against his palm. If he was quick, he could deal with her before she had a chance to phone the guards. That assumed she didn't have a phone upstairs, it assumed the shotguns were loaded, and it also assumed he had the nerve to do it. Murder. Kill her, in cold blood. Blow her away. Then spend a million years trying to wipe his prints and DNA off every bit of the house. It was a bit different from pocketing a few knick knacks, when you thought about it.

He was still lying on the ground, grovelling in front of her. He got up slowly, picking up his bag as if it was nothing of note.

'It's the middle of the night. Where were you going?' She didn't sound panicked, which was something.

'I was looking for the toilet. I got confused about which stairs it was off.'

'The back stairs.' She pointed. 'Down there.'

'That explains why I couldn't find it.' He tried a smile. 'Sorry for disturbing you. And for stepping on the dog. Sorry about that, Oscar.'

The mutt gave him a wall-eyed glare.

'I'll head down there, so. Sorry again.' The toilet wasn't a bad plan, actually. The tension was squeezing his guts. He needed a crap. He walked away in the direction she had indicated, waiting for her to call him back to ask for a better explanation, or to tell him to empty his pockets, and what's in that bag?

She said nothing. He risked a look back at her as he turned the corner to go down the narrow back stairs, and she was standing in the light, leaning over, talking to the dog. He allowed himself a small grin of triumph as he headed into the dark. They were like children. They couldn't imagine you would do them wrong, so they believed every word you said to them. Fools. He was glad he had taken advantage of her now. He'd have kicked himself twelve ways to Sunday if he'd left empty-handed because of what? An attack of conscience? She wasn't even nice to him.

*

In the morning, he came downstairs carrying his bag to find his hostess in the hall. 'Ah, you're up at last. Did you sleep well?'

What time she got up at, he couldn't imagine. It was only seven o'clock. 'I didn't, no. I think the roof is leaking, to be honest with you.'

It had started raining heavily while he was taking his celebratory shit, the water gurgling in cast-iron drainpipes and spilling from unreliable guttering. He had got back to his room to discover the bed was saturated, the ceiling still dripping. The remainder of the night he spent curled up on the floor, trying to find a position where his bones didn't ache and the draught from under the door didn't cut through the one blanket he'd been able to salvage.

'Oh dear.' She didn't sound surprised. 'I've had breakfast already. But there's some porridge if you'd like.'

'No. Thank you.' He'd yak if he tried. 'I'll get something later.'

She was looking thoughtful. 'I don't suppose – I shouldn't ask, but maybe if you would – if you have a head for heights which I must admit I don't—'

Payment for the night's board. He put the bag down, resigned. Always leave them grateful. 'What can I do? Is it the roof?'

'Could you see if there are many slates gone? The man who looks after it is away.'

'How do I get up there?'

'Through the attic. But you'll need to get the ladder. Cormac always uses his own.'

'No problem. Where is it?'

'It's in the shed.' She gestured vaguely to the back of the house. 'Out there. The door is jammed, though. You'll have to go out the front door and walk around. And I think it might be quite near the *back*.'

*

He was true to his promise, getting back to Dublin in record time with the radio blasting dance music and the heater blowing out a fug of hot air. He'd earned his money, that was for sure. First getting the fucking ladder out from what turned out to be a barn the size of a bus garage, full to the roof with junk. *'Shed' my arse.* Then getting it into the house while Clemmie waved her hands and shrieked warnings to him every time he came near a light fitting. Then propping it up on the rotting floor of the attic, discovering that the rungs were shaky in the extreme, and making it out onto the leads of the roof in time for the rain to start again. He had taken shelter by a chimneystack and enjoyed an illicit cigarette, thinking of her waiting patiently for him to return. She would think he was doing a thorough job if he didn't hurry back. Another cigarette put manners on the hunger that was beginning to twist at his stomach. He didn't waste any time looking for missing slates. It was something of a surprise to find there were any up there at all. A deep breath, then back down the stairs with the ladder. He took it back to the shed, jamming it in as best he could between a knackered old Riley with deflated tires and a load of rusty milk churns.

The relief of getting on to the M50, within reach of civilisation. The joy of seeing Dublin spread out before him as he came over the mountains, the Pigeon House towers striped red and white in the distance, Howth Head glowing green behind them. The fucking sun came out and everything. Welcome to the Promised Land, my child.

In his case, welcome to the Sundrive Road. There was a house there, a small one, not the kind you'd notice, and it was the home of the finest fence he'd ever met, a fat man named Ken who had every book you could imagine on antiques and never needed to consult one of them. Anthony didn't ask what happened to the things he brought him. The fat man paid cash and that was all that mattered to Anthony. That and getting rid of the stuff before the guards came calling.

Ken's wife was a comically small woman, a little elf of a thing. Would he have a cup of tea? And a sandwich? He practically took the hand off her; he was desperate for something.

Ken was scratching himself in the front room, layered in cardigans and jumpers as if he was capable of feeling the cold. The room was hot anyway. He drew the blinds without getting up from his chair.

'Stick the light on there and let's have a look at what you've got.'

Anthony sat on the other side of the coffee table and dug in his bag, setting out his bundled-up dusters where Ken could reach them. The fence tapped his fingers against his belly, waiting for his wife to come back with the tea.

'Tell me about the house.'

Anthony described it in as much detail as he could. Ken listened, asking questions, thinking. The Purdeys had him shifting in his chair with what could only be excitement.

'Shame you didn't find out anything about the paintings. Never mind. I'll make a note.'

Mrs Ken rattled in with a tray and handed Anthony a mug and a ham sandwich. Ken got the same, and a plate of biscuits. He needed to keep his strength up, Anthony reflected. Poor man couldn't be expected to wait until lunch.

As soon as the door closed behind her Ken's pudgy fingers went to work, unexpectedly delicate as he began unwrapping what Anthony had brought him. The first thing was the silver sauce boat. Even though he knew what was inside each parcel, Anthony still felt a thrill as the last fold of yellow cloth fell away – to reveal something that was definitely not an eighteenth-century sauce boat.

' . . . the fuck?'

Reverently, Ken set a wooden teapot-stand down on the table. It had been crowned with a plastic measuring jug. 'Well. Very interesting.'

'I don't understand it. I don't know what happened.'

The fat man was at work on the next parcel. He looked down at the contents without showing them to Anthony. 'What's this supposed to be?'

'Two Dresden figurines.'

'Two wooden dolls.' He held them up. They were hideous things, home-made, with crudely painted faces.

The next parcel was the silver dish ring, or rather a stainless steel dog bowl.

'I don't fucking believe this . . .' Anthony picked up one of the smaller packages and started ripping, pulling it apart recklessly, careless of the contents, which was a mistake. It was not a fine little carving of a mouse asleep inside a walnut shell. It was a hen's egg, and it broke. He could feel the blood beating in his head, the rage pushing against the bones of his skull. 'She sent me on a wild goose chase. She had me up on the roof cooling my heels while she was downstairs going through my bag. The fucking bitch.'

'You wouldn't be up to them,' the fat man observed in much the same tone as if he'd said the sky was blue.

Together, they unwrapped every parcel on the table, revealing every piece of junk that Anthony had carried away from Clementine Hardington's house. Chipped brown side plates dating from the 1970s. A lump of coal. Two wooden spoons. Orange plastic egg cups that were supposed to be salt cellars. Six green tiles masquerading as framed miniatures. Old matchboxes filled to the brim with rice to make them as heavy as the snuffboxes he'd assumed they were.

'This is a nightmare.' Anthony couldn't stop staring at the junk on the table, as if he could make it change back into riches if he only looked hard enough. 'I'm embarrassed, Ken.'

'So you should be.' He settled back in his chair, lacing his fingers over his paunch. 'Ah well.'

'Is that it?'

'Doesn't make any difference to me. You're the one who's out of pocket.' He yawned. 'You shouldn't be surprised. There's a reason they've held on for so long. They don't give it up easily.' He nodded at the last parcel, the smallest, which Anthony was clutching. It should have been the ivory samurai, upright and noble. 'Open it.'

It was tightly wrapped, folded in on itself, and he struggled to undo it, pulling the material apart eventually so what was inside bounced out and landed on the table where it spun around and around. Ken picked it up.

'What's this? A shotgun shell?'

Anthony shook his head, his mouth suddenly dry. 'It's a message.'

He knew in his heart that even if he had realised what she was planning – even if he had been as angry with her then as he was now – he would never have been able to pull the trigger. He knew it just as well as he knew that if she held the gun, she wouldn't hesitate. That was as much her legacy from her ancestors as the crumbling stones of the house, the acres of boggy parkland, the fine art and furniture and woodworm and all.

And as far as Anthony was concerned, she was welcome to the lot of it.

*

Jane Casey was born and brought up in Dublin. After an English degree from Oxford and an MPhil from TCD in Anglo-Irish Literature, she worked in publishing for ten years. *The Reckoning*, her third novel, will be published in July 2011. Married to a criminal barrister, she lives in London.

Part II:
Thieves Like Us

Irish Hard-Boiled Crime:
A 51st State of Mind

by Declan Hughes

Irish people can be especially prone to magical thinking, to put it at its kindest. We seem extremely reluctant to relinquish our belief in phenomena that neither experience nor reason will justify. The most notable and poignant example of this is our relentless credulity regarding the existence and quality of the Irish summer.

Although year after year, a solitary sunny day is followed by unending weeks of overcast skies and squally rain, hope springs infernal. In my case, this belief, or 'superstition', took root when I was thirteen, during the (genuinely) long hot summer of 1976. Every morning I would assemble a lunch and spend the day on Whiterock beach in Dalkey, alone or with friends. I swam and read and looked longingly at girls in bikinis and wondered how that, and everything else, was going to go. And that's pretty much how I spent my subsequent teenage summers, often in delusional defiance of the weather. I never got a job, because I didn't drink back then, could get all the books I needed from the library, experienced a certain amount of success in finding out more about those mysterious bikini-wearing creatures, and didn't want anything else money could buy as much as I wanted to be on the beach and in the sea, even if the rain fell and an east wind tested your faith in the Irish summer to the limit.

There was music in the air during that time, of course, and for all that punk rock had happened and post punk followed in its wake, and for all that I had developed a ferociously puritanical line in rock snobbery which permitted me to like virtually nobody except the Clash and Bruce Springsteen (which was convenient, since I could barely afford their records, let alone anyone else's), the soundtrack I still associate with Whiterock during those years was the Eagles' *Hotel California*. (You didn't have to buy *Hotel California*: in the late '70s in South Dublin, it played for free from every shop doorway and bedroom window). Cowboy boots and flared Levis and plaid and cheesecloth shirts and droopy moustaches and long hair were the order of the day for the half-generation ahead of me, and their musk of patchouli oil and dope smoke seemed like an intoxicating promise, a hazy benediction from alluring adepts of a laid-back cult I longed to join. The cult did not just dream of America, and more specifically, California; it seemed to believe it was already living there. And as I gazed out to sea on whichever blue sky day I could find or recall, I knew I was worthy of confirmation in their faith, for that was where I believed I was living too. The Ireland that presented itself to us day-to-day in the '70s was still run by priests and nuns and decrepit old bogmen in tweed suits, and claimed by murderous bigots intent on shooting and bombing everyone who disagreed with them into a fantasy vision of the glorious republican past; nobody who dreamt of truth, beauty, youth and love could tolerate either as a reality.

My play, *Digging For Fire* (1991) was, among other things, a dramatisation of some of these cultural contradictions. During a long drink-fuelled row in the pub, Danny, the aspiring writer character who should in no way be mistaken for the author but who is evidently ventriloquising many of his opinions, says:

'. . . I grew up with the TV on, (and I'm not unique in this), with England and America beaming into my brain; I never had a single moment of, I don't know, 'cultural purity'. I didn't know where I was from . . .'

Moments later, this exchange occurs:

Danny: And what about the people who don't want to live in a village? The people who left before their village suffocated them? Is village life supposed to be the most authentic, the most Irish?

Breda: It's also about having a sense of place—

Danny: And what happens when you don't have a sense of place? When I arrived in New York for the first time, and as the cab swung past that grave-yard and around the corner, and I got my first glimpse of the Manhattan skyline, I felt like I was coming home. The landscape was alive in my dreams, the streets were memories from a thousand movies, the city was mine.

Rory: Well, you have a sense of place, Danny. It just happens to be somebody else's place.

Danny: No it doesn't, it's as much Ireland as Dublin is; millions of Irish went out and invented it, invented it as much, probably more than any ever invented this poxy post-colonial backwater.

Breda: So what's the problem? You don't like it here, fine, you don't live here; you feel at home there, great, you live there. What's the big deal?

Danny: The big deal, the big deal is, that there is as much here as here is . . . and I don't believe the here you're describing exists here. To me, here is more like . . . there.

Pause.

Emily: Danny, are you on drugs?

In the introduction to the published text of the play, I put it like this:

'The experience of growing up in Dublin in the '60s and '70s was not unlike the experience of growing up in Manchester or Glasgow, or in Seattle for that matter. The cultural influences were the same: British and American TV, films and music. You read Irish literature, but mostly for the past; to discover the present, you looked to America. Irish writers flicked through the family album; American writers looked out the window. You knew you would go to America one day, to work, or for a holiday, or just to get the hell away from home, or maybe you lived in California or New York already, in your mind . . . and if you felt your cultural identity dwindling into a nebulous blur, well, you believed that what you had in common with others was more important than what set you apart, and you knew there were millions like you all over the world, similarly anxious to be relieved of the burdens of nationality and of history. You were tired of hearing about those who didn't learn from history being condemned to repeat it; you sometimes felt the opposite was true, that it was those who were obsessed by the past that were doomed never to escape it, to replicate it endlessly, safe and numb within its deadly familiarity.'

So when, at the age of sixteen or seventeen, I started to read Ross Macdonald, for all the talk of white stucco and bougainvillea, of canyons and freeways, I felt I was reading, if not quite an Irish writer, certainly someone capable of speaking more directly to me than any Irish writer of that time. Indeed, there is one aspect of Macdonald's work that connects very easily with traditional Irish experience. All the Lew Archer novels follow a similar pattern: hired to find, invariably, a missing girl, Archer finds that the truth lies ten, twenty, thirty years in the past, buried deep in the secret history of a dysfunctional family. Maybe I was not as consciously aware of this aspect of Macdonald's novels – what you might call southern-Californian family Gothic – as I subsequently became, but I think it accounts to some extent for why they made such a deep impression on me. Because of course, we are no strangers in Ireland to the troubled family plot: the feuds and fallings out, the secrets and lies, the who-didn't-say-what-to-whom-and-now-never-will.

There have always been plenty of skeletons in the Irish closet, and for a long time, we didn't even hear them rattle. Or at least, we said we didn't. 'Whatever you say, say nothing', has ever been the national motto. We lie to each other because we lie to ourselves. By the time I was coming of age, there was a sense that all that lying was taking its toll: Irish literary culture seemed an endless, exhausted riffing on the identity variations: Who are we? No, who are we really? What were we like when we were kids? What are we like now? Is anyone looking at us? Why isn't anyone looking at us? We're still very popular (among ourselves). Aren't we? The questions had grown weary through repetition; the answers could no longer be provided by looking inwards. Irish writing felt as if it was eating itself.

Macdonald, whose volume of autobiographical fragments was called, after Fitzgerald, *Ceaselessly Into The Past*, held an equally tragic sense of the difficulty escape from the past entailed, but at least the possibility, the (American) dream of Gatsby-esque self-reinvention was in sight. The future was at hand, and all was not futility.

As a writer setting out on a circuitous route that would eventually lead to my writing hard-boiled crime novels, Macdonald was one of my guiding spirits; the others, inevitably, were Dashiell Hammett and Raymond Chandler, the first and second persons in the blessed trinity of American hard-boiled crime fiction. But it wasn't Macdonald's family plots in the first instance, any more than it was Hammett's terse, Hobbesian fatalism, or Chandler's quixotic romanticism, that spoke so clearly to me; as much as what they said, it was the way they said it; it was above all else a question of style.

In *The Simple Art of Murder*, Chandler calls Hammett's style the American language, and says '. . . at its worst was almost as formalised as a page of Marius the Epicurean; at its best it could say almost anything . . . ' Chandler felt there was more to be said than Hammett felt the need to say, and added wit and lyricism to the mix; Macdonald refined the strengths of both with subtle intelligence and psychological acuity, and brought the hard-boiled crime story to a peak that remains unsurpassed. Not that any of this occurred to me back then: I just felt the way I felt when I heard *Jumpin' Jack Flash* and *Gimme Shelter* and *Honky Tonk Woman* for the first time: this is the stuff, I thought, this is henceforth the control in the experiment. I found the spare, insistent rhythm and pulse of the language every bit as intoxicating as the guns and the girls, the murk and the mayhem, the haunted carnival of death and delirium that noir descried behind the gossamer-thin veil of reality. I was the man Geoffrey O'Brien wrote about in *Hardboiled America*, who read this fiction 'as another might read a lyric poem – because its images sustain the life in him'. It was reality to me – more real than the everyday speech I heard around me. The

American language was my language, a language I felt more truly at home in than my 'own'. Moreover, day by day, it was modifying the way my 'own' language was spoken.

Roy Foster has talked about Daniel Corkery issuing 'literary visas' to the Irish writers of which he approved, namely those who wrote exclusively about the (Catholic, nationalist, rural, Gaelic) Irish identity he believed defined the essence of the nation. Everything I'd ever written had been at odds with the idea that you had to fulfill a certain set of criteria in order to qualify as Irish. In the theatre, that had by and large meant rejecting the native tradition and looking to England and America for models of the kinds of plays – urban and suburban, classless, deracinated, indifferent to the 'national question' – that I wanted to write.

In crime fiction, the situation was more complicated. There simply was no native tradition to draw on. I turned to America, not just for reasons of style, or because of the evident parallels between Californian and Irish family Gothic, or because novels based on the premise that the society they dealt with was deeply corrupt resonated more than somewhat to an Irishman; ultimately I turned to America because that was where, creatively, imaginatively, essentially, I had been living all along.

(I suppose it's possible to read the forgoing as a form of solipsistic delusion, a post-modern fantasy essayed by someone – a writer – who doesn't have to live in the 'real world'. But there is a case to be made that since the emigrants who fled to America after the famine attained a degree of power, and what we call 'Irish-America' became a force to be reckoned with politically, culturally, emotionally, 'Ireland' has effectively been the Fifty-first State of the Union. Without America to embrace (and contain) its huddled masses, not to mention its restless, disaffected malcontents; without America to be its friend at (international) court; without America to serve as a reminder throughout the disastrous first forty years of independence that Irish people could be competent, successful, could even rise to the highest office in the land; without America to provide money, in the form of commercial investment and, prior to that, in the form of cash wired to the old country from Uncle Paddy and

Aunt Mary in Boston and Philadelphia and New York; without America, not just imaginatively, but in the all-too-real word, Ireland would have found the struggle to exist at all very difficult indeed, perhaps impossible.)

For a while, I felt like someone with a guitar in the 1950s, waiting for rock and roll to break out. I knew it must be possible to write hard-boiled crime fiction set in Ireland. I just wasn't sure Ireland knew about it yet. I wrote a play about Dashiell Hammett, and a violent comedy about Dublin gangsters, all the time waiting for the time to be right – waiting, if you will, for reality to permit the kind of fiction I wanted to write. And then a couple of things happened at the same time: money, and peace. Money, in the shape of the economic boom of the '90s, raised the stakes. Not alone was there full employment and reverse emigration, there was also an explosion in illegal drug use, and a consequent rise in organised crime, as drug gangs enjoyed their own kind of boom.

The peace agreement that followed the IRA ceasefire lowered the stakes in another way. Prior to that, the Troubles seemed to undermine the degree to which crime fiction could work effectively: how could the deaths of one or two people be compelling when the IRA were slaughtering ten or twelve at a time? Removing political violence from the national scene enabled common or garden crime to be seen for what it was – and enabled those of us who wanted to write crime fiction that was political with a small 'p' to do so.

The American template suited the Irish times. The task was to employ the American model but to imbue it with a distinctive Irish feel. Perhaps a good analogy would be with jazz – a distinctively American music that, of course, was created using European instruments. When a European musician plays jazz, he negotiates a tradition that is at once alien but his own; he pays homage to Louis and Dizzy and Miles, but he must transcend mere pastiche; no matter whose shoulders he first stands on, he must eventually walk on his own two feet.

I created a detective – Ed Loy – and a first novel – *The Wrong Kind of Blood* – in which Loy returns to Dublin from twenty years in LA, where he has been working as a private investigator, to bury his mother; by the end of the book, he has discovered the secret behind his father's disappearance – he has, literally, dug them up. A loy is a spade, as *The Playboy of the Western World* tells us, and that Oedipal drama formed part of the deep Irish background to the novel. And if there was a sly wave at the shade of Sam Spade in there also, well, however presumptuous, that was the homage.

Loy having an American past was no mere contrivance, of course. I graduated from university in 1984 and helped form a theatre company called Rough Magic; everyone in Ireland who graduated the same year and didn't form a theatre company had to leave the country, because they didn't have a semi-glamorous way of being unemployed. Emigration was my shadow life, waiting for expression. I felt I lived somewhere in between the two countries, and Loy, who moves to Dublin but is drawn back to LA, at first emotionally, and, later in the series, physically, seems to do the same. He is an insider, because he was born and brought up in Dublin, and an outsider, because he has been away so long that the streets seem alien to him when he returns. He is an Irishman and an iconic American figure. Like Danny in *Digging For Fire*, he feels there is here and here is there; his fate is to roam between the two, and to find, inevitably, that the American Dream no more guarantees personal reinvention or flight from the burden of history than the Irish tradition ensures a firm sense of community, solidarity or identity. He knows what he does, but has only a fleeting sense of who he is, or where he lives.

As Henry Vaughan put it, in lines that could form an epigraph to any of the Loy novels:

He knows he hath a home, but scarce knows where; He says it is so far,

That he hath quite forgot how to go there.

*

Declan Hughes was a co-founder of, and award-winning writer with, the theatre company Rough Magic. He is the author of five Ed Loy novels, which have been nominated for the Edgar, CWA New Blood Dagger, Shamus and Macavity awards. *The Wrong Kind of Blood* won the Shamus for Best First PI Novel. His most recent novel is *City of Lost Girls* (2010).

Taken Home

By Alex Barclay

The National Guard was not pursuing Turnball Stackett. That would imply knowledge of his whereabouts. They were hunting him, searching for him, at the mercy of him. Turnball Stackett, nineteen years old, skinny, bendy, horse-toothed ranch hand, drunkard, convict, state penitentiary fugitive. Turnball Stackett, child rapist and killer.

But the manhunt of Turnball Stackett is not the story. Not to me. It was only in the final hours, when the law had all but gone, that our paths crossed. It was the night of 20 July, 1929, in Witlock, Kansas.

Witlock was a town made like hay while the sun shone, like the plans had been sketched on a napkin in a bar to preserve some ingenuity. But a man anxious he might forget the random scattering of a general store, a drugstore, a post office, a clinic, two bars, one way in, and one way out, had no business making a plan. The night I heard the name Turnball Stackett, I was just as confused.

I was fourteen years old. I was standing in the doorway of Nancy's Bar in my white nightgown, the headlights of the pickup truck behind me turning my bones black.

Not more than an hour earlier, I had wheeled my sister Hessie's ravaged body to our neighbours' ranch in her red Radio Flyer wagon. Hessie was nine years old.

'He's gone and kilter,' Mr Glessing had said. He was standing over us in the fading light.

'Kilter . . . ' I said.

Mrs Glessing stared at her husband, her eyes like pitchforks. She lay a hand on my forearm, and turned kinder eyes to me. Her hands were cold and pink. She had been peeling vegetables for canning. There were splashes of water on her apron. There were old tomato stains, and frayed edges, and two tight knots from when there was more of her. I buried my cheek against her side, and she held it there.

'Your sister's gone,' she said.

Killed her. He's gone and killed her. The Glessings knew.

'I'm so sorry, Ruthie,' said Mrs Glessing. 'I'm so sorry.'

Joel, Buddy, Ruthie, Timmy, Hessie, Bobby, Little Lamb and Little Mae. That's who we were. Sweet, tender Christian names with a sour chaser from our father, Henry Lowell. If the same fool who had created the ideal of Witlock had another napkin, he could have drawn the stick-figure figment of the Lowells: a line of straight backbones and semi-circle smiles, and sharp splayed fingers, and no hearts, or flesh.

'Where's your mama?' said Mrs Glessing.

'Away,' I said.

Mama had never been the same since Little Lamb was born. None of us were. He nearly killed her. She was a long time in the hospital. She came home the summer I turned twelve, to spend it in a shuttered room. Then she left, for a different kind of hospital. It was Little Lamb's second birthday before she returned. And when she did, she didn't know who I was. Though all her children in some way died during that time, to my mother I had never been born. Some misfire in her brain had erased me from her memory. Or maybe it was easier for my mother not to know the new wife her husband had taken, and easier still not to have given birth to her.

Little Mae was born just five months after my mother's last visit, but no-one cared to calculate, and she was as loved as any child could be.

Everything carried on. The passing weeks were marked by Church, and the Sunday visitors to the home they thought we lived in. I would try to hold the gazes of the visiting children, like a tooth to a string to a doorknob.

Whatever was in my eyes turned theirs away. When she was eight years old, Hessie once asked me did I think that there were any other girls that meant as much to their fathers as we did to daddy. That night, with my forehead pressed against my clasped hands, I prayed to God that there were none.

*

Mr Glessing took my dead sister in his arms, and carried her up the steps into the house, with Mrs Glessing behind him.

'So, help me God,' he was saying. 'So, help me God.'

Unseen, I ran for the back of the pickup truck, and wept quietly all the way to Witlock.

*

'Hessie . . . ' said Mr Glessing, as he stepped into Nancy's bar ahead of me. 'It's Hessie.'

My father stood up, his fists twitching, his thumbs grinding against his curled forefingers. He was so handsome. I could always see how handsome my father was.

'Turnball Stackett . . . ' said Mr Glessing. 'He's here. He took your Hessie. Lowell, he's killed your little girl.'

Mr Glessing took a step forward, and I was no longer hidden. Everyone turned to the door. My hair rippled in the wind above me like I was drowning. My lips parted, but there was nothing I could say.

Everyone stared at me.

Mr Glessing turned. 'Oh, Lord,' he said, 'why didn't you stay at the ranch?' His face was desolate.

My father grabbed his gun, and walked toward us. His eyes were alight. He pushed his rough hand under my arm pit, and half-lifted me into the night. He shook off his red plaid shirt and wrapped it around me like a blanket. He picked me up, and sat me in the truck between him and Mr Glessing.

'We need to take her home,' said my father.

'Mrs Glessing will look after her,' said Mr Glessing.

'My daughter will go home,' said my father. 'And she will stay home. They will all stay home.'

'Yes,' I said. 'Thank you, Mr Glessing, but—'

'They belong at home,' said my father.

I looked up at him. The edge of his right nostril was rimmed with dried blood. The same blood was on my nightgown, and under his nails, and brightening the pale hay on the floor of our barn.

'Ruthie,' said Mr Glessing, as he fired up the engine. 'Did you see which way the bad man went?'

'I don't know,' I said. I could see the edge of daddy's shirt shaking against my chest. I could smell his sweat. 'I don't know.'

'It's shock,' said Mr Glessing. 'That's what that is.' He was talking to my father over my head. His breath was hot on my scalp. There were railroads of stitches there. There were traces of my father's dark travels all over my body. One night, Hessie had sat at my back by the fire, and counted the outside scars. She made it a game, called them out the way daddy called nails and bolts and screws at the general store.

'Cigarette burns. Number: three. Check.' she said. 'Light up a Lucky!'

She ran her finger across my back. 'Buckle imprintations. Number: four. Check.' She stopped. Her hand was resting gently on my bare shoulder, by the fresh, even dashes of a downturned crescent moon, the fine work of 'Rowlings' Denture-makers of New York City!'

'Imprintation is not a word,' Hessie had said.

'No, it is not,' I said. And the game was over.

*

Mr Glessing brought the pickup truck to a stop outside our house. Lights burned in the windows. Bobby appeared on the front porch, with Little Lamb held high in one arm, and Little Mae cradled in the other. He was white-faced. He walked down the steps, and I took Little Mae from his arms.

Joel was a silhouette by the barn with a pitchfork. He ran to us.

'I'm sorry,' said Mr Glessing. 'I'm sorry for your loss, son.' He shook his head. 'Turnball Stackett . . .'

Bobby's expression lifted. I could see a flicker of relief. Then his eyes met mine. He looked toward my father, who had wandered over to the porch, and was studying a broken handrail.

'Do you want to come with us, son?' said Mr Glessing to Joel.

I answered for him. 'No,' I said. 'We need Joel here with us . . . in case . . . '

Joel nodded. 'I'll stay, if you don't mind, Mr Glessing.'

'That's fine by me,' said Mr Glessing. 'I understand.'

I turned to him. 'But Mr Glessing, maybe you should stay with Mrs Glessing,' I said.

'Ruthie, if a man can't leave his wife alone in the house without fearing for her life, it's a sorry world we live in. And Stackett will be the sorriest man living in it. And dying in it. And it will happen tonight, so help me God.'

And it did happen that night. At the hands of Henry Lowell. Turnball Stackett, staring with his drunk and scared eyes, had risen slowly from behind a bale of hay in his father's barn. Holding his bony white arms high in the air, he denied all knowledge of Hessie Lowell's death. When Mr Glessing accused him again, Stackett again denied it. The third time, Henry Lowell, who had been thrusting the barrel of his gun toward him at each denial, pulled the trigger, and blasted him backward. Henry Lowell was a hero.

*

It was a week of bad men and good, of innocent and guilty, their names in the same pot, boiled down, a stew the bitter taste of which only the Lowells knew.

Not one piece of himself did my father kill along with Turnball Stackett. He saw no reflection in Stackett's moonshine face.

*

Alex Barclay is the author of the Joe Luchesi novels *Darkhouse* and *The Caller*, and the Ren Bryce novels *Blood Runs Cold* and *Time of Death*. *Blood Runs Cold* was the winner of the inaugural Ireland AM Crime Fiction Award at the Irish Book Awards (2009).

The Troubles I've Seen

by Colin Bateman

From a very early age I was fascinated by writers and the whole process – in fact, I probably read more biographies of writers than their actual books. I grew up reading science fiction and loved all the history of it, the pulp magazines and the writers who turned out millions of words every year. That, to me, was writing – not some boring work of literature, but someone who got paid by the word. There was some crossover from the science fiction magazines to crime magazines, and there was also a connection through Marvel Comics, which I collected avidly.

So the first things I tried to write were science fiction short stories. I was a member of the British Science Fiction Association and had a short story accepted for their fiction magazine, *Tangent*, but before the story was even published, a combination of puberty and punk rock happened! (I don't know if it eventually did appear – those amateur magazines would only ever last for a few issues.) So pretty quickly science fiction and comics got dropped in favour of the Sex Pistols and The Clash, and then by the time I was seventeen I was working full time as a journalist, writing about punk rock (yes, for the selfsame weekly paper), and I even managed a couple of bands, set up a small label and released two of their singles. I was, and remain, a hopeless business-man, but I am kind of fascinated by the business end of entertainment.

I worked my way up from reporter for the *County Down Spectator* to sub-editor, and ended up deputy editor, but really I wasn't a very good journalist.

I was never interested enough in chasing stories, or, to be frank, in other people. I was a self-centred egotist from early on, although I'd precious little to be self-centred or egotistical about. When I wasn't doing ordinary reporting, I wrote a column. In the early days I used to put on my CV that I wrote a satirical column, but that was rather bigging it up. Essentially I just took the piss out of the local town, and there were a few surreal touches to it from time to time. It became very well known and a talking point in the town, to the extent that fifteen years down the line people still stop me and talk about it, and sometimes they have no idea that I've gone on to write books. I'd always wanted to write novels, but had usually given up very quickly, but getting such a reaction gee'd me on to making a serious effort to actually finish a book. And I suppose it also coloured how I write, in that I was always going for the laughs. I'm still doing that, and I love doing it, but it's a blessing and a curse in that even when I write something more serious – like *Orpheus Rising* – it still gets a wacky cover slapped on it.

So, I was still very keen on writing fiction, but had that dilemma every young writer faces – what to write about. There were half-a-dozen attempts at a punk rock novel, which were really thinly veiled accounts of my teenage drinking years that will, thankfully, never see the light of day. The journalism was certainly giving me more confidence with words, but I still couldn't settle on what I wanted to write about. There was a Troubles-set story I kept trying to write which did eventually turn into *Divorcing Jack*, but that was only long after . . .

I was always a home town boy. Never been to college or lived away from home. Always loved America and had been to New York a few times, and Florida, but then I went to Uganda. Yes, local paper with foreign correspondent shocker! I went out to report on a local charity working out there, and as a result of that I got offered a Journalists' Fellowship to Oxford University. It was only for three months and the plan was to network, meet important people and think about possibly making a go at journalism over there. Instead I just partied the whole time; cramming what other students drank in three years into a matter of weeks! But it did expand my horizons a lot, and fired me up with ambition, if not for journalism, then for writing. Actually, instead of writing the thesis I was supposed to write during this time, I wrote a radio play (gone forever). When I got back, I immediately entered the *Observer* 'Young Travel Writer of the Year' competition with some of my Ugandan stuff and became a finalist, and they jetted me off to South Korea for the 'final challenge' with five other aspiring travel writers. To cut a very longwinded story short – one of them became my girlfriend and it was she who turned me on to the novels of Robert B. Parker. It was one of those light bulb moments – I really liked his style and decided that was how I was going to approach my own writing. Keep it simple. Tell the story. Make it funny.

In saying that, I've never been one to sit down and say, 'Now I'm going to write this type of book or another.' So the fact that *Mystery Man* has turned out the way it has, for example, is pure chance. I know now that it's a broad comedy, definitely the least serious of any book I've written, but I didn't necessarily plan it that way. Even going back as far as *Divorcing Jack*, which some very kind people have described as groundbreaking – mostly close family members – in the way it tackled the Troubles, I wouldn't have had the balls to sit down and say 'Now I'm going to write something that's never been done before,' nor the confidence. When I was writing it, my only ambition was to get to the end of each chapter. You never know if what you're writing is any good, and whether the humour is going to work.

Okay, maybe that's not entirely true. I had a pretty good idea the humour in *Divorcing Jack* would work, because some of the better lines were reworked from various bits of journalism I did over the years, and it was getting laughs from those that inspired me to use them. I had no idea if they would work in the context of a thriller, though. *Divorcing Jack* is basically *The Thirty Nine Steps* with one-liners.

I can look back and see that it might have been considered groundbreaking, but I genuinely didn't think about it at the time or even consider that there might have been dangers associated with it. It was written in 1992 when the worst of the Troubles were over; if I'd attempted it twenty years before, then I can see how it could have been more radical. If it was anything, it was a rebellion against other books dealing with the North – the thrillers written by journalists who'd spent a few weeks here, who maybe got their facts right but didn't get the feel of the place. It was just another backdrop; in a small way possibly it was also a reaction to my own background as an Ulster Protestant and feeling that Ireland, or Northern Ireland, always meant Literary Ireland, it was about poets and playwrights and history, not about today or what former punk rockers were thinking. There are probably a lot of parallels between how the arts and terrorists were looked upon – the IRA with their sophisticated cell structure and meticulous planning, the Brighton bomb being planted something like a year in advance – and on the other side the UVF, who always gave us the impression of just being a crowd of drunks killing the first Catholic-looking passer-by they chanced upon. The four best known Ulster Protestants are George Best (a drunk), Alex 'Hurricane' Higgins (a drunk), Van Morrison (a curmudgeon) and James Galway, a flautist who'd once played in a Protestant flute band and scored his biggest hit with *Annie's Song*. There was nothing high culture about Northern prods. *Divorcing Jack* is, I think, a balanced book, in that it has a go at both 'sides', but if anything it was one of the first to have a Protestant as the leading character, and making him smart and funny and flawed was probably my way of sticking up for where I came from.

And so to overnight success . . . or not. Every writer has their war story and mine is an odd one. You could almost call it clichéd, because in the public eye or 'the Hollywood version' this is how writers get discovered. But actually it happens so rarely that you can't really call it clichéd, if that makes sense. *Divorcing Jack* was written in 1992, and I posted it to a Belfast publisher, figuring they could only get about one book per week, so that there would be a better chance of them reading it. I didn't let friends or family read it because I was kind of embarrassed by it – I mean, how can you judge? That publisher kept it for six months and only sent it back, unread as far as I can determine, after I contacted them several times.

Enlarging my scope to the whole island of Ireland, I then sent it to Poolbeg, who were then the largest publisher of fiction in Ireland. They actually gave me the first positive feedback, although I think from quite far down the ladder. When it went upstairs, the person in charge quite liked it but didn't think there was a market for 'a Unionist thriller'. I have to say, I fully agreed with them. Luckily *Divorcing Jack* wasn't that. I next went through the *Writers and Artists Yearbook* and sent *Divorcing Jack* off to every agent I could find. Every single one rejected it. One did contact me to say how much he enjoyed it . . . but didn't think he could sell it. So didn't try. There were wee hints in there that people were getting it, just not enough.

I gave up on *Divorcing Jack* at this point, but had enjoyed writing it enough to start my next book, which would become *Cycle of Violence*.

Me and my best mate Dave were going through what you might call a barren period as far as meeting girls was concerned. At least, we would meet them, and then they would run – we used to sing a version of the Motown song *My Girl* on our long lonely walks home from the pub, 'What Girl?'

But then I did meet someone, Andrea, who became the first person to read *Divorcing Jack* and she absolutely loved it. She came up with the revolutionary idea of not bothering with tiny local publishers, but aiming high. So I sent it off in a plain brown envelope to Harper Collins, one of the biggest in the world. It went into their slush pile, which I always imagined to be like an aircraft hangar, which they paid some student to hoke through from time to time, really just to be able to say that they still accepted unsolicited manuscripts. They hadn't found a book in this way for ten years.

So it was a huge stroke of luck when this student just happened to pick up my manuscript, and liked it enough to pass it up the line until eventually it reached the man who would become my first editor, Nick Sayers. He phoned me one day when I was working in the paper – but there was no sudden eureka moment. He said he liked it and would be taking it to his bosses to see if they could make an offer. It was a gradual thing over a number of weeks. The BIG moment came a few months later. *Divorcing Jack* would probably have slipped out just as a first novel without much fuss or promotion – but they entered my original, misspelt manuscript for something called the Betty Trask Prize. This was for the best first novel of a 'romantic or traditional nature', which *Divorcing Jack* probably wasn't. Now, a prize with 'Betty' in the title shouldn't be that important, but this one was, not least because it offered a cash award that was then second only to the Booker, and a lot of free publicity. *Divorcing Jack* went and won it, and this time I did jump up and punch the air, because really it changed my life completely. My writing career was off to a flying start.

Before *Divorcing Jack* came out I was asked if I wanted to be sold as a crime writer, and I said no, I wanted the freedom to write whatever I wanted. I don't know if this subsequently helped or hindered my career. It's also true that I haven't written anything that doesn't actually have a crime in it. So I am a crime writer, even though you won't always find me in that section in the bookshop, and I'm always referred to as such. I don't think being a 'crime writer' has helped me as much as just being from Northern Ireland – we are a tiny little place, so if you stick your head above the parapet you do tend to get well known.

I talked earlier about admiring the pulp fiction writer ethos, turning out a high volume of work and getting paid by the word, and that was pretty much how *I Predict a Riot* got started. I happened to meet Austin Hunter, the then editor of *The News Letter* – which has always billed itself as Ireland's oldest morning newspaper – in a second-hand bookshop in Bangor, and he asked me if I was interested in writing a column for the paper. I countered with, 'No, but I would be interested in writing some fiction for it.' I think at this point I had delivered *Belfast Confidential* but it was a year from publication and I was looking around for something different to do. Austin very bravely went for it – I don't think anything similar had ever been tried in a local newspaper. At that point there was no thought of turning it into a novel. We agreed that I would write something akin to a soap opera, something that reflected the 'new Belfast': the money, the property, the upward mobility. And that's pretty much how it started – fun, hopefully funny, but pretty much throwaway stuff, to be read the same way you read a football report or a cartoon strip. It was called 'Belfast City Limits', and it appeared every Friday.

Problem was, I loved doing it, and was writing two or three episodes a day. The plan was that it would run for several months, and then they'd review it – now, appearing on a weekly basis, that's only a dozen or more episodes, but I was enjoying it so much, and had created all these characters, I couldn't just leave them high and dry. So I ended up writing about one hundred and thirty chapters in a really short space of time, which they were never going to be able to use. The fact that the crime that dominates the book and the police officer who investigates it doesn't actually happen along until a third of the way through pretty much reflects how I write – by the seat of my pants, no plan, no outline.

It's a dangerous way to do things, and the length of the finished book shows how far you have to go to tie everything up, but I think it's one of my best, and I think from time to time about revisiting some of those characters. 'Marsh' Mallow would do well as a standalone character, a retired cop looking for something to do. I'm not so keen on the title, *I Predict a Riot* – it actually works for the story, but being a well-known Kaiser Chiefs song I think it was a bit of a desperate move. The original title of 'Belfast City Limits' was dropped because of our experience with *Belfast Confidential* – a book with 'Belfast' in the title will certainly sell well in Belfast, but nowhere else.

You would think, with our 'exciting' past, that Northern Ireland would be a commercial enough subject – but actually it can be the kiss of death. Whether people across the water – where the main market is always going to be – have Troubles fatigue or were never interested is debatable, I just know that research has been done that shows that whatever media you care to name, sales dip significantly when we are featured. I know that national newspaper sales always fell when we were mentioned, and I know of a BBC series set here whose viewing figures dropped away to virtually nothing before the opening credits were even over. When I came to write *Murphy's Law* for Tiger Aspect/BBC it was made very clear that while they didn't mind Jimmy Nesbitt's character being from Northern Ireland, and while they wanted my Northern Irish voice, they most certainly didn't want anything set over here. Of course, when it comes to television, it's a problem all the regions face. BBC Wales is an example. It is hailed as a major success because it makes *Dr Who* and all its spin-offs, but I'm pretty sure that there are no Welsh writers involved in it. 'Local' or regional dramas, of which we used to be guaranteed at least a series or a couple of one-offs every year – one thinks of the wonderful work Robert Cooper did when he ran the drama department in Belfast – are simply not being made and writers are not being nurtured the way they used to be.

Mystery Man, which started my latest series, is different from my norm in that it happened almost by chance. I was launching *Driving Big Davie* at No Alibis mystery bookstore in Belfast and I always prefer to read the opening chapters in books, because they're self explanatory. However, as the first chapter of *Davie* was virtually all about masturbation and some family members were going to be in the audience, I couldn't quite bring myself to read it. I knew this a couple of months in advance so I had time to come up with a short story, 'The Case of Mrs Geary's Leather Trousers', which was set in the bookstore, and really meant only as a bit of a throwaway entertainment.

When I did read it, it got the best laughs of almost anything I've done. When I came to launch the next book then, *Belfast Confidential* I think, and being spoilt by getting so many laughs for 'Mrs Geary', I decided to try and repeat that success by writing 'The Case of the Fruit on the Fly Over'. And that went down just as well. So I enjoyed writing them a lot, and began to think about perhaps publishing them through No Alibis, or maybe writing six or seven others to make a collection. But then common sense prevailed, because there's really no demand for short stories and while I like small press books and limited editions, I still have to eat. The interesting thing is that while the first two short stories make up the start of the book, the actual character of the bookseller/private eye only really developed once I got into the novel proper. If they had remained just short stories the characters would have been funny without any depth, which now, hopefully, they have.

Mystery Man was by far the lightest thing I'd written, and it was fun to do. And even though I've written sequels, I'm already a little bit wary of getting trapped into writing purely comic novels. I think I upset my publishers a little bit a few years ago because they went and rebranded me as BATEMAN and gave me a 'wacky' new look for *I Predict a Riot*, and then the next book I delivered was *Orpheus Rising*, which was anything but wacky but which they still had to shoehorn into the brand. So in a way I feel I owe them a couple of lighter ones. There's a Charlie Drake movie from the '60s which has always stayed with me – he played a comedian who was driven mad because when he tried to become a straight actor the public kept laughing at him, and that's a little bit how I feel sometimes. There are always going to be laughs, I think, but I do like to try different things.

Or I may be talking bollocks. I'm not very intellectual about these things. I just keep writing until I stop.

*

Colin Bateman is the author of twenty crime novels, including *Divorcing Jack*, *Orpheus Rising* and *Mystery Man*. *The Day of the Jack Russell*, the second in his Mystery Man series, won the Last Laugh Award for best humorous crime novel of 2010 at Crimefest. His next novel, *Nine Inches*, featuring the return of his hero Dan Starkey after a six-year absence, will be published in November 2011.

The Exile

by Paul Charles

'You should write a piece on the subject of exiles,' the editor of this anthology suggested.

I sat intrigued for a few moments.

'Well, you know,' I began, 'that's probably not a bad idea because the main character in both my detective series are exiles.'

'Yes, squire, that's why I thought you might be interested in covering it,' he replied in an editorial kinda way.

As I walked along Dublin's crowded streets on my way to a reading I was doing that evening with Gentleman Sam Millar, my head was filled with the editor's words and ideas were sprouting as fast as new detective TV shows.

Not until this invitation had I considered how many characters in my two detective series, Camden Town's Detective Inspector Christy Kennedy and Donegal's Inspector Starrett, were members of the displaced; either forced or self-imposed exiles. So this is a golden opportunity for me to examine how being an exile helps shape some of my characters and in a way, as it's a path I've trodden myself, allows me to examine how being an exile might have shaped my own life.

Detective Inspector Christy Kennedy was originally from Portrush and is now living and working in Camden Town. Also in Kennedy's team are: DS James Irvine who, with his non-intentional, near-perfect take on Sean Connery's accent, reveals his origins clearly, and Desk Sergeant Timothy

Flynn, is a long time Camden Towner, but is originally from Ballymena in Northern Ireland. The protagonist in the most recent Kennedy mystery, *The Beautiful Sound of Silence*, is twice exiled; once in his teens to London, in his twenties to Berkeley in California, and eventually, a few years before our story begins, he returns to London rather than his place of birth. The rest of the regulars: ann rea; DS Anne Coles; DS Dot King and Dr Leonard Taylor, are all English, although Dr Taylor is consciously based on, and named after, my hometown boyhood family doctor. From the Donegal series, Inspector Starrett is an exiled exile; he's originally from Ramelton. He had to hightail it to London in his late teens where he remained for several years before returning to Ramelton to take up a new career as a detective in the Gardaí. Dr Samantha Aljoe, Starrett's temptress, and pathologist, is originally from the Home Counties, but now finds herself based in Donegal, working out of Letterkenny General Hospital.

Originally, I myself am from a wee village in the wilds of County Derry called Magherafelt. I moved to London in 1967 when I was seventeen years old. I was on the Beatles' trail. Sadly I was to learn that they'd split up only months previously. London, in those (pre-Ryanair) days was twenty long, gruelling hours away. London in those days still had signs in guesthouse windows declaring, 'No Blacks, Dogs or Paddies'.

For all that, I realise, and accept with hindsight, that I enjoyed a comparatively easy exile.

In the generations before mine, families used to grieve children emigrating, the way they grieve the dead. Even as late as the '50s and '60s it was the same. Agreed, maybe we're not discussing flitting to London here, but if someone moved to Australia or America, well then, quite simply it meant there was a very good chance that their family would never ever see them again.

When I left Magherafelt to go to London, I hadn't realised I had an accent, but when the reply to each of my questions was, 'Pardon?' I soon got the picture.

Talking of which reminds me of an enlightening and revealing incident I was involved in shortly after I moved to London. The other participant was also an exile, albeit from a different country than mine. At the time I was working in Chessington and living in Wimbledon. One beautiful spring evening I was queuing for a ticket at Chessington railway station.

'Could I have a single to Wimbledon please?' I asked the man behind the grille when I reached the head of the queue.

'Where would you like to go to, sir?' my fellow exile asked back.

'Wimbledon please.'

'I know you want to buy a ticket, but where would you like to go?' he inquired impatiently as the queue behind me grew equally impatient.

'WIM-BLE-DON,' I tried again, this time as slowly and as clearly as my Ulster accent would allow.

He rolled his eyes and the queue tutted as one in sympathy with him.

I regrouped quickly and hit him with, 'Wimbledon, you know, the place where they play the tennis?'

'Ah,' he replied with theatrics John McEnroe would have been proud of, 'you mean Vimbledon, don't you?'

I fast learned it was important to have illustrations for locations or alternate words lined up for what I was trying to say, if only to avoid similar embarrassments. If I was moping for the security of my home to start with, then the above only served to increase my homesickness a few degrees above chronic.

Neil Diamond dealt with his homesickness (and believe me, it is an illness) by writing the soulful, *I Am, I Said*. I dealt with mine by writing home every night and by listening to *Astral Weeks* every waking hour God sent me. *Astral Weeks* is the masterwork of Van Morrison, one of Ireland's most famous exiles. Mr Morrison also happened to name one of his companies Exile Productions.

Much and all as I enjoyed the above recuperative medicine, if I had been able to afford the price of the ticket, I really would have returned home and stayed. It's as simple as that. I realised of course that that would have been, to some degree, an admission of failure, a consideration Starrett reluctantly admits in *Family Life*. Although all bar one of the above listed cases of exile were self-imposed, I would still argue that in each case the subject really had no choice in the matter.

At home, just before my own departure I'd been deliriously happy managing a wee group called The Blues By Five (there were five of them and they played the blues), and dating a girl of my dreams. The 'a' as opposed to 'the' is a conscious choice. I was to come to realise that the intensity of our relationship was based most definitely on the fact that I was leaving and when I left, 'we' would be no more. My departure was clearly her failsafe safety net. Anyway, I persuaded myself to stick out my exile in London until Christmas, by which point I would be able to afford a trip home. A few days before I commenced the long hard journey via Heysham, I met a wee girl, another exile, from County Clare and she was quite taken by my desert boots and thought that my accent was funny rather than difficult. So, as I spent my Christmas in Magherafelt, I found myself being preoccupied about meeting up with her again in London upon our return.

When I returned to London for the dying days of '67, I discovered the homesickness wasn't quite so bad; the sting of Neil Diamond's classic lyric, 'I've never liked the sound of being alone', had all but disappeared. With my newfound confidence, I started going to gigs in the famous Marquee Club, in Wardour Street, to see and hear some of the 'underground' groups I'd previously only read about in music papers like the *MM* and the *NME*. We're talking about groups like Spooky Tooth, Cheese, Jethro Tull, Skid Row, The Nice, Traffic, The Faces, Granny's Intentions, the amazing Taste, and Joe Cocker. Then I discovered the Royal Albert Hall – such a perfect arena for music – and I saw The Dubliners there and realised I was not alone. The accents at the Dubliners' patriotic concert betrayed at least another 5,000 similarly afflicted exiles. I also remember seeing Crosby, Stills and Nash doing a perfect concert at the Royal Albert Hall; that was the first time I'd ever seen the sound and the lights being monitored and controlled from amidst the audience. It made perfect sense they'd want to do that; I'd just never seen it done before.

The weeks stopped dragging; my letters home grew less frequent. I went to see Manchester United play Chelsea and felt a surge of National (Northern) Irish pride I'd never experienced before when I bore witness to George Best's genius as he absolutely destroyed the Chelsea defence. It was sheer unadulterated pleasure watching him perform magic in front of my very eyes.

On one memorable occasion around this time, I returned home to the fast-growing Magherafelt to discover my parents had moved from the house I'd grown up in and departed for London from. Of course I was aware such a move was taking place in my absence, but I was totally unprepared for the stark reality of it all. I felt very displaced and out of sorts for ages. I couldn't work out if my mini-trauma had to do with me not having been able to say goodbye to my old bedroom and all the 'stuff' I'd left behind, or about the fact that life in Magherafelt was happily going on all around and without me.

I had so many great memories about our old house in Beechland. Memories, for instance, like watching my father's workmates digging the garden during their lunch-break. It started off as a fun thing, with them mimicking my father in his lone task, but the proceedings grew very serious as, man by man, they clearly felt an unspoken need to help my dad complete the task by the end of their break. Or the hours I'd spend with my father in his workshop as he meticulously solved the puzzles of carpentry, while creating some useful pieces of furniture for our, or a neighbour's, house. All the while I'd incessantly question him about everything under the sun while savouring the aromas of wood chippings mixed with my father's unique, smoking-hot, brew of wood glue. Then there was the time my mother walked up and down, and up and down, the garden path behind me, strenuously supporting my bicycle as I tried in vain to learn to cycle on two wheels. Much later there was my cram-swotting to the sounds of Dylan; the music etched its way into my brain, the physics and chemistry didn't. Another memorable occasion was when I helped my father build a pigeon loft. Consequently the new adventures we enjoyed when my father became a 'pigeon fancier' were totally different to anything we'd ever experienced before. This was an entirely new scene to us; a semi-secretive world of breeding, racing and showing the pigeons and, more importantly, lots of time for vital father/son bonding.

But all of that was gone, disappeared from my life, and the usual overwhelming feeling of belonging I'd always enjoyed on my return trips from the

'Big Smoke' started to weaken somewhat. I suppose the move from my original home to my parent's new house underlined my rite of passage and all of these memories were ready to be filed as part of my youth.

I mention all of this only because when I started to flesh out Christy Kennedy's character, I imagined he'd have similar experiences. Christy borrows a lot from my father. They are good men and both enjoy the quality of modesty. The main difference between them is that my father loves solving the puzzles of carpentry and how things piece together, whereas Christy Kennedy's passion is piecing together the clues and evidence in order to solve the mystery of the crime he's investigating. They both however approach their task in the same meticulous manner. Kennedy's father, like my father, fought in and survived World War II and ably carried all the baggage that that entailed. A foreign country, in constant physical danger, was most certainly another more extreme type of exile, even to the point where sometimes you have to trust your life to fellow exiles. Such experiences, particularly as a seventeen-year-old, must, to varying degrees, shape and mould one spiritually and mentally, and the ripple effects surely must reach your children, if not generations beyond them. As I say, I had it easy. But from the way my father describes his war experiences to me, he always felt that there was something beyond himself; something indefinable, some reserve you didn't even know you had, but at the moment of desperation, it became available to you to dip into. My father's war-time experiences provided a vital back story for *I've Heard The Banshee Sing*.

Kennedy is from Portrush. Not quite Belfast, I know, but still another world entirely from Magherafelt. The 'wee Port' is real, very real, particularly to the youth of Ulster. I've always felt an overwhelming need to make my mysteries real. In a way what I try and do is the opposite of what Norman Mailer mastered in *The Executioner's Song* and Truman Capote achieved with *In Cold Blood*. They took a true story and wrote it to read like a novel. I like to take a fictional idea and endeavour to make it read like true crime.

So, to do this, I need to feel I actually know Christy Kennedy. I need to feel that Inspector Starrett could be a friend of mine. I actually need to believe that he's romantic and naïve. Just saying so is not enough, if you see what I mean.

Like friends, I hope to get to know them better as time passes. Like friends, they try not to disappoint you, but equally, like friends, they won't always do the things you want them to do and, particularly in fiction, I love those moments.

You give your characters a believable past and, I kid you not, they will help you write your mystery.

Talking about writing, as I mentioned earlier, I got through the exile/home-sickness phase helped immensely by the cushion of music, and I suppose I've got music to thank for ending up a crime writer. As I mentioned earlier, I was managing a wee group just before I left Ireland. Indirectly, that was how I really came to start writing. The wee group, The Blues By Five, were primarily a relief group to the main attraction, one of the many legendary Irish showbands. Anyway, part of my job as a manager was to ring up the local newspapers and magazines and blag journalists into doing a write-up for my band. So, fast-forward to the time I'm living in London, some of the same journalists would ring me and, 'Paul,' they'd start, proving they'd at least remembered my name, 'Taste are due to play the Marquee Club at the week-end, would you ever do us a favour and go along and have a wee chat with Rory and do a review of the show for us.' I readily obliged, happy to have a chance to return their many favours. But then, after a few trips to Wardour Street, I actually started to enjoy the process of writing and quite fancied taking it further. Every serious attempt ended up in the wastepaper basket until, many years later, I discovered, through detective fiction, the reason to keep the writer and (hopefully) the reader, turning the page, was the need to try and discover who did it, how they did it and why they did it. Between the lines you also, as a writer, enjoy the golden opportunity of exorcising your own demons.

So, exiles, let's talk about exiles.

There's this story Starrett tells about a Donegal man he once knew. This particular man moved to London when he was a teenager and sold *The Evening Standard* outside Camden Town tube station for years. Monday to

Friday, week in week out, he regaled his regulars with the charms of Donegal and how, when he lived in Donegal, he used to be a barber and sure didn't he cut the hair for Donegal's good and great and he'd name-drop people like Gay Byrne, Daniel O'Donnell, Sean Rafferty, Phil Coulter, and the likes. He'd inform all who'd listen about how much he wished he was back there in the auld country. Time passed, your man eventually retires to the land of his dreams, Donegal, and takes up his old trade, and as he's trimming hair, he'd entertain his captive audience with stories about how absolutely wonderful London was and sure didn't he used to sell his papers to, and be on speaking terms with, the likes of Alan Bennett, Gerry Rafferty, Julian Cleary, Christy Kennedy and Boy George. He'd bore his customers about how much he wished he was back there in London again. Aye maybe a case of the home is where the heart isn't, but definitely a case of the other's man's grass always being greener.

As we've seen, exiles tend to enjoy their own company; again they have to learn to.

In their initial early days, exiles think a lot, they have a lot of time to do so. For instance, you might spend time pondering on the thought that some people emigrate in the hope of what they're going to find; others move on because of what they're leaving behind. I'll let you be in my dreams if I can be in yours, Bob Dylan said that.

Being an exile is all about survival. Exiles learn that in order to secure their survival they need to put an order to their mind. A similar order, you would imagine, which just may come in handy to a detective.

When you are an exile, absolutely everyone is a stranger.

Some people became exiled because they were bored at home and London was on paper, not to mention the telly, an exciting adventure.

Lots of exiles travelled to London without having fixed up anywhere to stay. Police would pick them up and then try and get a nun to claim them and set them up. Apparently one of the secrets about being a happy exile is to excel at something or other, sport, music, writing, art, acting or whatever. It's a way of distracting attention from the fact that you're, 'not from these parts'. This way it's like you're not trying to fit in with your surroundings, you're making your surroundings fit in with you.

The pleasure and the pain of moving from a small village where everyone knows everyone's business and the total anonymity you encounter as an exile when you first arrive in London is totally perplexing but at the same time exhilarating.

Equally, supposedly, once you move to London from a small town it is near impossible to relocate, with any degree of success, back to your original home-town. This knowledge must temper an exile's personality either directly or indirectly.

Exiles fall into the Sunday morning rituals with other like exiles who also don't have families or benefit from real home comforts. You learn to study your fellow exiles carefully, because there is a good chance they are migrants who, without any family ties or principles to hold them back, can and will move on at the drop of a hat. So, what I'm saying is, you need to choose your friends carefully. On the other hand, non-exiles meet down the pub for their regular pints and there are 99 chances out of a 100 that they'll also be there the following week. Actually, I'm not really sure I believe that part, but that's my point here; maybe one of my detectives, Starrett or Kennedy, just might.

Does being an exile make you melancholy? Does it heck as like? As I have already said, it does make you happy in your own company and from the outside this can make you appear to be naval gazing. Kennedy frequently uses this valuable space to review his current case in detail.

The upside of being a self-imposed exile is the pure unadulterated joy you feel when you go back home for a visit. Kennedy, in one (and only one) adventure had occasion to return to Portrush while working on a case (*I've Heard The Banshee Sing*). ann rea, because it was she, as a journalist, who uncovered the Portrush connection to Kennedy's investigation, accompanies Kennedy in a professional capacity. Kennedy enjoys showing her around his early haunts, like Barry's Amusements; the basket ball court up on Ramore Head where his father once took him to see the Harlem Globetrotters play; the West Strand where he'd once saw Belfast beat group The Wheels perform on the beach, sponsored by *The Belfast Telegraph*; the harbour; the caravan parks; Kelly's; the entrance hall (for that is all that is still standing) to the Arcadia Ballroom, and the sand dunes. The latter, by the way, in a very non-professional manner. Coincidently it was during *I've Heard The Banshee Sing* that Kennedy had to cross the border and visit Ramelton, in County Donegal, where he met up with the aforementioned Starrett for the first and only time. This meeting was the genesis of the Inspector Starrett series, which as I say, allowed me to investigate the exile's perspective from another angle.

A good friend of mine recently asked me why the murderer in one of my books was such a likeable person. Well, again, that's because I was trying to keep it real. Just because a person murders someone it doesn't necessarily mean that in other areas of their lives, they're not a nice person, if indeed perhaps even a perfect family man or woman.

People murder for various reasons: love (or lack of it), greed and injustice seem to be the main causes.

Exiles with their lack of roots, their distance from families and absence of loved ones who really care for them, seem to be a ready target for injustice.

Starrett is motivated by injustice. He wants to discover the identity of the real murderer rather than have someone innocent put in the frame. He wants to protect the innocent as much as he wants to detain the guilty. The reason for this will become apparent in the third book of the Starrett series, but it's to do with a great injustice he himself experienced when he was first exiled and led by blind faith.

Kennedy, as I said, is intrigued by both the puzzle of the crime and the harm humans are capable of doing to each other.

I still don't fully understand the impact being an exile has had on my own life, or on Kennedy's life, or on Starrett's situation for that matter. I would guess, from experience, that it most certainly had a life-changing impact on their lives and their approach to work. But in a way, I suppose it's a lot like asking the question: how much has a tree been impacted by its environment, locale and the changing weather conditions? Like people, no two trees are the same. So where does the uniqueness come from? Starrett's point of view (more than Kennedy's) would be, yes, the bark of the tree is battered and bruised by the journey, the branches will twist and turn in their own unique growth, sprouting this way and that in a desperate need to reach for light. Yet deep inside, the basic, admittedly ever-growing, core of the tree is as it was, and as it always will be, as it continues its seasonal growth. Kennedy wouldn't be so sure. If they ever meet up again in Ramelton's Bridge Bar, over a glass of red for Kennedy and a pint of Guinness for Starrett, Kennedy – while admitting that the voice he has always heard in his head, the voice that has always guided him, has always been the same, has never changed, always remained true – would suggest that who you are must surely have been tempered by your experiences and by those fellow travellers you came into contact with.

'Yes, but then bejeepers, at what point in your life are you ever really you? You know, when you're seventeen, twenty-one, forty, fifty, sixty, or seventy? Or, are we all really just works in progress until the second before we die?' Starrett would reply.

They'd lose me at that point in the conversation and I'd allow myself to be distracted by the two new characters who'd just arrived at the bar. I'd be thinking, 'Now what's their story?' I'd wonder where they came from, how they met up, how they connected and grew to know each other. Say, for instance, one of them was from Burford in the Cotswolds and the other was from Delft in Holland. What paths would those two exiles have taken in order to end up in Ramelton in the Bridge Bar on the same night as Starrett, a rare breed of exile himself in that he returned to his hometown, Ramelton; Kennedy, originally from sixty miles along the coast, but exiled in Camden Town; and myself, from about fifty miles up the road, in the general direction of Lough Neagh, and now happily living in exile wherever I go.

I'd also be thinking, 'Most of the people in this bar are probably, or perhaps have been at one time or other in their lives, exiles. And you know what? Maybe the moment we leave our parent's house and that house ceases to feel like home, right there, right in that exact moment, that's when we all become exiles.

*

Paul Charles has published nine novels in his Inspector Christy Kennedy series, which are set in London. He has also published two novels in the Donegal-set Inspector Starrett series. His most recent novel is *Family Life* (2009).

The Executioners' Songs

By Niamh O'Connor

There are some hard and fast rules of thumb that always seem to apply when it comes to identifying the true crime cases that have captured the public imagination in this country.

First, there is always a BIG central character whose plot to kill cannot be put down to a moment of madness, or a crime of passion.

Their motive is always contrived, and never mitigated by the depressing inevitability of violence that tends to go hand-in-hand with alcohol, drugs, abuse, or deprivation in the background.

Take Catherine Nevin and Sharon Collins, both convicted of soliciting to kill, and in Nevin's case also of murder. Both are examples of women who had it all and simply wanted more.

Catherine Nevin owned Jack White's pub in Brittas Bay, County Wicklow and counted among her friends some of society's most influential people – a judge, a Garda inspector. But she had her husband Tom (54) bumped off in 1996, after trying for almost ten years to hire someone to kill him. She'd approached so many men to do the job for her, that three of those who had refused came forward after Tom's murder to testify that he had died in exactly the way she proposed – in an apparent botched robbery of the pub. Nevin was motivated by greed. She didn't want to leave Tom because it would have meant halving their assets.

Four books published on the case show the intense interest that exists:

The Black Widow (O'Brien Press); *The People Versus Catherine Nevin* (Gill & MacMillan); and *Will You Murder My Husband?* (Mercier Press). The fourth, *Catherine and Friends* (Liberties Press) was actually published ten years after the trial concluded.

Sharon Collins was cast in the same character-mould. Like Nevin, the Ennis mother of two was in her forties at the time of her crime. Collins wanted to have her aging property magnate partner, PJ Howard, and his two sons, Robert and Niall, murdered, because when PJ cancelled their planned marriage, it muddied her inheritance rights.

After arranging a marriage cert by proxy on the internet, Sharon Googled a contract killer, and, calling herself 'Lyin Eyes' began to plot with an Egyptian national living in LA, who worked as a poker dealer. Essam Eid travelled from LA to Ireland, bringing Ricin – one of the most deadly poisons known to man – and was all set to execute the targets, but instead approached the younger Howards to offer them the chance to buy themselves out of the hit.

As if the story didn't have enough sensational twists, PJ Howard actually stood by Sharon, convinced she'd been set up, and after giving evidence supposedly for the State in the Central Criminal Court, walked down from the stand and planted a kiss on her lips!

Two books were published following the guilty verdicts handed down in the Central Criminal Court: *The Devil In The Red Dress* (Maverick) and *Lyin' Eyes* (*The Sunday World* newspaper, later published in *Blood Ties* by Transworld Ireland).

The most engaging true crime stories tell us something about human nature, because unlike novelists, true crime writers can't rely on the whodunit element to keep a plot suspenseful, so the story is all about why.

Take the case of the Scissor Sisters, Linda and Charlotte Mulhall, who killed their mother Kathleen's toy-boy lover Farah Noor, after a drink- and drug-fuelled party in March 2005. On the face of it, the story shouldn't have had the x-factor because of the prostitution, drugs, and alcoholism in the women's backgrounds.

In Linda's case, her ex had been jailed for cruelty to her children. But even without a sensational motive for the crime, the reason their story was so incredible was that nobody shouted 'stop'. It's hard to imagine how three female members of the same family could be present in a pokey flat while a man was being killed, and that afterwards all three could reverse the usual dignity afforded to the dead so as to chop him up to get rid of the body, dumping Noor's body parts like household rubbish in the Grand Canal, and transporting his head away in a schoolbag on a bus so he couldn't be identified.

The books that followed the conclusion of this case were: *The Torso In The Canal* (Maverick House); *The Scissor Sisters* (Merlin); and *The Scissor Sisters* (The Sunday World, later published in *Blood Ties* by Transworld Ireland).

Another category of crimes that tend to captivate are those that rock middle Ireland. When certain crimes arrive in the suburbs, people sit up and take note. There was huge coverage of the murder of Brian Murphy – a teenager kicked to death outside Annabel's night club on the southside of Dublin – because of the savagery and social classes involved.

In exactly the same way, the case of seventeen-year-old Raonaid Murray, who was knifed to death yards from her home in Glenageary, still dominates the headlines, although the crime remains unsolved. The randomness of the crime, coupled with the fact that her parents were good, hardworking people, meant she could have been anyone's daughter, and made the story utterly compelling.

A sub-category of this middle-Ireland section is the kind of story that shows the gap between justice and the law, and makes the blood of middle Ireland boil. Take Majella Holohan's infamous victim impact statement about her son Robert, killed by his neighbour, Wayne Donoghue, who claimed it was horseplay that had gone wrong. Normally a child murder is off-limits. But this case broke the mould, because Majella was so determined to tell the court who her dead son was. She felt his identity was being lost throughout the clinical process of the trial, which had defined the eleven-year-old by his ADHD and dyslexia. The fact that trashing the victim's reputation is what is required in criminal law when proving provocation was cold comfort to her.

After Wayne O'Donoghue was convicted, Majella used her VIS to describe who Robert really was – a loving boy, who tried to make her scrambled eggs when she was sick in bed, and who loved the rides in Euro Disney.

Having corrected the record as to who her son was, she listed the questions raised, not solved, by the criminal justice system. Why was semen found on her son's hand? Who kills out of horseplay for throwing stones? And what happened?

She was accused of subverting the trial process. She was pilloried by the lawyers. How dare she criticise the system? So hers became a story of a mother against the system. David and Goliath.

One book was published on the case: *Afraid Of The Dark* (O'Brien Press).

It is widely acknowledged that because of what Majella did, Siobhan Kearney's family were denied their right to have a voice and to make a VIS in court. Thirty-eight-year-old Siobhan was murdered by her husband Brian Kearney (51) on 28 February 2006, his forty-ninth birthday.

Kearney tried to fake her suicide in their home, and after locking her in the bedroom, left their three-year-old son alone in the house with her and went out to work.

Again, a couple with seemingly everything – a beautiful house in upmarket Goatstown, a hotel in Spain, and a successful business.

And why did he do it? Because she was going to leave him; he was under financial pressure.

It didn't take a behavioural scientist to read from the way the family walked arm-in-arm into the Central Criminal Court each morning that they had a lot to say. Yet the judge exercised his discretion and refused them the right to speak when the trial had concluded.

The law has even since been changed to tighten up the judge's right to restrict even the reporting of a VIS.

Generally the cases that capture the public imagination will also involve a perpetrator who has managed to dupe everyone into believing they are an ordinary Joe, sometimes involving someone who has never been in trouble with the law.

Wicklow carpenter Larry Murphy had never come to the attention of Gardaí until he raped a woman he abducted in Carlow and was in the process of strangling her in the boot of his car in the Wicklow mountains when he was spotted by two men 'lamping' foxes, who recognised him. When he was put in prison for another crime, women stopped disappearing. It turned out he could be linked to the locations and dates where three other women had disappeared, never to be found, who disappeared over the course of six years in the Leinster area – American Student Annie McCarrick, who went missing from Enniskerry, County Wicklow; Jo Jo Dullard, hitchhiking home in Moone, County Kildare; and Deirdre Jacob, a student teacher who vanished in Newbridge, County Kildare.

In a sinister twist, Murphy had been a classmate of David Lawlor, another rapist who murdered Marilyn Rynn (42), a civil servant who never turned up for Christmas dinner in her parents house in 1996. Rynn had been getting the Nitelink home after the office Christmas party on 21 December when Lawlor, a married telecom worker who happened to be on the same bus, decided to follow her.

There have been numerous books on the cases of the missing women including: *Predator: Larry Murphy* and *Ireland's Missing Women* (*Sunday World*); *Missing* (Gill & MacMillan); *Where No-one Can Hear You Scream* (Gill & MacMillan).

Another seemingly ordinary Joe was Joe O'Reilly, the successful advertising executive who murdered his wife Rachel, the mother of his two young sons. He fantasised to such an extent about replacing her with his mistress, Nikki Pelley, that after he murdered Rachel, he treated the members of her family to grisly re-enactments of what he said the killer must have done, showing them exactly how she must have died.

Several books followed O'Reilly's conviction in the courts: *Joe And Rachel: Murder In The Naul* (first published in the *Sunday World* and later in *Blood Ties* by Transworld Ireland). *The Suspect* was published by Maverick House.

Another advertising executive turned wife-killer was Eamonn Lillis, who murdered his former James Bond model wife, Celine Cawley, on the deck of their salubrious Howth home.

The huge surge in interest in the whole area of true crime can be pin-pointed to a certain date in Irish criminal history: 26 June 1996, when Veronica Guerin was gunned down in cold blood. The vivacious reporter who'd infiltrated the underworld's murky depths to name and shame drug barons had paid the ultimate price for door-stepping drug baron John Gilligan at his multi-million pound equestrian centre to ask about the fortune he'd made from the misery of heroin addiction. Suddenly, the subject of true crime zoomed horrifyingly close and personal for the public, and rocketed to the top of politicians' and newspaper editors' agendas.

Although *The General* had been published by O'Brien Press before the Guerin murder, Veronica Guerin's murder prompted intense interest in the whole area of Irish true crime, and the book resulted in a Hollywood movie of the same name, directed by John Boorman.

But perhaps the strongest sign that the interest in books on these cases has been sated was the publication of only one book following the conclusion of the Eamon Lillis trial, despite the wipe-out newspaper coverage: *Death On The Hill* (O'Brien Press).

Personally, I've turned from true crime writing to fiction to get around the restrictions of libel law, while highlighting the shortcomings in the justice system. My first novel, *If I Never See You Again*, was published by Transworld Ireland in 2010.

It's a path pioneered by *Sunday Independent* journalist, and Irish Book Award winner, Gene Kerrigan, whose true crime book, *Hard Cases,* gave the ring of authenticity to crime novels like *Little Criminals*, *Midnight Choir*, and *Dark Times In The City.*

*

Niamh O'Connor is a crime reporter with the *Sunday World*. She published a number of non-fiction crime titles before publishing her first novel, *If I Never See You Again*. Her latest novel is *Taken*.

The Truth Commissioners

by Gerard Brennan

So, where are we now? What exactly is going on with Northern Ireland, aka the Six Counties, or The Province, or The North of Ireland, in 2011?

Nineteen ninety-eight saw the signing of the Good Friday Agreement, a historical moment, which many believed would be the foundation for peace in our politically conflicted statelet. But things didn't go quite according to plan. Deadlines for decommissioning were missed, which held up British demilitarisation. The Royal Ulster Constabulary became the Police Service of Northern Ireland, marketed as Catholic-friendly, but did not gain immediate support from Sinn Féin. Power-sharing between the DUP and 'Sinn Féin-IRA' became a major obstacle. Due to a lack of progress, the Northern Ireland Assembly was suspended from 2002 until 2007 and political control was maintained through the Northern Ireland Office. In short, there was nothing straightforward about the Northern Ireland peace process.

Finally, though, it looks like we're actually getting somewhere.

The St Andrew's Agreement in October 2006 aimed to tackle the various political stalemates. It was successful in that it led to the restoration of the Northern Ireland Assembly and in May 2007, Ian Paisley of the DUP was elected First Minister and Sinn Féin's Martin McGuinness was elected Deputy First Minister. That they were able to work together, given each man's role in the Troubles, was something close to spectacular. In fact, they got on so well that, in typical Northern Irish humour, they were soon nicknamed The Chuckle Brothers. Paisley retired as a political hero a little over a year later and his successor, Peter Robinson, now serves in his place with McGuinness still in post as Deputy First Minister. The chuckles have considerably lessened, but the politics continue to progress.

And there you have it. A brief history of the Northern Ireland peace process. We are most definitely experiencing the post-Troubles era.

The threat of terrorism is still present in the form of dissident paramilitaries, but they have very little support in mainstream society. A hell of a lot of EU money has been poured into conflict resolution, through various cross-community projects, targeting those who live in areas where sectarian hatred is rife. Since the end of the bombing campaigns, the economy has experienced a property boom and a property crash that contributed greatly to the current credit crunch. A new generation is coming to the fore that, given the luxury of dual nationality (a choice between considering themselves Irish or British), has instead become comfortable with the idea of being *Northern Irish*. The world has moved on, and the dinosaurs that grumbled about 'Sinn Féin-IRA' and 'DUP sell-outs' are facing extinction. The next generation could well grow up in a society that no longer dwells in tribal politics. Perhaps they'll discover that they've always had a shared national culture. Maybe they'll embrace it. And with any luck, the generation after that will never fully grasp what all the fuss was about.

But right now, and apologies if this seems facetious, this crazy wee statelet is a hotbed of inspiration for the new breed of Northern Irish crime fiction writer that has exploded onto the scene in recent years.

Although the topic of Northern Irish politics is pretty much a flogged-out dead stallion, there is one Northern Irish writer who is still making it interesting, entertaining and funny. Derry man Garbhán Downey spent many years as a political journalist and got to know our complicated system inside-out, warts and all. Quite recently, he gave up his life as a hack to focus on writing full-time. Of his seven books written to date, *Yours Confidentially – Letters of a Would Be MP* (2008), is the most recent and most relevant to the current climate. It's a political satire set in modern Northern Ireland that cuts very close to the knuckle and boasts a wonderful cast of unwitting cameos from the likes of Gerry Adams, Ian Paisley Junior, Gerry Kelly and Sammy Wilson.

We meet a handful of Downey's recurring characters in *Yours Confidentially*. The protagonist, Shay Gallagher, has been building his political career as an independent since Downey penned *Private Diary of a Suspended MLA* (2004). Gallagher is now a contender for promotion to Minister of Parliament and a seat in Westminster. A move like that would earn him some serious firepower, and being a rare breed of politician who actually cares about his constituency, he would more than likely use it for the greater good. However, the problem with Shay is, he's just too damn honest. Wary and distrustful of computers and the thought of emailing, he has committed many of the honest thoughts he wishes to share to paper. These letters, to his politician fiancée, colleagues and friends, have been copied and held under lock and key for safekeeping. But, of course, they don't stay there, which is how they make up the entire structure of the book.

Luckily, Shay has subscribed to his Agent, Tommy Bow-Tie's '90 Per Cent Rule':

[T]here is no harm, occasionally, in planting a little white lie in a story – i.e. a 10 percenter – if it can help you undermine the other 90 percent or, alternatively, give it legs at later stage.

It's an interesting theory, and much of the book's plot hangs on its relevance.

First and foremost, *Yours Confidentially* is a political satire, and a hilarious one at that, but it's also got its darker serious side. Downey presents us with the highly believable world of behind-the-scenes deals, backhanders and criminal influences on government. And there are fascinating insights into how the characters deal with each other on a personal level. Something as simple as Shay being addressed by a highly ranked officer in the Police Service of Northern Ireland as '*Shay, a chara*,' is full of wonderful implications. Their familiarity, trust and loyalty towards each other born of a shared background summed-up in a Gaelic phrase that means 'Dear Shay'. Also, it's interesting to note that the phrase is derived from *cara*, the Gaelic for 'friend'.

Another novel, deeply entrenched in the world of Northern Irish politics, though written in a very different tone, is *The Truth Commissioner* (2008) by David Park. This serious and thought-provoking literary work wrestles with the thorny issue of *The Disappeared*; the victims of violence killed during the height of the Troubles, whose remains have never been found. In Park's Northern Ireland, a Truth Commissioner has been drafted in to act as an impartial judge of sorts in a process where the victims' family confront those involved in the killings. The process is a hearing, something similar to a court case without a sentence, held at Stormont (Belfast's parliamentary building), which is intended to aid the healing of those affected by the past.

Although there is a lot of potential in this premise, it becomes more of a backdrop in this novel. Park writes a tale about people rather than reporting on an imagined situation. He devotes a huge amount of time to the thoughts of the novel's four central players; an ex-Provisional IRA man turned politician, an Irish immigrant living in America trying to escape a mysterious past, an ex-RUC officer who bent the rules once or twice, and the Truth Commissioner himself. Each player is deeply haunted by both their past and their present and each one plays their part in uncovering the truth behind one of the disappeared.

Park's ability to keep this story deeply rooted in humanity lends a wonderful level of understanding to a topic that is fraught with too much inherited subjective opinion. *The Truth Commissioner* strips back all the bullshit and presents us with the raw materials of the situation – people. People who made decisions that they thought were for the greater good, but had resounding and permanent consequences. People who live with regret, guilt and fear. People who are flawed, fucked up and fragile.

This book isn't sympathetic to any 'side' or political ideal. It is what it is, and that's its greatest strength. The bittersweet final scene, where a bulldozer awaits first light to get to work on an excavation, leaves the reader melancholic but just a little bit expectant and hopeful. It is a new dawn that brings a chance to dig up and acknowledge the past, so that tomorrow can be faced with dignity. To this reader, it is symbolic of the challenge that all of us affected by the Troubles must conquer in order to move on:

> 'And then in the first true light of morning a yellow digger trundles along the pitted track and when it reaches the end of the bog it stops its engine and waits. Soon others will arrive with their transit vans and equipment, their thermal-imaging cameras and their marking poles. But for the moment the driver sits alone waiting in his cab and as the rising wind snakes around him he shivers against the coldness of the morning and, pressing his hands together as if he's praying, lifts them to his mouth and tries to fill them with the warmth of his breath.'

The subject of the Troubles is close to the heart of those who've lived through it, but what about those who've witnessed the media coverage over the years but have never really been affected by it? For argument's sake, let's split them into two camps; the English and the Americans.

This is a horrible simplification, but it's one that the publishing world subscribes to. Case in point: Stuart Neville's debut novel was known as *The Ghosts of Belfast* in its Soho Press US edition, whereas Harvill Secker, an imprint of Random House, opted to title the UK version *The Twelve* (2009). That's down to the belief that UK readers will be turned off by the very thing that turns on the US readers; Northern Ireland, and all the connotations those two words bring.

But I think Neville's debut has gone a long way towards skewing those dated connotations. If the media storm it has created in the early days of its publication is anything to go by, this will be one of the most far-reaching novels to come from the post-Troubles boom to date. And deservingly so, I should add.

Gerry Fegan is an ex-IRA hit man who is haunted by his past in more ways than one. Twelve, in fact, in the shape of the ghosts of the people he has murdered in his bloody career. Now he drinks himself to sleep every night in an effort to evade the screams of those he killed. But the ghosts offer a glimmer of hope. Fegan figures that the ghosts see him as an extension of the guns or bombs that killed them. He's a machine of death, bred to kill. But the ghosts want the blood of the men who pulled the triggers. And so starts the novel's main plot thread, a bloody revenge campaign that threatens to derail the peace process of Northern Ireland.

Whether the ghosts in *The Twelve* are metaphorical or actual manifestations is a moot point, though their presence does extend the book's readership to fans of the horror genre and all the subgenres in between. However, in a sharp marketing decision, it was sold as a thriller, first and foremost, which now pits Neville's book against the usual troop of ex-SAS 'writers' who usually dominate the shelves.

The Twelve won the *LA Times* Crime / Mystery Novel of the Year award in 2010, and Neville's literary credentials were further burnished by the publication of his follow-up novel, *Collusion* (2010). That novel also features the killer Fegan, but explores more deeply – as the title suggests – the malevolent forces at play during the darkest periods of the Troubles. At the time of going to press, *Collusion* is in the running for the *LA Times* Crime / Mystery Novel of the Year award for 2011.

Perhaps the broad generalisation affecting the title of Neville's debut could go some way towards explaining the varied levels of success Adrian McKinty experienced with the release of his novel, *The Dead Yard* (2006).

The Dead Yard is the second of McKinty's 'Dead' trilogy featuring Michael Forsythe, which is bookended by *Dead I Well May Be* (2003) and *The Bloomsday Dead* (2007). In America, *The Dead Yard* was picked as one of the twelve best novels of 2006 by U.S. magazine *Publishers Weekly*. Not the best crime novel. The *best novel*. And the audiobook version won audiobook of the year. But the UK edition just didn't attract the level of kudos or sales it deserved.

The Dead Yard follows Michael Forsythe as he infiltrates a terrorist cell in Boston with links to the Real IRA known as The Sons of Cuchulainn. He's just spent five years in the Witness Protection Programme since the lethal act of vengeance that was *Dead I Well May Be*. After a brush with the law in Tenerife he comes under the scrutiny of some British intelligence officers who see potential in him as an undercover agent. His criminal past can only help make him more convincing in his role and very early on, he proves his worth by spotting an assassin at his first stop in Boston:

'He was a hard bastard who'd entered with some kind of automatic weapon under his raincoat, which he kept buttoned despite the heat. A dead give-away. His face was scarred, his hair jagged, and either he was from Belfast or he worked twelve hours a day in a warehouse that got no natural light. Tall, stooped, birdlike. About fifty. An old pro. The dangerous type. Sipping the urine-colored Schlitz. Not nervous. Calm. Smoking Embassy No. 1 cigarettes, which I don't think you can get in this country, so that solved the nationality question.'

Along with an action-packed storyline, McKinty brings the reader a lot of food for thought when he sets the Northern Irish protestant, Forsythe, amongst the catholic Real IRA sympathisers. Forsythe's removed perception of the sleeper cell and the members' ideals, sheds a cold and unromantic light on the subject of dissident Irish Republicanism.

So, if *The Dead Yard* explores the mindset of the absentee freedom fighter, and reflects on it unfavourably, I suppose that it's a positive sign that it's made such an impact in America. All those Irish-American sympathisers of the cause could maybe learn a thing or two from Michael Forsythe's personal opinions. The war's over lads. Time to wise up and move on.

Now, if only the UK could show the same level of interest. Maybe they could learn from it too.

Probably one of the simplest yet most striking references to a paramilitary organisation in Northern Irish crime fiction can be found in Brian McGilloway's *Borderlands* (2007). This is the first in the growing series of Inspector Ben Devlin novels set in Lifford, a town on the Free State side of the border between County Donegal and County Derry.

The plot revolves around a body found on the border, which becomes a Garda investigation due to the fact that the victim, a teenage girl, was a Lifford resident. Of course, during the investigation there is a certain amount of coop-eration between An Garda Síochána and the Police Service of Northern Ireland in both an official and unofficial capacity. Due to this very clever choice of set-ting and situation, McGilloway has really got the best of two worlds at his dis-posal. Not many police procedural series can explore two different police forces in the kind of detail that the Inspector Devlin books present. And with juris-diction complications and politics between the two forces, McGilloway fairly makes the most of his premise.

But let's get back to how McGilloway handles paramilitaries in *Borderlands*. As well as pulling in favours with his contacts in the PSNI to get to the bottom of Angela Cashel's murder, Inspector Devlin reaches out to a priest with some links to the Provisional IRA. His request for help is answered by a phone conversation with an unidentified Provo, who helps in a very minor way. He confirms that a murder linked to the Cashel case was not one of *The Disappeared*. But what is most interesting about the exchange is that it is conducted on a patchy and static-drowned mobile phone line, giving the impression of a physical distance between Devlin and the IRA. Symbolically, it is a form of lip-service to a time gone by.

And on the topic of history, there's also a lovely reference to the old RUC in there. It's worth mentioning for the sake of balance. In an interrogation room scene, McGilloway mentions an infamous technique used by the former Northern Irish police force. Devlin notices the plastic chair on the suspect's side of the table in a PSNI station and speculates on how the RUC used to cut two inches off the front legs of the chair so that the suspect could never find a comfortable sitting position for the duration of the questioning. Such a simple idea, but a powerful image giving just a small but discomforting taste of empathy for those questioned in the pre-PSNI days.

It's quite fitting that the last book explored in this short study should be *Mystery Man* (2009) by Colin Bateman. Back in the nineties, Bateman led the way in Northern Irish crime fiction with the release of his debut, *Divorcing Jack* (1995). Since then, Bateman has penned over twenty novels. *Mystery Man*, his most recent, marks yet another stage of evolution in both his writing style and the sub-genre of post-Troubles crime fiction.

Bateman's Dan Starkey series saw him tackle the Troubles and post-Troubles issues to lesser and greater degrees in seven brilliant novels. Starkey was a blazing, sometimes controversial moral conscience, speaking out against terrorism, dodgy politicking and the crime spawned when the two are combined. *Mystery Man*, on the other hand, is cut from a very different cloth.

This novel steps away from all things Troubles-related and takes on an entirely different plot to anything Bateman has done before. Amateur detection, hypochondria, book signings, poetry retreats, ballet, murder and German Nazis all contribute to this flat-out comedy. It struck me once or twice that it was the kind of story that could have been set anywhere, but I'm not sure that it would have been as good if it had. You see, the whole concept of the novel is a little bit meta-fictional. Most of it is set in Bateman's favourite real-world bookshop, No Alibis in Belfast. Many of the situations could inspire the phrase, 'Sure it would only happen in Belfast, like.' And although there are precious few swipes at the type of people who give Northern Ireland a bad name, they're still there, and I imagine Bateman is still smirking as he types them.

Mystery Man and its sequels *The Day of the Jack Russell* and *Dr Yes* are the most light-hearted of Bateman's work to date, though coming from the mind of a Northern Irish writer, the series does have its black moments. The protagonist does get caught up in a multiple-murder investigation, after all. But they're books born of a time when things around Northern Ireland are a little less grim. They're much less a work of in-the-trenches humour than their predecessors, and maybe that's because we've all begun to drag ourselves off the battlefield and towards something a little less chaotic.

The future looks good for Northern Ireland, the peace process and the crime fiction movement that has grown from it. This chapter explores only a small portion of the post-Troubles literary phenomenon. As well as the authors mentioned here, we can't ignore the works of Sam Millar, Paul Charles, Jason Johnson, John McAllister, Ian Sansom and the host of emerging writers on their way up through the publishing ranks.

A decade from now, I hope we'll still be hearing from the leading lights in post-Troubles crime fiction, though by then I'd prefer that the 'post-Troubles' tag is out-dated. I hope that we'll simply be talking about Northern Irish crime fiction and that above all else this will denote a brand of literature of the highest quality. It'll be a brand that exists not because of, or even in spite of, a history of violence, but one that simply is. And I hope it becomes a brand that will carry as much weight as it deserves to.

*

Gerard Brennan co-edited *Requiems for the Departed*, an anthology of crime fiction based on Irish mythology. His novella, *The Point*, will be published in September 2011 by Pulp Press. He lives in Dundrum, County Down, with his wife, Michelle, and their kids, Mya, Jack and Oscar. He blogs at *http://crimesceneni.blogspot.com*.

Escaping Irishness

by Ingrid Black

Burning books has been frowned upon since that unfortunate business in 1930s Germany, which is a pity because there are many published volumes for which consignment to the flames would be richly deserved. (I should know, I've written a few of them.)

Personally, I'd reserve a special place right at the top of the pyre for a book entitled *Being Irish*, which came out – *escaped* might be nearer the mark – around the time of the millennium. Basically it was a collection of less-than-groundbreaking reflections by a hundred people, famous and otherwise, on what it meant to them to be one of God's chosen people.

They didn't put it quite like that, of course, but there was no mistaking the assumption underlying a depressingly large proportion of the contributions, namely that being Irish was an awe-inspiring achievement altogether, and that those born under a green star were sensitive, poetic souls with a superhuman capacity for empathetic engagement with the world, intimately connected to history and their native land, thirsting for justice and peace like no race before, which was why everybody else on the planet secretly wanted nothing more than to be Irish and spent every day in deep mourning because they were not.

It made *How The Irish Saved Civilisation* look modest by comparison.

It would be gratifying to report that this nauseating exercise in collective navel-gazing had more contributors than it did readers, but honesty forbids. Soul searching tomes about the search for identity will always draw a crowd, rather like car crashes, especially in Ireland where national traits are cultivated the way some countries grow rhubarb.

As one of the book's few sensible essayists put it: 'The only unique thing about the Irish, perhaps, is their utter conviction that there is something unique about being Irish.'

Hear, hear. Indeed, one might almost say that more nonsense has been written about Ireland than about any other country, were that not to risk falling into the trap again of treating the Irish as if they were unprecedentedly unique. It could be that such books have a higher purpose, which is to foster a sense of community and togetherness in a scary, fragmented world. The problem is that, by creating a checklist of qualities which go into making up Irish identity, a feeling of inadequacy can easily be engendered in those who fail, in their own eyes, to measure up to the national ideal. Inclusion becomes exclusion. Solidarity becomes segregation. And if that's true of being Irish, then how much more true it is of being an Irish writer? The term 'Irish writer' itself can be problematic. What is an Irish writer – a writer who happens by birth or accident or choice to be Irish? If that's all it is, then it's as meaningless a phrase as 'tall writer' or 'blue-eyed writer'. If something else is meant, then we're back in the realm of expectations and demands. The humble scribbler who only wants to be left alone to work is being asked to tick those damned boxes again. Writers have always had a central place in Irish affairs. It was dreamers such as Yeats and Lady Gregory who helped invent the idea of Ireland as a nation in the first place. 'If you would know Ireland body and soul you must read its poems and stories,' Yeats said. 'They are Ireland talking to herself.' The creative project in those early days was explicitly nationalistic. It might almost be said that they were making up Irishness as they went along, and it probably seemed churlish, not to mention unpatriotic, at the time to demur.

Thus Irish writers who followed were expected, to varying degrees, to partake in the same mission. The Matter of Ireland predominated. The English had misrepresented and abused the native Irish for centuries. The writer's job was to reclaim and remake that identity, taking it out of the hands of the oppressors and giving it back to those from whom it had been stolen, and it was too important a task to be taken trivially, which is why so many humourists were despised and marginalised when they dared turned the satirical tables on Irish life.

For many authors, the business of being an Irish writer was so onerous a responsibility that the words themselves became almost secondary. They were ambassadors for a burgeoning nation's desires and dreams. In a way, it was an inevitable part of belonging to a small country, where everybody seems at times to be looking over everybody else's shoulder, but it's a burden which must have put off countless hopefuls from ever taking up the pen. Dennis Kennedy, former journalist turned history academic, touched on that in his own contribution to the *Being Irish* collection. He recalls what happens in Flann O'Brien's *The Poor Mouth* when the hero, Bonaparte O'Coonassa, is chased across the Paradise of Ireland by a great hairy beast called the Sea Cat that threatens to eat him alive.

On being asked to describe it, Bonaparte draws an outline which, surprise, surprise, 'bore a close resemblance to the pleasant little land which is our own.'

Anyone foolish or brave enough to have left the cosy fireside of Irishness and wandered away from the tribal camp into the uncharted dark, only to be pelted with proverbial rocks for his pains, can be forgiven a little shudder of recognition there.

Sometimes the idea of Ireland just won't leave you alone.

Complicating this still further was the English language question. The poverty-stricken, rain-sodden residents of Corkadorkey in *The Poor Mouth* are visited by Gaelic speakers from Dublin who tell them that not only should every word they utter be in the native language, but that the language itself should be the only subject of conversation. It's a clever satire of fanaticism, all the more effective for not being very far from the truth.

Even today, there's a residual feeling among many Irish people, whether they speak Gaelic or not, that those who do are somehow more real and authentic than the rest, and that something is missing or diminished when an Irish person speaks English.

Stephen Dedalus, meeting an Englishman in Joyce's *A Portrait of the Artist as a Young Man*, torments himself with the suspicion that he is unable to use the identical words with the same confidence. 'My soul,' he says, 'frets in the shadow of his language.' Irish writers were expected to labour under the same sense of dislocation and loss. Even if they gloriously overcame it, they were still meant to be aware of the struggle. But where did that leave writers who had no interest in Irishness as such, not even their own? Who were Irish by definition, but never gave it a moment's thought beyond the biographical facts? Who weren't tormented? Who felt no national burden? Who simply didn't fit into those neat Protestant/Catholic, urban/rural, North/South classifications? Who didn't feel a part of that club? Who saw the English language the way Indians see cricket – as something which may have come originally from England, but what of it, let's just play. The charge against writers who won't align themselves to the great Irish project is that they've forgotten where they came from, but isn't that half the fun? It's enormously liberating sometimes to ignore the past and reinvent oneself anew.

It would be easy to say that, for long periods, the only way to escape Irishness was to escape Ireland, and many writers did just that. (Not just writers either. Generations of Irish people have managed to forge new identities through emigration.) But physical distance was never a prerequisite. Others stayed and just stubbornly ploughed their own furrow. Not fighting against the prevailing cultural climate necessarily, merely ignoring it, because it wasn't relevant to them, it didn't speak to what was happening inside their heads.

Crime fiction was one such escape route, because, the odd literary maverick aside, it had never been a particularly popular native form.

Why that should be is hard to say. Some have speculated that the reason there was so little Irish crime fiction in the past was because murders were a rare event, which even if true, is an odd argument, because murder did still happen, even if proportionately less of it than in other territories, and violent death is by its very nature horrible and fascinating. There has always been more than enough of it around to imprint itself on the consciousness of alert writers.

Moreover, why assume a straight causal link between crime statistics and crime writing? English rural society in the mid-twentieth century was not noticeable for its high homicide rate either, but that didn't stop Agatha Christie from littering St Mary Mead with corpses. The impulse to fictionalise extreme human behaviour is not dependent on newspaper headlines.

Whatever the reason, crime fiction was certainly not established in Ireland in the way of fantasy or the ghost story. Aspiring fabulists had Lord Dunsany, Sheridan le Fanu and Bram Stoker to show them the way. For the most part, Irish mystery readers up until quite recently had to look further afield, chiefly America, to satisfy their imaginative needs. Whatever disappointment they felt about that was more than compensated for in the sense of liberation provided by sidestepping the suffocating insularity of so much Irish fiction.

Importing these genre conventions into an Irish context was a way for writers who felt out of place with the prevailing culture to reclaim the ground under their feet, make it their own again, even recreate it from scratch. They were freed from the tyranny of authenticity. Dublin didn't only have to be Joyce's city. It could be Sam Spade's and Hannibal Lecter's as well. Why not? It's public space. It's up for grabs.

Mingled with that was also the pleasure of sticking out a cheeky tongue at one's forefathers, and there's nothing wrong with that either. Women found the same escape from the demands of femininity in crime fiction. Female characters could be whatever they wanted to be. They could behave disgracefully. They could break the rules.

Crime stories are the perfect medium for remodelling the world in this fashion, because they are at heart fairytales. They share the same familiar quality as myth. The details change from country to country, retelling to retelling, but they give shape to the identical shadows and impulses. If the Brothers Grimm were alive today, they'd be collecting newspaper clippings about modern-day Rumplestiltskins and wicked stepmothers and witches in the wood enticing children to step across the threshold and have some candy.

My, my, grandmamma, what big teeth you have.

There's also a powerful element of wish fulfillment within the hardest, most cynical crime fiction, which suits the writer out of sorts with his surroundings. There has to be. Fiction is impossible without fantasy. Most crime, after all, is a fairly prosaic affair. Writing and reading about it would be dullness personified for everybody concerned.

So the writer sexes it up, in that ugly but undoubtedly useful phrase. Serial killers are, thankfully, rare beasts; when people do kill, they tend to do it rather unimaginatively and get caught easily as a result. The annals of the mystery novel would be a poorer place without the criminal genius who toys with the police, but how many exist outside the head of the nerdy, wouldn't-say-boo-to-a-goose author at his laptop? Likewise, the fictional conceit of tracking every criminal conspiracy to the very top of society is usually just that: fictional. Government ministers and property developers and bishops can be thoroughly unpleasant individuals, but outside of the pages of crime fiction they rarely organise gangland hits or run international drugs cartels. Making them do so in works of the imagination – and better still, getting their comeuppance – is generally a sign of a writer's private political daydreams coming out.

Huge numbers of crimes also go unsolved, which would make for frustrating endings. Hercule Poirot gathering the suspects in the drawing room and admitting that his little grey cells have packed up on him and he hasn't got a clue whodunnit would be amusing once or twice, but readers would soon grow weary of the joke.

And so would the author, if truth be told.

Modern crime writers might like smugly to imagine that they've grown out of the cosy conservative certainties of the Golden Age – that criminals will be caught and punished, and the natural social order restored, and then it'll be high tea on the vicarage lawn at four as usual – but narrative resolutions make their own demands and have their own satisfactions. As John Connolly once said: 'All crime writers are secretly moralists.' Since this isn't a moral world, they're going to try and put it right on the page as best they can, in weird and murky ways sometimes, and often unsatisfactorily for the protagonists because the wicked do escape justice; but there aren't many amoral crime writers around who actively egg-on their most villainous creations. Even lamenting the failure to apprehend the guilty is a conservative resolution in itself, and maybe it's the best we can hope for as readers in a system where the real criminal justice system too often works to the advantage of perpetrators.

Where crime fiction has an advantage is in fixing these archetypal patterns onto a recognisably solid physical environment. One of the undoubted pleasures of the genre is to explore the particularities of place. As a reader, what first attracted me to John Sandford's Lucas Davenport series was not so much some sketchy tease of a plot on the back of a shiny paperback, the details of which I can't even remember now, but the prospect of getting an impression of Minneapolis-St Paul, about which I knew precisely zilch. Patricia Cornwell's early Scarpetta novels might have been sold on their gruesome forensic accuracy, but seeing Richmond, Virginia up close was as much of a draw for me.

Like its Irish cousin, Scandinavian crime fiction is enjoying a surge of popularity at the moment for the same reasons. It's a chance to inhabit alien territory for a while, to see beyond the regional clichés of blond manic depressives killing themselves whilst wearing chunky knitwear (though if, along the way, a few blond manic depressives kill themselves whilst wearing chunky knitwear, who's complaining? It's all good clean fun).

In truth, it's impossible to know how accurate to their settings these books are without heading to the locations with a stack of paperbacks, a map, and the obsessive determination of a trainspotter who hasn't had a girlfriend since junior school. But the real thrill is that it doesn't matter a jot. If the setting comes alive on the page, and the book stays in the memory, it ought to be job done for writer and reader alike.

When it comes to home turf, however, doubt too often sets in. An Irish writer wanting to set a thriller in Dublin will feel constrained by the demands of verisimilitude, usually because he knows some parochial smart alec will delight in scanning the book for factual inaccuracies and, on sniffing them out, gleefully take the opportunity to dismiss the publication out of hand. A certain type of Irish person can be extremely possessive like that. They take slights against the country personally. They're easily offended.

Others simply can't understand why a writer might want to run away from Irishness rather than wrapping themselves in it like a flag on St Patrick's Day.

I had the experience of a sub-editor correcting the references in one of my novels to the 'Dublin Metropolitan Police' and trying to change it to 'Garda Síochána', as if I didn't know that the DMP had disbanded in 1925. I wanted to escape from the associations which the words 'Garda Síochána' conveyed. 'Dublin Metropolitan Police' had a neutral ring about it which felt right. Dublin could be just another city. Its police force could be just another police force. So I put them back in their old headquarters at Dublin Castle, because that was an aesthetically satisfying location to me, regardless of the fact that it's now home to the Revenue Commissioners, amongst others, and hosted regular sittings of the Mahon and Flood Tribunals into various grubby financial dealings by politicians.

Who wouldn't prefer the fictional alternative?

Not that there's anything wrong with a writer wanting to set down on the page a city he knows and loves exactly as it stands in real life. Joyce always said that if Dublin were to suddenly vanish, it could be recreated using *Ulysses* (though imagine if the city planners accidentally picked up *Finnegans Wake* instead. The resulting mess doesn't bear thinking about!). The important thing is not to let a preoccupation with accuracy become a fetish, because that's missing the whole purpose of fiction. The joy of it, too.

Crime novels aren't journalism, thank God, and writers sell themselves short when they try too hard to make a case for their books as mirrors held up to the society in which they live. Crime writers in Ireland are particularly prone to this special pleading. To listen to some of them you'd swear they were writing socio-political critiques of contemporary Irish mores rather than novels. The suspicion must be that they're still trying to court the approval of certain critics who were always sniffy about crime fiction anyway, and will only lower themselves to take notice of it if they can be persuaded first that it has 'something to say'. By which they generally mean something uninteresting. Such as chest-beating, tub-thumping analyses of what it means to be Irish. The best novels don't have clunkily linear messages to convey. They don't make excuses for existing. They simply are.

Just as freeing oneself of the burden of speaking for Ireland is, for an Irish writer, the start of being able to speak for oneself, so giving up the futile effort of trying to win over the skeptics could well be the making of many a crime writer. Why expend all that energy sucking up to reluctant readers who have to be convinced they'll learn something sociologically beneficial before opening the cover of a book? Who cares what they think? They're the modern equivalent of the island-shaped Sea Cat. The only safe course is to stay away from those claws.

*

Ingrid Black is the pseudonym of Eilis O'Hanlon and Ian McConnel, a husband-and-wife writing team. The Ingrid Black novels feature former FBI agent Saxon, and Grace Fitzgerald, Detective Chief Superintendent with the Dublin Metropolitan Police Murder Squad. The most recent Ingrid Black novel was *Circle of the Dead* (2008).

The Black Stuff: A Conversation with John Banville

by Declan Burke

My favourite John Banville novels have always been those in which Banville employed the thriller / mystery framework, as he did in his debut, *Nightspawn* (1971). He returned to the crime/mystery genre again in *The Book of Evidence* (1989), *Ghosts* (1993) and *The Untouchable* (1997), before assuming the open pseudonym of Benjamin Black to write historical crime novels set in 1950's Dublin, the first of which, *Christine Falls*, was published in 2006.

There followed a number of hugely enjoyable literary spats, most notably at the 2009 Harrogate Crime Writing Festival, when Banville was perceived by his peers to be dismissive of the crime novel after claiming to be 'slumming it' when writing crime fiction.

So where, exactly, does John Banville stand on the subject of the crime novel?

Declan Burke: Is it the case that Benjamin Black writes crime fiction and John Banville narratives of crime?
John Banville: Well, if you've done your research, you've probably come across me talking about Georges Simenon. That was really the start for me, because I had never read Simenon before 2003, when John Gray at the *New York Review of Books* sent me two or three of his novels. One of them was *Dirty*

Snow, which I think is a masterpiece – that was the first Simenon I read. It's set in an unnamed Belgian city, probably Liege, where Simenon was born. It's set during the war, among low-lives, thieves, murderers, sort-of collaborators, but they're only collaborators-for-gain, they have no politics at all. It's a frighteningly dark, savage book, although unusually for Simenon, it's a little bit overwritten towards the end . . . This was one of what he called his romans durs, his 'hard' novels, and I was just bowled over by it. I thought, if he can do this kind of thing, in this very direct, story-telling way, then I want to try it.

At that point I had written a television script, a three-part mini-series for RTÉ, but it was becoming apparent that it wouldn't be made, that there wasn't enough money for it. So it struck me one day: 'I know what I'll do, I'll turn this into a novel, try my hand at doing that Simenon thing.' I mean, I haven't got Simenon's extraordinary gift for brevity, for spareness. He can set a scene in a couple of sentences and do it magnificently. And yet these are not really crime novels. They are about criminals and crimes take place in them, but they're not Maigret, they're not detective novels. I don't much like Maigret, I've never actually succeeded in finishing one of them . . . but these other novels were amazing. But then, I've always been reading people like that. I think one of the great novels is James M. Cain's *The Postman Always Rings Twice*. Again, it's not a detective novel . . . It's a dark, ugly book, but very powerful . . . What I'm saying is that the genre's a blur, and I don't like to think in terms of crime fiction and straightforward fiction, or mainstream fiction. I've been reading for years now Richard Stark's books, the Parker books, and I think there are a half-a-dozen of those books that can stand with any of the best fiction.

DB: A radical claim . . .
JB: Well, I don't think it is . . .

DB: What I mean is, the literary mainstream would perceive that as a radical claim.
JB: You know, I did an interview with Richard Stark, Donald Westlake, a couple of years ago, and I liked him enormously, he was wonderful. A real old-

style gentleman. And I was looking forward to many years of friendship with him . . . He died on New Year's Eve [2008], of course, which was terribly sad. But I think . . . I mean, he was terrible on titles, but *Slayground* is amazing, it all takes place in a funfair, and *The Jugger*, again, amazing . . . I asked him why he picked the name Stark and he said, 'Well, y'know, I wanted to write starkly.' So I don't think that genre comes into it . . . I mean, the Chicago University Press, of all places, is now re-issuing the Parker books . . . (laughs). Westlake said he never thought he'd see his books advertised in the *New York Review of Books*.

You know, this is not a pose that I'm taking. I really don't make those kind of distinctions between genre and other writing. There's just good writing.

DB: It may not be a pose, but you did say at one point that the Benjamin Black persona was 'an experiment'. Has the experiment been a success?
JB: I don't know yet. I can't feel as strongly about the Benjamin Black books as I do about the Banville books. I feel differently about them. To me, the Benjamin Black books are like doing carpentry, they're like a well-made table, an elegant chair. They're good, honest, straightforward . . . In that they're much closer to my literary journalism, my reviews. I get pleasure from those, but it's a craftsman's pleasure. I don't get any artistic pleasure. And that's the way I like it. And that, of course, immediately contradicts what I was just saying about not differentiating between genre and other fiction, but I just see it as a different type of writing. I write Benjamin Black books from up there [taps his forehead], I write John Banville books from down there [taps his chest]. That doesn't mean that I hold the John Banville books lower or higher than the Benjamin Black books, I just see them as different. I write completely differently as Benjamin Black. I write straight onto the screen, there will be no versions of it . . . I do one big revision, where I get rid of as much rubbish as I can, and then it's done. I write very quickly as Benjamin Black . . . I mean, I'm going to do two Benjamin Black books this year, one over the summer and then one later in the year.

DB: Do they both feature Quirke?

JB: No, Quirke is in one of them. The other is about a wonderful story that my accountant told me, about Princess Margaret and Princess Elizabeth being sent here during the Blitz, it was all top secret . . . His father [the accountant's father] was a Guard in Clonmel, and he knew about it. So I have a wonderful plot there. I was about to sign a contract with BBC Film to do it some years ago, but then all the fuss about the Queen's butler kicked up, so they wouldn't touch anything to do with the royalty . . . So, anyway, I'm going to turn that into a novel.

DB: Is it possible to write crime fiction in this day and age in a non-ironic way? Are the parameters too narrow?

JB: I wouldn't consider the Benjamin Blacks ironic . . .

DB: Not even *The Lemur*?

JB: Well, I'm not even sure if *The Lemur* should have been published as a book, because it was a serial for the *New York Times*. It was written in a very formulaic way . . .

DB: I presumed you were playing with the formula, the conventions . . .

JB: I was, I had great fun, although it was slightly disappointing that it all had to be written before the series began to run. I had the wonderful notion of myself on a Friday evening sitting at the desk thinking, 'These people want 15,000 words by tomorrow morning . . .' (laughs). And then, I'd never written anything as Benjamin Black that wasn't set in the 1950s. It was easier, but . . . The Quirke novels are much more fun, trying to trawl through my memory. I mean, I was about eight, nine, ten at the time that the Quirke novels are set. So, I'm dredging up bits of my past. For weeks I'll be trying to remember something. For example, in those days cars didn't have indicator lights, they had little yellow-orange arms that went out to the side. I spent *weeks* trying to remember what they were called. And then my pal Harry Crosbie said, 'They were trafficators, don't you remember trafficators?' Yes! Trafficators . . .

(laughs). So I have a lot of fun, not quite researching but just digging through my own memories and so forth.

Also, I have a great interest in the human backdrop to the 1950s. It's a curious period that nobody deals with very much, but I think it's a fascinating period. I mean, the 1950s is why we're here. You can trace the Celtic Tiger and all its madness right back to those times of deprivation, when the whole country was just waiting for a party. Even people who didn't live through it lived with the aftermath of the '50s, the post-war depression . . . But when I was doing *The Lemur*, it was set in the present day, in New York, which I thought I knew until I started trying to write about it. And then you realise you know nothing . . . But no, I had a lot of fun doing *The Lemur*, although I don't know that I would do it again. I think that Benjamin Black is more comfortable with the past. In fact, when I think of Benjamin Black and Quirke, I often mix them up in my head . . .

DB: The form of the crime novel – are the parameters too rigid because of readers' expectations? Does that reflect the public's reaction to crime itself?

JB: I don't think so. Certainly Benjamin Black's kind of crime novel is a kind of fairytale. Even though I don't have an ambition to write about a detective who knows everything and follows up clues . . . I mean, poor Quirke is a bit of an idiot, like the rest of us, stumbling around missing the point most of the time. But because everything is going to be explained at the end, it can't really be life-like. I think that's the essential thing about it. In life, nothing is explained. Or if it is, it's usually wrong or mistaken or mendacious . . . And you do have to stay within certain conventions. There has to be a plot. There has to be strong characters. There has to be – Hitchcock used to call it a McGuffin – a disappeared person, or some hook to begin with. So one is certainly working within the conventions. But that's very interesting, because writing as John Banville brings with it its own conventions as well. The point about novels is that they have a beginning, middle and end, even *Finnegans Wake* has a beginning, middle and end, even though Joyce tried not to have .

. . but there is. And we don't get that in life. We can't remember our birth, we don't experience our death, all we have is this mess in the middle. So it's the case that the novel, and certainly the crime novel, is a kind of fairytale. But that doesn't mean that it's not true. You know, it may not be factual but it can still be true. I think that's the case with all our literary output.

DB: When you say fairytale, do you specifically mean the kind of medieval parable of Charles Perrault, for example? Don't go into the woods because you don't know who's hiding out in there . . .

JB: Well, they are fantasies. They're fantasies about how life can be solved. There is a crime, there is a criminal, who generally has to be the most unlikely person you'd suspect of a crime . . . Again, these are the conventions we work inside, and that I enjoy working inside. Now, my brother [Vincent Banville], who has been writing and reading crime fiction most of his life, will say to me, 'Oh, I can spot the crook straight away.' But I'm not terribly interested in, y'know, the kind of Agatha Christie story where there's eleven people there and they all have a motive for murder. That doesn't interest me at all. But there does have to be some suspense, and some reason for the reader to keep going that's more than just the interesting characters and the dialogue. There must be a need to get to the end and find out what happened. And that's a kind of childish desire, but then there's a kind of childish desire in reading that kind of book (laughs). At least, that's how Benjamin feels anyway.

DB: The strong central character is vital, though. If you take out a fascinating central character, then it's just like reading a game of Cluedo . . .

JB: Well, I used to devour Agatha Christie's books when I was a kid, but I never found them believable for a moment. And Sherlock Holmes is another timeless character, but he's not human. He's a very clever man, but again, he's not very believable. I much prefer to write about characters who could actually exist. I mean, there could be a Quirke, there could be a Phoebe, there could be a Silver Swan . . . So it's a desire to work within a convention, to obey the rules of the convention but not be tied down by the rules of the convention.

DB: What was it, if it was one thing, that your John Banville novels didn't give you that you found in Quirke?

JB: (long pause) I don't like writing John Banville novels, I hate them. I mean, I think they're better than anybody else's (smiles) but they're not good enough for me. I don't have that feeling with Benjamin Black. I quite admire the Benjamin Black books. As I began by saying, they seem to me decent craftwork. And that's a pleasure that I don't get from the John Banville novels.

DB: I've read that you cringe when you walk by a bookshop or a library, knowing the Banville novels are in there on the shelves, imperfect . . .

JB: 'Yes, but that's a kind of sickness, you know? Perfectionism is a flaw in my mental make-up, but it's there, and there's nothing I can do about it. It makes me try very hard indeed, and hence it will take four or five years to do a John Banville book. You see, what I started doing with Benjamin Black, I went to stay with a friend of mine in Wicklow, I had a room there, and I sat down one Monday morning and thought, 'I don't know if I can do this.' And when I stood up again I'd written almost two thousand words. It was unbelievable. I assumed at the time it was because I had the TV script as a framework, as a starting-point, so I was quite worried again when I started *The Silver Swan*, but that rolled along quite well. I just found I was writing quite fluidly, quite fast.

The one difficulty I find is that it's quite difficult to do humour in crime writing. I don't know why. Elmore Leonard does it quite well, but that's more wit than humour. For some reason, the conventions of crime fiction don't allow for humour. I keep brooding on that, but I can't figure out why it is. But again, you have to work within cliché to a certain extent. The hero of the crime story is always the kind of Al Pacino character, with the divorced wife, with a kid who loves him but hasn't forgiven him for leaving his mom . . . y'know, there all these conventions. Again, you have to work within those. Like poor Quirke (laughs), with his maximum troubles. But I liked the notion of making him a flawed sinner, like everybody else. I suppose that's one of the things that drives him, because the pervading effect of the 1950s was guilt. We were all guilty. We didn't quite know why, but we all felt deeply guilty, because the church had instilled guilt into us from an early stage. And that's a very useful thing for a character to have, it's a very strong motive . . . It's very useful when it comes to Quirke, in *Christine Falls* especially he's soaked in guilt. Everybody is. They all think they're going to hell (laughs).

DB: Which, to be fair, was a very real fear at the time.
JB: Oh yes, it was. It was indeed. Of course, things are different now, there isn't the same sense of guilt as when I grew up in the Wexford of the 1950s. It was quite something.

DB: To go back to a question I touched on earlier. You say you write from the heart as Banville—
JB: Not from the heart. From the solar plexus.

DB: Okay, but the difference between Black and Banville . . . Is crime writing less of an art than literary fiction? And can it be art at all?
JB: I think Simenon made real works of art in half-a-dozen of those romans durs. Those books are as good as anything by Camus or anybody else. And real existentialism, written by a man who was himself very dark, very troubled. I do think they are works of art. Can I do it as art? I don't know. A friend of mine says that I became Benjamin Black for the same reason as Beckett wrote in French. Beckett said, *Pour écrire sans style*, 'To write without style'. And that may well be the case, because the Benjamin Black books are writing degree zero, there are no linguistic pyrotechnics, just the straightforward narrative. Which, as I say, is what I enjoy.

DB: I think you're being disingenuous there . . .
JB: 'Well, in a way it's not for me to say. I'm the last person who should say, because the only person in the world who can't read my novels is me. Everyone else can read them; I can't. Even when I'm writing them I'm not reading them, because, y'know, I carry all the baggage of producing them. So I can't judge.

DB: When John Gray at the *New York Review of Books* sent you the Simenon novels – did he think you'd respond to the Simenon novels given the crime narratives of *The Untouchable*, say, or *The Book of Evidence*?

JB: He may have, yes, although I don't think he was thinking about my work. I think he was just putting me in the way of a very good writer. But that may have been in his mind . . . Certainly, yes, *The Untouchable*, and especially *The Book of Evidence*, are crime books. They have higher ambitions, I suppose, but they are essentially books about people who have committed crimes.

DB: Can you see yourself repeating the point of view of *The Book of Evidence*, say, and writing from a killer's perspective?

JB: No, I don't think I'd do that again. I think I did everything I had to do in that story. Although, if I thought there was something more to be done, I would do it. But I thought that Freddie Montgomery was enough (laughs) for three books. Three books are enough for any one criminal.

DB: When it was first announced that John Banville was turning his hand to crime writing there was a certain amount of resentment, that it was simply John Banville trying to earn an easy buck, and doing so under a pseudonym. But surely all writers adopt a persona to write?

JB: Oh yes, of course. In fact, I have to give a talk in Milan in June, and the theme they have for it is 'The Invisible'. And what I'm going to write about is precisely that. About how the person who does the writing is not the person who has his breakfast beforehand, or has a glass of wine with his tea. When I'm doing readings, or signings, I can see the disappointment in people's faces – and I think all writers feel this – that I'm not the person they expected. And I always say to them, or I always mean to say to them, 'The person who wrote that book is not here. The person who wrote that book ceased to exist when he stood up from the desk. I know no more about him than you do. The only evidence of him in existence is this document in your hand.' So, being Benjamin Black was just another extension of that.

DB: Is it possible to twist that even further, and say that the Benjamin Black who wrote *The Silver Swan* was not necessarily the Benjamin Black who wrote *The Lemur*, or *A Death in Summer*?

JB: No, he wasn't . . . I'm actually not that confident about the Benjamin Black who wrote *The Lemur*. I thought that he was straining, mostly because of being uncertain of the milieu. He was having to do things that were really not to do with the book itself, or to do with the serialisation, because the *New York Times* is obsessive about facts. The fact-checkers would ring up and say, 'You said in this that in the old days, if you wanted to go to Trinity College, you had to get permission from the archbishop. We can find no record of this. You actually had to get permission from your local bishop.' And you're thinking, how on earth did they find out about that? And why they want these things to be so factual . . . I kept saying to them, 'Look, this is fiction. This is not a news report.' And then, the conventions were extraordinary. You could say that someone was black, but having said that, you couldn't at his or her next appearance comment on the fact that they were black. You could only do it once. And I suppose when you think about it, y'know, if it was a white character, you wouldn't say, the second time they turned up, 'The white guy walked into the room . . .' But the point I was making was that John Glass [protagonist in *The Lemur*] was an Irishman, and he grew up in a country where there were very few black people, at least there weren't when he was growing up. So he would be fascinated by this. I mean, I don't resent that they had their rules, and if you agree to do something, you have to abide by the rules . . .

DB: The great crime writers tend to de-glamourise the places in which their novels are set – Raymond Chandler's Los Angeles being the classic example. But there's very little that's glamorous about 1950's Ireland . . .

JB: (laughs) Well, it can only be glamourised . . . No, that's true. One of the things that I decided when I started out writing as Benjamin Black was that I wouldn't write in clichés. But I also decided, and most importantly, that I would not give the characters the benefit of my hindsight. They would be absolutely people of their time, as we are people of our time. We can't know what the world will be like in forty years' time, or how people will think. And to be realistic, and to be convincing, and honest, to be true to the book I was writing, I had to have the characters accept what was happening in the time they were living in. So there's no commentary on how guilty they were, say, because that's not how people think at all.

People thought in the 1950s that, 'this is the way the world should be. There are things we don't like about it, but essentially, this is how the world is.' That was an important decision I made. So I can't glamourise or de-glamourise that world; it simply is that world as we know it. Now, having said that, a friend of mine, Harry Crosbie, made a wonderful suggestion. He said, 'Why don't you give him a car? You could give him an Alvis.' You wouldn't know what an Alvis is, but they were *serious* cars. The best of English craftsmanship. So I said, 'That's a wonderful idea.' So I had Quirke in St John of God's drying out [in *The Silver Swan*], and Phoebe comes in, and either Phoebe says to him or he says it to her, 'We're going to go to Crawford's Garage out in Earlsfort Terrace and buy an Alvis.' And I suppose, Quirke is quite a wealthy man, he would be very well paid, so he can afford to buy a fancy car. So that's quite glamorous. But of course, Phoebe had to teach him to drive (laughs).

DB: Given the backlash that occurred when it was announced John Banville would be writing crime fiction, were you surprised by the Edgar nomination for *Christine Falls*?

JB: 'Well, one of the problems was that I didn't know what the Edgar was (laughs). Editors came on the phone cheering, but I didn't know what it was. I was certainly pleased, and I was sorry I didn't win it, I would have really liked to win a prize for the Benjamin Black material . . . Actually, my worst experience, in terms of the backlash thing, happened when I was in Mantua last year, or the year before, at a literary festival. There was a panel discussion on crime writing, with Dennis Lehane, George Pelecanos and Michael Connelly, which was going out on the radio, going out live. But the festival organisers had told me that I'd be coming on to do a very short interview, and then I'd leave. And I didn't know that these three guys were going to be on this panel, I thought I was just doing a very quick interview. And so my publisher came up and said, 'Great, we have to leave now.' And I said, well, I'd really like to stay, but they'd pre-booked me somewhere else. And that all came out as, y'know, I was too good for those guys, when in fact it was snobbery on behalf of my Italian publisher. Because, apparently, they say that in Italy that kind of crime writing is despised, and they didn't want to have me 'tainted' (laughs). Tainted by George Pelecanos!

DB: Why did it take so long for the genre of crime fiction to take off in Ireland?

JB: I think the more interesting question is why it did take off when it did. The North had been going for thirty years, there was lots of violence, we had drug gangs here . . . I think it's more that up to the early '90s, literature in this country was the higher stuff. We had all these Nobel Prize winners, everyone was writing in the grand tradition, everyone wanted to be a prize-winner. Then, with the sudden growth of popular culture in the early '90s . . . I always say that modern Ireland began in 1993, when Bishop Casey was outed. People who are interested in sport say no, it was the Italia 1990 World Cup, but certainly a whole new generation of people emerged who weren't interested in higher art, weren't interested in these stylists, were far more interested in society, in manners, in the ways in which we actually live. And I think that that's where the crime novel came from. I think there was a kind of commitment to investigating a new Ireland, and Roddy Doyle was very instrumental in that.

Roddy was the first Irish writer really to write about a whole class of people who had been ignored before this. I think he opened the way for much of the new kind of literature, which wasn't self-obsessed, which wasn't concentrating on language and style, which was really telling stories and was really engaged with society. Engaged with character, engaged with modern pressures, and that's where the crime novel comes from. Even though he didn't write crime books, he loosened things up. He freed things, so people could say, 'Hey, let's do something that the old guys haven't done.' I'd imagine that's one of the reasons why there was resentment towards me, if there was resentment. It was as if, y'know, 'You're supposed to be one of *them*.' As if I was an old guy putting on leather gear and going out to nightclubs and so on . . . That wasn't how I saw it, but I can imagine how other people could have seen it that way.

DB: Is Benjamin Black an alternate ego, a doppelganger, or just another facet to John Banville?

JB: I really don't know. I don't know yet . . . He's still relatively young. I'm not trying to evade the question, I just don't know how to answer it. As I've said before, he works so differently to the way John Banville works, but then John Banville the writer works quite differently to John Banville who's not writing. You see, there used to be just two of us in the room, now there are three of us. Me and these other two . . . It's funny, but RTÉ did a documentary last year, and they had this wonderfully clever conceit – I'm a child when it comes to technology – where they had me sitting at my desk writing, but they also had me walking around the room at the same time. And four or five people actually said to me, 'You know that bit where you're sitting at the desk? Who's the other guy dressed the same as you, walking around?' (laughs) I just said, 'I don't know.' But then, I'm not sure who the guy sitting at the desk was, either. I'm really not certain about most of the things I do.

You asked me earlier, did the experiment work, and I said, 'I don't know.' I suppose it's like the French Revolution, it's too early to say. I may end up making a fool of myself. On the other hand, I have this notion that there'll be a dictionary of Irish writers published in 2050 (laughs), and under 'Banville, John' it'll say, 'See Black, Benjamin'.

*

John Banville was born in Wexford, Ireland, in 1945. He worked in journalism for many years, and still reviews extensively. His novels include *The Book of Evidence*, *The Sea* and *The Infinities*. Under the pen-name Benjamin Black he writes crime novels, the latest of which is *A Death in Summer*. John Banville won the Man Booker Prize for his novel *The Sea* (2005).

The Craftsman

by Stuart Neville

Albert Ryan watched his long fingers in the mirror as he buttoned his shirt collar. They showed no signs of bending to age, moving with the same deft grace they always had. Last winter, an ache had settled in the ring and little finger of his left hand. It had neither worsened nor improved since then; it lingered like a dinner guest oblivious to the hour.

He hitched up his tie knot, Double Windsor, smoothed the collar's wings, and ran his hands down his breast. The tie's silk whispered on his fingers. A Taoiseach had given it to him. He couldn't remember which. Either Haughey or Fitzgerald, they swapped office like a game of musical chairs back in the Eighties. Albert only remembered the presentation box – Italian, the politician had said – and Celia's eyes when he showed it to her. She had kissed him like he was the only man in the world. It had been a Saturday night. They made love. She clawed the back of his neck and bit his chest. She insisted he wear it to Mass the next morning.

Now he admired it in the dressing table mirror. It was a fine thing, black with navy and silver detail. A craftsman's work if ever he'd seen it. Twenty-odd years old and it looked like it had been woven yesterday.

Celia's voice drifted from the grand old bed like paper on a breeze. 'Bertie?'

He stood, smoothed his Gieves & Hawkes shirt over his stomach, still flat and hard after all these years. His hands travelled to the small of his back, made sure the holster was secure. 'Yes, sweetheart?'

'Why are you all dressed up?' she asked.

Albert watched her in the mirror. She smiled in the glass. Today was a good day, all things considered. Yesterday had been bad. She had soiled herself, and they had both wept as he cleaned her. But this afternoon she could see him, know him, talk to him. He hoped she didn't remember the day before.

'I'm heading out for a wee while,' he said.

'Into town?' she asked.

'No, love,' he said. 'Into Dublin.'

'Oh? What for?'

He turned from the mirror. Her head tilted on the pillow, and her eyes glittered like a girl's. He so wanted to press that pillow into her face. Spare her from the bad weeks and months ahead. She frowned, seeing his heart like she always did.

'Such a saggy face,' she said, pouting.

He had been jowly since his early thirties, despite his athletic build. He looked like a forlorn bloodhound by the time he met her at a party in Malahide, she a decade younger than him at twenty-six. Still now, he had no idea how he'd won her, only that she had stroked his cheek and called him 'saggy face'.

'Go back to sleep,' he said. He approached the bed. Portraits of Christ and the Virgin hung over it; smaller images of her favoured saints stood on the bedside locker; her Rosary lay pooled on the blankets. Celia had gathered God close to her since the diagnosis. Sometimes she cried out for forgiveness in her sleep.

He touched his fingertips to her lips. She dutifully pursed them, but there was no moisture, no warmth. Only the gesture, and that was enough.

In a way, she was still as beautiful as that day in Malahide when she'd made him blush by letting her hip brush his groin as she slipped past. There had only ever been Celia. She was the all and everything he knew about women. Still as beautiful, yes, but now cut from wax, a hollow mannequin modelled on the woman who had claimed him wholly thirty years ago.

'What are you going into Dublin for?' she asked. She stretched under the bedclothes, a long and languorous wave along her body, as if this were any lazy day. Only the crease on her forehead betrayed the pain it caused her.

'To see a man about a dog,' he said, feeling a small but rapturous peal of mischief in the teasing.

She smiled, showing her missing teeth. 'My daddy used to say that. When he was keeping secrets. What secrets are you keeping, Albert Ryan?'

He sat on the edge of the mattress, leaned down, and kissed her forehead. Her skin felt so thin and dry he imagined his lips pressed against her bare skull. Still, he kept his mouth there, letting his fingers tangle in her hair.

'No secrets from you, sweetheart,' he said. 'Never have, never will.'

And wasn't that his great mistake?

She knew. All along, she knew what he did. He trusted her because she loved him, and he loved her. He would never have believed a vulgar sickness could render love and trust meaningless.

'The doctor,' he said. 'I'm going to see him.'

'Why?' Her head turned so that the loose skin on her cheek wrinkled against the pillow.

'To kill him,' he said.

'But why?'

Such sadness in her eyes. He turned away. 'You said things.'

'What things?' she asked.

'About what I do – what I did – for a living,' he said.

'I didn't,' she said. 'Did I?'

'You did, sweetheart.' He placed his fingers against her cheek. He felt her remaining teeth through the thin curtain of flesh.

'I didn't mean to,' she said.

He smiled down at her. 'I know.'

'You mustn't,' she said, her mouth pinched with regret. 'He's good.'

'I must.' Albert stood. 'Sleep now. I'll be home soon.'

*

He walked the ten minutes to the DART station in Dun Laoghaire, overlooking the bay. The pistol nestled snug in the hollow at the small of his back.

It was an excellent weapon, small, designed for concealment, and handmade to order by an Austrian gunsmith. A first-rate artisan, now dead some ten years, and the work hadn't been cheap. The pistol's chamber held one .22 calibre round. Albert had loaded it with a hollow-point. The same Austrian had made the round, also an exquisite thing. The bullet was soft lead, cast in a fluted jacket that would allow it to split into pieces on penetration of the subject, each fragment taking its own trajectory through flesh and organs. The pistol had a low velocity, so close range was preferable. A clear shot to the temple would be best.

When Albert boarded the train, a kind young fellow vacated a seat for him. He considered protesting – even at sixty-six he was probably fitter than this youngster – but it would serve his purpose better to play the weak old man. He sat down and thanked the boy.

The weapon did not rub or bulge. A soft buckskin holster held it secure. A fine craftsman from Walsall, near Birmingham, had made it. The best leatherwork in the world came from Walsall, as grey and oppressive a town as Albert had ever seen. He remembered collecting it from the workshop, and the warm velvet scent of the place. The holster seemed so insignificant amongst the saddles and bridles, but the craftsman had dedicated as much care to this small piece as he had the grandest items. It was beautifully stitched, and even bore a delicate brand in a Celtic pattern. Age had given it a deep red lustre, and he always admired it for a moment or two before inserting the pistol and sliding it down behind his waistband, affixing the loop to hold it in place.

Albert Ryan admired nothing more than craftsmanship, for he too was a craftsman. Skill and care in one's work gave a glimpse of the divine to anyone with the eyes to see it. He had owned many beautiful things in his life. The Aston Martin V8 had been the most treasured among them. He remembered Celia giggling and gripping his arm as he pushed it hard along a coast road in Antrim, across the border in the North, hedgerows whipping by on one side, the North Atlantic disappearing to infinity on the other. She had not asked questions when he left their hotel alone that night, or when he returned two hours later. And she did not protest when he forbade her to listen to the news the following morning. For all her girlishness, which she never lost as the years burnt away, Celia had flint at her centre. He loved her for it.

He caught himself smiling and brought his hand to his mouth. A young woman smiled back at him from the seat opposite. He considered ignoring her, but for some reason he said, 'Good memories.'

Her smile broadened for a moment, lighting sparks in his stomach, before she returned her eyes to her paperback.

Fool, he thought. This was why no one hired him any more. He had softened in his later years. That was why the money had dried up and he had to sell the damn car. That was why he had to sell their home with the sea view, the home Celia loved more than anything, and take a miserable flat that overlooked nothing but other anonymous apartment blocks. Their wonderful things never seemed at home in the new place, so selling them off didn't matter so much. Hardly anything mattered after Celia started bleeding from unspeakable places.

He disembarked at the Grand Canal Dock station and walked the short distance to the bus stop. The traffic would be slow to the clinic in Rathgar, but he didn't mind. Time had taken on a strange elasticity these past few years, even more so since Celia fell ill. A few minutes here or there wouldn't matter.

Albert was gambling on the slender doctor, a handsome man wearing well in his young middle age, to leave the clinic at a normal hour. Ideally, he would study a subject for days, maybe weeks, before carrying out an action, but the matter was urgent.

He considered it as he climbed aboard the bus and took a seat. The doctor would always nod and smile as Celia rambled, as she was prone to do these days. Sometimes she would recount her time in London, working as a secretary in the Irish embassy, or perhaps Paris. She had only been stationed there a few months, but she still found delight in recalling her walks around Montmartre.

On occasion, her memories were more delicate. The visiting nurses blushed as she boasted of her husband's prowess as a lover. 'Oh, those hands,' she told them. 'And he was never selfish. He always put my pleasure before his own. A wonderful thing in a man, that, you'll be lucky to find the same.'

Albert had smiled weakly as the nurses tried not to snigger.

But this morning had been unfortunate. She had been speaking quite coherently about the importance of discretion when working at a consulate, the doctor giving her his most patronising smile as he examined her, his skilled fingers dancing across her body.

'Of course,' she had continued, 'discretion has been my greatest talent. All these years, and no one ever suspected anything of him. To think those hands, those giving hands, could have done such things. But he always kept them clean. I never once saw blood on them. Not a drop. Even that time we had to go away. Where was it, Bertie? Lebanon?'

And that had been enough to end the doctor's life, whether he understood the implication of her ramblings or not. Albert knew it only took one loose thread for everything to unravel. It may have seemed random nonsense from a dying woman, but if the doctor picked at it, if he thought about it at night as he waited for sleep, he might just get a hold of that thread and start pulling.

And that could not be. Albert knew the procedure. At the slightest risk of exposure, they would close him down. That's what they called it. Closure, as if he were a shop going out of business. One day, one evening, one morning, he would simply be gone. And then who would take care of Celia? They would send her to some desperate grey place where no one cared about their work. She would die there, alone and frightened, in pain, wondering why her Bertie did not come for her.

No. Not while he had strength in his hands and iron in his chest.

'I love her too much to let her die like that.'

'Excuse me?' the plump woman next to him said.

He stared at her for endless seconds. Had he said that aloud? Good God, his careless mouth!

'I'm sorry,' he said, bowing his head respectfully. 'I was daydreaming.'

She gave him a thin smile and turned her attention to the Dublin suburbs slipping by the window.

He reached beneath his overcoat and pinched the flesh below his ribs, hard. He had to focus, sharpen his mind. Killing must not be a reckless venture. He had learned that early on, and taught it to others. Care and skill were second to only one thing: the will to do what other men can't. But will without craft is empty bluster. Many a man forgot that to his cost.

Thank Christ, Albert's stop approached. The fat woman might take exception to the sweating old fool beside her, she might remember him when she saw the news that night, and all would be lost.

Albert hoisted himself from the seat and made his way to the front of the bus. His feet shifted for balance as it slowed and stopped. He thanked the driver and stepped down. The woman did not watch him from the window as the bus pulled away, leaving him in tree shade on this pleasant avenue.

The clinic stood opposite, an old Victorian house converted to provide the best medical care to those who could afford it. It was in that building that a great tube had swallowed Celia while she trembled. This practice had eaten the last of their savings. The doctor's visit this morning had cost a fortnight's rent on their miserable flat. It had cost the doctor much more.

Albert entered the small park opposite the clinic, found a bench with a reasonable view of the building, sat down, and waited.

*

'Mr Ryan, are you all right?'

He seized the wrist, claimed the assailant's balance. Light and oxygen screamed into his brain, dragged him from sleep, battering his heart with adrenalin.

Dear God, the doctor, staring down at him.

Asleep.

Albert sucked air in hard through his nose, letting its coldness blast away the murk behind his eyes.

He had fallen asleep.

How long? The sun had moved below the rooftops, no longer warming his face. An hour? Maybe more. He released the doctor's wrist.

Dr Moran swayed and regained his balance. He blinked down at Albert, his mouth open.

'I'm sorry,' Albert said, feigning weakness and confusion. 'You startled me.'

'That's okay,' Dr Moran said. 'I didn't mean to scare you. I was just about to get into my car when I saw you sitting here. Are you all right? Do you need help?'

He went to put his hand back on Albert's shoulder, but seemed to think better of it.

'I'm fine,' Albert said.

'And Mrs Ryan? Any change?'

'No,' he said. 'She's the same.'

'So what are you doing here?' The doctor sat down beside Albert. 'Did you want to see me?'

Albert pulled back his sleeve, saw his bare wrist. He'd forgotten his watch. 'What time is it?' he asked.

'Just gone six,' Dr Moran said.

'Stupid old man,' Albert said.

'What's wrong, Mr Ryan? Why did you come here?'

Albert sighed, leaned forward, and reached inside his overcoat with his right hand. The early evening air chilled his midriff as he pulled the pistol from the holster. It was small enough for his left hand to conceal it from the doctor's view.

'Mr Ryan?'

He gave the doctor a soft smile. 'My wife rambles. I suppose it's those patches for the pain. What are they, morphine?'

'Fentanyl,' Dr Moran said. 'Stronger than morphine. I wouldn't prescribe them if they weren't necessary. She's comfortable, isn't she?'

'Oh, yes.' Albert nodded. 'But it does leave her a little confused. And then she talks. Old memories and such. Sometimes they aren't her own. She can't seem to keep them straight, keep her memories and her fantasies apart.'

'It's a common side-effect.' The doctor put his hand on Albert's shoulder. 'Is that what's bothering you?'

'In a way,' Albert said. 'Tell me, do you save many? The people you treat. How many do you save?'

'Some,' the doctor said. 'Not enough.'

'You're a good doctor,' Albert said. 'You're a craftsman, like me. Well, like I used to be.'

'What did you do before you retired?' the doctor asked, leaning back in the seat. 'I wondered what Mrs Ryan meant by the blood on your hands. I couldn't decide if you were vet or a butcher.'

A dry laugh rose up from Albert's belly. 'Neither,' he said.

'Then what? I wondered if you'd been in medicine, a surgeon maybe, but I don't think so. You'd know about Fentanyl, for one thing.'

Albert closed his eyes, committed himself, and opened them again. 'You're a good man. We have much to thank you for, Celia and I. It makes me so sad to do this.'

'Do what?'

Albert brought the small pistol up to the doctor's temple. 'This,' he said.

It sounded like a snare drum. Birds scattered.

*

The bed was empty save for a pale yellow stain.

'Celia?' Albert called from the doorway.

He stepped inside. The dressing table drawers stood open, their contents spilling over the edges. Powder and perfume coated the surface beneath the mirror. Panic flared in Albert's breast, a wild fluttering thing. He willed it to be calm.

'Celia?' he called again.

'In here, Bertie.'

Her voice came from the en suite bathroom. It was stronger than he'd last heard it, but metallic, like a rusted blade. Albert passed the bed, registered the smell of stale urine, just another odour of the unwell. Steam warmed his face as he looked in.

Celia leaned against the basin, one hand gripping its edge, a stick figure in her scarlet evening gown. Its straps clung to the bones beneath her tracing-paper skin. He'd forgotten how tall she was.

She applied lipstick, running the stub across her mouth, and dropped it to clatter in the basin. She pinched a tissue between her lips, leaving a deep red kiss on the white paper. The tissue fell from her fingers and wafted to the tiled floor. It soaked up a brighter red from the small puddle it settled in.

'Sweetheart, you're bleeding,' Albert said.

'Am I?' She looked down. 'Oh,' she said.

'Where from?' he asked.

'I don't know,' she said, turning her attention back to the mirror. 'It doesn't matter.'

Albert noticed the pink blotching on her upper arm. 'Where's your patch?' he asked.

'I took it off when you left,' she said.

'But the pain,' he said.

She eyed him over her naked shoulder. 'It doesn't matter,' she said. 'How do I look?'

'Beautiful,' Albert said.

Celia smiled. Lipstick stained her remaining teeth. Love burned in him like an African sun. 'Beautiful,' he said again. 'What are you doing?'

She turned back to her reflection. 'Getting ready,' she said.

'What for?'

'You killed that nice doctor,' she said. It wasn't a question.

'Yes,' he said.

'I'm a sick woman, and I cost that young man his life. For nothing. Just some words.' Her knees buckled, and she grabbed the basin's edge. She straightened. 'I will die,' she said.

'Darling, don't.' He took a step towards her, slipped on her blood, steadied himself with a strong hand against the wall.

'I will die and nothing will stop it,' she said. 'I will only get worse. I will ramble more and more. What about the nurses? What about the cleaner? What about dear Finula from downstairs? When she reads to me, what if I say something to her? Will you kill her too?'

'Of course,' he said.

'Why?' Celia asked. 'What for? What good could it do?'

'To protect you,' he said. He moved closer. 'I only had one talent in life.

God help me if I can't use it to protect you.'

He went to put his hands on her shoulders, but she pushed the gown's straps aside, let the dress fall to her waist.

'Look,' she said.

'Darling, don't,' he said.

'Look.' Her reflection stared hard at him. 'Look at me.'

Albert looked. He studied the greys and purples of her skin, the places where his hands had once found ripe flesh, the sad remains of the breasts that had caused him to gasp when she first revealed them to him three decades ago.

'Don't,' he said.

'You're protecting a skeleton,' she said. A tear escaped her. 'I'm dead and rotting. I should be in the ground already, not lingering here.'

Albert put his hands on her waist. Her hipbones felt like shards of porcelain beneath the fabric of her dress. He kissed her neck and raised the dress back up, slipping the straps over her brittle shoulders.

'Don't,' he said.

Celia watched the reflections of his hands. 'Oh Bertie, the things you've done with those,' she said. 'We'll go to Hell, you know.'

He slipped his arms around her, his nose and mouth pressed to the nape of her neck. He smelt her sweetness through the decay, still there, underlying the rot.

'Don't,' he said.

'I'll go to Hell,' she said. 'I'm damned for knowing what you've done. I will burn for ever and nothing can save me. Not even you.'

His tears slicked her loose skin. 'Don't,' he said.

'But did God give you that talent?' she asked. 'I used to wonder about that. It used to keep me awake at night. If God gave you that talent, that craft, how can he damn you for using it? I used to tell myself the people you killed must have deserved it. They had to, or you wouldn't have done it. They were criminals. They were murderers and thieves, and they deserved to die, so you used the talent God gave you. And so we wouldn't go to Hell.'

Albert raised his eyes from her neck, met hers in the mirror. 'Come back to bed, love.'

'No.' She smiled and tilted her head. 'Not now that I'm all gussied up.'

She winced at the pain it caused in her neck, and Albert gripped her shoulders to steady her.

'Your God-given talent,' she said. 'That was how I lived with it. But now you've done something awful to that poor doctor just because my mouth ran away with me. He was good. He didn't deserve to die, but you used your talent on him. So now I know I was wrong all those years. It doesn't matter where your talent came from. We're damned, and that's all there is.'

'Don't talk this way,' Albert said. 'Please.'

'I won't have anyone else die because of my blathering.' She stared hard at him, her eyes clearer than they'd been for a year. 'Do you hear me, Bertie? Not a single person. So I have one thing to ask of you.'

'What?'

She reached up to lace her fingers with his. 'Such beautiful hands; such a terrible craft.'

She turned in his arms, using his thick body for support. Her cheek met his. She ran her fingers along his jowls. 'Such a saggy face,' she said.

'What do you want?' he asked.

Celia pressed her lips to his. He tasted her lipstick and remembered every kiss they'd shared, from every darkened corner to every sun-washed beach. Her lips moved across his face, gathering the tears from his cheeks as if they were salted jewels.

'Such a saggy face,' she said. She smiled and rested her forehead against his.

'What do you want?' he asked.

She kissed him again, hard and final.

'You know,' she said.

He shook his head. 'I won't,' he said.

She reached for his hands, brought them to her throat. 'You will, Bertie,' she said.

Her life pulsed against his thumbs.

'No,' he said.

'Yes,' she said. 'It's your talent. I trust you to do it well.'

Warmth lurked in the hollows beneath her chin.

'I can't,' he said.

'Yes you can,' she said. 'You're a craftsman. You can do—'

She went light and loose as a bag of twigs.

He kissed her once. 'I'll see you there,' he said.

*

Stuart Neville's debut novel, *The Twelve*, aka *The Ghosts of Belfast*, was the winner of the *Los Angeles Times* Mystery/Thriller of the Year Award in 2010. Its sequel, *Collusion*, was published in 2010. Stuart lives in Northern Ireland.

Part III:

Kiss Tomorrow Goodbye

Brutal, Harrowing and Devastating

by Gene Kerrigan

There was silence after the shot. Seconds passed, then the screams began, distant and incoherent. The sound of a car, screeching away from a standing start. There was a lot of joyriding in the neighbourhood around that time, so the sound of squealing car wheels wasn't a novelty. Some nights the kids would steal a car and drive around in circles until a busybody called the police. When a squad car showed up the kids waited patiently, revving the engine, lingering until the cops got close. Then, when they might have left it a little late, they'd hit the metal and the chase was on.

They almost always won.

They'd lose the cops and head back towards the neighbourhood, dumping the car when they became bored with the chase.

One night the chase ended outside my house and the flames from the abandoned car lit up the front bedroom until the fire brigade arrived to sweep up. It must have been exciting for the kids, to stand some distance away and watch the drama they had created, to hear the whoosh as the car took light and to watch the fire brigade at work. Besides, some kids argued in righteous tones, by totalling the car you were doing right by the car owner. After an hour or two of speeding around the city, maybe after a few bumps and sideswipes, the stolen car was more than a bit shabby. The owner could claim compensation for the damage, but the car would never be the same. Made more sense to total it, let the owner claim the full whack. And it was more fun that way.

That night, squealing tyres after the sound of a shot suggested something more than a routine joyride.

It must have been about one in the morning. Back then (it was the mid-1980s), I did a lot of writing in the small hours. I left the typewriter, hurried to the front door.

There was a playground across from the house where I lived. During the day the smaller kids scrambled up and down the monkey puzzle, played on swings and the roundabout or played football or tennis on the spaces marked out on the taracadam. In the far corner of the playground was a sandpit where the younger kids frolicked.

At night, the older kids gathered in the playground and drank Scrumpy Jack. Sometimes they lit bonfires in the sandpit and stood around, keeping warm, beer and cider in hand.

That night, I could see figures running back and forth behind the playground railings.

In the distance, from a road that led away from the playground, the sound of the car with the squealing tyres. Definitely not a chase – it was a getaway. Then there was a smacking sound. I think it was a parked car being sideswiped as the getaway driver misjudged his steering on the narrow, curving road.

I thought I made out what a young woman was screaming, but it seemed outrageously unreal.

'They shot him! They shot Robert!'

She screamed the same thing again, and this time there was no doubt.

His name wasn't Robert, but the rest is as it happened.

I rang 999 and told the operator there was a shooting, that someone was hurt. Then I crossed to the playground, climbed through a gap where a railing had been removed. There were several young people there, male and female. The girls were crying, the boys were standing around, faces tight. There was a young man lying face down on the tarmacadam.

I didn't see any blood. There was no horror or fear on the faces of the victim's friends – just a stricken emptiness. They looked down at the young man and they looked away.

The police had another young man in custody by the time of the funeral.

When the funeral Mass ended, seven or eight of Robert's friends left the church. The usual ceremony continued, the family following the coffin from the church, faces stiff as they struggled to keep utter despair at bay – accepting commiseration from friends and neighbours as the coffin was loaded into the hearse. As was the tradition, the hearse would drive slowly to the deceased's home street and stop for a moment outside his house, before the drive to the cemetery.

Robert's friends had left the church to fetch their horses.

At that time in Dublin a lot of working-class kids had developed an unusual urban hobby–horse riding. They bought the old nags at irregular horse markets around the city. They didn't have standard horse-keeping skills or facilities, and some horse lovers worried about the horses' treatment. Even a loving owner could damage a horse out of ignorance. The kids sometimes left their horses tethered in fields close to the estate, sometimes they kept them in the back garden. It was not unusual to see a young man lead his horse up the front path and around the side of the house, much as he might put his bicycle away.

As Robert's funeral procession prepared to move off, his friends returned on horseback and reined in off to one side. Their leader was guiding his own horse single-handed, his other hand leading Robert's horse by the reins. He nodded his respects to Robert's family and they nodded back. As the funeral procession set off, family and friends walked behind the hearse. Then, with a word from their leader, the horse riders wheeled in behind the other mourners and set off as formally as a squad of cavalry, the leader still holding the reins of Robert's rider-less horse. The moment was part of – and simultaneously apart from – the society in which it occurred. A desperate moment of dignity, and acknowledgment of personal identity, snatched from a dreadful and pointless tragedy.

The killing had something to do with an argument over, I think, a motorbike, perhaps some other trivial thing. The killer stormed away from the playground that night, went to someone's house and borrowed a shotgun, came back to the playground in a car. Got out, pointed the shotgun through the railings and fired. He was known to the victim's friends, so he was easily caught and convicted. My memory of it is that he was sentenced to about three years.

*

People commit murder for trivial reasons, some in anger or in desperation; some callously, with cruel or greedy intent. We live in cities where gangs kill to protect their market share of the businesses that service us with drugs, prostitution and cheap stolen goods. Drug gangs use the pubs and streets as battlegrounds, and bankers and financial hustlers steal more in a day than has been stolen by all the burglars in the history of the nation.

Crime fiction springs from such aspects of how we live, and at its best it will reflect and explore these things. At its worst, it will exploit them.

Some years ago, in a magazine specialising in the genre, the British novelist David Peace laid down some rather strict criteria for crime writers:

> 'Crime is brutal, harrowing and devastating for everyone involved, and crime fiction should be every bit as brutal, harrowing and devastating as the violence of the reality it seeks to document. Anything less at best sanitises crime and its effects, at worst trivialises it. Anything more exploits other people's misery as purely vicarious entertainment. It is a very fine line . . .
>
> I believe the crime writer, by their choice of genre, is obligated to document these times and their crimes, and the writer who chooses to ignore this responsibility is then simply exploiting, for his or her own financial or personal gratification, a genre that is itself nothing more than an entertainment industry constructed upon the sudden, violent deaths of other, innocent people and the unending suffering of their families'. (*Crime Time* No. 27, 2002)

I think Peace has a point. We are not fictionalising sport or politics, romance or show business. We are dealing in matters that have dreadful real-life equivalents in shredded lives and traumatised families – those of our neighbours. Where I think Peace may be over-strict is in treating crime fiction as a single genre.

Readers find it handy that books are separated into categories. 'I liked that one and I'd like something else in the same vein.' For publishers, genres are a useful marketing tool – their covers, titles and blurbs say, 'If you liked that you'll love this'. This can't be avoided, and there's no compelling reason why it should be.

One problem, though, is that bookshops, the media and critics treat crime fiction as an undifferentiated genre. It's all 'Crime Fiction', as though the author of *Midsomer Murders* might take a break and scribble an episode of *The Wire*.

Far from being a coherent genre, crime fiction over the years developed a seemingly infinite array of subgenres, most of these in turn sub-dividing into potentially lucrative product lines – the classic mystery, the genteel puzzle, the hardboiled thriller, the heist novel, the comic caper, the deadly serious caper, the historical mystery; the police procedural, the forensic procedural, the serial killer thriller, the psychological thriller, the courtroom drama, the revenge story, the chase novel, the ex-Special Forces guy helping a friend in trouble thriller; old-fashioned noir, neo noir, noir pastiche, the private detective, the lawyer detective, the amateur sleuth, the writer detective, the reporter detective, the priest detective, the obsessive-compulsive detective, the gay detective, the suspiciously overcompensating straight detective (Is that a gun, Mr Spillane, or are you just happy to be slapping women around?); the crime scene investigators, the pathologists, the cold case specialists, the missing person specialists, the profilers, the behavioural analysts; the boy detective, the pensioner detective, the detective who sits at home and cogitates while the laconic sidekick does the legwork, the blind detective, the detective in a wheelchair, the fat detective, the thin man, the angst-ridden detective, the alcoholic detective, the paranormal detective; the evil (but sophisticated) serial killer, the charming psycho, the complex thug, the ice-cold hit man, the morose hit man, the cheerful conman, the comic gangsters, the lone professional criminals – and the perennial Detective Inspector Plod, patiently hunting clues to not-too-dissimilar murders, through a dozen not-too-dissimilar novels, one after the bloody other.

And this is not to mention the slightly precious literary crime novel, usually featuring quantities of snow as a metaphor for something or other.

Traditionally, crime fiction divided into two camps. The longest-established is the classic mystery story. Typically, the gifted amateur sleuth (Sherlockian or Marple-ish) follows red herrings through twists and turns before solving the brain-teasing puzzle.

Famously, Raymond Chandler credited Dashiell Hammett with developing a more realistic, hardboiled crime fiction, in which Hammett 'took murder out of the Venetian vase and dropped it into the alley', and thereby 'gave murder back to the kind of people who do it for a reason, not just to provide a corpse'. He suggested that if writers of crime fiction wrote about the kind of murders that happen, 'they would also have to write about the authentic flavour of life as it is lived. And since they cannot do that, they pretend that what they do is what should be done'.

This differentiation between classic mystery and hardboiled was valid then and remains so – up to a point.

And it's true that the classic mystery was generally conservative, and the hardboiled crime novel often challenged the cosy consensus. The classic mystery – sometimes referred to as the 'cosy' – described the disruption of a genteel world, usually by a murder. A super-smart detective assembled a list of suspects, finally zeroing-in on the killer. The crime was solved, the disruption remedied and order restored.

The hardboiled school isn't so much about a mystery – though there may be one. The crime has disrupted society, as in the classic mystery. But unlike the 'cosy', the hardboiled novel sees this cracked, disrupted society as the reality – and the cosy consensus as a sham. The detective explores this reality, and is under no obligation to put things back together.

In the hardboiled novel there may well not be any detective, much less a super-sleuth. The police may play a subsidiary part – if any. The Blaxploitation movies of the 1970s sometimes ended with bodies lying all over the place, as the good guys and the bad guys fought it out. The cops arrived only as the credits rolled. Their role was to sweep up the corpses.

The cosy-versus-hardboiled duality survives, but the relationship is a lot more complex than it was in Chandler's day.

Chandler deconstructed the classic detective mystery sixty-six years ago in his essay, 'The Simple Art of Murder'. That essay is best remembered for the famous romantic passage about the 'mean streets' down which a man must go. Much of the essay, though, was devoted to trashing A. A. Milne's *The Red House Mystery*, a crime fiction classic of the old school. Chandler was irritated that an example of 'an arid formula which could not even satisfy its own implications' should still be in print so long after its 1922 publication. I wonder how he'd feel to know that two new editions of that book, one hardcover and one paperback, were published in 2008, eighty-six years after first publication. And two more in 2009 (paperback and Kindle). And in 2010. And before that in 2007. And in 2004. And in 2001, and 2000, and 1987 . . .

There are at least two reasons for the popularity of the 'cosy' mystery story. People like the challenge of trying to solve the puzzle. And people like to be comforted. That has always been the attraction of the 'cosy' crime mystery. A crime ruptures society's values, the detective – the agent of comfort – mooches around in search of clues, examines the suspects to ascertain who has betrayed the common values – and pounces. All is explained, the guilty party is removed from the midst of the good people. Order is restored, the comfort blanket has done its job.

The best of this kind of story can be hugely entertaining, especially when it revolves around engaging characters, from Sherlock Holmes to Poirot, from Columbo to Jessica Fletcher. And for them, David Peace's strictures are too demanding – readers experience such stories as puzzles, and understand them to be far removed from reality. They bear the same relationship to real crime as Mills & Boon stories bear to real romance – a reassuring yarn set in a fantasy world that looks only a little like ours.

Unfortunately, behind every successful larger-than-life mystery fiction stands a horde of smaller-than-life sleuths solving humdrum mysteries. This ensures that a large percentage of crime fiction is hardly any more plausible than a game of Cluedo.

We are awash with the likes of gruff but lovable Detective Inspector Plod, hugging the bottle of single malt his creator gave him, along with some off-the-shelf 'personal demons' to haunt him. Or maybe the writer makes him a fan of Mahler – or Buddy Holly – something 'characterful' to take the bare look off him. This distinguishes Detective Inspector Plod from Detective Inspector Trudge, tucked between similar covers one shelf up, or Detective Inspector Slog, ensconced on the shelf below.

For my own part, I don't see the point of such mystery stories without the entertainment provided by larger-than-life characters. Or, better still, without some new way of using the old formats. Yet the shelves sag with the chronicles of Detective Inspector Plod (UK) and stern-jawed crime fighter Clint Furnace (USA) – and they are hugely popular. Much of it – today as in the past – amounts to little more than a series of laboriously contrived puzzles, chases or dilemmas, to be engaged in by interchangeable protagonists, while the reader tries to guess who did it, or why or how, or if they'll get away with it.

There's a reason for the repetitiveness and predictability of much crime fiction. It sells in trailer-loads. Readers enjoyed Detective Inspector Plod Solves a Murder (in which the gruff but characterful copper almost has an affair with his pretty Detective Sergeant, Imelda, and then thinks better of it). So, they're delighted to see a brand new volume arrive, Detective Inspector Plod Solves Another Murder (in which the killer taunts the gruff but characterful copper by sending him email clues about the identity of his next victim). Ben Yagoda's description of such stories applies: 'Similar things happen in similar ways', and many readers like a predictably satisfying experience.

Over.

And.

Over.

(Obviously, crime fiction isn't alone in this – it's a danger common to all genre novels. Conventions become clichés, shortcuts become over-familiar beaten paths.)

It asks too much of publishers and television producers to suggest they ignore the reliable cash-flow to be found in that market. And such products can coexist with fictions that might say something different, or say the same thing in a different way.

Your first ten Detective Inspector Plod mysteries may perform limply in a crowded market – but one day you may write your breakout novel – at which point readers will not only buy your next novel featuring Inspector Plod, they'll also seek out your backlist, and soon you can afford a flat overlooking the Thames, next-door to Jeffrey Archer.

Happily, the better writers are still finding interesting things to do with the classic formats – whether these involve the amateur sleuth, the private detective, or even good old Detective Inspector Plod.

For instance, the crime novel provides a perfect fictional route into societies that might otherwise remain vague to us. The Scandinavian sub-genre is an obvious example. David Downing's series about reporter detective John Russell is steeped in the atmosphere of Nazi Germany. James Church's Detective Inspector O series is set in present-day North Korea. On the surface, Matt Rees's Omar Yussef series is as old-fashioned as they come – an amateur sleuth solving mysteries. But Omar Yussef is an elderly teacher, a Palestinian, alert not only to the oppression of his society but to its shortcomings. Such novels bring us into these societies in a unique way.

The mystery format is from an old tradition, but such writers are doing something new. Nothing in a hardboiled novel has shocked me as much as a plot development in the first Omar Yussef story, *The Bethlehem Murders* – indeed the shock effect would be lessened within a hardboiled setting.

The division today is not between the traditional 'cosy' and the hardboiled. It's between books that merely exploit crime as material for entertainment, and books that entertain but also have – as Raymond Chandler put it – 'the authentic flavour of life as it is lived'. The division is between the books in which murder is merely an exciting development and those in which 'murder is an act of infinite cruelty'.

Where the genre has really degenerated is in the growth of a kind of mutant crime fiction, an amalgam of the old 'cosy' with surface elements of the hardboiled – and it is here that Peace's worries are more than justified.

*

In 1981, Thomas Harris published his second novel (his first was an efficient but unremarkable terrorism yarn). *Red Dragon* is a superb thriller. And there's more to it than that. It's about how humans struggle to overcome our capacity for evil. Nature, one of Harris's characters supposes, is indifferent to our moral striving, nature is bereft of morality. In nature, 'there is no mercy. We make mercy, manufacture it in the parts that have overgrown our basic reptile brain.'

Red Dragon and *The Silence of the Lambs* (the former is the better book) feature Hannibal Lecter. He is already in prison, captured by criminal profiler Will Graham. Graham is successful because of his empathy with monsters such as Lecter, his ability to understand his own capacity for evil, while still suppressing it. The men he hunts have been unable or unwilling to stifle that urge to gorge without scruple. Flawed humanity is Harris's subject. He exalts humanity over nature, positing that we seek to be greater than our origins, larger than our fate.

In both books, Lecter has a minor but crucial role – the sophisticate who abandons the constraints humanity has developed and gives free rein to the savagery his nature is capable of. His cruel crimes are approached at an angle. Harris skilfully horrifies us, without wallowing in the gore. In the two Lecter books that followed, the monster took centre stage – unfortunately. The latter books flaunt Lecter's gruesome eccentricities. They lack the moral centre of the first two books.

Perhaps Anthony Hopkins's bravura performance in the movie version of *Lambs* is to blame – he was stunning, but lacked the subtlety of Brian Cox playing the role in the movie version of *Red Dragon*. Hopkins's Lecter made the killer a kind of celebrity cannibal, his lines repeated with glee. Lecter acquired the status of a bogeyman – a Jason Voorhees, Michael Myers or Freddy Kreuger figure. We're invited to enjoy being scared by the monster. This may have influenced Harris.

Worse, the success of *Silence of the Lambs* created a tiresome parade of serial killer fictions – each more eccentric and cartoonish than the last, trying to clamber onto the Lecter bandwagon.

Agatha Christie wrote *Who Killed Roger Ackroyd?* Edmund Wilson, in an impatient dismissal of the novel, wrote a famous article titled 'Who Cares Who Killed Roger Ackroyd?' And who indeed cares how grotesque (but charming) the latest imitation Hannibal Lecter is?

The grotesque (but charming) serial killer is just part of a mainstream crime fiction that combines the cosy conservatism of the classic mysteries with the surface detail of the old hardboiled school. In place of the hardboiled novel's moral toughness, there is glamour and unrestrained bloodletting – and corpses used as decorative devices.

It's a kind of bastard grandchild of Agatha Christie and James Hadley Chase. There's a body in the library, alright – but it's been ripped from crotch to larynx, its eyes gouged out and its guts spread around the room. The bizarre (but cultured) killer has left a quote from *King Lear* stuffed up its rectum.

In the glossy fictions, there's more blood on view, and characters swear and screw and belch – and the corpses are dissected in loving detail. But at heart these would-be tough-guy productions are just as much a part of the Cosy Squad as Miss Marple was. Glamour and gore attract the crowd, and the detectives provide comfort by slickly (whatever the implausibility) bringing order back to a disrupted world.

The detective may even be our old friend Detective Inspector Plod – or, in an American incarnation, the likes of pseudo-glamorous Lieutenant Horatio Caine. In which latter case the job of making him 'characterful' will consist of Horatio repeatedly putting on and taking off his shades, while mumbling quips that even the old Bond movies would have scorned.

We might paraphrase Chandler: 'The glamour merchants have given murder back to the kind of people who need a corpse to spice up their glossy dramas'.

(Of course, while some of the worst influences on crime fiction come from American television, so do some of the best – *The Wire, The Sopranos, Breaking Bad*).

Over most of the past decade, the *CSI* television franchise has dominated and set the tone for crime fiction. Watched in 200 countries, the show has a global audience of countless millions. The demand is insatiable, and when people are not watching one of the three separate *CSI* series on television they're playing one of the seven *CSI* computer games ('You've experienced the thrill of the show! Now it's time to live it!'); or reading one of the three dozen *CSI* comics. Or playing with *CSI* toys (maybe a DNA lab or a forensics lab). Or attending the travelling exhibition, *CSI: The Experience.*

Perhaps even reading one of the two dozen *CSI* novels in print.

The show itself (and its imitators) features what are essentially models with police badges, standing in cool poses at designer crime scenes in picturesque locations, beside stylishly arranged corpses.

The creator of *CSI*, Anthony Zuiker, pointed out that the show was no big deal when it began in 2000. Along came 9/11 – a major disruption of the world as people understood it. Zuiker says: 'People were rushing to us for their comfort food. There was a sense of justice in *CSI* – it helped to know that there were people like our characters out there helping to solve crimes.'

Comfort food – precisely. It's the very definition of the old 'cosy' mystery – the comfortable world is disrupted by a crime, the detectives identify the killer and order is restored. Reassurance sells – be content, you live in the best of all possible worlds; the folks in power are honest and competent and will take care of you.

This market is so buoyant that some leading sellers can't keep up, so they create fiction factories – with the supposed writer sometimes merely tossing out rough plots to the team of elves who provide the actual words, and the book is marketed under the established brand name.

(It's worth noting that there's long been another side to the market for literary comfort blankets. Paranoia, too, sells – be apprehensive, you are being manipulated by powerful, unseen forces that pull the strings of the puppets supposedly in power. Witness Robert Ludlum and Dan Brown, and their many and varied imitators. The bonus is that the reassurance market and the conspiracy market reinforce each other.)

There will always be the formula fiction factory franchises. And victims despatched in exotic ways by colourful hit men, 'ordinary' heroes who turn out to be former Special Forces assassins, characters recycled from other novels, from old movies, from processed television drama. There will always be the Lecter lookalikes; and the glamour parade in which models with badges adjust their cool shades; and the mystery draped in modish cultural references (Agatha Christie on steroids); and, God help us, the Proust-length saga that over countless sequels tediously unwraps a little more of the inner life of the unremarkable character that is Detective Inspector Plod.

The crime fiction equivalents of Mills & Boon may sanitise crime, but they are relatively harmless. The fictions that deal in grotesque villains and exotic forms of murder, the stylish festival of gore, will continue to profitably glamorise and exploit crime, and obscure its reality.

*

Raymond Chandler's summing-up of the private eye subgenre is celebrated: 'Down these mean streets a man must go who is not himself mean, who is neither tarnished nor afraid.' Personally, I like some of my heroes tarnished and occasionally afraid. But in that same essay, 'The Simple Art of Murder,' Chandler wrote something more to the point:

'The realist in murder writes of a world in which gangsters can rule nations and almost rule cities, in which hotels and apartment houses and celebrated restaurants are owned by men who made their money out of brothels . . . It is not a very fragrant world, but it is the world you live in, and certain writers with tough minds and a cool spirit of detachment can make very interesting and even amusing patterns out of it.'

Crime is often a distorted version of the behaviour held in high regard within a society. Ambitious and able people who never learned the skills of capitalist buccaneering become ghetto entrepreneurs. They source and distribute an illegal product – and as they prosper they pick up the business skills they need. They merge and split and fight to protect and extend market share – and they do it without the benefit of lawyers. Limited their lives may be, but some are far tougher, brighter and ultimately more successful than the idiots in the

Financial Centre to whom they sell cocaine. Those clowns first blew up a credit bubble and then blew up the economy.

From the early 1990s, as the Irish economy began to rev-up, so did the criminal gangs, growing in confidence and savagery. While the banks were overseeing complex tax frauds that cost the exchequer billions of euros, the gangs were building their own business networks. To write fiction about Irish crime is to write about Irish society – in its brutality, its irrationality and its injustice.

The bad guys are often chasing the same things as the rest of us – they want to pay off the mortgage, get a better car, a bigger house, more time in the sun, enough money to do well by their loved ones, and themselves. But – like the pillars of society who benefitted from the massive tax frauds – they want these things faster, without boring effort. They pursue them using the means within their reach. These little criminals have friends and family and finer feelings, and they'd shoot you in the head if you stood between them and whatever matters at the moment. Some of them are nice people, when they're not shooting someone in the head.

The more sophisticated criminals, operating from swish boardrooms, have delicate feelings, and they'd destabilise an entire society if they saw the chance of a financial killing. Some of them are thoughtful people, when they're not condemning countless thousands to anxiety, pain, stunted education, deprivation of medical treatment, the dole or suicide.

When we tackle these subjects in crime fiction – whether through the mystery story or the hardboiled, the allegorical or the realist – the conventions (and clichés) of crime fiction have an enormous gravitational pull. It's easy to find yourself, with the best of intentions, drawn deep into the land of Detective Inspector Plod.

Raymond Chandler offered a guiding principle. Admirable crime fiction, such as that written by Dashiell Hammett, he said, is of course made up – but it's 'made up out of real things'. And that remains, for me, the measure and the challenge of a crime novel: to avoid contrived puzzles, rehashed plots and cliché characters, to make an entertainment out of 'the authentic flavour of life as it is lived'.

It's not as easy as it looks. We succumb to cliché, we trivialise, we sanitise, we sensationalise. When we fail it's because we forget the look and feel of violence, the look and feel of life. We forget the attendant details – for me, the pathetic romance of the funeral of that young man shot in a playground. The damaged, limited lives, and another young man willing to kill so easily for such shallow reasons. And the leader of a small group of young men, holding his dead friend's horse by the reins, exchanging mute gestures of respect with the family of the dead boy – each seeking to extract from a miserable tragedy some small sense of majesty and meaning.

Which, after all – heartbreakingly but magnificently – is perhaps what both writing and living are about.

'Crime is brutal, harrowing and devastating for everyone involved, and crime fiction should be every bit as brutal, harrowing and devastating as the violence of the reality it seeks to document. Anything less at best sanitises crime and its effects, at worst trivialises it. Anything more exploits other people's misery as purely vicarious entertainment. It is a very fine line . . .'

*

Gene Kerrigan is a Dublin journalist. His third novel, *Dark Times in the City*, was judged the best crime novel of 2010, at the Irish Book Awards. It was also shortlisted for the Crime Writer's Association's Golden Dagger. His fourth novel, *The Rage*, will be published in June 2011.

The Killers Inside Them

by Gerry O'Carroll

A short while after I retired from An Garda Síochána, I began writing a weekly column in the *Evening Herald*; then, in 2005, my autobiography *The Sheriff: A Detective's Story* was published. Following the publication, my agent and mentor, Robert Kirby, began suggesting that I should try my hand at a bit of crime fiction. When I mentioned this to the editor of the *Evening Herald*, Stephen Rae, he agreed wholeheartedly, convincing me that I had the Kerryman's gift for storytelling – that I was a born *seanchaí*.

I thought about it for a time and came up with a thousand reasons for putting it on the long finger. I realised that there's a world of difference between penning an autobiography and venting into the imaginative realm of crime fiction. After all, I didn't have to think up the stories in *The Sheriff*, I just had to retell them. It was a daunting challenge, and as I am basically a lazy-minded individual, I didn't relish the prospect of the blood, sweat and tears that such an undertaking would undoubtedly involve, and I discovered over time that my apprehensions about the disruption to my tranquil, rural retirement were well-founded. No matter what excuses I invented for procrastination, Robert, who always flattered me that I was a natural-born storyteller with twenty-four years' experience as a detective, finally persuaded me that I was ideally placed to give it a go.

A number of other factors spurred me on. Firstly, I was delighted and relieved that *The Sheriff* had gone down so well and had made it into the Top

10 in the best-sellers list. It got good write-ups, with some critics going so far as to suggest that I showed promise as an author. Another, more compelling motive for writing my first novel, *The Gathering of Souls*, came from much closer to home.

I have the good fortune to have been born in the lovely town of Listowel in County Kerry, which is often referred to as the 'Literary Capital of Ireland'; the town hosts the annual Listowel Writers' Week, one of the most important literary festivals in Europe. This small north Kerry town has spawned a host of famous, talented writers that include the prolific, internationally renowned playwright and author John B. Keane, Dr Bryan MacMahon, George Fitzmaurice and Maurice Walsh, who wrote *The Quiet Man*. In a town so steeped in literary tradition, I was only too well aware that *The Sheriff* would face its ultimate test at the hands of Listowel's searchingly honest but merciless townspeople, but thankfully my fears were without foundation: there was an exceptionally well-attended book launch in St John's Art Centre, and *The Sheriff* sold out in the town's bookshops. I had raised my head above the parapet and proclaimed myself a writer in my hometown – always a risky venture – and had lived to tell the tale. There was no begrudgery at all, and I was overwhelmed by the generous and warm response and the flood of congratulations I received.

A few weeks later, while I was still basking in the glow of my modest success, I was suddenly brought down to earth with a bang. While walking through the town one afternoon, I was approached by a leading member of the Listowel Writers' Committee. From the uneasy way he fumbled his words, fidgeted around and shuffled his feet, it was obvious to me that something was bothering him. Then, having paid me some polite compliment about my book, he rambled on about the proud heritage of famous Listowel writers before finishing with the barbed comments that one swallow doesn't make a summer, and one book doesn't make a writer. I got the message loud and clear that, unless I wrote another book, I would never be accepted as a serious writer in the Listowel literary circle. I would always be known as a one-trick pony. If I ever needed motivation, this was it.

From an early age, long before I joined the Gardaí, I was addicted to reading about the dark and violent world of serious crime. It was a passion I shared with my father, who was a voracious reader and devotee of crime fiction. By my early teens, I had read everything I could get my hands on by authors such as Raymond Chandler, Agatha Christie, Georges Simenon, etc. Unbeknown to my father, I had also gained access to my father's stash of *True Detective* monthly magazines, which I kept hidden because, under the Draconian censorship laws of that era, such publications were considered a threat to the moral fabric of Irish society and were banned. The graphic and gruesome photographs in these magazines – of some naked, murdered women and of the bullet-studded bodies of hoodlums at the scenes of police shootouts – both repelled and fascinated me in equal measure. In my childish daydreams I scoffed at the idea that I would ever settle for the mundane life of a bank clerk or a bricklayer. No, I was going to be a detective with a badge and a gun, upholding the law and bringing villains to justice, just like the big heroes in the magazines, and I fulfilled my dream when I became a member of An Garda Síochána in 1967. I served for thirty-four years, twenty-four of them as a detective, and I was involved in the investigation of more than ninety murders, as well as bombings, kidnapping, political assassination, disappearances and other serious crimes. There is an old Chinese curse that says, 'May you live in interesting times', and if you were to read even a brief resumé of my experiences in the police, you would agree that I was well and truly cursed, but many of these experiences, however painful, were to become grist to the mill when eventually I started to write *The Gathering of Souls*.

Robert Kirby, my agent, had secured a publishing deal and I got the green light to begin work on the book. Robert felt that I would benefit from the advice of an established crime writer, and he introduced me to John Matthews, an English writer who had already received critical acclaim for a number of thrillers including the hauntingly atmospheric novel *Past Imperfect*. John was generous with his advice and cautioned me on the snags and pitfalls I would encounter on my maiden voyage in that perilous realm of crime fiction. I am deeply grateful for his kindness and patience and encouragement.

After meeting a 'real' writer, I was fired up with renewed zeal, and the plot and characters began to take shape.

Around this time, Robert introduced me to Jeff Gulvin, another English crime novelist. Jeff is a gifted and prolific author with twelve books to his credit, including the bestseller *Storm Crow*. He came to meet me in Dublin to discuss plans, and from the very beginning we got on well together, became friends and developed a good working relationship.

My ultimate plan was based on a psychopathic serial killer of young women with the main plot centred on the frantic hunt for the kidnapped wife of the detective who is leading the investigation. When I was racking my brains for a plot, the more I thought about it, the more it seemed the obvious choice to feature a serial killer, because for many years there had been widespread speculation that a serial killer was operating in this jurisdiction, and I had often spoken out publicly about my concerns regarding the existence of such a killer. There was no other rational explanation for the disappearances, between 1993 and 1998, of six young women in the Leinster area of the country. Of course, as I expected, the official response from the authorities was to rubbish my claims, but some years later, owing to growing public concern and fear, the Garda commissioner announced the establishment of a special unit named Operation Trace to investigate these disappearances.

This was also a subject I could write about from my own personal experience because in 1976, I had played a pivotal role in securing the conviction of Ireland's first serial killers, the two Englishmen John Shaw and Geoffrey Evans, who had abducted, tortured, raped and murdered two young women – one in Wicklow and the other in Galway. John Shaw admitted to me during questioning that they intended to kill one young woman a week for as long as they could. Thankfully they were caught sooner rather than later and are still in prison, having now achieved the infamous distinction of being Ireland's longest-serving prisoners.

I gathered further material for my fictional villain from my dealings with another evil psychopathic killer to whom I devoted a chapter in *The Sheriff* and to whom I refer to as 'the man with a thousand faces' in my novel.

I have to confess that there were times when I became strangely unnerved as the thin line between reality and imagination became blurred and distorted. My encounters with these killers gave me an invaluable if terrifying insight into the warped minds of those evil psychopathic creatures who masquerade as 'human' beings. I remember clearly looking into the eyes of one of those cold-blooded killers and asking him how he could still function after the diabolical crimes he had committed. His reply was as chilling as it was revealing. In a calm and matter-of-fact voice, he explained to me that he was able to bury all his problems in his mind. His exact words were, 'I feel terrible about it, but I have it all deep in a cavity in my brain.' In my portrayal of a serial killer I have tried to capture the essence of one of the darkest forces in human nature. In his book *Beyond Good and Evil* (1886), the philosopher Friedrich Nietzsche issues a chilling warning of the potential danger in dealing with such malevolent beings. He writes that 'whoever fights monsters should see to it that in the process he does not become a monster, and when you look into the abyss, the abyss also looks into you.'

Having settled on the plot, my next task was to assemble a cast of characters to people my creation, an exercise which was immensely exciting and satisfying. I discovered that one of the great pleasures of fiction writing is having the freedom to flesh out and bring to life, on the page of a book, living, breathing people. My two main characters in the book are Detective Sergeant Joe Doyle and Detective Inspector Moss Quinn who, although partners and best friends, are as different as chalk and cheese. Joe is a grizzled old veteran, coming to the end of his career, a fists-and-boots policeman from another era. A hard-drinking single man from the bogs of Kerry, he regards with contempt the new namby-pamby, kid gloves, official regulations for dealing with prisoners in custody. He is regarded by the criminal fraternity as somewhat of a dinosaur, but they still fear and hate him because of his explosive temper and his none-too-gentle methods. Moss Quinn, on the other hand, is a young ambitious inspector, married with children, urbane, sophisticated and articulate, with a university degree and a future ahead of him. Although polar opposites, they are joined at the hip in friendship, and even if at times they may disagree with each others' methods, they are united in their uncompromising war against the bad guys. I am hoping to expand the characters of Doyle and Quinn in a follow-up novel, as my publishers, Liberties Press, have expressed an interest in at least one other book. They want me to do for Listowel and its environs what Ian Rankin's Rebus did for Edinburgh! I am grateful to be afforded the opportunity, and I would like to thank Seán at Liberties Press for their support and confidence in me.

I conclude with a special thanks to my friend and collaborator, Jeff Gulvin, for his professional guidance and advice, for giving so generously of his time and especially for his invaluable editorial reviews and insights. I am especially indebted to him for his advice on my use of dialogue, an aspect of writing that I had so much to learn about. Of course, we had the usual disagreements and differences of opinion, and we had to deal with the inevitable tensions and strains that occur in a working relationship. Indeed, there were times when I became lazy and disheartened and very close to throwing in the towel, but Jeff's judicious use of the carrot and stick approach to my intransigence kept me on track and on schedule.

Entering the world of creative writing has been an immensely satisfying and exciting experience. Writing has given me a new lease on life and a freedom to roam in the boundless universe of my imagination. It is my protection and shield against the debilitating, life-sapping melancholy we mortals all experience in our so-called 'golden years'.

*

Gerry O'Carroll served with An Garda Síochána for thirty-four years, twenty-four of them as detective. His first book, *The Sheriff*, was a non-fiction account of his career in policing. His debut novel, *The Gathering of Souls*, was published in 2010.

A Shock to the System

by Arlene Hunt

When I was a child of about eleven or twelve I found myself hanging from a set of monkey bars at my local primary school. I was no doubt showing off. If memory serves, I was trying to impress a boy called Paul Doyle with my daring and skill. Paul could swing in a perfect arc and land with a roll and a flourish. I, being far more ungainly, could not.

This lack of coordination did not dissuade me in the slightest. That day I leaped like a demented howler monkey and landed so badly I managed to completely rip the ligaments in my right ankle to shreds.

'Jaysus,' Paul said, 'that was terrible.'

Then he saw my foot and he blanched.

The pain was immediate and intense. Within minutes my foot had swelled like a zeppelin.

I managed to make it the half-mile home, but no amount of cold water or elevating my foot dulled the pain. I whinged miserably, and after a quick trip to Doctor Pippet in Wicklow town – who gazed at my now shiny purple foot with detached amusement – it was decided I should be brought to Loughlinstown hospital.

I'm telling you all this because none of it really mattered. Not the spectacular jump, the subsequent agony, not the giddy trip to the big smoke, none of it. What has stuck with me since that day was the registration number of a car.

FSI 168.

I cannot tell you the make or model of the car to which this registration belonged, only that the car itself had been involved in a crime – an abduction I think – and the newscaster on the car radio said we should look out for it.

FSI 168.

As soon as I heard that I forgot all about my tears and gripped the window with my sticky hands. I was convinced I would spot this vehicle and all would be saved. I interviewed myself as our car hurtled along. Yes, I was very brave, I told interviewer me. I had indeed the great presence of mind to memorise the number. Why yes I had been hurt earlier that day, jumping in a remarkable act of skill and daring. The family of the rescued person wanted to give me a pony? Yes I would gratefully accept. I was magnanimous in my self-praise, humble, even as the villains were being hauled off to jail, angry and bitter, no doubt, at being thwarted by a young girl, her eager eyes and her purple swollen foot.

Alas, it was not to be. I was not Nancy Drew and I solved no crime that day.

From an early age I had a genuine interest in crime. Back then I lived in a foster home with Kitty and Peter McWilliams. Peter was ex-army and from an early age – when he wasn't chasing me with earwigs and spiders – he would regale me with tremendous tales of murder and mayhem in the jungles of Borneo and of shootings and beheadings in Malaya. He would talk of torture and fighting, of testosterone-filled mess halls and violence. And, of course, being a child I lapped it up. He was an endless talker, I an endless listener. He would puff contentedly on his pipe and say, 'The thing is, mate, them facking Nips really knew how to skin a man . . .'

When not learning how to skin folk properly I also kept Kitty company. And there were two things Kitty liked: a half bottle of Stout daily, and cop shows.

Under her expert tuition I immersed myself in *Hill Street Blues*, *Magnum PI*, *TJ Hooker*, and Edward Woodward's *The Equalizer*. I loved crime shows; all of them: Agatha Christie, *Murder She Wrote*, *Charlie's Angels*, *CHiPs*, it mattered not how kooky or ridiculous the plots. I revered Dirty Harry, and thought Charles Bronson rather cool actually; I fell in love with Tom Selleck weekly, and Poncherello, with his shiny teeth and knee-high boots, made me swoon. *Knight Rider* was cool, the *A-Team* were d.e.a.d.l.y. Oh, how would they trick Mr T into flying this week? 'Who loves you, baby?' Kitty and I would say, winking at each other, 'Book 'em, Danno!' we would shriek over cups of hot chocolate.

It would be safe to say I liked my crime like I liked my toast, hot and easily digested. There would be a villain and he would be caught every time. Those were the rules. The good guys would save the day. That was how it was supposed to be. Real life crime never really penetrated. I lived in the countryside, in a picturesque village called Redcross. We didn't even lock our doors, for Heaven's sake. The one time I did engage in a criminal act – stealing a tube of Bubble-Up from Mrs Collier's village shop – Kitty frog-marched me all the way back down to the shop to make my weepy confession.

(I was a rubbish criminal. Kitty discovered my crime because like a fool I stood at the side of the house, blowing reams upon reams of bubbles, which promptly blew past the front door leading Kitty to come investigate.)

Because real crime held no place in my imagination it came as a quite a shock to me when I realised that crimes happened to actual people and that murder was not neat and solved by nosy, bespectacled authors. I had equated murder with television and film, with glamour and fast cars and growly mustachioed men, with big hair and t-shirts asking, 'Who shot JR Ewing?' It never occurred to me that I might need to be careful with the life I had been granted. It didn't seem to occur to any of my peers to be more careful with ourselves either. Why would any of us need to keep in touch with our parents, or carry mobile phones, or have curfews or any of the things I now impose upon my own child?

Maybe I choose to look back on my youth through slightly rose-tinted glasses, but at the risk of sounding like an old fart, it did seem a more innocent time, the days did seem sunnier, and the people more open and trusting. Crime, when it happened, was shocking, rare and mostly confined to the city. What did a country gal like me know or care about stuff like that?

Of course, innocence and naïvety are like Bubble-Up bubbles, they don't last long and when they're gone, they're gone for good.

The murder of Bridie Gargan was the first case I remember being inter-ested in. Certainly it was the one that made me realise murder was very real and that it could be horrific and vicious and arbitrary. It was not sanitary. It could, and did, happen to anyone.

Bridie Gargan worked as a nurse in St James Hospital. On the 22 July 1982, Bridie had finished work and was on her way home to Castleknock when she decided to stop in Phoenix Park to enjoy the July sunshine. While sunbathing she was set upon by Malcolm MacArthur, an on-the-skids playboy who wanted to steal her car. He forced Bridie into the car and told her to lie down on the back seat. He told her that he wanted to tie her up. When Bridie became upset and refused to lie down, MacArthur savagely beat her with a hammer. A passer-by tried to come to her aid, but MacArthur leaped into the car and drove away, with Bridie smashed and dying on the back seat.

It seems unthinkable, does it not? MacArthur did not know Bridie, nor hold a personal grudge against her; she had what he wanted and that was all the reason he needed to attack her.

In the ensuing chaos MacArthur ended up driving Bridie to a hospital, but once there he changed his mind and drove away again. I wonder, if she had been treated might she have survived? Impossible to know, but the questions remain. MacArthur eventually abandoned the car he had been so willing to murder for, with Bridie still in it. She was only twenty-five when she died.

MacArthur also killed a man by the name of Donal Dunne. He travelled outside of the city to do this, making his way down to Offaly, supposedly to buy a shotgun. He shot Donal with his own gun and stole his car. This was later found abandoned on Dame Street in Dublin.

As bloody and vicious as Malcolm MacArthur was, his crimes might not have caught the public's attention so vividly had he not sought refuge at the home of Patrick Connolly, the then State's Attorney General. Once the press got hold of that detail, the case became red hot. Connolly was subsequently to lose his job over it. Charles Haughey called the case 'grotesque, unprecedented, bizarre, unbelievable'.

I was fascinated by the case, and filled with what ifs. What if Bridie hadn't pulled in? What if it had become cloudy? What if the man had managed to make MacArthur leave the park? What if they had found the car sooner? How was it possible that Bridie had been chatting with friend and colleagues only hours before her attack, unaware Death was waiting in the wings? Who decided what little action could cause such an outcome?

'She got an awful death God love her,' Kitty said that evening, glancing at Bridie's photo in the *Evening Press*. 'And she with her whole life ahead of her.'

She looked at me.

'You never know the minute or the hour. Remember that. The minute or the hour.'

That sentence was the one that scared me. No, I wouldn't know, just as Bridie had not known when she pulled into the Phoenix Park and thought it was a beautiful day to sunbathe.

Nothing is more frightening to a parent than the thought of losing a child, under any circumstances. But surely having a child kidnapped or stolen away must be the cruellest of acts. The idea that people are out there, waiting for an opportunity to snatch a child and do with them what they like, genuinely frightens me.

My custom as a child was to wander as far from my home as often as I could. I had a fold-up bike and with this machine my boundaries were greatly explored. I could leave my home at nine o'clock on a Saturday morning and be gone until nine o'clock Saturday night. I often returned filthy and starving, and I'm sure Kitty must have been worried sick on more than one occasion about my prolonged absences.

But it was normal for me and normal for she. Lots of parents shooed their children out the door; most were relieved not to have children under their feet.

'Just tell me where you're going,' Kitty would say as I hopped on my bike for another excursion.

And I'd give her some irritated and quite useless reply. Useless because I never really knew where the hell I was going until I got there.

'I need to know in case something happens to you.'

What did *that* even mean? I would wonder, pedalling away. What could possibly 'happen' to me? That I cycled across busy main roads, played in ruins that were death-traps, petted all the dogs I met, spoke cheerfully to strangers and frequently attempted to swim in dangerous rivers seemed reasonable to me. So what was that woman expecting to 'happen'?

In my youth people who snatched children for nefarious deeds did not exist, they were as real to me as the bogeyman. And since I did not believe in bogeymen, I did not believe in perverts. No, it wasn't even that I didn't believe in them; I had no concept that such a person could exist.

In 1986, a few days before Hallowe'en and not long after his thirteenth birthday, the disappearance of Philip Cairns was to open my juvenile mind to the very real possibility that bogeymen existed.

Philip lived in Templeogue, a lovely, safe, middle-of-the-road suburb in Dublin. He had just started secondary school that September and at 12:30pm on 23 October, he returned home for lunch. At 1:30 he shouted his goodbyes and left home to walk the quarter of a mile back to school. He never made it.

A massive search began. Phillip's shy, smiling face peered from the pages of every newspaper. His schoolbag was found days later in a lane near his home. It was a busy lane, so why had the bag not been spotted before? Was the child-snatcher playing mind games? Was it a warning? Parents became fearful. Philip had been snatched in broad daylight. Why had nobody seen anything? Where was he? Who had him? Gossip was rife. In the playground of my school theories abounded: he had been stolen by gypsies; by a mad kidnapper; there was talk of 'cults'; there were vanloads of kidnappers roaming the countryside, just waiting to catch unwary children – for what purpose we did not know, only that these things were self-evident. We traded stories of near misses and what ifs. Suddenly we children eyed-up strangers with more suspicion, we stayed closer to home. We had no choice, really, as our parents became more demanding of our intentions.

'Where are you going?' Kitty would now demand. 'And what time will you be back?'

I was outraged by this intrusion upon my freedoms. Demands for times and locations were followed up by, 'Don't talk to anyone you don't know. Remember Philip Cairns? That could happen to anyone.'

As I cycled away I would promise myself only that should anyone stop in a van and try snatch me, I would fight them to the death. As comforting thoughts went it wasn't a very good one, but it was all I had. I am sure Kitty slept better in her bed knowing that too.

Philip Cairns was never found. There is no closure to his disappearance. His poor family was never allowed that measure of kindness. The not knowing is surely the most painful part.

Over the years many murders have entered my mind and taken up permanent residence therein. I think about the person at random moments. Not to belittle the death of anyone of course, but it's just that some deaths rattle you to the bone and they are not so easy to leave behind. Some deaths make you question everything, the good in people, the point of it all, they just catch you off guard.

I remember vividly how I felt upon hearing the news that the bodies of Imelda Riney and her three-year-old son Liam had been found in County Clare. Even though this happened back in 1994 I can still remember the sensations running through my body. My hands balled and I felt physically sick. I don't know why I was so shaken by that particular case, perhaps because my own daughter was also three at the time and the idea that anyone could harm a child of her age left me furious and uncomprehending.

The more I read about the case the more I empathised with Imelda Riney. She was a young woman, separated from her husband and living alone with her two sons in a beautiful, peaceful part of Ireland. From the moment she and Liam were reported missing I followed the news doggedly, hoping the outcome might be good.

It was not to be. A little over a week after being reported missing, Imelda, her little boy and the body of a local priest, Father Joseph Walsh, were discovered in a shallow woodland grave.

I know it seems strange, because I did not know them, but when I listened to the news that day, I cried. I kept thinking of Imelda and what she must have gone through knowing that the man who had her in his clutches was going to harm her and her son. As much as I tried not to, I imagined her fighting to protect her boy, as any parent would fight to protect their child.

Brendan O'Donnell, the murderer, was only twenty years old when he committed those heinous acts. He was caught after abducting another young girl, eighteen-year-old Fiona Sampson. He dragged Fiona, barefoot and bleeding in her nightdress, through the woods for miles as Gardaí and her father gave chase. Finally he tried to hijack a car at gunpoint from a farmer called Eddie Cleary. Mr Cleary grabbed the gun, and after a struggle O'Donnell was apprehended.

O'Donnell gave evidence in court that made my heart ache. After abducting Imelda and Liam on 29 April, he had forced Imelda to drive them to Cregg Woods in her car. He told her he was going to shoot her. She fought him, and he shot her in the eye. He then led little Liam over to his mother's body and shot him in the side of the head. He said this made him 'feel very happy, a good feeling'.

What can you do with someone like that? He showed no remorse and had he not been captured he would, without a doubt, have killed again and again. The humane part of me wants to understand the circumstances that can foster and breed such malevolence. He was a disturbed individual whose childhood had been bleak and horrible. His mother had died while he was a youth and he had been physically abused by his father. In many ways his story is a textbook case. Maybe I should have some sympathy for this man. But then I think of Imelda, knowing she was going to die, fighting for her and her son's life. I think of a grown man placing a bullet in the head of a three-year-old child or shooting an unarmed priest and I feel nothing except murderous contempt and vengeful intolerance. I think of Imelda's other son, left behind without his mother and brother and my sympathy becomes harder and harder to locate. What could drive someone to commit such an act and can there really be any understanding of it? Maybe some people are plain evil.

I still think of Imelda and Liam, not often I admit, but on occasion. My daughter will be eighteen this year, a grown woman. Liam should be a grown man. There but for the grace of God.

There have been plenty of horrific killings in this country. Murders that shake the nation, like that of Veronica Guerin, a brave reporter who doggedly chased freewheeling scumbags, despite being threatened, shot and assaulted. Veronica was gunned down in her car on her way back from court and her murder sparked the biggest outcry I've ever seen.

When Veronica was killed the whole country seemed united in condemnation. Politicians came out and spoke angrily. The words, 'a line must be drawn,' were said over and over by various mouthpieces. The Criminal Assets Bureau (CAB) was set up to target the crooks and hit them where it hurts most, in their wallets. But as long as there is money to be made there will always be crime and no amount of bravery, foolhardiness, laws or convictions will ever remove the motivation for the hardened criminal to act as he sees fit.

With money as a goal and various criminals fighting for turf, it is not surprising that gang-related killings are on the rise. But it is not just gang members who die, and to that end nothing could have horrified me more over the last few years as the brutal slaying of Anthony Campbell.

On 12 December 2006, twenty-year-old Anthony Campbell, a football-loving, hard-working young man, was carrying out a plumbing job in a house in Finglas. The house in question belonged to a gangland crook called Marlo Hyland. On that morning, Hyland was asleep upstairs when gunmen entered the house and executed him.

They also shot and killed Anthony Campbell, the only son of Christine Campbell. He was an innocent bystander. Anthony's boss, who had gone to collect supplies for the job, made the gruesome discovery upon returning to the house. Anthony was found slumped in the hallway by a radiator. He had tried to shield himself from the shot; a bullet wound was found in his hand.

That detail breaks my heart. That poor young man, he knew what was coming. I was sickened by this act, everyone was. By all accounts, Anthony was a decent, much-loved and loving young man. He was kind and good-natured and he too had his whole life ahead of him. From everything I've read about him, we have lost a good member of society.

It was the callous nature of his shooting that got to me. I try to comprehend it, but there is no bottom line here. He was without worth or value to whomever entered that house that day. There was no compassion in the heart of that killer; nobody with an ounce of mercy could have carried out such a cold-hearted act.

Of course the bandwagon was rolled out in force, more 'lines were to be drawn'. Scumbags killing scumbags was one thing, but killing innocent civilians was another. But as I sit here today on a bright sunny afternoon, I can type the names Shane Geoghegan and Roy Collins and think, where were the lines this time? What, if anything, has changed since Anthony's death?

Shane was killed in a case of mistaken identity, and Roy was murdered only last week, gunned down by cowards in an attempt to intimidate a family. Again, both men were valued members of their communities. Their loss is our loss. We should be outraged at their deaths, we should be angry and disgusted at the apparent lawlessness of the gangs who appear to operate quite freely. We should be demanding more of our politicians. Sound bites and talk of 'lines drawn' don't mean diddly squat if there is no lasting change.

I cannot think of a more devastating blow than to lose a loved one to murder. I do not know how anyone could get over it. I'm not sure I could. Waking up every day, knowing that someone you loved has been ripped from your life because somebody else decided their fate.

There will of course always be killing: humans are capricious and reactionary. We are jealous and fearful and emotional beings. Who amongst us has not entertained the thought of throttling someone at some point in our lives? Fortunately, most of us exercise a certain level of restraint whereby we can rein-in our baser selves.

I jest about the throttling, sort of, but really all of us have the capacity to slip across the line. We should recognise that and be respectful of it. There is however something deeply repugnant about a person who takes the life of another with *sang froid*.

That's the difference for me. I can wrap my mind around the idea that someone might kill another in the heat of the moment. That a person can weigh up an option and decide, coolly and calmly, to end the life of another person is beyond my ken. I could not, even if it was my worst enemy, imagine murdering a person, taking away their futures, ending their hopes and dreams. I do not have the capacity to inflict that sort of pain. I cannot understand how anyone can take pleasure in death or be immune to grief and suffering. I abhor torture, in all its guises.

I understand now why Peter joked about death and violence, it was his way of coping with the horrors of war. A nurse at his nursing home once blithely said, 'It takes a certain type of man to do what he did.' Yes, lady, it does, but without men like him, people like us might not live the lives we do. War is ugly and horrific and death is a part of it. I'm going to use Orwell for this one: 'People sleep peaceably in their beds at night only because rough men stand ready to do violence on their behalf.'

When I was a tomboy, riding around the wilds of Wicklow with my dog Pharaoh at my side, blathering away to strangers and forgetting to go home at the right time, my skewed view of murder lay in fiction, or 'la-la land' as Kitty called it. With my head in the clouds I thought I could understand killing and bloodshed and explosions that overturned trucks but never seemed to hurt anyone. Yeah, the butler did it, in the library, with a candle-stick. Ho-ho-ho. Don't drink the milk, B.A., there are sleeping tablets in it.

I knew nothing of grief, nothing of brutality, nothing of pain and death. I had not given birth to someone for whom I would lay down my life. I had not watched grieving fathers and mothers plead for information as they held photos of their slain children in shaking hands. I had not kept an ear half-cocked, hoping to hear good news in a case where I suspected there would be none. I had not watched parents tear themselves apart searching endlessly for missing children. I did not know the details of death, how a person suffers, how fear floods the body, how a body breaks down. I did not know people could linger on, incapable of asking for help, dying one second at a time. I did not know there were paedophiles in the world. I did not know jokes about men skinning 'Nips' were a coping mechanism. I did not know life was cheap to some.

I only knew that the good guys would win in the end. As an adult I'm still hoping that is the case.

*

Arlene Hunt is the author of six novels, including the well-liked QuicK Investigation series. She lives in Dublin with her husband and daughter. Her latest novel, *Fair Game*, will be published in 2011. You may contact her at *www.arlenehunt.com*

'The Murder Capital of Feckin' Europe': The Crime Narrative in Irish Theatre

by *Sara Keating*

[The] impulse to protect the criminal is universal in the west [of Ireland]. It seems partly due to the association between justice and the hated English jurisdiction, but more directly to the primitive feeling of these people, who are never criminals, yet always capable of crime, that a man will not do wrong unless he is under the influence of a passion, which is as irresponsible as a storm on the sea. If a man has killed his father, and is already sick and broken with remorse, they can see no reason why he should be dragged away and killed by the law.

J. M. Synge, *The Aran Islands*

The story that prompted this observation was recorded by J. M. Synge in his 1907 ethnography *The Aran Islands*. The story itself – 'of a Connaught man who killed his father with the blow of a spade when he was in passion' – had such significance for the writer that it directly inspired his 1907 play *The Playboy of the Western World*, which became the foundation text of twentieth-century Irish drama. This controversial story of patricide has resonated throughout a century of Irish plays, providing a metaphor for overthrowing post-colonial oppression in the years before Irish independence and a metaphor for conquering the conservative ideologies of de Valera's Ireland as the country moved towards the millennium.

Taking its cue from Synge, Irish theatre finds no shortage of criminal activity throughout its various genres. Genre in the theatre tends to be defined more by form – realist, expressionist, absurdist – than by narrative content. So, while the crime narrative in film and fiction certainly has its idiosyncratic structural and stylistic techniques, in theatre the 'theatrical crime thriller' does not exist formally as a genre.

Instead, it is through plot, theme and tone that the crime narrative finds its expression, and it is Christy Mahon's brutal familial murder that set a template for the twentieth-century Irish playwright, whose dramas are set in motion, whose tragedies are brought to catharsis, by and large by the domestic crime. Indeed, in plays by writers like Synge, John B. Keane, Tom Murphy, Marina Carr and the plays of other writers throughout the century, it is the family home that is the scene of the theatrical crime – the site of parricide, filicide, general murder, incest – and blood-relatives that provide its main victims. The Irish family home is a place where a father can set his children upon each other (*A Whistle in the Dark*) or where a man can kill a stranger to ensure he keeps his home (*The Field*) or where a pimp can kill the woman who stands in the way of his pipe-dreams (*The House*). These are plays that stand alone as visceral violent crime dramas, but that can, like Christy Mahon's crime, also be read as microcosms of the nation; a nation itself founded on an act of violent bloodshed. (Indeed, in his film noir-inspired play, *The Blue Macushla*, Tom Murphy went so far as to makes gangsters out of Republican heroes.) And they can also be read as criticisms of a nation that imagined itself more in line with literary ideals; that refused to take account of its 'dysfunctional, impoverished reality'.

However, as Ireland began to realise itself as a modern nation in the late twentieth century, so Irish playwrights began to take interest in using the crime narrative in a different context. Inspired by American film, international crime fiction and the changing face of Ireland as it moved towards the millennium, playwrights like Declan Hughes, Gerard Stembridge, Conor McPherson and Mark O'Rowe began to explore the neglected urban life of the nation. Irish drama thus found itself re-invigorated by contemporary crime narratives set in modern Irish cities, which drew on a key influence of mass culture and the cinematic tradition to create a highly stylised, yet realistic, representation of the complexity of modern Irish life.

It is firstly, however, the plays of Martin McDonagh that provide a full picture of the extent to which the crime narrative has infiltrated Irish drama since the early twentieth century and the effect this has had on a contemporary generation of writers. Although his Leenane Trilogy was written in the late 1990s, his extensive post-modern poaching of key plot points from other, earlier Irish plays, draws attention to the disproportionate amount of domestic discord and criminality in Irish drama. Indeed, McDonagh uses a single community – a fictionalised version of a real Connemara village, Leenane – to create a condensed and concise version of the unlawful, immoral characterisations and illicit plots that Irish theatre relies on. Indeed in *The Beauty Queen of Leenane* the central crime of matricide recalls the parricide of *The Playboy of the Western World*. The loy that Christy Mahon's father uses to kill his father, however, is replaced by a poker, with which the sexually-repressed, forty-year-old virgin Maureen, the 'beauty queen' of the title, beats her mother to death.

In many ways, the real tragedy, the real victim, is Maureen. While there is no argument that can really condone her torture of her elderly mother, Mag, her rage is understandable. After brutally and deliberately sabotaging her daughter's one chance at happiness, there is no doubt that the vile Mag deserved it. Indeed, if Mag were not so infirm, there is no doubt that she would be capable of similar sins: murder is logical when living among the depraved. It is the simultaneous monstrosity of the victim and the horror of the crime (along with McDonagh's highly stylised language and absurd dialogue) that sustains a tragic-comic effect in this brutal execution; a tragic-comic effect that is carried through to the rest of the trilogy where crime upon crime is layered upon Leenane, 'the murder capital of feckin' Europe'.

A Skull in Connemara, the second play of the trilogy, borrows its title from a vague reference in Beckett's *Waiting for Godot*. In the last lines of Lucky's rambling, nonsensical speech, he declaims ' . . . I resume alas alas abandoned unfinished the skull the skull in Connemara.' In Beckett the 'skull in Connemara' is suitably allusive, suggesting a looming threat in the western landscape; in McDonagh it refers to the unfinished matter of yet another murder. The play, like *The Beauty Queen of Leenane*, takes place in a cottage in remote Leenane, in which Mick Dowd, gravedigger, is preparing to disinter bodies from the graveyard to make way for the latest batch of local corpses. There are two central mysteries at the heart of the plot. Firstly, what does Mick do with the unburied skeletons? ('Skitters' them to pieces and dumps them in the lake.) Secondly, did Mick kill his wife or was it an accident? (It turns out that it was sort of both: Mick's murderous intent was forestalled by the intervention of fate.) It is the inept local policeman and wannabe detective Thomas Hanlon who is charged with unravelling the root of these questions. However, he is so preoccupied with late-night crime on TV (*Hillstreet Blues* and *Quincy* provide his crime-busting models of choice) that he cannot even see, let alone solve, the crimes going on under his nose. In typical McDonagh fashion, we aren't given any definitive answers: no arrests are made; no bodies are repatriated to their resting ground. What we understand for certain, however, is that 'if it's a murderer ye've always wanted living in yere midst, ye can feckin' have one.' If Leenane is, indeed, as Tom's younger brother Mairtin explains, a community so bored that any crime will do nicely for a bit of excitement, then one of the locals will surely oblige; locals like Valene or Coleman Connor.

It is the plight of the warring Connor brothers that provide the conclusion to the Leenane Trilogy; the final proof, if any were needed, that the fictional Leenane is, as Father Walsh says, the murder capital of Europe. Drawing influence from Tom Murphy's play, *A Whistle in the Dark*, the play opens on the eve of the brothers' father's funeral. The action soon reveals that Coleman killed his father after a lifetime of abuse (another nod to *The Playboy of the Western World*); but more specifically because he said 'me hair was like a drunken child's.' Valene, holding the moral high ground over his younger brother, blackmails Coleman out of his inheritance with the threat of handing him over to the police. Valene's strategy fails, however, because Coleman has long ago embezzled the insurance money. As the brothers turn on each other with murderous intent, the suicidal local parish priest and illegal *poitín* smuggler, Girleen, intervene, but their own skewed morality manages to goad the brothers on rather than dissuade them.

If the Leenane Trilogy, produced individually by Druid Theatre between 1996 and 1997, suggested that late twentieth-century Ireland was still in thrall to a rural imagination, the late 1990s also saw an explosion of playwrights constructing new theatrical realities that took account of contemporary Irish life in the city and, with it, the crime that accompanies urbanisation. In the 1996 play *The Gay Detective*, for example, Gerry Stembridge used a detective plot to suggest how the burgeoning Celtic Tiger modernisation was also encouraging social change in Ireland, most notably in the liberalisation of homosexuality laws. Set in a shadowy Dublin underworld, the play combined social commentary with the noir crime narrative, as the hero of the play, gay detective Pat, uses his position to solve a series of homophobic crimes, including several incidences of 'queer-bashing' and the double-murder of a prominent, closeted, homosexual TD and a rent boy. However, solving the crime is the least of Pat's worries, as he is forced to dodge the prejudices of his peers, and Pat ends up finding the culprit, but leaving the police force. Homosexuality and the crime narrative are in this case incompatible.

They also prove incompatible in the work of Mark O'Rowe, who also began to use the crime idiom to interrogate configurations of masculinity and reflect the changing social landscape of late twentieth-century Ireland.

O'Rowe describes himself as an 'urban writer, specifically a Dublin writer, and, more specifically, a writer from Tallaght.' O'Rowe's journey to the theatre came through film, when, imagining a future as a Hollywood film director, theatre seemed a more realistic option or at least a good starting point; at the very least you could rent a school hall or a pub and get a few of your friends to put your play on. O'Rowe's first play, *The Aspidistra Code* (1996), was a blend of kitchen-sink drama and gangster play, following the plight of a family as they are pursued by a loan-shark, Drongo, and defended by an modern urban Robin Hood, known as Crazy Horse. Much of the humour in the play comes from the fact that the criminal underworld dragged on stage in the shape of these two grotesque criminals is one that comes with its own strict ethical codes of honour: as Drongo says, right before he raises a gun to complete his hit: 'Without moral values, ethics, etiquette, principles, we are without rules. I have to do my job. I have to do my job and I'm sorry, mates. I'm sorry for you. But if I don't stick to my rules, then what am I?'

O'Rowe's second play, *From Both Hips* (1997), was another family drama, this time shaped into a comic thriller of violence and vengeance and which also ended with a dramatic shoot-out. The play centres on petty criminal Paul, who has been accidentally shot by a nervous policeman and member of the Drugs Squad, Willie. As Paul threatens revenge of the most malicious kind – tabloid exposure is as vicious as any violence – Willie comes up with an idea that is less as 'eye for an eye', more of a 'hip for a hip'. It is O'Rowe's plays, *Howie the Rookie* (1997) and *Terminus* (2006), however, that create the most original marriage of crime narrative and theatrical exposition in Irish drama. Using the monologue form to inhabit a series of characters – to portray their criminal exploits from the inside-out – *Howie the Rookie* and *Terminus* occupied a peculiar space between comic crime caper and poignant tragedy, in which an odyssey through an unnamed city, a fictional Dublin, becomes a journey into a grotesque underworld in which the characters seek redemption. As O'Rowe explains: 'In the early plays like *The Aspidistra Code* or *From Both Hips*, you had violent characters seen from normal people's perspectives. It was with *Howie the Rookie* that I really had to question myself. It's not the kitchen sink element, the people in the house who are witnessing this. It's actually the people who commit. They're the people I'm interested in.'

Howie the Rookie splits the story between two characters: The Howie Lee and The Rookie Lee, united by 'their namesake in Lee-ness', Bruce Lee. These are characters who 'enjoy bein' after people', and who see sex as a way of proving their prowess and their masculinity. The Howie Lee narrates the first part of their shared story; it is the story of a debt of honour between friends that must be repaid, which ends in the accidental death of The Howie Lee's young brother Mousey. In the second part of the play, The Rookie Lee takes up the narration, recounting how The Howie comes to his defence in an attempt at finding redemption for the sacrifice of his brother. Juxtaposing a stylised Dublin idiom – full of formal syntax and poetic flights – O'Rowe establishes an almost mock-heroic presentation of the men: men who are using crime, violence, are even prepared to murder, in order to preserve their reputations. Encountering grotesque characters like Peaches and his sex-mad sister Avalanche, big-time crime boss Ladyboy and his fighting piranha fish, joy-riders Ginger Boy and Flann Dingle, O'Rowe creates a world full of vivid danger and endless moral temptation. But the play is not necessarily about character. It is, like conventional Hollywood crime thrillers, all about the momentum of the story, and O'Rowe's heightened prose is constantly pushing with forward momentum, on and on, until the inevitable finale, the ultimate sacrifice: the death of The Howie Lee.

As petty criminals, common thugs, on the verge of committing a heinous crime, the characters in *Howie the Rookie* find echoes in O'Rowe's 2003 film *Intermission*, which has at the heart of it's multi-themed, Robert Altman-influenced plot, a bank heist in which a pair of bored supermarket workers find themselves embroiled in a quest for vengeance being worked out between Irish music-loving detective Jerry Lynch and a domesticated professional thief Lehiff, who was played by Colin Farrell. However, O'Rowe returned to inhabit the mind of a deranged serial killer, known only as C, in his 2006 play *Terminus*. The interweaving plot-threads in *Terminus* are shared between three characters, each narrative thread resonating with familiar crime narrative elements. In the first story, told by A, a mother, trying to redeem herself after stealing her daughter's boyfriend, is drawn into the lair of a lesbian crime gang who are about to perform an illegal abortion. In the second story, told by B, a lonely young woman breaks into a building site at night and climbs a crane, from which she is either pushed or falls to her death. In the third story, told by C, a painfully shy man makes a pact with the devil: trading his soul, and the souls of all the victims that he kills, for a beautiful singing voice. Crafted in metered verse, in *Terminus* O'Rowe uses the urban forms of slam poetry and rap to find a distinct literary voice in which to make his trademark heightened language and his earthy contemporary crime plot compatible. With high-speed car chases, murdered hitchhikers, and, eventually, the disembowelment of the serial killer, *Terminus* is a blend of crime narrative and supernatural horror. It proved again how far O'Rowe was prepared to go, not just in presenting atypical narratives on the stage, but in inhabiting those stories from the inside.

Conor McPherson's early monologue plays set a similar precedent, using first-person narrative confession or recollection to tell stories set in modern Dublin. Like O'Rowe, the first-person narrative provides an inherent pace and drama to the characters' unfolding odysseys through modern Ireland. The supernatural influences referred to in the plays hark back to ancient Irish traditions. However, the supernatural beings that appear in the stories are drawn straight from vampire and horror films. In these early plays, the crime narratives and quests of revenge or fulfilment are played out in contemporary situations by usually adolescent, usually substance-abusing young men.

Part coming-of-age drama, part comedy crime caper, *This Lime Tree Bower* (1995) is set in a small seaside suburb of Dublin, where three men – brothers Frank and Joe, and their sister's boyfriend, Ray – find their lives thrust together by an unexpected series of events, which centre around the robbery of a local bookmakers. The crime, like the crime at the heart of his 1994 play *The Good Thief,* is a crime with a moral intent: to rob from the rich (the bookie) to give to the poor (Frank and Joe's debt-ridden father). Although, like many of McPherson's plays, *This Lime Tree Bower* is more concerned with the act of storytelling than the story itself, the play prefigures McPherson's 1997 film *I Went Down,* whose story of loan-sharks, road-trips, and gang-related revenge, is a typical comedy crime film. However, the supernatural elements of plays like *St Nicholas* (1997) and *The Seafarer* (2006) tend to eclipse McPherson's crime narratives, and the appearance in the plays of vampires (*St Nicholas*) or the devil himself (*The Seafarer*) do bring the plays closer to the horror genre more than crime. But it is important to take note of how the plays rely on narrative mystery, plot suspense and a noir-ish atmosphere for their effect.

In Northern Irish drama, the crime narrative has for long been intertwined with the politics of various paramilitary organisations and their political goals. However, since the late 1990s, Northern Ireland has moved towards increasing stability and playwrights have found the crime narrative to be increasingly useful in exploring – indeed, debunking – the issue of now-defunct paramilitary organisations. Martin McDonagh's 2000 play, *The Lieutenant of Inishmore*, is set on the small Aran Island of Inishmore, where émigré island man, Mad Padraig – one of the members of one of the many republican splinter groups who populate the play – is due to visit home.

Early on in the play we get to see Mad Padraig at work, torturing a drug-addict who owes him money. The scene confirms McDonagh's satirical view: politics in relation to Northern Ireland has given way to petty crime; drug-dealing, gun-running, and not a single political belief between any of the characters. The rest of the play, which involves a gun-toting soldier-girl, several murders, and the death and resurrection of a cat, continues this deflationary attitude to the current situation in Northern Ireland; that political violence and terrorism has become so irrelevant that its proponents will start gang-wars and killing sprees over the death of pet.

Rosemary Jenkinson's 2006 play, *The Bonefire*, takes a similar parodic view of paramilitary violence, applying it in this instance to loyalist organisations. Set on the eve of the Twelfth of July in a flat in the notorious Annadale complex in Belfast, a group of 'UDA' wannabes get dragged into the crossfire of a paramilitary gang war they know nothing about. The petty crimes that fund their cocaine-furled lifestyle include social-security fraud, selling weapons locally and low-level drug dealing. However, the main point that Jenkinson, like McDonagh, is trying to make, is that political convictions have become irrelevant in post-ceasefire Northern Ireland: it's all about petty squabbles and material greed now, as a typical exchange has it:

> **Leanne:** Why are we ever flying that Israel flag from the top of the flats?
> **Tommy:** Well, now. It's because the Catholics is flying the Palestinian flag.
> **Leanne:** Well, you wouldn't be too happy if them Israel folk came wailing around our walls in their skull-caps would you?
> **Tommy:** Look, it's just a flag isn't it? We have the English flag but I don't expect them to be taking over Annadale tomorrow.
> **Leanne:** They already did . . . In the sixteen hundreds . . .

It would be a crime to conclude this essay without making reference to the early plays of Declan Hughes, who, with his Ed Loy series, has become one of the most significant Irish crime fiction writers to emerge over the last five years. If Loy's very name reveals Hughes' theatrical origins (the loy was Christy Mahon's weapon of choice for murdering his father in *The Playboy of the Western World*), so Hughes's plays were heavily marked by the influence of crime fiction and film noir. For Hughes, the influence was inevitable: the world, he says, has 'been colonised irrevocably by the first beam of light Hollywood had shone on us.'

I Can't Get Started (1990), a fictional bio-drama based on Dashiell Hammett's writing career, reflected the emerging playwright's interest in crime fiction. *I Can't Get Started* demonstrated an astute understanding and sardonic exploitation of early twentieth-century crime narratives, using the very crime conventions that Hughes satirises, complete with a hard-drinking anti-hero who turns good at the end, and the two types of women prevalent in crime fiction: 'good old girls' and 'femme fatale types'. Hughes presents us with an arrogant, alcoholic, past-his-sell-by-date writer, who literally can't get started on his new book. Hammett wants his work to take a more literary turn; he is 'through with all that hard-boiled crime stuff, it's a menace.' However, Hammett finds himself haunted by future characters, in the shape of Daniel Webster, Private Eye, who pursues the plot of a typical hard-boiled crime thriller in front of the audience's eyes. 'I need you to leave me alone, Dan,' Hammett implores the imaginary detective. 'You're a relic from a stupider age. A fossil. An outmoded myth.' However, Hammett actually needs Dan more than he knows, because when Dan figures out the mystery of the multiple murders he 'does what the detective always does at the end of the story. He explains what everything means.' This crime mystery has been 'the story of a woman who loves too much a man who cannot love at all'; just like Hammett's own life story and Hughes's play.

Hughes's 1998 play, *Twenty Grand*, is a less self-conscious transfer of the crime-fiction narrative to drama for the stage. The play is set in crime-boss Frank 'Sinatra' Hackett's nightclub headquarters as he prepares to transfer power to his son-in-law, Tommy Dalton. Again Hughes writes with his tongue in cheek – these are herbal-tea-drinking, stammering gangsters – but, with its bank heists and its battles between virtue and vengeance, the plot enacts a traditional crime narrative, complete with last minute plot-twists, whose denouement brings the play to a violent, bloody close.

Since this relative explosion of contemporary crime drama on to the Irish stage in the 1990s, there have been many other crime plays. *Rank* by Robert Massey, which features money-laundering suburban-dwelling taxi-drivers; *Noah and the Tower Flower*, which tells the story of a recovering drug-addict drawn back into crime in Ballymun; and *Homeland* by Paul Mercier, which enacts an odyssey of political corruption, prostitution and property swindles in contemporary Dublin, are just some of the many examples.

What these plays will contribute to the canon of Irish drama on a broader scale remains to be seen, but they surely will, as the plays of the 1990s did, continue to engage with Synge's observations about the 'impulse to protect the criminal in the West' or Martin McDonagh's assertion that, in dramatic terms, anyway, Ireland is the 'murder capital of feckin' Europe'.

*

Sara Keating writes about theatre for the *Irish Times*. In 2006 she received a PhD for her research on contemporary Irish drama. She teaches courses on Irish theatre at Trinity College and University College Dublin.

A Dangerous Hope

By Andrew Nugent

I was lucky; I got two university educations. In the first I was trained in UCD and Kings Inns as a lawyer, a trade which I plied for a couple of years. At the end of my second sojourn in the groves of academia, I was pronounced a competent theologian by Strasbourg University – a fine Reformation foundation – and a tolerably safe one by the Roman authorities. I had been required to swear a few lurid oaths in Latin to reassure the appropriate Roman Congregation on that score. They are – or certainly were in those days – inclined to fret about such matters. This second university career coincided with my late adolescence – i.e. my mid-twenties – the immediate aftermath of the Second Vatican Council, and also with the Student Revolution of 1968 in France. I can say been there, done that; and they were exciting times. My next novel revisits Strasbourg and '68, of which I have vivid memories.

I should explain at the outset that – as a very late vocation to the order of crime writers – the only crime writer I feel qualified to write about is myself. So the requirements of both vanity and humility are perfectly satisfied if I confine myself to doing just that.

When I came back from my studies, and for the next quarter century, I became engrossed in school work and confined my writing to fairly frequent articles in the areas of spirituality-lite and pastoral theology. It was only in 1999 – just ten years ago, and I in my early sixties – that I began to write fiction. By then I had been living in Nigeria for nine years, as Novice Master in a foundation of my home abbey. The people were beautiful and my novices were wonderful, but the climate, food, diseases, corruption, scorpions, snakes and road accidents were eventually catching up with me. I was looking forward to a well-earned sabbatical leave.

Instead, 1999 was my *annus horribilis* – as the dear Queen would say. My two companion (Irish) monks died within four months of each other, both from complications of malaria; and in the middle of that, my own younger brother back in Ireland also died. He was only in his fifties and we were very close.

Those three deaths were like repeated hammer blows – tough to take. What could I do? There was no pub to go to, to drink a few pints and drown my sorrows. There was no TV where I could watch Manchester United and forget my sadness. So I began writing. I thought at the time that this was just to distract myself and to escape from a painful situation. I certainly never imagined that what I was writing could ever be published – which is quite an interesting way to write a book.

With time I discovered that I was not writing to escape anything or any-where. On the contrary, I was writing out of a need to go deeper into myself and, equally, out of a desire to communicate with other people in a more meaningful way.

There is the maxim familiar to all writers: Write about what you know. For once, I did not feel inclined to write about religion. It was not that I had ceased to show reverence to God, but I was much less certain that I knew what He was up to, in my own life or in the whole wide world. 'No harm too!' I seem to hear my built-in Greek Chorus warbling.

So, apart from religion, what else did I know about? I knew about the law and lawyers. So I wrote *The Four Courts Murder*. Then, I had lived a long time in Africa and had come to love the Nigerian people, so I wrote *Second Burial*, or *Second Burial for a Black Prince*, as it is called in the US. This is a story about Nigerians living in Dublin's inner city. It was written, at least partly, to per-suade readers that black people, too, laugh and cry, have feelings and hopes and fears, that they are capable of extreme courage, generosity, intense loyalty, and love. Finally, as I had worked for most of my adult life in a boys' boarding school, I knew something about that species too. So I wrote *Soul Murder*, which celebrates the many good qualities of teenage boys – warts, moods, nerve-jangling music and all – and it also touches on some delicate and important issues.

In the last decade I have also written a spiritual book, *The Slow-Release Miracle*. To my considerable surprise I was to discover that all four books – both murder and mysticism – came from the same place within myself, and that if I had not started to write the novels, I would never have been able to write the spiritual book either, or a further chapter of autobiography contained in a collective work of 'ten monastic journeys', which appeared in 2008.

John McGahern, the Irish novelist, once said to a friend of mine, 'I write to know what I am thinking.' This is so true. Writers can expect people in their own circle to enjoy psychoanalysing them on the basis of what they write. It is, I suppose, one of the legitimate uses of literacy – a free ride on somebody else's literacy. But, more often than not, it is a fairly superficial exercise where it is not downright codswallop. Interpretation requires a minimum of empathy and a spiteful reader usually finds what he is looking for.

But for an author himself – and no doubt for a thoughtful and unbiased reader too – what he writes can be truly revealing. In retrospect – I mean re-reading – I seem to have had two major preoccupations in what I have written so far, one negative and one positive. These are envy and hope. They are, when you think of it, two sides of the same coin, which we call desire. A wise abbot has defined a monk as 'one who desires and who desires to always go on desiring.' Perhaps, until we get to be really wise, this desiring business can be both hazardous and ambivalent – but it is always worthwhile. Anyhow the only alternative is to be dead. So, yes, I am interested in desire, and I should like to say something about these two forms of desiring: envy and hope.

*

Envy is defined as the resentful or unhappy feeling of wanting what somebody else already possesses. The Book of Wisdom says that 'Death came into the world through the devil's envy' (Wis. 2: 24). This was interpreted by some of the Fathers of the Church to mean that the demons were envious of humankind's vocation to become divine, as adopted children of God. So they became the sworn enemies of every human person, seeking – by temptation – to wreak soul-murder on a massive scale. St. Cyprian of Carthage, in particular, teaches that envy – not money or pride – is the root of all evil. He warns the Church and the Christian community against it.

As a pragmatic fact, there is much envy in ecclesiastical and religious circles, as also in the academic world, where, not just by coincidence, the academic bonnet mimics the monastic hood. Just think of the novels of C. P. Snow.

According to St John the Evangelist, the prototype murder in human history – which should surely be of interest to crime writers – was caused by envy. 'Cain cut his brother's throat simply because his own life was evil and his brother lived a good life' (1Jn 3:12).

Without asking readers to buy into all that stuff about the Bible and demons, and the Fathers of the Church, we can consult John Cassian, one of the pioneers of desert monasticism – a believer himself, certainly – but a hard-nosed realist when it comes to human behaviour. Cassian describes envy as the 'hidden snake-bite'. It is all the more pernicious, he adds, because it goes unrecognised and unacknowledged, even by the people themselves who are most addicted to it. Cassian concludes bleakly that envy – of all the vices – is the most difficult to remedy and is, in fact, practically incurable.

Envy is also an unnatural vice, according to the wisdom of the desert fathers. It does not even feature on the list of *logismoi*, the normal danger areas associated with natural urges like sex and other physical appetites, or the natural reactive drives, like anger and sadness.

As I have said, very few people will admit, even to themselves, that they are consumed by envy. So the disease runs rampant and is very difficult to eradicate. We have only to look at contemporary western society to be convinced: Envy has become a way of life, almost an art form, if not actually a religion. Is that not what the current catastrophic economic turmoil – with its immense number of victims worldwide – is basically all about? Envy and its elderly ugly first cousin – sheer greed.

There is a rich vein here for crime writers to exploit. I would contend, moreover, that, while people who write crime should not be sanctimonious moralisers – nothing could be more tiresome – crime writers must be moralists. That is to say that they should have a definite ethical sense, if only because they are practically the only source of moral imperatives that a lot of people even half-listen to in contemporary society. They must stand up and be counted. They must be *engages*, if they are not themselves to become *des salauds*, as Jean-Paul Sartre did not hesitate to call the gutless and spineless of another age.

In *Soul Murder* I have suggested that some of the most egregious cases of sexual predation, especially in respect of younger or otherwise vulnerable people, are not motivated so much by lust or even by the allure of money – for instance, where the dominant person coerces the other to engage in prostitution and to hand over all or part of her/his earnings – but by envy, by the cruel use of power to destroy innocence, to deflower, to deprave, to humiliate, to drag somebody down to one's own level. This is indeed the very definition of soul murder.

Both from the point of view of the victims and of the perpetrators of these crimes, it is important to recognise the true dimensions of the trauma inflicted, as also of the malice that can inspire it.

It was a blog-reviewer called Anne Brooke who helped me to identify another, perhaps even more fundamental reason, for which I write murder mysteries. She wrote (on a website called It's a Crime or a Mystery):

'I really enjoyed [*Second Burial*], which I reviewed for Mystery Scene last year. What's interesting about it is that, in spite of what sound like very dark themes, it's very hopeful and almost light-hearted in an unusual way.'

I believe that this is exactly what I am trying to do, to 'give an account of the hope that is in me' (1P 3:15). This is not at all a question of being manipulative with readers, or propagandist, or moralising – still less of telling them edifying tales. Indeed, some of my tales, as I have been told severely on more than one occasion, are distinctly less than edifying.

But it is my deep conviction that life is that slow-release miracle, where people find themselves caught up in all kinds of difficult situations, and even tragedies, which they quite frequently do not understand themselves. Yet, in their very bewilderment, such people can grow and deepen, and thereby create a meaning for what is negative, destructive, and meaningless in life, and even in death.

My publishers classify me as a crime writer. I am acutely aware that some addicts of crime novels must find me disappointing because I am not so much interested in solving crimes, as in understanding victims and survivors. These are the true heroes of my books in the sense that Joseph Campbell uses the word in his seminal work, *The Hero with a Thousand Faces*. It is they who have to undertake the difficult, hazardous, and transformative itinerary towards a goal. The police, I think, have a different role. Not heroes, nor even anti-heroes, they are mentors, sages, interpreters, guardians. The Irish police force is called the Garda Síochána, guardians of the peace. It is an honourable title, and besides, I am sure that the Garda detection rate is right up there, in line with international standards.

Once again, it is a blog-reviewer who expresses the point very accurately. I only have her first name, Meen, and I know that she is Dutch, and lives in Ireland. (In parentheses, I should say that I do pay attention to reviews by bloggers, both favourable and hostile – and I have got a few terrible ones – because there is a strong possibility that the bloggers have, at least, actually read the books).

Meen writes of my murder mysteries:

'These books are not exactly police procedurals, even if the investigators are members of the Gardaí. The author is more interested in human rela-tionships than investigative procedures.'

She is kind enough to add, 'and for me, this really works' and to say encouragingly, 'I'm already looking forward to the next one.'

This irenic addendum makes it easier for me to plead, 'Guilty as charged'.

My cops are three in number, one female and two males. One is sixty-ish, one fifty-ish, and one in her late twenties. I get the impression that they are absolutely atypical because all three are happily married to partner No. 1, and the spouses get to feature in the books as well. None of them is hard-boiled or world-weary, none of them chain-smokes or drinks heavily, eats only junk food, or habitually sleeps in their clothes, and none of them has ancient parents who I can use to pad out the pages by interminably dragging them off to the home for the bewildered.

If they are a tad laidback, it is not their fault. It is because I want victims and survivors to hold centre stage. It is they who have to embark on the hero's journey, to grow, to develop, to deepen, and to be transformed. Because – what do you know! – that is the way it is in real life.

I make honourable amends to the Gardaí, as best I can. They do investigate, and they do solve cases, and they do arrest the villains – well, those villains whom I have not disposed of myself before they can get to them. But, in addition, in the context of the heroes' journeys, the police people become real persons and they get to do things less clockwork and more humanly meaningful than mere investigation.

And where is hope in all this? Precisely, hope is the dynamo for action and for the journey. Meaningful action becomes possible, not so much on the basis of investigation and problem solving, but much more in terms of sensitivity in relationships, listening, and obedience to the voice of the Spirit. Jürgen Moltmann says, in his splendid book *The Theology of Hope*, 'Meaningful action is possible only against a horizon of expectation.' Hope is that horizon of expectation, and only those who have that horizon of expectation – however shadowy and incoherent it may be – will have the courage and dynamism to embark on the hero's journey.

Our culture is short on hope. Living for a time in a third world country, I am struck by the contrast between the vibrant hope of those who have nothing and the hopelessness of those with too much. There is more spiritualstarvation in the northern hemisphere of our planet than physical hunger in the poorest parts of the world.

The symptoms of hopelessness are everywhere to be seen in our western world: addiction, suicide, obsessive greed for everything from food to money, perversion and trivialisation of sex, devaluation of marriage and of all enduring personal commitments, crisis in the religious ministry, abdication of parenting – and even of reproduction, to the point of zero growth levels in population, so that, especially in Northern Europe, whole nations have become like colonies of octogenarian lemmings, hobbling headlong into the sea. All of this betokens a society which has massively lost hope.

Of course, hope is dangerous. Hope threatens the precarious security of the present moment, the gratification of bread and circuses now. Hope is inseparable from growth, change, and creative insecurity. Hope is for those who travel light, risk-takers, pilgrims. Our culture craves absolute security now. This is our Achilles' heel. The terrorists have understood that.

So that is why I am so attracted by those who embark on the hero's journey. Maybe they refuse the call the first time it sounds, as Campbell recognises as almost paradigmatic, and most often they are forced by a cruel fate to answer the summons – as, for instance, the case of the survivor who feels duty-bound to seek the difficult and dangerous path to avenge a loved one by bringing his killer to justice. There is much more at stake in a human tragedy than a routine police investigation and a fair cop at the end. All that is merely the little story.

I choose young people for my heroes because, for all their faults and failings, they most spontaneously have that audacity of hope. Things may not turn out very well in the end. In some cases, there may be no happy ending. The hero's journey may not turn out to be a triumphal progress but, on the contrary, a veritable way-of-the-cross, spiralling down to disintegration and death. This, too, is a fact of life. Ultimately, none of us is going to get out of here alive. And this, too, is integral to the awesome audacity of hope.

*

Andrew Nugent's murder mysteries are all autobiographies which feature a trial lawyer, monk, missionary, or headmaster. In his forthcoming novel, *1968*, he is a student at Strasbourg University, where his better self gets murdered. As an author, he is less interested in what happens to killers than in the heroic journey of victims and survivors.

Walking the Tightrope:
The Border in Irish Fiction

by Brian McGilloway

Almost my entire life, I have lived in places marked by duality. I grew up in Derry or Londonderry, a city bisected by the River Foyle, where your religion and political allegiance could be assumed from which name you gave the place. Derry, in many ways, for years operated as a microcosm of what was happening nationally. So close to the border that the Sunday afternoons of our childhood inevitably involved cross-border trips for Chef Brown Sauce, among other things, there were even plans at one stage to run the Irish border up the river and split the city literally between the North and South of Ireland. This plan is not as ludicrous as it sounds, perhaps, for the border runs along the river for most of the twenty miles from Strabane to Derry, veering wildly off to one side just before it hits the city, then correcting its course a few miles further down on the far side of the city limits.

Later I moved to Strabane, which sits to one side of the fledgling River Foyle, while Lifford sits across the water. I remember as a child crossing the border checkpoint here – The Camel's Hump, as it was known. The journey was memorable due in no small measure to the huge Army hangar that squatted on the border. There could be no doubt when you had crossed into 'the South'.

Of course, the problem with this was that 'the South' was actually, geographically, to the North, and the North to the South, due to the decision to excise Donegal from Northern Ireland despite its place in the province of Ulster. All of this made some sort of absurd sense to us when we were young. My own children, however, struggle to grasp it because the border as a physical entity no longer exists. You can cross from Lifford to Strabane without ever encountering a checkpoint now – unless police have wind of imminent dissident terrorist attacks, or some agricultural scare necessitates a border patrol. In fact, now the only way to tell when you have left one country and entered another is by the slight change in the quality of the tar surfacing the roads and the fact that one territory uses miles per hour on signage, and the other kilometres.

Indeed, crossing the bridge from Strabane to Lifford is as easy as crossing the bridge from the Waterside to the city-side in Derry – which perhaps explains my own fascination with borders and why I choose to set my crime series in the borderlands of the Lifford/Strabane area.

The border in the Devlin series represents various things. The borderlands are the grey area that most of us inhabit, the distance between what we'd like to do and how we'd like to be, and what we actually do and who we actually are. And perhaps spurred on by notions of the border as a frontier, elements of the Wild West have surfaced more than once in the Devlin novels: *Bleed A River Deep* concerns a gold mine, a modern day gold rush and features, on the first page, one of the main characters 'with a gun in his hand . . . Only five years old and a little under three feet tall, he had a cowboy hat tipped back on his head, his hair strands of fine spun gold, hanging in his eyes.'

The border also operates for me as a reflection of how things have changed. When I began writing the first book, I deliberately set out not to write a political novel. Despite this, in each book I find elements of the Troubles appearing. *Borderlands* touches on 'the disappeared', common in the border areas in the 1970s. *Gallows Lane* concerns men who use religion as a front for violence and the image of Cuchulainn. *Bleed A River Deep* concerns itself with the smuggling of people and laundering of fuel across the border by individuals desperate to establish criminal empires. And in all the books, the developing professional relationship between Devlin and Jim Hendry reflects something of how I see the developing relationship between North and South impacting on the ground. Devlin crosses the border frequently into the North; having spoken to officers on both sides of the border, that is not unusual. One mentioned his happiest memory of cross border co-operation was when the Guards visited the RUC station at Christmas with crates of Guinness.

Border settings feature prominently in a number of the most recent Irish crime novels, with four books released in the past three months in Ireland (including the third Devlin novel, *Bleed A River Deep*) which utilise border settings. Declan Hughes' *All The Dead Voices* centres around the present-day effects of a botched assassination attempt on a judge near the border in South Armagh during the Troubles. Lying in wait for a judge making his way from Dublin to Belfast, near Newry on the border, the IRA bombers discuss the politics of the Troubles. In one striking passage towards the end, following an act of extreme violence, Hughes captures the dual nature of the aesthetically stunning border area and the horrifying events which occurred there:

'After the fire and the smoke, and the debris and body parts scattered about the fields, amid the sulphur and burning flesh, and the savage whooping and hollering of Ice, Red stared across the fields, the heartbreakingly beautiful hills and fields of South Armagh. Was it then that he understood that only great and lasting dishonour and shame would be gained if they won the land back by this kind of slaughter.'

The republican heartland features more extensively in Stuart Neville's *The Twelve* (*The Ghosts of Belfast* in the US) which reaches its climax in the border-straddling farmland of Bull O'Kane – a prominent republican who shunned the political in preference to the criminal. Within the book he is connected with fuel smuggling, dog fighting and dodgy land acquisitions through intimidation, as well as being implicated in numerous murders, of course. Many of the activities of Bull O'Kane would not be out of place in Toby Harnden's *Bandit Country*, a seminal work of non-fiction on the paramilitary campaign in South Armagh. Indeed, it seems wholly appropriate that the book should end on the border, for the protagonist, Gerry Fegan, inhabits a number of borderlands of his own, both moral and psychological.

Smuggling of people across the border is a key plot element of Adrian McKinty's *Fifty Grand*. However, and fittingly for an Irish writer no longer living in Ireland, the border in question is between Mexico and the US rather than in Ireland. Nevertheless, in a visceral, brutal opening scene, the border crossing is inextricably linked with exploitation, violence and ultimately death, despite the fact that the actual border itself is an abstract:

'We made it,' he said again.

I peered through the window and wondered how he could be so sure. It looked like fucking Mars out there. A thin brown sand worrying itself over a bleached yellow ground. Nothing alive, all the rocks weathered into dust.'

It seems clear to me why crime writers might be attracted to border settings – the demarcations of power, clashes of cultures, jurisdictional conflicts, crimes, murders and various forms of smuggling all sit easily in a crime narrative. I did wonder how non-crime writers who choose to write the area might approach it. The truth of the matter is, though, that the border isn't really used in crime fiction any differently than it is in non-genre writing. And the more I read in other forms and genres, the more I became convinced that any book set on the border must have an element of crime about it for, in literature at least, the two seem almost synonymous.

Indeed, the themes and issues present in almost any texts written about the border seem to feature commonalities with Irish crime fiction. Unsurprisingly, the border is most obviously associated with the Troubles. Cross-border killings and the divisions between North and South and, by extension, Catholics and Protestants, feature in all works. Alongside this, normal crime, especially smuggling, is again a common feature and, with this, an awareness of the differences in standards of living between the two territories. It is perhaps understandable, when a country has been split in two, to a degree arbitrarily, that writers should be aware of and exploit the inherent absurdity of the formation of the border and the quirks and peculiarities of its location. And, if the place itself is peculiar, this is reflected in the characters who people the fictional landscape, the secrets and long-running feuds between the families who reside in border areas which are fodder for border writers. Taken together, then, murders, social division, criminal activity fuelled by economic disparity, long-buried secrets, all viewed with the blackest humour, seem to me the obvious ingredients of any crime narrative and key features of Irish crime fiction in particular. I would contend that the border setting itself can not be described in any terms other than those which we usually associate with crime.

The divisions between North and South, Protestant and Catholic, and the attendant violence this bred would appear to be the most obvious trait of border fiction. For years the border has been the crack in the pavement through which people could disappear to evade justice. Those on both sides who wanted to carry out cross-border raids exploited long-running animosity between the two police forces on either side. If ever something would help reinforce feelings of social division and the tribal mentality of both religion and politics in Ireland, surely a border crossing would do it. And this is reflected in the literature of the place.

Eugene McCabe's beautiful short story 'Heritage' begins with Eric O'Neill recalling how 'a week ago he had watched a gun fight between British soldiers and gunmen across the river in the Republic.' The story itself involves Eric having to deal with a death threat against him and his growing knowledge of his father's involvement with a Catholic neighbour. McCabe's strength in the piece, as in all his work, is his understanding of the complexities of relationships. Most tragic of all is the unrequited nature of Eric's relationship with Rachel, with his being unable to touch her because his mother has brought him up to believe it is morally wrong. Most robust in defence of this morality is his uncle George. He thinks nothing, however, of killing two neighbours with farming implements in revenge for the murder of fellow UDR men. The story perfectly encapsulates the absurdity of the religious division, and of course the tragic consequences of that absurdity. The seeming contradiction of religious hatred and the inherent hypocrisy are illustrated in one scene when

Eric goes to church. After the service he stands in the church yard with a friend, looking across the river which marks the border to 'the lime-washed Catholic church half a mile away . . . a full congregation funnelling through the square porch separating their graveyard.

'Bees from a hive,' Eric said.

'Wasps,' Joe said.'

It works best though when viewed through Eric's eyes; his connection with the place, and with nature highlighted from the start; his natural empathy with other creatures seen both in his affinity with the birds of the area and his protection of the otter during the ill-fated hunt. He will not leave the border area because this is his land, he suggests at the opening, prepared instead to face certain death from neighbours. The closeness of the two churches, and the passing reference to the graveyard, seem to sum up McCabe's depiction of the area in one scene.

Colm Tóibín recalls, in *Bad Blood*, his reportage piece on the summer he walked the border, how murder squads used it for cover. In one particularly strong section, he mirrors McCabe to an extent, placing together two murders in one area, one that of a RUC officer, the other an IRA volunteer:

'One was a Catholic, the other a Protestant; one lived just south of the border, the other just north of the border; both died violently of bullet wounds in the same year, 1986, within a few miles of each other, one in April, one in July. Both had large funerals. It is possible that the man who died in July had been present as the first one died; it is even possible that the man who died in July was killed in reprisal for the first death; it is also possible that neither of these things is true; but it must be said that some people believed them.'

The RUC officer, John McVitty, was murdered while working in the fields with his twelve-year-old son. Tóibín notes that the IRA had escaped across the fields into the South after the shooting. (This is just one of many incident where Tóibín mentions the border being used as an escape route – another details the horrific murder of a delivery man who was shot twenty-one times in the grounds of a primary school while the children were there.)

The second killing, that of Seamus McElwain, was allegedly committed by the RUC or SAS. Shot and wounded while he and another man, Sean Lynch, were crossing a field armed with rifles, he lay in a ditch and was questioned by the SAS for twenty minutes before the RUC arrived. Tóibín tells us that McElwain 'had been shot first in the legs, then left there and was later shot in the stomach and then in the heart.' Killings then were committed not just by terrorists, nor was the traffic always from south to north. Tóibín recounts various incursions over the border, when, for example, Peter Robinson led a group into Clontibret. Likewise he mentions British incursions into the south.

(This latter idea is even used by Ian Rankin in his thriller *Watchmen*, which features a scene where Special Branch officers cross into the South on a raid, the border's function here being seemingly to create a sense of dislocation, to portray for the reader, a man out of his depth. The eponymous Watchman, Miles, finds himself aghast at the realisation that his colleagues in the RUC plan to execute a supposed IRA cell, one of whom protests during the raid: 'You're way out of your territory. You better get the hell out of here. This is an international incident.' Rankin makes much of the incongruity of a group planning murder complaining about their enemy's failure to respect international boundaries.)

Vincent Woods's powerful drama *At the Black Pig's Dyke*, also uses the border as a setting. Merging the ritualistic killings of the mummers, straw-clad men who moved from house to house performing simple dramas at Christmas with modern-day terrorists enforcing their criminal activities and indulging their personal proclivities and animosities through murder, Woods paints a bleak picture of border Ireland. The plays of the mummers invariably involved a fight between St Patrick and St George, which would result in the death of one. A doctor would be called who would produce a magic remedy and raise the dead to life before a final scene of reconciliation. In Woods's play, though, the mummers use their travelling troupe as cover for other activities. The dyke of the title is the border, steeped in blood. At various points we hear of murders, including that of Jack Boles: 'he was lying in a puddle of water outside the byre door – his face from me – and the water near as red as the berries on his lips. He'd been stuck in the neck like a pig; and his hands – his hands that played the melodeon – were slashed to ribbons like he'd tried to ward off the blows of a knife.'

Later, spurred on by the constant references to the wren offered as a symbol of betrayal, the mummers surround Hugh Brolly, who has been doing cross-border runs for them smuggling items. On his last run, sickened by events, Brolly had abandoned the van and contacted the police. The mummers taunt him with a variety of names:

'Traitor.

Collaborator.

Informer.

Grasser, squealer.

Dirty bastard.

Double dealer.

Judas fuckin' Iscariot.'

This final insult is seemingly the worst – as always in border literature, the violence is tied inexorably with religious references.

One of Brolly's tasks in the play is to smuggle across the border. Inevitably with cross-border literature, smuggling and the financial disparity between the two territories is a common feature. Throughout his book, Tóibín cites people commenting on using the border to their advantage, agricultural grants in the North being significantly more generous in the mid '80s:

'The locals made a good living out of the smuggling industry; those who were prepared to take the small risk involved in carting farm machinery, spare parts for cars, alcohol, tobacco, and electrical goods across the border, or those who conveyed animals across in the dead of night could make a lot of money without much work.'

Spike Milligan's novel *Puckoon*, dated now and bordering on offensive in its portrayal of the Irish, features smuggling of a different variety, where the locals are trying to bring a dead body over the border for burial after the boundary commission draw the border through the area in such a way that the church is on one side and the graveyard the other. When the procession first reaches the border they are stopped by the customs official who questions their wish to 'bury an Irish citizen in what is now British territory', Milligan, with a sharp eye for the absurdity of the border's location in places continues:

'I presume the deceased will be staying this side permanently?'

'Unless someone invents a remarkable drug – yes,' answered the priest.

'Then,' went on Barrington, he will require the following: an Irish passport stamped with a visa, to be renewed annually for the rest of his –' Barrington almost said 'life' – 'stay,' he concluded.

Consequently, bodies and explosives are smuggled back and forth across the border in the coffin. Mix-ups and shootouts ensue with a comment that would only have been possible in the 1960s following the failed border campaign of the late '50s:

'They must have been the IRA I suppose Sergeant?' said Lt Walker.

'Oh yes sur,' was the confident reply. 'No one else fires so many rounds and misses.'

One area where Milligan is spot on, though, is the unusual consequences of the border. After seeing the Boundary Commission all close their eyes, grip the pencil and draw the last few miles blindly onto a map, we hear of two incidents which illustrate the resultant confusion. In the first, a collision between a car and a charabanc full of passengers leaves the charabanc driver lying on the border.

'Now his legs were being sued by the passengers of the charabanc, and his top half was claiming damages from the car driver. The solicitors predicted that the case would last three years because of the travel involved.'

This is followed by the local publican complaining that the border runs through his pub, isolating one tiny section from the rest.

'That two square feet is in Ulster, where the price of drinks is thirty percent cheaper. Now every night me pub is empty, save for a crowd of bloody skinflints all huddled in that corner like Scrooges.'

Tóibín mentions a similar real life example:

His name was Felix Murray, I discovered, and the border ran though the house in which he and his two brothers lived. These days, he said, all three of them slept in the North, but there was a time when one of them had slept in the South . . . there was a sofa in the kitchen, he pointed out though the window, where you could sit and let the border run through you.

They got their dog licence in the South, he said, it was cheaper, but their television license in the North where it cost less. Their electricity was connected in the South, but their water in the North, he said . . . the postman came every day, one from the North, one from the South. The southern one came earlier.

When asked by Tóibín what is the worst aspect of the living arrangements, the man made pointed comments that it's the number of people who stop at the house to ask him questions: 'That was the worst thing, he said, and looked at me frankly. I understood, I said. I took his point.'

The border isn't always an abstract concept – in Shane Connaughton's 1991 novel *The Run of the Country*, one of the more memorable incidents occurs when the cross-border train runs through a drunk who'd fallen asleep on the tracks. A semi-autobiographical piece about growing up in a border village with his Garda father, Connaughton's work is more about the blossoming of first love and presents an Ireland of the 1950s. Even here, though, the Troubles are not far away; the book opens:

He could see the soldiers coming, hear their shouts, and he saw the sunlight breaking silver on his father's cap-badge. His father knew the terrain, and scoured it daily for armed republicans.

The first hint that these were different times comes several lines down when, commenting on how quite the soldiers have had it, guarding the border 'until such times as the Troubles ends', the narrator comments, 'The games on the lawn were the closest these Free State soldiers ever got to war. The IRA never fired at their own.' How that changed would affect Irish society, and those who choose to write about it, in ways we are still only coming to grips with.

The world Connaughton creates is very much of the period, where the Troubles are signified by an uneasy truce. In common with much border literature, at one point, the narrator comments on the land belonging to Protestants, 'and they'll only sell it to their own.'

Later in the story, to interrupt a fight in a bar, the owner plays *The Soldier's Song*:

> Everyone got to their feet and, exhausted, were glad to stand to attention. The Catholics couldn't show disrespect for their own anthem in a Protestant hall. The Protestants, whose secret allegiance was to the Queen, had on the southern side of the border to pay respect to Dublin or risk the consequences of their peculiar political position. Dixon had come up with a musical masterstroke. The fight was over. It was a ritual. Like Sunday Mass or a football match.

Certainly, during the period of the story, the border is a different place to that of more recent popular fiction. At one point, the narrator comments, 'Partition was a legal fact, but along the Border fact melted into fantasy.'

Yet, despite this claim, the same traits of border literature exist: religious intolerance, political uneasiness, issues of land-ownership, and, of course, unapproved roads being used by the locals to evade Customs and police and smuggle goods – in this case American jeans, boots and butter among other essentials:

> The road they were on was a tightrope. Cavan one minute. Fermanagh the next. Customs men lay in wait. Squad cars patrolled. His father's eyes scowered the land for his precise location. A lark, a hare, a stone . . .

It is perhaps this idea of a tightrope which best symbolises the border: walking between counties, countries, traditions, religions, police forces, political allegiances. For Connaughton, the border is adolescence; the area between youth and adulthood, a time of rebellion. For Tóibín, it represents bad blood, with the requisite letting of that blood on both sides; for Milligan it is the absurdity of the personal and the political; for Woods' the repetitive rituals of violence that allow no prospect for progress or peace; for McCabe the secretive nature of relationships and the inability to trust even those closest to you.

None of these ideas would be out of place in any work of crime fiction.

*

Brian McGilloway is author of the critically acclaimed Inspector Benedict Devlin series. He was born in Derry, Northern Ireland in 1974. After studying English at Queen's University, Belfast, he took up a teaching position in St Columb's College in Derry, where he is currently Head of English. His latest novel is *Little Girl Lost*.

A Series of Unfortunate Events:
The Ridiculously Short History of Irish
Crime Cinema

by Tara Brady

Nineteen ninety-eight. Dublin. Members of the public are bombarded daily by headlines detailing the criminal capers of comic-book monikered villains. National TV spews forth any number of foxy forensic scientists, crumpled sleuths and maverick lawyers, all of whom are seen to work above and beyond their remit. Clatters of smart stiletto heels form excited lines around book shops for Patricia Cornwell's latest Kay Scarpetta adventure, *Unnatural Exposure*. The author, partly inspired by the quadrillions of units sold to Irish fans, has chosen to set the novel between Richmond, Virginia and Dublin, Ireland. A nation rejoices.

Within six years, in a not entirely unrelated development, Ireland is named the best place to live in the world, according to a 'quality of life' assessment by everybody's favourite right-wing bible, *The Economist*.

Centuries after a happy, random bunch of Ice Agers hailing from Spain, Portugal, Scandinavia and North Africa got together and made the Irish, their offspring have finally found their groove. We, the people of Ireland, have elected to live in a permanent state of Hibernocriminophilia. Since 1990, we have decided our presidential contests by plumping for the candidate who most closely resembles Ms Scarpetta. The nation that can crow about nine

Nobel prizes for literature now boasts an entire school of hip young crime-writing gunslingers: such gifted indigenous Chestertons as Ken Bruen, Declan Hughes, Brian McGilloway, Arlene Hunt, Colin Bateman, Adrian McKinty, Tana French, John Connolly, Gene Kerrigan and Alex Barclay.

In turn, the Irish public devour the genre and all its bastard spawn: forensic and police procedurals, courtroom and legal drama, hard-boiled and gumshoe thrillers, anything sparked into life by somebody doing stuff they're not supposed to.

The statistics are impressive. Within an ill-defined release territory comprising the UK, Republic of Ireland and Malta, *Gone, Baby, Gone*, Ben Affleck's widely acclaimed adaptation of Denis Lehane's book of the same name, took more than 50 percent of its box office receipts from the Republic of Ireland. The most startling aspect of this particular figure is that it is by no means atypical; crossover crime titles such as *Tell No One* and *Alpha Dog* have been known to play in Irish cities for months on end.

There is a neat dovetailing of interests at play here; crime may pay in the Irish market, but not nearly so handsomely as cinema. Irish cinema admissions per capita, we are frequently reminded, are the highest in Europe, hitting a whopping 4.3, in comparison to the EU average, which stands at 1.96.

Adhering to a precedent established by Hollywood in the '30s, recessionary times have furthered the stampede. Admissions for January 2009, a traditional dead zone for cinema attendance, were 2 percent up on the previous year. Indeed, more than 1.7 million Irish punters – that's coming up on half the population – went to their local cinema that month.

Looking at the figures, one might reasonably assume that some nifty indigenous procedural would be a permanent feature in the average Irish picture house. Sadly, things haven't quite worked out like that.

The plucky Irish can take credit for a great many innovations and achievements – surfing, splitting the atom, saving civilisation's bacon through centuries six to eight AD – but genre cinema, for as long as we've had such a thing, has seemed beyond our capabilities.

Letters? We're all over those suckers. We're a nation of storytellers and all that. Big elaborate squiggles down the margins of religious treasures? You better believe it. Movies? We don't really do movies. The story has, perhaps, begun to change, but only just; feature films have never really been our bag.

We have, to be fair, produced the occasional internationally renowned film director in a lineage dating back to Rex Ingram. We may even have delivered the odd cinematic visionary. You would have to go at least as far as Iran to find a visual stylist in the same league as Neil Jordan. Jim Sheridan's *Get Rich or Die Tryin'*, a vehicle for rapper 50 Cent, is far from the director's best work, but it's difficult to think of another director who could have rendered Fiddy's shower-stabbing scene as a mighty Grecian relief.

The history of Irish cinema is, nonetheless, a strange, disjointed affair; the history of crime narratives in Irish cinema is, consequently, even patchier. For much of the hallowed century of cinema – that giddy epoch after 1894 – Irish cinema was about as fecund as the Irish space programme.

How to say this politely? Indigenous cinema has always been a problem for us. There are a million reasons why. We can take it all the way back to the Bronze Age and speculate that visual arts have never really been our strong point. Our museums play house to robust, practical things – flat axes, daggers, pots – featuring few of the fruity embellishments one finds in, say, contemporary Iberian remnants.

Many of our deficiencies as a filmmaking nation, however, can be attributed to the relative size and newness of our state. Film production only really kicked off here in 1916 and was plagued by bleakly comic misfortunes from the get-go.

The story of early Irish cinema coalesces into a sad litany. The US-owned Kalem Company, an imprint that pretty much constituted the entire Irish film industry for three years, would produce more than thirty short sentimental diaspora 'dramedies' in Killarney during the early twentieth century. Unhappily, Kalem shut down all Irish operations following the outbreak of World War I. The Film Company of Ireland, founded by the American lawyer James Mark Sullivan, was similarly ill-starred; their entire early production catalogue was destroyed in the 1916 Rising, while their audacious efforts to produce an Irish *Birth of a Nation* were plagued by censorship disputes and poetic tragedy. The first print of Mr Sullivan's lost epic *Ireland: A Nation* went down with the *Lusitania*. Sullivan, like his predecessors at Kalem would, having lost his wife and child during the Irish Civil War, eventually abandon the country and its blighted film industry.

The unfortunate man's experiences rather set the tone. Irish cinema had started as it meant to go on – messily and desperately in need of foreign patronage. Historically, our best-known films, our weightiest contributions to the cinematic canon – John Ford's *The Quiet Man* (1952) and Robert Flaherty's *Man of Aran* (1934) – are not, in fact, ours at all.

The foundation of the Irish Free State in 1922 would only derange matters further. The embryonic republic was not inclined to fritter away resources on such frivolities as the Nickleodeon; the Arts Council was founded as late as 1951, the Irish Film Board, or Bord Scannán na hÉireann, did not emerge until 1980.

Further east, the revolutionary fervour of the '20s-inspired young Russian artists to throw fabulous new shapes across the canvas, the plate and the big screen. Our very conservative insurrection found cultural expression in retro forms and preservationist tendencies. Cinema, embraced and valued as a potent propaganda delivery system by Stalin – Kino Massam, as they say – was, for Irish authorities, a sinister foreign import bearing suspiciously little resemblance to William Butler Yeats's Cathleen Ní Houlihan, or the keening, peat-stained spirit of a rural Christian nation.

The conservative nature of Ireland's revolutionary fervour was never going to prioritise or promote cine-literacy. There were pragmatic considerations, of course. Films were often regarded with the same protectionist distrust that governed the trade of cattle and coal.

There was, moreover, something godless about the entire blasted medium. The newly perfected Irish constitution may not have mentioned religious strictures directly, but it did not take long for repressive Catholic doctrine to attach itself to the document. 'I want everybody to realise what this Constitution states about authority . . . that authority comes from God,' suggested Éamon de Valera, the most influential politician of the state's first half century 'That is . . . fundamental Catholic doctrine, and it is here. It is true doctrine.'

We, the brand-spanking-new nation of Ireland, were fighting for our right not to party. Early Irish forays into filmmaking – see, but only if you must, the Church-sponsored non-fiction infotainment produced by the National Film Institute after 1943 – were noted neither for their radical ideas nor good vibes.

For decades, Irish authorities strove to defang the medium. One of the first pieces of legislation passed by the newly established Irish Free State was the 1923 Censorship of Films Act, establishing the post of film censor. In the decades that followed, successive state-appointed, draconian moral guardians, believing the public to be one episode of *Dallas* away from eternal damnation, sought to 'protect' the populace from materials deemed 'indecent, obscene or blasphemous'. In the decades before the comparatively recent (now total) liberalisation of film classification, Irish censors banned more than 2,500 films and hacked into an additional 11,000.

The grim history of Irish censorship has been well documented elsewhere, not least by such learned folk as Ciaran Carty and Kevin Rockett. For movie buffs, it's a roll call of minor atrocities: *Brief Encounter* and *Casablanca* were re-cut to preclude the possibility of adultery; a 'materialistic view of the origin of life' was removed from the Rites of Spring section in Disney's *Fantasia*; *Jules et Jim* was banned outright for its 'depiction of . . . troilism'.

Oddly, against this unhealthy, festering backdrop, many crime-themed movie imports survived with relative integrity. Crime fictions have always tended toward an inherently moral universe and a dark-hearted inversion of the Cinderella Principle. The genre's inclination to reward virtue and punish the wicked was not without its charms for the Irish morality police. The occasional racy film noir, a subspecies noted for admonishments against wayward women, could pass, only partially molested, into Irish picture houses.

This was not, alas, enough to spark an indigenous response to the form. There were no Irish equivalents for such robust British titles as *They Made Me A Fugitive*, *Brighton Rock*, *The Long Good Friday*, *The Lavender Hill Mob* and *The Ladykillers*. Why would there be? Irish cinema, until the 1990s, was practically an oxymoron. The burgeoning industry was characterised by fits and starts, a bewildering sequence of international patrons (John Huston, Gregory Peck, Roger Corman, John Boorman) and tax breaks.

Talented filmmakers battled in the margins to produce an Irish canon: George Morrison's *Mise Eire*, Louis Marcus's *Flea*, Peter Lennon's *The Rocky Road to Dublin* are all still worth putting one's hand up for.

The establishment of the Irish Film Board in 1980 inspired a small body of technically compromised but angular curios from daring people who, in earlier times, might have channelled their energies into intricate flying machines. Despite admirable efforts from Irish film scholars, nobody has ever really bought the notion that these efforts – which have not exerted a particularly lasting influence on Irish cinema – constituted a New Wave. At any rate, the idiosyncratic talents to emerge during these years – Bob Quinn, Cathal Black, Joe Comerford – displayed no real interest in genre. The mechanisms of genre would inspire the French masters of the real New Wave: Godard, Truffaut, Rohmer, Rivette, Resnais, and Chabrol all knew their flicks. Ireland was different. Social realism was the order of the day and Irish cinema limped through the '70s and '80s without producing anything that might be mistaken for a crime flick proper.

Sadly, genre cinema, the very scales and arpeggios of the tenth and liveliest muse, continued to elude us until recently. Our national inadequacies were poignantly brought into focus with oddities such as *Cry of the Innocent*, a messy thriller co-written by Frederick Forsyth, then a tax exile in Ireland, and the release, in 1988, of *The Courier*, a rare Irish attempt at a commercial, straight-world form. This muddled tale of a motorcycle courier who gets mixed up with Dublin's underworld, a flop by any register, displays no affinity for the beats or rhythm of a drugland thriller. More depressingly, the film is indicative of a culture that lacks the cinematic grammar or maturity to knock out a reasonably enjoyable B-picture.

Everything changed as the twentieth century ground to a close. Where to begin? Multinational investment. Economic prosperity. Diminished Catholic influence. Liberalisation. Swinging from chandeliers. For the first time ever,

Ireland looked like a modern European country, with yachts and Starbucks and everything. The terrifyingly backward theocracy represented in Lennon's *The Rocky Road to Dublin* – a grim 1968 study of a country untouched by the grooviness elsewhere – had almost entirely disappeared. Non-nationals actually wanted to live here. Who knew?

The Celtic Tiger, as nobody likes to call it, had a mad, inconceivably positive influence in cultural terms. A newfound national desire to strut found new forms of expression in glassy, steely architecture, satirical post-cubist canvases, snarky blogs and bestselling works of chick lit.

Irish cinema, meanwhile, had already started producing the sort of film you could show to outsiders without causing you to curl up and die with embarrassment. There were international productions such as *The Commitments*, *Far and Away*, *Braveheart* and *Saving Private Ryan*. There were Oscars for Jim Sheridan and Neil Jordan, and additional Academy nods for Terry George (writer of Sheridan's *In the Name of the Father* and writer-director of *Hotel Rwanda*).

On the back of these successes, the Irish Film Board was rebooted in 1993 (following a six-year hiatus) and promptly started bankrolling what, for the first time, looked like a coherent national cinema.

Infrastructure created production, which in turn created an improbable new genus of Irish movie star. This was quite a turn up for the books. The Irish were not unaccustomed to homegrown thespian talent. David Kelly, to name a fine example, has rarely been off our screens since he messed up the wall in *Fawlty Towers*. But there is something qualitatively different about the international standing of say, Brendan Gleeson, Cillian Murphy, Jonathan Rhys Myers and, of course, Colin Farrell. These guys are Proper Movie Stars. They play sheriffs and spacemen and naughty English monarchs. They pop up at the Oscars. They feature highly on Dishiest Men in Western Europe polls.

There follows a pleasing snowball effect in terms of industry. Movie stars, as everybody knows, make movies.

There was more. The emergence of the Irish crime film, like its literary equivalent, was hugely influenced by political developments in Northern

Ireland. For decades, conflict in that region had exerted a strange dialectical affect on Irish fictions. On the one hand, the 'Troubles', as we quaintly called them, inspired tetchiness about representations of violence. When censor Sheamus Smith banned *Natural Born Killers* in 1994 he cited the violence 'which is made light of' and 'the fact that we are living in a violent society in Ireland'. Conversely, the situation in Northern Ireland has also ensured that the Dionysian impulses that informed the fictional cops and robbers, sleuths and dames of elsewhere, have frequently been sidelined by politics.

Neil Jordan, to cite an obvious example, has consistently worked classic crime structure into such fascinating treatises on violence, politics and gender as *Angel*, *The Crying Game* and *Breakfast on Pluto*. With these films, the director, who knows enough about the genre to get away with remaking Jean-Pierre Melville's *Bob Le Flambeur* as *The Good Thief*, has produced work that is simply too complex, too infected by realpolitik to be read as true crime.

Others have floundered where he has scored international success. Recent attempts to wed Irish politics to genre have produced such uncertain entities as *Resurrection Man* (loyalist butchery in the 1970s), *An Everlasting Piece* (comedy wig-manufacturers), and *Divorcing Jack* (comedy journalists).

Indeed, it would be 2009, fifteen years after the initial ceasefire in Northern Ireland, before *50 Dead Men Walking*, a film dealing with a real-life informer's experiences, emerged to buck the trend and score a modest financial success in Irish theatres. If previous films touching on the subject utilised genre tropes to make politically minded films, *50 Dead Men* utilised politics to enhance genre tropes. Tellingly, perhaps, the film was made by an Außenseiter: the Canadian director Kari Skogland.

South of the border, a rapidly changing society produced a strangely Gothamite criminal underclass. A new breed of journalist – scoops such as Paul Reynolds, Veronica Guerin, Paul Williams – would emerge to keep track of colourfully nicknamed Dublin gangsters. The public was enthralled. Filmmakers were keen. Adopted Irishman John Boorman was the first to respond with *The General*, a fine, award-winning drama based on the life of tabloid criminal anti-hero Martin Cahill.

The success of Mr Boorman's picture would inspire a raft of true-life crime flicks. Martin Cahill would inspire a second theatrical release (Thaddeus O'Sullivan's *Ordinary Decent Criminal*) and a TV special (*Vicious Circle*). These competing representations were new but not novel. The Cahill of the movieverse owed something to the twinkly-eyed savagery found in Jimmy Cagney's Irish-American mobsters and G-Men. *The General* was prepared to acknowledge Cahill's folkloric charm – two wives, cheating the IRA, swindling the Catholic Church, playing cat-and-mouse with local law enforcement – but not entirely at the expense of his villainy. *Ordinary Decent Criminal*, by contrast, turned the capering up to eleven with a broadly comic Kevin Spacey in the lead. The impossibly beautiful Pennsylvanian actress Linda Fiorentino was improbably cast as his working-class Dublin wife.

The murder of journalist Veronica Guerin would inspire a second flurry of movie activity; Joan Allen would play the late crime reporter in *When the Sky Falls* (2000), Cate Blanchett would do the honours for Joel Schumacher's *Veronica Guerin* (2003).

For better or worse, we finally had the know-how to produce commercial cinema. Now we had to make good our escape from the shadow of historical drama. Our new knack for form, a welcome respite from the civil strife that has informed Irish cinema from *Shake Hands with the Devil* to *The Wind that Shakes the Barley*, would produce fine Irish horror movies (*Dead Meat, Isolation*) and slinky polysexual romantic comedies (*The Trouble with Sex, Goldfish Memory, About Adam*).

The single biggest impetus for the development of Irish crime cinema was not, however, indigenous to the region. In 1992, a young former video store clerk named Quentin Tarantino would make his directorial debut with *Reservoir Dogs*. By the end of that taut ninety-nine minutes of heist-movie heaven, the shot that killed Mr Orange would reverberate any place where images moved. It is impossible to overstate Tarantino's influence in the development of an indigenous crime movie, just as it is impossible to overstate his influence on cinema generally.

Tarantino changed everything. He made Miramax one of Hollywood's most powerful players; Bob Weinstein, co-creator of that studio, called him their Mickey Mouse. He inspired new models of distribution; suddenly, the big players were beating a path to Sundance on the hunt for This Year's Tarantino, a ritual which continues to deliver such crossover critical wows as *Little Miss Sunshine*, *Juno* and John Carney's *Once*.

It was Tarantino who paved the way for a whole new genus of gabby, cine-literate indie filmmakers. Robert Rodriguez, Kevin Smith, Eli Roth, Kevin Williamson and a host of others could only have emerged in a post-Tarantino universe.

The Tarantino alchemy – grafting bubblegum conservation to genre, tricking with chronology in new and exciting ways, a Mametian use of profanity as punctuation – would soon become the condition to which all crime movies aspired. Regretfully, as the wave of *Pulp Fiction* clones released throughout the nineties demonstrates (*Things To Do In Denver When You're Dead*, *The Boondock Saints*, *Two Days In The Valley*) being Quentin Tarantino is harder than it looks.

In Ireland, the first recognisably post-Tarantino product to hit multiplexes was *I Went Down*. The film was director Paddy Breathnach's second foray into seamy underworlds, following on from his 1994 no-fi, neo-noir *Ailsa*. But four years after *Pulp Fiction* (1994) had firmed popular notions of the Tarantino template, there was a hip new grammar in play.

The pitch – two mismatched, reluctant rogues bond during small-fry criminal activities – echoed a new international vogue for talky, soulful villains. The Beckettian rhythms of playwright Conor McPherson's script suggested, also, a potentially prosperous cinematic seam suited to Ireland's theatrical bent.

It was a minor breakthrough of sorts. Since *This Other Eden*, Irish cinema has sought to translate stagecraft into film, to little avail.

This groundbreaking marriage of genre and gab was an overnight sensation with native audiences; *I Went Down* quickly became Ireland's most successful independent film when it was released in 1997. Positive American notices praised its zeitgeist-surfing universality. The *New York Times* trumpeted the absence 'of Irish movie stereotypes' and 'a spare and quizzical indie spirit'.

By 2003, a decade after the release of *Reservoir Dogs*, Tarantino's influence had become unavoidable in both Irish theatre and cinema. Many (perhaps too many) short films began with men in suits discussing their favourite fast food. Many (far too many) plays featured scenes in which some unfortunate villain gets noisily tortured.

But one young playwright did demonstrate a genuine ability to successfully meld Tarantino's temporal experimentation and pop-cultural lexicography with an undeniably Irish (indeed, undeniably Dublin) verbal irreverence. Mark O'Rowe, raised in Tallaght, a working-class area of west Dublin, had already established himself with Tarantino-influenced plays such as *Howie the Rookie* when he embarked on his first cinema feature. Directed by John Crowley – a veteran of the Abbey Theatre and the Royal Shakespeare Company – the accomplished, rambunctious *Intermission* took its cue from *Pulp Fiction* as it wove together a collection of loosely connected stories into one satisfying whole. There were more culinary jokes – one of the characters recommends pouring 'brown sauce' into tea – but they seemed so authentically Hibernian that few critics felt the need to make unflattering comparisons to Travolta's remarks about Burger King.

Colin Farrell, already a Hollywood star, returned home to play a hoodlum who sets off the action by punching an apparently innocent women in her unlucky face. The narrative frame then pulls out to discover an arrogant police officer (Colm Meaney), a shy woman embarrassed by her wisp of a moustache (Shirley Henderson) and a depressed supermarket employee (Cillian Murphy).

The film received excellent reviews in both the United States and the United Kingdom: Anthony Lane, the notoriously unhappy critic of the *New Yorker*, remarked that 'the great thing about *Intermission* is that you barely have time to spot the gaps'; Roger Ebert, the dean of American reviewers, called it 'a virtuoso act from beginning to end'. Yet, for all the praise, *Intermission* failed to launch a renaissance in Irish crime cinema and it was another six years before Crowley and O'Rowe returned to theatrical features (with *Is Anybody There?* and *Perrier's Bounty*, respectively).

The latter, another Dublin-based crime caper starring Cillian Murphy, marked a step backwards into the bewildering, uncertain tone of Irish crime flicks of the '80s. An odd spiritual subplot featuring Jim Broadbent as a dying man failed to gel with the low-rent gangsters found elsewhere in the script.

The work of Martin McDonagh would further Tarantino's influence on Irish culture. The playwright's unique fusion of the patois of John Millington Synge and Tarantino-brand pop culture rap had already earned McDonagh a Tony award when he assumed writing and directing duties on the Oscar-winning 2006 short *Six Shooter*, a blackly comic, existential shoot-'em-up.

By 2008, McDonagh finally delivered a crime feature. *In Bruges*, like *I Went Down* and *Intermission*, was seen to bridge the gap between Vladimir and Estragon and John Travolta and Samuel L. Jackson. Brendan Gleeson and Colin Farrell offer us a tolerant yin and an intemperate yang. Gleeson plays Ken, an embodiment of 'ah sure' Irishness, a mutual correction for Farrell's Ray, a hero for every Irish tourist who ever looked at a wondrous spectacle before dismissing it as 'shite'. *In Bruges* dumps these two bungling killers in the tranquil medieval enclave of the title – an unlikely refuge after a hit goes horrifically, devastatingly wrong.

In Bruges proved rather too specific for international tastes – the film took only $33 million worldwide – but it was a critical favourite and a domestic smash. Colin Farrell won a Golden Globe for Best Actor in a Musical or Comedy for his role, while Martin McDonagh's script was nominated for an Oscar and he actually took home the BAFTA Award for Best Original Screenplay.

Elsewhere, the new Irish crime flick was already evolving into other forms, blossoming into such previously unimaginable sub-genres as the Godardian burglar romp (*When Brendan Met Trudy*, 1998) and the paranoid property thriller (*Alarm*, 2008). In keeping with accepted Tarantino usage and our capacity for post-colonial irreverence, capering became the order of the day. In a nation defined by centuries of occupation, where crooked politicians were re-elected because, not in spite of, their foibles, the comic scam was always going to have a very broad appeal.

If early Irish crime films – Vinny Murphy's *Accelerator* (1999), Paul

Tickell's *Crush Proof* (1998), Fintan Connolly's *Flick* (2000) – were still hung up on social deprivation, Shimmy Marcus' *Headrush* (2003) heralded a new, absurdist direction.

Marcus's award-winning keystone-criminal drugs caper followed lovable losers Gavin Kelty and Wuzza Conlon to Amsterdam where, they imagine, one big pharmaceutical score can solve all their financial and romantic troubles. The film's loose-limbed, episodic buffoonery takes in a transvestite drug-lord played by Huey Morgan, BP Fallon's New Age dope peddler and Steven Berkoff with dangerously flared nostrils.

Man About Dog (2004) established the knockabout crime caper as a thrusting new indigenous sub-genre. This shaggy-dog story about three West Belfast ne'er-do-wells and a greyhound, penned by Pearse Elliot and directed by Paddy Breathnach, would take more than €2.5 million at the Irish box office.

Tellingly, when Elliot attempted to introduce weightier themes into his similarly structured follow-up, *A Mighty Celt* (2005), native audiences showed far less interest. Northerners, it would seem, are still required to be cute and cheeky if they want to attract mainstream movie fans in the Republic.

For all these developments, there remains a strange disjoin in the Irish film industry. We currently boast one of the most exciting documentary sectors in Europe, yet no producer has thought to link impressive young practitioners of vérité – say Joel Conroy (*Waveriders*) or Ross Whitaker and Liam Nolan (*Saviours*) – with literary true crime epics like *The Burning of Bridget Cleary* or *Unsolved: Nine Irish Murder Files*.

Similarly, in the feature film sector, why hasn't somebody thought to attach Ireland's horrormeister Ed King (*Dead Meat*) to a Tana French novel? What might an idiosyncratic young talent like Donal Foreman do with Declan Burke's *The Big O*?

It's in that spirit that *Savage*, the most critically successful indigenous crime film to emerge in recent years, marries Irish realist tendencies and recognisable movie beats. Bolstered by a career-making performance from Darren Healy, Brendan Muldowney's 2010 urban vengeance drama functions as the 'Irish *Taxi Driver*' within a distinctly dirty Dublin milieu. Similarly, PJ

Dillon's *Rewind* (2010) is an authentically gritty Irish noir set in Dublin's post-boom suburbs.

It's a badly needed blueprint. Irish chick lit, the hot cheerleader to Irish crime's crumpled Emo outsider, has already produced *PS, I Love You*, a major motion picture starring Oscar winner Hilary Swank. But the Irish film industry simply hasn't moved to capitalise on new developments in crime fiction.

Meanwhile, Ireland's hottest young camera-slingers are retreating further into dark comedies (*Eamon, A Film With Me in It*), social realism (*Kisses, WC*) and Northern Ireland (*Five Minutes of Heaven, Hunger*).

As budgetary constraints and recession start to eat into the Irish Film Board, one can't escape the feeling that we may have missed the boat, yet again.

*

Tara Brady is a film critic with the *Irish Times* and president of the Dublin Film Critics' Circle.

Working-Class Heroes

by Neville Thompson

It's a funny thing, this, being asked to write a factual account of what its like being a crime writer in Ireland. It's funny because I've never thought of myself as a crime writer; I just thought I was writing stories of what I see around me on a daily basis. Maybe that's the point of it all, maybe that's the difference between Ireland now and Ireland before: crime today is just a way of life.

I grew up in Ballyfermot. In the 1960s, Dublin was a time of plenty, a Celtic Tiger before we knew what tigers were. Despite the fact that all my family seemed to have jobs, the area itself was always getting bad press. The Gala Cinema was a battle ground for gangs from every area of the city. I would hear my older sisters talking of the lads coming in from Bluebell and Inchicore. It was always exciting and whispered. There was something about whispered conversations that I knew was different and whispered conversations with the window open to hide the smell of smoke . . . well, they were the most exciting of all.

By the 1970s, the jobs had vanished, my older siblings had married, but Ballyfermot still remained the same. I know now the poverty of the area but at the time, living among it when no one had anything, it was never a problem. We were cocooned in our own area and happy as pigs in shite. I played football for teams in the lower end of Ballyfermot and so crossed the battle line of upper and lower. I was in the bastard zone, middle Ballyfermot, we could move between the two like ghosts in the night. I remember seeing the fights but never being involved. Was it crime? Undoubtedly. Did it seem like a crime? Never.

Upper knew not to go lower, lower knew the same, as did Palmerstown, Bluebell, Drimnagh, Inchicore, Walkinstown and Chapelizod. Everywhere was a battleground. But it was exciting. I remember the first night I had to jump out of the way of a stolen car. I was running from Markievicz Park to my Ma's. In those days, for some reason when alone, I ran everywhere. I wore a grey tracksuit after seeing Rocky and thought I was Ballyer's own Stallone. I would wave to people as I ran, punching the air. I hadn't fought in a ring since I was eleven; I got thrown out of the boxing club for kneeing Tommo Bates in the balls. It was only messing, he had tripped me up at the end of round one, but Lugs Brannigan barred me. Just as well, I was crap.

Anyway, I was jogging down Thomond Road when I heard a screeching sound. I looked up to see a car take the corner from Lally Road, like Starsky and Hutch did on the TV, the arse of the car was way across one side of the road. The car was a good hundred yards away from me and it was struggling to hold the road, first the front wheel on left side hit the kerb, then as it straightened, the back wheel on the right clobbered it. I looked at it, I was still jogging, and thought, 'Fuck, where's the driver?' For a moment it looked like there wasn't one, and then I saw his head, barely making it over the steering wheel. Music was blaring out of the car and I spotted that it was the Lally Road lads all perched inside. Fucking lunatics. Suddenly the car mounted the kerb and started coming down the pathway. Sparks were flying as its side tore the pebble-dash off the wall. It was flying and seemed stuck to the wall, the wall I was jogging along beside . . . flying in my direction. It was on its way, counting down . . . fifty, forty, thirty, twenty . . . it was stuck to the wall . . . it was racing . . . fifteen feet . . . they were screaming, hollering . . . ten . . . I was stopped, frozen . . . five feet and I jumped, not graceful, not a high jump, just desperate, over the wall straight onto my face, body down into the grass, my good tracksuit ruined. As they sped on I rose, my heart beating faster than I ever had before, and though I knew my Ma's hand-wash and mangle would never get the grass out of my tracksuit, I didn't care. I sat on the wall and watched them all take turns driving the car up and down the road. I looked up the road and older people, parents, were out with deckchairs and cans of beer, ready for the night of action, and we all cheered as the road became a racetrack and new heroes were born.

In the papers I read about the joy-riders and heard people giving out about the robbing that was going on, but though I understood the disgust I enjoyed the spectacle. I enjoyed the fact that our streets had become a rally track, I enjoyed the fact that we didn't have to go to a cinema to see a Bruce Lee kick – all you had to do was stand at the local Lido chip-shop for an hour.

I remember the first stabbing I ever saw. Well, I didn't see it, but it was the first that had affected anyone I knew. We all knew people were carrying, like they sharpened the metal hair-combs and the buckles on their belts. I was drinking and soccer was still my life. We travelled to Ballymun on the north side. Ballymun was the Ballyfermot of the north side and there was no love lost. Our team was an exciting band of alcoholics. Once we had a morning start we always had a chance to win, but the afternoon meant we had been drinking.

We changed in Ballyfermot and headed over in the cars to Ballymun. There was no way anyone was leaving their clothes in the 'Mun changing rooms, the robbing bastards would have had it all. The grey clouds sat over the depressing background of the high-rise flats. Even the pitch seemed an off-shade of grey, not green. We arrived and the drivers stayed with their cars. The pitch was in the middle of nowhere and on a hill. Mad Dog, one of our star midfielders, upset their fans by having a shite on the sideline, but they had no changing rooms so what did they expect? We went on the pitch and suddenly I saw him: Mongo, the legend. Mongo was a man mountain, from 'Mun but spending most of his life in Dundrum . . . the mental home. Trouble was, he got out at weekends and the manager of the team was too scared to stop him playing. We had a good-looking fella on our team and Mongo took a dislike to him. It was natural, poor old Mongo had spent a lifetime looking at his own ugly mug. Ten minutes into the match and Mongo has attacked our model, and was sitting on him beating him to a pulp. Mad Dog and myself ran over and tried to get Mongo off him but he was a strong bastard. I jumped on his back and bit down until he stopped, that meant me taking two lumps out of him. We were both sent off, and as we stood on the sideline we continued to beat seven shades of shite out of each other.

We all thought that was that until later that night, sitting in our local. Everyone was reliving the story and every telling of it got more graphic, by the end of the night it sounded like I had severed his head with my teeth. As we left the pub, well oiled, we were met by Mongo and two mates. They just started slashing everyone with blades. We quickly sobered up and regrouped; within minutes Mongo and his mates got the beating of their lives, two of our team had to get stitched up, one had had a Stanley knife with two blades in it ran across his face. The idea of the two blades was to leave a permanent scar.

It was funny but we never seen it as a crime, never felt the need to call the police . . . it was life.

The 1980s was a whole different ball game. Drugs had always been around, a bit of hash, a few tablets but nothing major . . . then the Dunnes introduced the city to heroin. Overnight the world changed, overnight people changed. It was the first time I ever seen whole areas devastated. Fatima was awash, so was Ballymun, lower Ballyer was gone mad too. There was a whole generation who first stopped playing football, stopped hanging around, stopped looking healthy and stopped living by the number one rule of the working classes . . . you literally don't shite on your own doorstep.

Maybe people had always taken drugs and maybe they had always been dying but suddenly they were doing it in the open. People were dying in doorways. Parents were having to clean the playgrounds of syringes before letting their children out to play. And the junkies were getting hounded out, everyone was turning on each other. There were marches on the houses of the dealers. Women screaming at the dealers to leave their kids alone, showing solidarity, only to have to go to the same dealer in the dead of the night to score for the son, who was too sick to move off his deathbed.

It was a horrible time. Banks were repossessing people's houses, every family was touched by the recession and no one seemed to escape the curse of drugs or emigration. Families were torn apart, communities were torn apart, the city was torn apart. But still it never registered as crime . . . it was life.

In the 1990s, the Tiger struck. We had U2, we had the saviours of the Third World, we had an economic boom and a great soccer team and people were coming home. It didn't really seem to matter that drugs had every working class area in its grasp. Ecstasy had us all loved-up, heroin brought us back down, hash kept us chilled, and cocaine was suddenly becoming acceptable. I walked my own area and the destruction was unbelievable. We had vast areas of skeletons, we had Dallas-proportion houses in the same areas as all the desolation and no one was taking a blind bit of notice . . . and then a reporter was shot dead. Suddenly the world sat up and took notice. It was funny the way the world only took notice then; it was a sickening act, but it wasn't the first one.

In the gangs people were getting greedy and guns became more readily available. With this availability came shootings and with the shootings came poor, cheap-shot reporting. Anyone in crime was bad . . . it was black and white.

After one such incident I decided to write a book about it, which became my first published work, *Jackie Loves Johnser OK?*

I had known a guy in my football days growing up in Ballyfermot, a header, but a decent skin. We all knew he was robbing but we also knew he was a laugh and a good man with the women. In Ballyfermot it didn't make him a hero or villain and I wanted to tell that type of tale. I realised that telling the story from Johnser's point of view only would make it a harsh and one-sided tale, similar to the papers. So I told it from Jackie's point of view too, and it became, for me, a love story, an everyday struggle in working-class Ireland. Yes, there was violence and crime . . . but more importantly, there was life!

The book hit a spot with a lot of people. Maybe it was the raw language, the sex, the violence – I can't be sure. I felt that I needed to write about the characters after the events in the book. Tara, Johnser's wife, had come across as a lunatic. So I wanted to show a different side, the tears of the clown, so to speak. I wanted to get behind the characters and continue their story. *Two Birds/One Stoned* was born.

The trend for me continued in *Have You No Homes To Go To?* I wanted to move away from Johnser and co., but continue with the struggles of normal life, such as money-lending. To others, money-lending might seem like a rip-off, but in a poor estate it can mean day-to-day survival. That book dealt with the problems of love, drinking and gambling, and along the way, a murder. But the murder was no more important than the stay-at-home son, or the money Simmo loaned. It was real, it may have been a crime . . . it was certainly life.

That process was repeated for my next two books. *Mama's Boys* was about two lads trying to get rich quick, and *Simple Twist of Fate* is about a girl growing up in Thailand. The fact that one story had drug-running and the other prostitution only went to show how lives could sometimes work out.

Meanwhile, out of the blue I'd gotten a call asking me to go into prisons and do workshops with prisoners. It seemed that they were reading my books more than any other fiction writer. My attitude was to go in and just do a workshop, nothing special, no special treatment, and to treat them the same as anyone else. Of course, looking out and seeing some of the most famous or infamous people in the country was a bit unusual, but I tried my best to just try and work with them.

Within a year they had written a play, within eighteen months a book of short stories of their experiences, their lives. It was fascinating. At first I got the stories they thought I wanted to hear, as if I was Paul Williams looking to do an exposé. I wasn't. I had met people, okay, dangerous people, but people – and I wanted *their* stories. Not Bonnie and Clyde, not all cops are pigs and all robbers scum: I wanted to know what made them tick.

The result, *Streetwise*, was brilliant. Guys telling honest stories, warts and all. Bravado left at the door. The stories came alive. Yes, there was violence, yes, there was drugs, but mostly there was life.

We all benefited from their honesty. They finally told their side, we finally got an insight into what went on to begin with (like the fact that some started their drug life at the same time we got holy communion for the first time). And for once we had authors writing about crime and not making money from it; all the proceeds went to charity. *More Streetwise* had a whole new batch of writers but still maintained the honesty and grittiness of the original.

And so it goes. My stories are about life, real life. The fact that crime happens in them is neither here nor there.

*

Neville Thompson was born in Ballyfermot, Dublin in 1961. His first two novels, *Jackie Loves Johnser OK?* and *Two Birds/One Stoned*, were Irish best-sellers. Thompson has also served as editor on *Streetwise*, a collection of short stories written by inmates of Ireland's Midlands Prison. His most recent novel is *A Simple Twist of Fate*.

Paper Tiger: An Interview with Tana French

In interview with Claire Coughlan

'Crime has become the genre that examines the tensions and fears of a society; it becomes a way of trying to explore it. I don't know about everybody else who writes crime, but one of the reasons I write it is that I find it really hard to wrap my head around the fact that one person can go out and kill another.'

Such is the reasoning behind Tana French's chosen genre. Being female and a crime writer or reader makes perfect sense, she says, as women are socialised to be aware of crime from an early age.

'You're socialised to have an emotional response, to be frightened; basically, you're socialised towards fear. I think that applies to both crime writing and crime reading – the majority of crime readers are women. Reading and writing crime becomes a way of trying to understand the incomprehensible. Because in crime writing, usually evil is exposed and punished.'

Beyond the broad strokes of the appeal of crime writing, Tana French's novels – *In the Woods* (2007), *The Likeness* (2008), *Faithful Place* (2010), and *Broken Harbour* (2011) – explore 'the tensions and fears' in the culture clash between the past and present; what happens when a past, that a newly wealthy country has tried to forget ever existed, collides head-on with the twisted, materialist mores of the present.

Crime fiction has become a means of understanding our new identity, says

French. 'Crime writing subconsciously becomes a way to explore the things that we can't deal with within our society. And I don't think we've dealt with the Celtic Tiger boom, never mind the recession – psychologically, just on the national psyche level. I think crime's the natural way, because a murder is a crack in the fabric of society, it's this huge chasm that opens up and through that crack surfaces the troubles and tensions and the unresolved questions that that society's been coping with.

'I have this theory that crime writing is one of the places where the crucial issues of any nation's identity get explored,' she continues. 'I think it's because crime writing is so high stakes – you're dealing with the worst thing that one human being can do to another, because it's almost always murder that you're dealing with in the crime novel. But also you deal with something that's very culturally specific, because the kind of murder you get is determined by the society in which it takes place. I mean, you don't get drive-by shootings in eighteenth-century Wexford, the same way you're unlikely to get a witch burning in, say, modern Dublin. I wouldn't rule it out totally, but it's kind of unlikely.'

Murder is by its very nature indicative of the kind of society that spawns it, which makes crime fiction a sociological microscope, more so than any other kind of fiction.

'Murder itself cuts across every cultural nuance, but the kind of murder is determined by the culture itself. Because of those things, crime fiction becomes a point of exploration of a society's deepest fears, of things that it hasn't assimilated. And God knows, over the last fifteen years, Irish society has just been avalanched with more than we can possibly assimilate in this lifetime.'

The clash between past and present has come to the fore in all three of French's books thus far. In *In the Woods*, there's the matter of a motorway versus an archaeological site; in *The Likeness*, the past of a 'Big House' owned by an Anglo-Irish Ascendancy family flips back on its current inhabitants; while in *Faithful Place*, the ghosts of 1980's recessionary Dublin are laid to rest.

'In *In the Woods*, there's the motorway versus the archaeological site: yeah, we need a motorway, but do we really have to scupper a priceless heritage that we can never get back? And usually the answer is no, but somebody was bribed to put it right there.'

The premise of *In the Woods* involves the body of a twelve-year-old girl found on a ceremonial altar on an archaeological dig. Rob Ryan, a detective with Dublin's fictional murder squad, is called upon to investigate, but the archaeological dig in question happens to back onto a wood which he went into as a child with two friends. Ryan himself was the only one who returned.

The site is now being excavated before a motorway is built over it, despite local protests. This, of course, has parallels with recent events in Irish history, where our cultural and national identity has held up 'progress', such as the construction of the M3 motorway in the Tara Valley, just over a mile away from the Hill of Tara in County Meath, an important sacral site associated with Indo-European kingship rituals.

In *The Likeness*, the character of Ned Hanrahan wants to buy Whitethorn Lodge – the 'Big House' now occupied by five PhD students at Trinity College – and turn it into a luxury spa hotel.

'We're still trying, as a country, to find a way to balance these things. You do get people like Ned who have completely bought into what the Celtic Tiger was selling, which is that we should be embarrassed about the fact that Ireland existed before the year 1996 or so. We should just pretend that it never existed, spend the money as fast as we can, run up our credit card bill, make sure everything's designer and forget everything else.

'And all of a sudden it's occurring to us that this might not be as everlasting as we were told. And that's another shock, coming on top of the shock of sudden riches, that we haven't assimilated. I think because we never got together a new Irish cultural identity within the Celtic Tiger, we were just so confused, this sudden recession is just such a shock; it's a double whammy.'

French mentions *The Wrong Kind of Blood* by Declan Hughes, in which a body surfaces on a building site, as a good example of a crime novel where the past and present also come together.

'I think that's huge for us, that identity gets created at the crossroads between past and present. That's how it's made, and if you try to ignore or suppress one or the other, you're going to end up with a very skewed, very unhealthy sense of self. I think that's what we did with the Celtic Tiger.'

Faithful Place is set 'right at the tipping point' between Ireland's economic boom and the current recession. 'I started writing it in January of 2008, so it's set in December of 2007,' Tana explains. 'Everybody I know knew that this wasn't going to last, but we had politicians getting up there and saying, "How dare you say that this won't last forever? If you say that, then you are responsible for the country losing jobs." All of a sudden, if you tried to be objective about the fact that, for example, property is insanely over-inflated, then you were somehow responsible for damaging this country.

'There was a distinct disconnect between reality and perception, and we were all being told that perception was much more important than reality. If you dared try and focus on what the reality was, you were somehow a bad person and a traitor to your country. No, everything was wonderful, property in Ireland was worth millions and we were all going to live happily ever after and buy a new iPod. And for a lot of us who weren't part of the Celtic Tiger – and it did leave most artists behind – we all knew that this wasn't real and couldn't last forever. And the end of 2007 was the point where it started to be like, uh oh, it's not going to last forever. A very precarious time, when people were starting to recognise that and starting to get frightened about it, and some people were getting a little bit *schadenfreude*, and a bit, "I don't care, I never got anything out of it anyway." '

Someone like Ned from *The Likeness* must be in a state of shock and paralysis now that the party's over, economically speaking. French pronounces that he's most likely 'banjaxed'.

'I think someone like that would have to get over the shell-shock first. There's an entire chunk of a generation who bought into this and invested their minds and their futures in what the government told them was happening. The government, the media, the banks, the property developers – a lot of people had a vested interest in claiming that the Celtic Tiger was going to last forever. And there are a lot of people, I think, who are in their twenties today, who staked the way they think on this, and who did fall for the idea that the one important thing in our society is money.'

Her analogy for Ireland's recently squandered wealth is an apposite one. 'We're like a family who's been desperately poor for generations and suddenly wins the lottery. No, they're not going to have a healthy way of dealing with money, they're just not. It can't happen.'

'It wasn't everybody, though. Some people did go, "Hang on a second, actually, that sounds like a load of bollix and I'm not following it." Here's something else that I talk a lot about in *The Likeness*: knowing what you want. Not what you're told that you want. And that's something that *The Likeness* characters, in particular, are very, very aware of: What do I want and what am I prepared to sacrifice for it? Once you know that, you may not end up getting it, but at least you're not going to wake up going, "Hang on a second, what the hell happened with my life?" And I think people who got suckered into being told what they wanted are having that horrible wake-up call, because not only did they get told that they wanted the IFSC job, but now it's gone and they're going, "But hang on, I didn't even want it that badly."'

In *The Likeness*, Detective Cassie Maddox, another detective from the fictional murder squad – who was Rob Ryan's sidekick in *In the Woods* – is sent undercover to Whitethorn Lodge, a house in County Wicklow which has fallen into the possession of five Trinity students. Their mantra of 'no pasts' and their closely guarded isolation goes horribly wrong when one of them – who happens to be Maddox's doppelganger and has been using the moniker 'Lexie Madison', which was Maddox's previous undercover identity – is found stabbed to death inside the ruins of an old Famine cottage. These ruins were the shells that remain of old dwellings which dot the Irish countryside, which were abandoned by Irish emigrants in the 1840s during the Great Famine. Maddox, *The Likeness*'s narrator, who is also part-outsider by dint of being part-French, observes that most people who've been brought up in Ireland don't even notice these ruins anymore.

French herself was brought up in Malawi, Rome and the US – due to her father's job as a development economist – before returning to Dublin in 1990, as a teenager, although the family spent summers in Dublin when she was a child. It's this outsider's perspective that she applies to her novels, which are full of observations and nuances that someone who has lived here continuously all their lives might somehow miss.

In fact, the mantra of 'no pasts' in *The Likeness* is something that was echoed by newly flush Ireland during the boom years, and we're still very much a teenage nation, with all the lack of identity which that entails, argues French.

'We're a really new country, and we went through the equivalent of being young teenagers where the fact of admitting that they have parents almost kills them with embarrassment. They'd prefer to think that they sprang fully fledged from I-don't-know-where.

'And I think we went through the equivalent, where it was just so embarrassing to admit that we had had any kind of past. Also, to be fair, our past wasn't necessarily all that much fun. So, I think there was this drive to go, "No, we're really, really cool now." '

'I think that the harder you fight against the fact of having a past . . . it's the same with the characters in *The Likeness*: the more they try to suppress it, the more explosively and dangerously it comes back to claim its place within their identity.'

But for the Whitethorn Lodge inhabitants, who reject everything about the New Ireland that they're supposed to embrace, it all goes grotesquely wrong. Why?

'They make the mistake of thinking that something can be eternal. There's no room for growth there. And if you don't allow for growth, you are going to implode and it is going to be a really ugly picture.'

Identity shifts from novel to novel in French's books: whereas the narrators of *In the Woods* and *The Likeness* have been Rob Ryan and Cassie Maddox, respectively, *Faithful Place* features Frank Mackey, Maddox's former undercover boss, who appeared as a peripheral character in *The Likeness*. French's fourth novel, *Broken Harbour*, features Mick 'Scorcher' Kennedy, who had a supporting role as Frank's nemesis in *Faithful Place*.

French employs the device of shifting narrator identities from novel to novel because she is interested in the 'big turning points' in people's lives and most people don't have that many, were she to focus on just one character for a series.

'If you use the one narrator, you have to keep dumping the poor guy into these life-changing situations and he's going to end up a nervous wreck, or you have to go with the smaller ups and downs, which is what most series do. And there are writers who do that really beautifully, but it's just not what captures my imagination, so I swap narrators.'

Broken Harbour is set on a fictional 'ghost estate', a feature of Ireland's post-Celtic Tiger era landscape, empty housing estates which were built during Ireland's property boom and were often only partly inhabited. It's set, French says, 'somewhere out past Balbriggan [north County Dublin], on one of those half-built estates, one of the quarter-inhabited ones. A family has been attacked and the father and two children are dead, the mother's in intensive care and Scorcher, who is still not one hundred percent back in everyone's good books after making a mess of the case in *Faithful Place*, has been assigned this case with his rookie partner. And of course, it ends up getting tangled up with Scorcher's own personal life because Scorcher's got a history with this location in this previous incarnation – before it was an estate it was a place where people went on their summer holidays. He's got a bit of history there and what with that and everything else, the case sucks him in.'

The explosion of crime fiction in Ireland in recent years has coincided with a new appraisal of what it means to be Irish, which in turn has seen the genre occupy a more central position on the Irish literary spectrum.

'I do get a lot of readers who go, "I don't usually like crime novels, but I like this one," and it's great, and I'm like, "Now read more of them, because there are loads of great ones out there."'

'The walls are coming down, and it's a lucky moment for me and for Alex Barclay and everyone else who's doing it. We're so new; we haven't really got an identity as a genre. People are much more open to the idea that it's genre but it's not "just" genre. The boundaries around crime that used to keep it segregated off – there's "girly crime", which has to be the more cosy, psychological stuff and there's "guy crime", which has to have a gun on the cover and a hero called Jack who shoots people – all of those boundaries are breaking down; it's not so limited.'

Despite that, snobbery is still a factor when it comes to genre fiction.

'I think we've picked a lucky moment to start writing, the Irish new wave. Like I said, the boundaries did start to come down – Dennis Lehane being one of the cases in point, with *Mystic River*. That's a family saga, it's social history, it's a coming of age story, it's everything and a crime novel. Anybody who still felt any kind of snobbery or "crime fiction can't be good literature," I think that book probably knocked that idea out of their heads. Look at *The Secret History*, as well; that's actually a great crime novel.'

The Secret History, Donna Tartt's 1992 campus novel about an insular group of friends, was reissued by Penguin a couple of years ago as a crime novel, as part of their 'Celebrations' series, whereas it was originally marketed as literary fiction. French herself has drawn comparisons to Tartt, particularly with *The Likeness*.

'That made my day,' laughs French. 'I love Donna Tartt . . . and here we're going back into the issue of identity. She launched that genre of writing about that age, you know, that early twenties stage. It may be that it didn't happen that way up until our generation, where there was a zone of late-college/post-college . . . You'd kind of grown up a bit and moved out of home, the primary influence in your life was no longer the family you were born into, but because we don't get married as early as our parents' generation did, you're not starting your own family yet; at the age of twenty two, you're probably not with the partner with whom you're going to spend the rest of your life. And so the most crucial thing in your life is your friends. They define you.

'I think Donna Tartt was one of the first to write about that, and about what an incredibly powerful, passionate and beautiful thing it is – but how that power can also go devastatingly wrong. Because there does come a time when you need to outgrow that. It's not that your friends become any less important; it's that other things become more important. I still have some of those friends and they still mean just as much to me, but now I've got a husband and he's the primary relationship. But if you don't let that happen, if you just hold on to this little bubble that the six or eight of you have created together, that power can implode and become a destructive force. I think that's what [Tartt] started off. And as our generation grew up, we've started writing about it as well. It's something wonderful; it's an amazing point in life.'

French's own cultural identity is mixed: her father is part-Irish and part-American and her mother is half-Italian, half-Russian. As a former stage actor, is French's professional identity as hybrid as her cultural one?

'Once an actor, always an actor. Also, I don't see them as in any way contradictory; I see them as intertwined. It's the same job; you're playing your narrator for a year and a half on paper, rather than for the six weeks on stage. It even involves the same kind of precision. You know, on stage a character wouldn't sit that way, a character would sit like this . . . it comes to be second nature. And writing's the same because I write first-person, so if my narrator would never use a certain construction, tough; I've got to find a different way to word that sentence. It really is about the same kind of rigour as acting.

'That is kind of fundamental to the way I write, because it's the same skill deep down. I don't start with a full plot – I know some crime writers who start with the whole plot outlined, and then they draw the characters out of what the plot requires. I envy it, because they're starting with a lot more organisation.

'I can't work that way. I don't know "whodunit" when I start writing. You start with the character of the narrator and the premise. The more real and three-dimensional this character becomes to me – and hopefully to the reader as well – the more I can draw the reader into their world, into their hopes, fears, traumas and tensions and all the rest. I think it's because that's what I'm trained to do. The plot springs out of the characters, rather than the characters springing out of the story. It's very much the same thing as acting.'

Given French's cultural background, it's interesting that she sets all her books in Ireland, when she could do what John Connolly or Alex Barclay have done and set them elsewhere.

'Dublin is the only city I know well enough,' French says. 'I know the small things about it, the quickest short-cut from A to B and what a "D4" accent sounds like, as well as the big things, like what kind of problems and tensions the city's dealing with. Unless you live somewhere and those questions are part of the air you breathe, every day, I think it's very hard to know what they are; how else would you know that kind of stuff? The media aren't going to give you a clear, fully textured picture; nothing is.

'I think you could probably write a very personal crime novel and set it in one family, in a city you didn't know as well, but I like stuff that has roots. And I care about the stuff that's confronting Dublin right now, the uncertainties, the challenges. I care about that, because this is my city and regardless of the problems, I love it. I just don't care about any other city that way.'

*

Tana French grew up in Ireland, Italy, the US and Malawi. She is the author of *In the Woods* (2007), which won the Edgar, Anthony, Barry, Macavity and IVCA Clarion Awards, *The Likeness* (2008) and *Faithful Place* (2010). *Broken Harbour* will be published later this year. She lives in Dublin with her husband and daughter.

Claire Coughlan has worked as a journalist for a variety of publications since 2003. She is a graduate of the MA in Creative Writing at UCD, and her first novel is currently under consideration. In 2009 she was awarded an Arts Bursary in Literature from Dublin City Council.

The Houston Room

by Ken Bruen

Och ochón.

That's Irish and roughly translated means:

Woe is me.

The song of me life.

The American elections were a week away and were we interested?

You betcha.

We are the 53rd State, we just don't shout about it, not too loudly anyway. I was in Garavan's, the truly last remaining old pub in Galway and horror, the rumour, it is being sold.

What hasn't?

Peadar, the current barman, knows my routine, I get there at 11.10. That's like ten minutes after opening, so I don't seem so . . . desperate.

Peadar looked alarmed, and Jesus, this is a guy who doesn't give a shite about anything.

Ever.

He beckoned me over, whispering

'There's a guy here, says he has to see you?'

I probably owed him money or worse, he owed me a beating. I said

'Fook 'im.'

Peadar nearly smiled, this is what he knew, smoke and side stepping. But, he pushed,

'This isn't the usual bollix, he's from Texas.'

He was kidding?

I said

'You're kidding.'

Nope.

Moved closer to me, added

'Young geeky looking guy, like a total nerd but generous, he's already bought everybody a jar.'

The fuck was this?

I said

'Send him over.'

Cautioned,

'After I get my first of the day.'

The so-called cure.

Yeah.

A pint of the black, Jameson chaser.

It took its own sweet time. The Guinness fighting for supremacy over the Jay and my insides rebelling against both, nigh roaring

'Enough, we've had enough, God damn it.'

The booze won.

Barely.

And I heard

'Jack Taylor?'

Turned to see this young kid, sixteen if he was a day, a shock of black hair falling over his forehead and thick black glasses. He was built like a starved greyhound, wearing chinos, a grey anorak (people wore them anymore?) and what can only be described as the newest Converse I've ever seen.

They glowed in their savage whiteness.

Lose the glasses and he would have been a good-looking guy.

He pushed out his hand, I took it grudgingly and he gasped

'Can I buy you a brew, damn, many brews.'

He launched into a frenzy of words that I'd no idea what he said. One of those amazing minds that the mouth just cannot keep pace with the thoughts pouring out.

And delivered with that Texan lilt that is so appealing, unless you're Bush. I held up my hand, said

'Jesus wept, take a breath, slow the fuck down, I've no idea what you're saying.'

He smiled, adjusted his glasses, his eyes dancing in his head from sheer life.

He tried again.

'I'm David Thompson, own a publishing company in Houston and I'm compiling a book of the detectives of European cities.'

He pulled out a moleskine diary, battered with notes and clippings all spilling out, said

'See, you're the first on my list.'

I signalled to Peadar, asked

'What are you having son?'

And got the look, he said

'I'm twenty-four years of age.'

I smiled, asked

'What's that like?'

He was thrown then smiled, said

'Oh they told me you were fast with words.'

I nodded at his glass, said

'Before Tuesday?'

He had a half of Smithwick's.

Before I could get to me wallet, he'd a fifty euro on the counter, said

'My treat Mr Taylor.'

'Jack, it's Jack.'

I clinked glasses with him, then

'How can I help you?'

His face was flushed from excitement, and he launched

'See, I want to do a book that is a cross between *The Wire* and *Southland*, follow you on a case, record the whole process.'

I lied.

'I don't currently have a case.'

I was supposed to be investigating a vicious debt collector who had beaten a young housewife half to death when she failed to cough up the weekly repayment. The Guards showed no interest and I'd been hired by the woman's father to attempt catching the thug in the act of intimidation.

His face fell. I rammed home

'See, this is what I do, sit on the stool, let the cases come to me and they do but just now, you are shit out of luck partner.'

He looked like a kid who had Christmas cancelled. I tried

'How about I make up some yarn, embellish it with local colour, the swans, tourist shite, and you're good to go.'

He was horrified, said

'But that's a lie.'

I drained my pint, sighed, said

'Then good luck with your project, be sure to try the soda bread before you leave.'

I was standing, shucking into my all weather Garda coat and he lit up, asked

'Is that item 1824, the famous coat?'

'No.'

Moving off, he laid a batch of fifties on the counter, a lot of them suckers. He asked

'Sure there isn't something?'

Fuck.

*

The money lender, name of Brown, had a flat on the dockside. Since the port literally dried up, new apartments had sprung up on the waterside. Brown was from the north of Dublin, grew up hard and violent. A lucrative drug business netted him his first fortune, then the money lending gig came down the pike.

With the recession and the banks bad fooked, desperate people did desperate things, like trying to save their homes, put food on the tables for their kids. Believing that short term loans would temporarily ease their woes.

The economy slipped closer to meltdown.

The 500 euro they'd borrowed with vig had to be re-negotiated. On Brown's terms. And then the skels bit, hard.

Collection day, Friday, they took the furniture, broke some bones to show their intent and in jig time, they owned a shit load of property.

The young woman in hock to them was beyond desperation, her father had pleaded, PLEASE.

Where I came in. I was giving David the short version as we headed down Shop Street, he asked

'Want to grab a ride?'

Jesus. I stopped, said

'Basic Irish-English lesson number one, a ride here means sexual intercourse. And I'm pretty sure you're not offering me that . . . least I fooking hope not, we've only just met.'

I swear on me mother's grave, he blushed and you know, that was the first indication I was going to like this kid.

I don't do like.

Ever.

I slapped him on the shoulder, said

'Don't sweat it, and does this mean you have a car?'

He looked perplexed, said

'Doesn't every body have a ride – oops, a car?'

'Yeah and leprechauns point you to pots of gold.'

We'd reached the docks. I pointed out across the bay, said

'Next stop, USA.'

Brown's apartment was on the ground floor, a pint from Sheridan's pub. A sign on the bottom floor, promised

'Let us solve your money problems.'

Brown lived above the small office he used. I said to David

'Follow my lead, if it gets hairy, run.'

He swallowed, asked

'Hairy?'

I sighed, said

'You see a hurley, take off.'

In the small office, a babe was seated behind a large desk, she was reading *Entertainment Weekly*. Must have intuited David was coming. She looked up, said

'Yeah?'

She wasn't chewing gum but her expression thought she was, boredom oozing from her over glossed lips. I said

'Financial packet for Mr Brown.'

Got her attention.

She hit the phone line, looked up, asked

'And you are?'

'Great news for Mr Brown.'

She spoke rapidly then listened, said

'Go through the back corridor, then up one flight to Mr Brown's apartment.'

David, with the kind of manners that get you hurt, said

'Thank y'all so much.'

She looked at me, asked

'Is he for fucking real?'

I said

'He's from Texas.'

*

Heading up the stairs, I said

'Lesson two, keep your fooking mouth shut, got it.'

'Yes sir.'

On the first floor, a man built like a shit brickhouse stood sentry outside a closed door. He was probably only in his thirties but his eyes were old; eyes that had never set on a living thing they didn't want to hurt, badly. He boomed

'Where are you going, shitheads?'

Nice manner.

I looked back at David, as if for guidance, then shot my boot forward, catching him full in the balls. He didn't go down so an elbow to the nose, followed by a kick to the head, for bonus. David let out a short gasp, stammered

'Was that necessary?'

I was down, going through the guy's pockets, pulled the Nine from his inside pocket. I put my fingers to my lips, said

'Shiss . . . h.'

He did.

I opened the door, a small man, in an impeccable suit, Armani? I know class as I've never been able to afford it. He was almost bald, with one of those horrendous comb-overs that defy belief. His face, lived-in would be a kind description, a nose broken, many times, and a thin mouth that would befit a cobra. Eyes that saw nothing but opportunity. He looked up, from his massive desk, littered with files, Mr Busy. Hissed

'The fuck are you two clowns.'

I could hear David's intake of breath. I had the Nine down by my side, said

'I'm the bearer of two kinds of news, good and awful.'

He was standing up, his hand moving surreptitiously to a drawer, he sneered

'I've news for you bollix, you're fucked.'

I kicked the desk with all my force, trapping his right hand in the drawer, then moved fast, got behind him, tore the drawer open, saw his fingers were broken, and the Glock. I pushed him on to the desk, removed the Glock, tossed it to David, going

'Catch.'

He didn't.

It fell to the carpet with a dull thud.

I said

'Oops.'

Pulled Brown to the front of the desk, said

'Ok, here's the good news, we're not going to kill you . . . today . . . and the awful news? You're outta business pal.'

I let go of his immaculate suit and credit to him, his shattered hand notwithstanding, he stood to his full five-six height, looked at us each in turn, said

'You're fucking dead, wanker.'

David asked . . . yah, believe it . . . asked

'What's a wanker?'

Brown laughed, said

'Where did you find this dipshit?'

Before I could answer, the door burst open and the bruiser charged through, using his elbow to casually knock David aside and hit me full frontal with his right hand. Following through with a punch to my chin, taking me off my feet, I sailed backwards, thinking

'Oh Jesus wept, we are so fooked.'

He stood over me, spat

'I'm going biblical on your arse, shithead.'

Brown was getting his act down, smirking, and preparing to wreak mighty vengeance.

A voice

'Hey.'

David.

The bruiser turned and got a shot of pepper-spray in the eyes. David was on his feet, gave another dose to Brown, then went

'Phew.'

I stood, grabbed the Nine, asked

'Is that legal to carry?'

He smiled, said

'I'm from Texas.'

*

Thus began the most unlikely friendship this side of the Shannon river. I asked him where he was staying, he said

'The G Hotel.'

Jaysus.

I asked

'How fecking gay is that?'

He was confused, said

'I'm confused.'

I shrugged it off, said

'It's a Galway thing, how would you like to bunk down with me?'

He muttered

'Really?'

Like he won the fookin lotto.

You'd think, and normally be right, a bedraggled soul like me, I'd live in a shit hole.

Nope.

A friend of a friend, yadda yadda, asked me to take care of his flash apartment in Nun's Island.

I did.

Stunning place, right in the centre of the city, with a roof garden from which you could see the ocean and yearn, the whole of the city in all it's un-innocent wilting beauty. I never had anyone to stay.

I don't do guests, ever.

Like I say, I was beginning to like the kid, maybe he reminded me of my dead surrogate son, Cody.

Maybe.

First thing he noticed when he entered the flat, was a huge framed portrait of Johnny Cash, with the lines underneath

'How well I learned that there is no fence to sit on, between heaven and hell.

There is a deep wide gulf, a chasm, and in that chasm is no place for ANY MAN.'

He emitted a low whistle.

That evening, I'd fixed some serious steaks, Irish mashed spuds, gravy and a shit load of brews.

The weather was unseasonably good and we were on the roof as evening fell, kicking back, sipping on long necks and David asked me

'Ever thought of getting married?'

Fook on a bike.

I told the truth, said

'There was an American lady, once, a mystery writer would you believe but . . . ah bollocks, I fooked it up.'

He thought about that, the dipping sun reflected off his glasses giving him an aura of blue light like finality and someone walked on my grave. I asked, in urgency

'You OK kid, I mean, health and all, you take care of that?'

He smiled, said

'Yah betcha.'

Then as I knocked the heads off two fresh beers, he said, more to himself

'There's a gal, I work with, named McKenna, I kina feel there might be something but she's an opera singer, smart as a coon hound and I don't want to . . . like, mess up?'

I said, with force

'Promise me this, you go back to Houston, you ask the lady out, ok?'

He nodded, delighted.

And that's when I told him about Michael, The Archangel of Galway.

*

After, so long after, me heart shrived, I'd see his face, not a line on it and his sheer joy at the story of Michael.

I read the blogs, the plaudits, the honours, the praise and they race across my mind like water on a Galway granite roof. The line that lingers is, 'He was our golden boy'.

He was.

Jesus, was he ever.

Innocence, if that means an unwavering belief in the goodness of people, or folk as he'd have said.

To a battle-fatigued cynic like meself, that is almost alien. But you know, for a wee while, oh Lord, so brief a time, I saw the world through his eyes.

Michael is a character that only Galway could produce.

A former Professor of Metaphysics (whatever the fook that is), he'd been married, a house in Newcastle, two perfect kids, until a drunk teenager killed his daughter and walked free from court.

Michael lost his way, and just about everything else.

No sign of him for nigh a year then he appeared, with, I kid thee fookin not, a six-foot wooden cross and tramped the town with it, saying

'I am Michael The Archangel, casting down into hell Satan and all evil drunk drivers.'

You'd figure he'd be a target for the thugs and riff raff who prey on the homeless and vulnerable.

Nope.

He had an aura that even the most ice-stone hooligan didn't want to fook with.

I took David to the Claddagh, we fed the swans then lo, Michael appeared, trailing that heavy cross behind him.

David was stunned, said

'I thought you were kidding me.'

As Michael passed, he suddenly stopped, turned to David, his grey weary eyes, fixed on the kid, said

'Beware the year of 2010, the year of Zen.'

David, momentarily stumped, rallied, asked

'What's the year of Zen?'

And Michael did something he'd never done in a decade of mad pilgrimage, he reached out a withered hand, put it on David's shoulder, said, rather intoned

'Zen is nothingness, your heart will bleed.'

And moved on.

David looked at me, visibly shaken

I had nothing.

We got the fook out of there.

*

Our last week was solely this

Grub on the roof, with the weather still holding

A gig at The Saw Doctors.

Teaching David how to play the spoons.

And David buying me all of Eoin Colfer's work, a real gift.

Time to go time.

I got us a cab to Galway airport, and we were silent all the way, despite the cabby trying to engage us in the latest Man U fiasco.

We weren't biting.

As he prepared to enter the departure gates, he did something very few men, never mind people have done.

He hugged me.

And it . . . felt right. Goddamn it to hell.

Said

'Jack . . . thank you.'

I said

Nothing

. . . nothing at all.

I couldn't.

Us Irish, gift of words.

Shite, not then.

I lowered my head and he walked away.

Did he look back?

I don't know.

*

Flash forward, 2010.

Ireland has been fooked and gone since that time.

I was in a new place, not a damn patch on my Nun's Island days.

I was up early, not industry, a bollocks of a hangover and the landline buzzed. Reluctantly I answered,

heard

'Is this Jack Taylor?'

A Texan lilt?

As it's not a TONE you'd ever forget, I won't anyway, muttered

'Am . . . yeah.'

'This is McKenna, David Thompson's wife, I found your number in David's new address book. I regret to tell you, David died yesterday.'

I dropped the phone.

I think, though I can't sweat on it, fell to me knees, and a wail emitted

'Oh Sweet Jesus no.'

Time after, I'd be in a pub, the other side of two Jameson, mellowing out and I'd tell me David story to a complete stranger and they'd always ask, always

'So what was he like?'

Jesus, didn't they hear me?

I'd sigh, go

'He was from Texas, what can I tell you?'

Written in Morocco, 2010

*

Ken Bruen is the author of twenty-six crime novels. He has been a finalist for the Edgar, Barry and Macavity Awards, and the Private Eye Writers of America presented him with the Shamus Award for the Best Novel of 2003 for *The Guards*, the book that introduced Jack Taylor. He lives in Galway, Ireland.

Afterword

From Chandler and the 'Playboy' to the Contemporary Crime Wave

by Fintan O'Toole

The end of the boom has made Irish crime writing better, reflecting the new reality as a kind of jigsaw without all the pieces, while drawing on the tradition of anonymity that was present in classic crime writing elsewhere, but absent from this country for so long.

Most potted biographies of Raymond Chandler will tell you that, in 1895, after his parents divorced, his mother took him from Chicago, where he was born, to London, where he grew up. In fact, the boy and his mother went originally to her own place of birth – Waterford, where they lived uncomfortably on the fringes of respectable Protestant society. It was from there that Chandler went to London, where he was supported through his English public-school education by his uncle, the Waterford solicitor Ernest Thornton.

It is tempting to imagine what might have happened had Chandler stayed in his mother's native city, and to fantasise about Philip Marlowe going boldly down Parnell Street and John's Hill. But of course, Chandler would not have been Chandler, nor Marlowe Marlowe, if that had happened. Early twentieth century Ireland was not the place where great crime fiction could happen. And the reasons it couldn't happen then are the reasons it may be happening now.

Crime stories thrive on a social condition that was emphatically absent in

Ireland: anonymity. Without anonymity, there is no mystery. And in Ireland, mystery was impossible. The archetypal Irish murder drama of the early twentieth century is Synge's *The Playboy of the Western World*, in which the 'murderer' almost immediately announces his guilt, the crime is endlessly spoken about and re-enacted and even the 'corpse' rises up to get in on the act. The comedy of the play, indeed, is that it is a murder mystery in reverse – the shocking revelation is that Christy did not in fact kill his Da.

And the archetypal late twentieth-century Irish murder story is John B Keane's *The Field*. In Keane's narrative, everyone knows whodunit and why. The drama lies not in the unravelling of a mystery, not in the struggle to uncover the truth, but in the refusal of the community to act on what it knows. The problem posed by Irish crime is not, as in the classic detective story, the acquisition of knowledge, but the assumption of collective ignorance.

Crime fiction is a function of something Ireland didn't have until recently – large-scale cities. As long ago as 1805, William Wordsworth could write of London, in his long autobiographical poem The Prelude, '*How often in the overflowing Streets/ Have I gone forward with the Crowd, and said/ Unto myself, the face of every one/ That passes by me is a mystery.*'

That mystery of unknown and perhaps unknowable faces is the material for crime fiction. The history of the genre is rooted in changing attitudes to the anxieties of anonymity. Walter Benjamin argued that while the 'original social content of the crime story was the obliteration of the individual's traces in the big-city crowd', the genre went on to lift that veil of anonymity by showing how the individual (the culprit) could be rendered knowable through the traces left by his crime. Arguably, the ground subsequently shifted back again, as crime fiction became less confident that it could console us with the idea that everything could be traced and named by the heroic work of the detective.

It is striking that the most successful Irish crime writer, John Connolly, who began his career just a decade ago, felt it necessary to set his books in the US and to insert himself directly into the American detective tradition.

Connolly presumably decided that Ireland, even in the Celtic Tiger years, was not the place for crime fiction. Yet it is equally striking that in the last few years, Irish-set crime writing has not merely begun to blossom but has become arguably the nearest thing we have to a realist literature adequate to capturing the nature of contemporary society.

Boom-time Ireland reproduced the social conditions that created crime fiction as a mass genre. As Denis Porter puts it in *The Cambridge Companion to Crime Fiction*, the explosion of crime fiction in nineteenth-century America was associated with rapid economic change: 'Old agrarian America had given way to a new, fast evolving social and material environment, characterised by monopoly capitalism, unprecedented wealth especially for the few . . . and the progressive massification of everyday life.' Sound familiar? Even more resonant is Porter's description of the background to the novels of Dashiell Hammett and Raymond Chandler – 'urban blight, corrupt political machines, and de facto disenfranchisement of significant sections of the population through graft and influence-peddling'. That fallen world is the universe of Declan Hughes's *All the Dead Voices*, of Gene Kerrigan's *Dark Times in the City* or of Alan Glynn's *Winterland*.

The dislocations of rapid social and technological change, experienced in boom-time Ireland, creates a sense of fragmentation in which everything has a sheen of mystery. Reality becomes a kind of jigsaw puzzle from which some key pieces seem to be missing. And at the same time, the cronyism and corruption of that same Ireland create a countervailing sense that everything is actually connected, that there is a pattern waiting to be discovered. The simultaneous existence of these two conditions is good for crime fiction.

If that were the whole story, however, what we'd be getting now would be simply a local version of the established international genre. That we're getting something rather more interesting than that is suggested by two intriguing ways in which the best writing is inflected by older Irish traditions.

One is the way the end of the boom has actually made Irish crime writing better. Hughes, Glynn and Kerrigan are not just among the first Irish writers to register the collapse of the Celtic Tiger. They also draw strength as storytellers from that implosion – the established Irish literary habit of drawing energy from entropy.

The other fascination is the way that new Irish school of crime writing preserves something from the days in which Irish crime writing was all but impossible. It is notable that Kerrigan and Glynn in particular don't pay much attention to the police and don't even pretend that there is a super-detective who can solve the city's mysteries. Kerrigan's central figure is himself a criminal; Glynn's is the sister and aunt of figures who have been up to their necks in the moral mire. Nor do they pretend that the revelation of the truth will make much difference to the corrupt worlds they evoke. In creating an Ireland with no faith in authority and no belief that the bad guys will be vanquished by naming their names, they get closer to reality than most literary fiction has managed.

*

This article first appeared in the *Irish Times* on 21 November 2009, and is reproduced by the kind permission of Fintan O'Toole and the *Irish Times.*

Irish Crime Writing 1829-2011: Further Reading

by Professor Ian Campbell Ross and Shane Mawe

The following list does not pretend to determine the 'best of' Irish crime writing. Instead, it offers a conspectus of Irish authors of crime fiction, writing in English and Irish, from the mid-nineteenth century to the present day, each represented by a single title. Although most titles are adult fiction, a sampling of crime writing for children and young adults is also included. As with other popular genres, crime fiction moves, sometimes mysteriously, in and out of print. Here, the publication details refer to the first edition but most of the following have been reprinted (often many times and under different imprints) and many are currently in print. For hard-to-find earlier works, we have given the URL for freely available online titles.

Allen, Liz. *The set-up*. London: Hodder and Stoughton, 2005.

Baker, Keith. *Engram*. London: Headline, 1999.

Banville, Vincent. *Cannon law*. Dublin: New Island, 2001.

Barclay, Alex. *Blood Runs Cold*. London: Harpur Collins, 2009.

Barry, Jack. *Miss Katie Regrets*. Dingle: Brandon, 2006.

Bateman, Colin. *Belfast Confidential*. London: Headline, 2005.

Benjamin, Peter. *High Ride*. Dublin: Pocket Books/Town House, 2003.

Birmingham, George A [*pseud.* of James Owen Hannay]. *The Search Party*. London: Methuen, 1909.

Black, Benjamin [*pseud.* of John Banville]. *The Silver Swan*. London: Picador, 2007.

Black, Ingrid [*pseud.* of Eilís O'Hanlon and Ian McConnel]. *The Dark Eye*. London: Headline, 2004.

Black, Sean. *Lockdown*. London: Bantam/Transworld, 2009.

Blake, Nicholas [*pseud.* of Cecil Day-Lewis]. *The Private Wound*. London: Collins, 1968.

Bodkin, M[atthias]. McDonnell. *The Capture of Paul Beck*. London: T. Fisher Unwin, 1909.

Bowen, Elizabeth. 'Telling'. *The Black Cap: New Stories of Murder [and] Mystery*. London: Hutchinson, 1927.

Boyne, John. *Crippen: A Novel of Murder*. London: Penguin, 2004.

Bruen, Ken. *The Guards*. Dingle: Brandon, 2001.

Burke, Declan. *The Big O*. Dublin: Hag's Head Press, 2007.

Campbell, Aifric. *The Semantics of Murder*. London: Serpent's Tail, 2008.

Carson, Paul. *Scalpel*. London: Heinemann, 1997.

Casey, Jane. *The Burning*. London: Ebury, 2010.

Charles, Paul. *I've Heard the Banshee Sing*. London: Do-Not Press, 2002.

Childers, [Robert] Erskine. *The Riddle of the Sands*. London: Smith Elder and Co, 1903.

Colfer, Eoin. *Plugged*. Dublin: Headline, 2011.

Collins, Michael. *Lost Souls*. London: Weidenfeld & Nicolson, 2003.

Connolly, John. *The Unquiet*. London: Hodder & Stoughton, 2007.

Crofts, Freeman Wills. *Sir John Magill's Last Journey*. London: W. Collins Sons & Co., 1930.

Cromie, Robert and S. Wilson. *The Romance of Poisons: Being Weird Episodes from Life*. London: Jarrold & Sons, 1903.

Cunningham, Peter. *The Bear's Requiem*. London: Sphere, 1990.

Curtis, Robert. *The Irish Police Officer: comprising The Identification and other Tales, founded upon Remarkable Trials in Ireland*. London: Ward and Lock, 1861.

Cusack Margaret Anne. *Ned Rusheen; or, Who Fired the First Shot?* London: Burns & Oates, 1871.

Davison, Philip. *The Crooked Man.* London: Jonathan Cape, 1997.

Dickinson, David. *Death in a Scarlet Coat.* London: Constable, 2011.

Dillon, Eilís. *Death in the Quadrangle.* London: Faber, 1956.

Donovan, Gerard. *Julius Winsome.* London: Faber, 2007.

Dowd, Siobhan. *The London Eye Mystery.* Oxford: David Fickling, 2007.

Dowling, Richard.*A Baffling Quest.* London: Ward and Downey, 1891.

Downey, Garbhan. *Confidentially Yours.* Derry: Guildhall, 2008.

Dunsany, Edward Plunkett, Lord. 'The two bottles of relish'. *Time & Tide*, 12 Nov. 1932.

Edwards, Ruth Dudley. *The Anglo-Irish Murders.* London: HarperCollins, 2000.

Ekin, Des. *Stone Heart.* Dublin: O'Brien Press, 1999.

Fitzgerald, Conor. *The Dogs of Rome.* London: Bloomsbury, 2010.

Fitzgerald, Nigel. *Suffer a Witch.* London: Collins, 1958.

Fitzgerald, Kitty. *Small Acts of Treachery.* Dingle: Brandon, 2002.

French, Tana. *In the Woods.* Dublin: Hodder Headline, 2007.

Fuller, James Frankin. *John Orlebar, Clk.* London: Smith, Elder & Co., 1878.

Galvin, John. *The Mercury Man.* Dublin: Townhouse, 2002.

Gébler, Carlo. *A Good Day for a Dog.* Belfast: Lagan. 2008.

Glynn, Alan. *Winterland.* London: Faber and Faber, 2009.

Griffin, Gerald. *The Collegians.* London: Saunders & Otley, 1829.

Hamilton, Catherine Jane. *The Flynns of Flynville.* London: Ward Lock and Company, 1880.

Hamilton, Hugo. *Headbanger.* London: Secker and Warburg, 1996.

Harrison, Cora. *My Lady Judge: A Mystery of Medieval Ireland.* London: Macmillan, 2007.

Hector, Annie (Mrs. Alexander). *A False Scent.* London: F.V. White & Company, 1889.

Heussaff, Anna. *Bás Tobann,* Baile Átha Cliath: Cois Life, 2004.

Higgins, Jack [*pseud.* of Harry Patterson]. *Day of Reckoning.* London: HarperCollins, 2000.

Hill, Casey. *Taboo.* London, Simon & Schuster, 2011.

Holland, Jack. *Walking Corpses.* Dublin: Torc, 1994.

Hughes, Declan. *All the Dead Voices.* London: John Murray, 2009.

Hunt, Arlene. *Undertow.* Dublin: Hodder Headline, 2008.

Joyce, Joe. *Off the Record.* London: Heinemann, 1989.

Kearney, Selskar [*pseud.* of Robert Brennan]. *The False Finger Tip: An Irish Detective Story.* Dublin: Maunsel and Roberts, 1927.

Kelly, John. *The Polling of the Dead.* Dublin: Moytura, 1993.

Kerrigan, Gene. *Dark Times in the City.* London: Harvill Secker, 2009.

Keightley, S[amuel] R[obert]. *A Man of Millions.* London: Cassell & Co., 1901.

Kitchin, Rob. *The Rule Book.* Brighton: Indepenpress Publishing, 2009.

Landers, Brendan. *Milo Devine.* Dublin: Poolbeg, 2001.

Landy, Derek. *Skulduggery Pleasant.* London: HarperCollins, 2007.

Leather, Stephen. *Dead Men.* London: Hodder & Stoughton, 2008.

Le Fanu, J[oseph]. Sheridan. 'The Murdered Cousin'. *Ghost Stories and Tales of Mystery.* Dublin and London: James McGlashan, William S. Orr & Co., 1851.

Leitch, Maurice. *The Smoke King.* London: Secker & Warburg. 1998.

Lover, Samuel. 'The Priest's Story'. *Legends and Stories of Ireland.* Dublin: W. F. Wakeman, 1831.

Lusby, Jim. *Making the Cut.* London: Gollancz, 1995.

McAllister, John. *Line of Flight.* Portishead: Blue Chrome, 2006.

McCaffrey, K. T. *The Cat Trap.* London: Robert Hale, 2008.

McCarthy, Ava. *The Insider.* London: HarperCollins, 2009.

McCarthy, Ellen. *Silent Crossing.* Dublin: Poolbeg, 2010.

McCarthy, Kevin. *Peeler.* Cork: Mercier Press, 2010.

McDonnell, Vincent. *The Knock Airport Mystery.* Dublin: Poolbeg, 1993.

McEldowney, Eugene. *A Kind of Homecoming.* London: Heinemann, 1994.

McGilloway, Brian. *Borderlands*. London: Pan, 2008.

McGinley, Patrick. *Bogmail*. London: Martin Brian and O'Keeffe, 1978.

McKinty, Adrian. *Dead I Well May Be*. London: Serpent's Tail, 2003.

Mac Liam, Seoirse. *An Doras do Plabadh*. Baile Átha Cliath: Oifig an tSoláthair, 1940.

McLynn, Pauline. *Right on Time*. London: Headline, 2002.

McNamee, Eoin. *Resurrection Man*. London : Faber, 1994.

Meade, Glen. *Web of Deceit*. London: Hodder & Stoughton, 2005.

Meade, L.T. [Elizabeth Thomasina Toulmin-Smith (née Meade)]. *The Brotherhood of the Seven Kings*. London: Ward Lock & Company Limited, 1899.

— and Robert Eustace. 'The Arrest of Captain Vandaleur'. *The Harmsworth Magazine*, July 1894.

Michaels, Sarah. *Summary Justice*. London: Frederick Muller, 1988.

Millar, Cormac [*pseud.* of Cormac Ó Cuilleanáin]. *An Irish Solution*. Dublin: Penguin, 2004.

Millar, Sam. *Bloodstorm*. Dingle: Brandon, 2008.

Molloy, Joseph Fitzgerald. *An Excellent Knave*. London: Hutchinson, 1893.

Moncrieff, Sean. *Dublin*. London: Doubleday, 2001.

Moore, Brian. *Lies of Silence*. London: Bloomsbury, 1990.

Moyes, Patricia. *Dead Men Don't Ski*. London: Collins, 1959.

Murphy, James. *Luke Talbot; or, the Cliffs of Mullawn-Mor*. Dublin: Sealy, Bryers & Walker, 1890.

Neville, Stuart. *The Twelve*. London: Harvill Secker, 2009.

Ní Dhuibhne, Eilís. *Dún an Airgid*. Baile Átha Cliath: Cois Life, 2008.

Nugent, Andrew. *The Four Courts Murder*. London: Headline, 2006.

O'Connor, Gemma. *Sins of Omission*. Dublin: Poolbeg, 1995.

O'Connor, Niamh. *If I Never See You Again*, Dublin: Transworld Ireland, 2010.

O'Duffy, Eimar. *The Bird Cage*. London: Geoffrey Bles, 1932.

Ó Dúrois, Seán. *Crann Smola*. Baile Átha Cliath: Coiscéim, 2001.

O'Faoláin, Seán. 'Murder at Cobbler's Hulk' (1971). *Foreign Affairs and Other Stories*. London: Constable, 1976.

O'Flaherty, Liam. *The Informer*. London: Jonathan Cape, 1925.

Ó Grádaigh, Eoghan. *An Fear Fada Caol*. Baile Átha Cliath: Sáirséal agus Dill, 1959.

O'Meara, Kathleen. *Narka the Nihilist*. New York: Harper and Brothers, 1887.

Ó Muirí, Pól. *Dlithe an Nádúir*. Baile Átha Cliath: Comhar Teoranta, 2001.

O'Neill, Desmond. *Life Has No Price*. London: Gollancz, 1959.

O'Neill, J. M. *Open Cut*, London: Heinemann, 1986.

O'Rourke, T. S. *Death Call*. Dublin: Breffni Books, 1997.

Ó Sándair, Cathal. *Réics Carló ar Oilean Mhanann*. Baile Átha Cliath: Oifig an tSoláthair, 1984.

O'Sullivan, J. B. *Backlash*. London: Ward Lock and Company, 1960.

Parsons, Julie. *The Guilty Heart*. London: Macmillan, 2003.

Payne, Harold [*pseud.* of George C. Kelly]. *Detective Burr: The Headquarters' Special; or, The Great Shadower's Baffling Case: A Story of False Clues and A Woman's Art*. Beadle's New York Dime Library 728. New York: Beadle & Adams, 1892.

Pearse, Patrick. 'An Bhean Chaointe'. *An Mháthair agus Sgéalta Eile*. Dublin: Dundalgan Press, 1916; trans. Joseph Campbell as 'The Keening Woman' in *The Collected Works of Pádraigh H. Pearse*. Dublin: Maunsel & Co., 1917.

Petit, Christopher. *The Psalm Killer*. London: Macmillan, 1996.

Pim, Shelia. *Common or Garden Crime*. London: Hodder & Stoughton, 1945.

Power, M[aurice]. S. *Children of the North*. London: Abacus, 1991.

Radcliffe, Zane. *London Irish*. London: Black Swan, 2002.

Reid, Desmond. *Bullets are Trumps*. London: Fleetway, 1961.

Ryan, William. *The Holy Thief*. London: Macmillan, 2010.

Smyth, Seamus. *Quinn*. London: Hodder & Stoughton, 1999.

Strong, L[eonard] A[lfred] G[eorge]. *All Fall Down*. London: Collins, 1944.

Thompson, Neville. *Jackie loves Johnser, OK?* Dublin: Poolbeg, 1997.

Tremayne, Peter [*pseud.* of Peter Beresford Ellis]. *A Prayer for the Damned*. London: Headline, 2006.

Trevor, William, 'Events at Drimaghleen' (1987). *Family Sins & Other Stories*. London: Bodley Head, 1990.

Twenty Major. *The Order of the Phoenix Park*. London: Hodder & Stoughton, 2008.

Ua Nualláin, Ciarán. *Oidhche i nGleann na nGealt*. Baile Átha Cliath: Oifig an tSoláthair, 1939.

Welcome, John [*pseud.* of John N. H. Brennan]. *Run for Cover*. London: Faber & Faber, 1958.

Wilde, Lady [Jane Francesca Wilde (née Elgee)]. 'The Holy Well and the Murderer'. *Ancient Legends, Mystic Charms, and the Superstitions of Ireland*. London: Ward and Downey, 1887.

Wilde, Oscar. 'Lord Arthur Savile's Crime'. *Lord Arthur Savile's Crime and Other Stories*. London: James R. Osgood, McIlvaine & Co., 1891.

*

Ian Campbell Ross has written, edited and translated books on Irish, British and Italian literature and history. His course on Detective Fiction was the first taught in Ireland and introduced Popular Literature into the School of English, Trinity College Dublin, where he is Professor of Eighteenth-Century Studies. *www.tcd.ie/English/staff/academic-staff/ian-ross.php*

Shane Mawe is currently employed as an Assistant Librarian in the Department of Early Printed Books, Trinity College Library. Along with crime fiction, he devotes a worrying amount of time and money to his other interests in music and sport.